A CHRONICLE OF ANCIEN[T...]

HENRY WILLIAMSON

A FOX UNDER MY CLOAK

ALAN SUTTON PUBLISHING LIMITED

First published in 1955 by Macdonald & Co (Publishers) Ltd

First published in this edition in the United Kingdom in 1996
Alan Sutton Publishing Limited
Phoenix Mill • Far Thrupp • Stroud • Gloucestershire

British Library Cataloguing-in-Publication Data

A catalogue record for this book is available from the British Library.

ISBN 0-7509-1214-6

Cover picture: detail from The Triumph of Death, *c. 1562 by Pieter Brueghel the Elder (c. 1515–69).*
(Prado, Madrid/Bridgeman Art Library, London)

AUTHOR'S NOTE AND DEDICATION

Many of the scenes in this novel are authentic, including those which are based on incidents
recorded in the Official History of the Great War, Military Operations, compiled by Brigadier-
General J. E. Edmonds, C.B., C.M.G., R.E. (retired), and Captain G. C. Wynne, The King's
Own Yorkshire Light Infantry – to whom grateful acknowledgement is hereby made.

Each of the characters in this novel had an existence in the 1914–18 war, though not all
necessarily acted or played their parts in the times and places mentioned in the story.

In particular, the author dedicates this volume to

CAPTAIN DOUGLAS BELL, M.C.

his old school-fellow and comrade-in-arms, wounded at Lone Tree during the battle of Loos,
1915.

Printed in Great Britain by
The Guernsey Press Company Limited,
Guernsey, Channel Islands.

INTRODUCTION

HENRY WILLIAMSON was a writer of tremendous energy and tenacity. He wrote over fifty books, innumerable short stories and articles in newspapers and magazines, and literally thousands of lengthy letters. Most of his books were long and there were several typescript versions for each one. His compulsion and need to write ruled the whole of his life.

His first book *The Beautiful Years* was published in 1921. In 1951, thirty years and thirty-five books later, there appeared the first volume of his long novel in fifteen volumes, *A Chronicle of Ancient Sunlight*, whose hero, Phillip Maddison, is based on Henry Williamson himself. Apart from being an absorbing story of the life of an extraordinary man, the entire *Chronicle* is a fictionalized social history of the first half of the twentieth century.

The first volume, *The Dark Lantern,* opens with a scene where a man called Richard Maddison is out collecting moths on a summer night when he is set upon by two ruffians. Richard Maddison is based on Henry Williamson's own father, William Leopold Williamson, and this scene and most of the characters and incidents throughout the entire series are based on real scenes, characters and incidents from Henry Williamson's own life, and that of his family and friends. The element of fiction and transposing of real events with imagined ones does, however, mean that nothing can be taken for granted.

William Leopold Williamson was a bank clerk by profession who, in May 1893, married Gertrude Eliza Leaver in a secret ceremony. This dramatic tale is to be found in *The Dark Lantern.* Their first child, Kathleen Mary, was born in 1894, while Henry William Williamson was born on 1 December 1895 at 66 Braxfield Road in Brockley, south-east London. A third child, Doris Mary, was born in 1898. Soon after, William Leopold bought one of the new houses being built next to 'Hilly Fields' in Lewisham, and so the family moved to 11 [now 21] Eastern Road, where the main part of Henry Williamson's childhood and adolescence was spent. A blue commemorative plaque was placed here in 1984 under the aegis of The Henry Williamson Society and Lewisham Council.

Henry Williamson's mother came from a family who had been farmers in Bedfordshire and the young Henry was very friendly with his Bedfordshire cousins in whose home he felt more relaxed; we find all the relations woven into the tapestry of the *Chronicle*. An earlier branch of the family had originated from Devon, which Henry Williamson always claimed as his spiritual home and where he was to live for the greater part of his life.

In 1907 he obtained a scholarship to Colfe's Grammar School in Lewisham. He was not psychologically suited to the strict discipline of school life, preferring to roam the countryside collecting birds' eggs, but he was not a disgrace either: he became Captain of Harriers [cross-country running] and was in the school rifle team. His feelings, friendships and adventures gave him plenty of writing material and are marvellously captured in an early book, *Dandelion Days,* and later in *Young Phillip Maddison*, the third volume of the *Chronicle*.

On leaving school in the summer of 1913 Henry Williamson became a clerk in the Sun Fire Insurance Company, which becomes the 'Moon' Fire Office in the *Chronicle*. In the early summer of 1914 he went on holiday to stay with his Aunt Mary Leopoldina [Theodora in the novels], who rented a cottage in the tiny village of Georgeham in North Devon. This holiday made a great and lasting impression on the young Henry Williamson. He loved the wild coastal scenery of the nearby Braunton Burrows and the cliff promontory known as Baggy Point. This idyllic impression was further reinforced because shortly afterwards the First World War broke out and soon Henry Williamson was a soldier in the battlefields of Flanders.

He had enlisted into the ranks of the London Rifle Brigade the previous January, and was mobilized on 5 August 1914, embarking for the battlefields at the beginning of November. This period is related in the fourth volume of the *Chronicle, How Dear is Life,* where Phillip actually joins The London Highlanders, who also leave for the horror of the trenches. The ensuing volumes, *A Fox Under My Cloak*, *The Golden Virgin*, *Love and the Loveless* and *A Test To Destruction,* are all devoted to coverage of the war, interspersed with scenes of amorous and hilarious adventures of home leave, and service in this country training to be an officer, many of them episodes which were personally experienced by Henry Williamson himself. These books are considered by many critics to be some of the best that have ever been written about the First World War.

The war affected him greatly, particularly the extraordinary Christmas Truce of 1914, when he discovered that the German soldiers – the enemy – were fighting for the same ideals as the British: God and their country. He realized the futility and destruction of war and this determined his life's work: to show the world, through writing, that truth and peace lay in beauty and the open air. This was reinforced when, in 1919, stationed in Folkestone with the Dispersal Unit, he discovered a copy of Richard Jefferies' book, *The Story of my Heart,* and read in rapt attention what was to him 'a revelation of total truth'. He began to write seriously from then onwards.

After demobilization in September 1919, Henry Williamson returned to live at his parents' house, where he behaved rather wildly for a few months. At the beginning of 1920 he obtained a job as motoring correspondent for the *Weekly Dispatch* and was soon having short nature sketches published in various newspapers and periodicals while he worked on his first novel. But he found life in the family home too narrow and frustrating because his father disapproved of everything he did. Finally they quarrelled irrevocably, and in March 1921 Henry left home for the cottage in Georgeham whose lease he took over for £5 a year. This period of his life is related in *The Innocent Moon*, the ninth volume of the *Chronicle*, although Phillip's courtship and marriage with 'Barley' and her subsequent death in childbirth soon after is a fictionalized version of what in real life was a frustrated love affair.

The Beautiful Years, the first volume of his tetralogy *The Flax of Dream,* was published that autumn. From then on Henry Williamson wrote and published a book (sometimes two books) more or less every year, almost to the very end of his long life.

In 1924 he embarked on an ambitious project: a novel depicting the life story of an otter. To procure material he joined the Cheriton Otter Hounds and at one of their meets he saw a beautiful young woman, Ida Loetitia Hibbert, whom he soon decided was his ideal partner. They were married in May 1925. She is Lucy Copplestone in the *Chronicle* and we first read about their courtship and subsequent marriage (and Henry's quarrels with her brothers) in the tenth volume, *It was the Nightingale*.

Tarka the Otter was published in October 1927 to much acclaim, especially after it was awarded the Hawthornden Prize for Literature the following year. A letter arrived from T.E. Lawrence, Lawrence of Arabia, who wrote to say he had 'sizzled with joy' on reading it, thus starting a correspondence and friendship between the two men.

With the £100 prize money Henry Williamson bought a field on the hill above Georgeham and built himself a Writing Hut which was to be his refuge throughout his life.

In *The Power of the Dead* Phillip goes off to learn farming from his uncle, Sir Hilary Maddison, who owns twelve hundred acres of downland with its own trout stream. In real life Henry and his wife and two sons moved to Shallowford in the village of Filleigh near South Molton in Devon, where there are, of course, several hundred acres of farmland and a trout stream. Henry set to work to improve the trout fishing and to write a book about another water creature, to be called *Salar the Salmon*. He published several more books and made two long visits to America, where his books had always been well received, at this time. His family increased and was complicated by the fact that his secretary, known in the novels as Felicity, also bore him a child.

In early May 1935 he wrote a letter to T.E. Lawrence asking if he might visit him to discuss a writing project for a friend, Victor Yeates, who had just died; Lawrence rushed out on his motorbike to send him a telegram in reply and as he returned had an accident from which he subsequently died. Later that year Henry was invited to visit his great friend Sir John Heygate, who was working in a film studio in Germany, and to attend the huge Nüremburg Rally being addressed by Adolf Hitler. Henry also saw and was greatly impressed by the German Youth Movement and the agricultural and industrial reforms Hitler was instigating. We must remember here that Henry had a German grandmother, and that his own ideas that 'truth and peace lay in beauty and the open air' coincided with what he saw happening in Germany. Later he was to call Hitler 'Lucifer', the fallen angel. This era is covered in *The Phoenix Generation*, the twelfth volume of the *Chronicle*.

Once *Salar* was published Henry Williamson felt he needed to move on to find fresh material. Two books, the charming *The Children of Shallowford* and the factual *Goodbye West Country*, relate the family's life at Shallowford in an interesting saga. Having seen the portents of war looming, he decided now to become a farmer and in 1937 bought a very run-down farm on the north Norfolk coast to which, amid much turmoil, the family moved. *A Solitary War* relates Phillip's [and Henry's] struggles to turn the 'bad lands' into a viable farming unit. Once in Norfolk Henry Williamson was persuaded to attend a meeting of the British Union of Fascists where he met its leader Sir Oswald Mosley. As a new farmer Henry felt the BUF's agricultural policy held the answer to the country's troubles, and Mosley became his new hero. Mosley is Sir Hereward Birkin in the *Chronicle* novels. *Lucifer Before Sunrise* continues the story of the farming struggle in wartime England. He also covers the farming era in *The Story of a Norfolk Farm* and *The Phasian Bird*.

It was a harrowing time for the family. Henry was exhausted and irritable, trying both to run the farm as a perfect system and to write to earn enough money to keep everything going. At the end of the war it was obvious that things could not continue as they were. The farm was sold but the tensions were so great that the family broke up. Henry returned to his field in Devon alone, although he always maintained close touch with his ex-wife and his children.

The last volume of *A Chronicle of Ancient Sunlight* also has Phillip returned to Devon, living alone on Exmoor. This tremendous novel, *The Gale of the World*, culminates in an epic description of the storm that led to the flooding and devastation of Lynmouth in 1953. Afterwards, Phillip, finding himself still alive, decides that he can at last start to write his Chronicle – opening with a shy young man out with his dark lantern mothing on 'the Hill' and including all his friends in ancient sunlight . . .

In real life, on his return to Devon Henry Williamson met and soon married his second wife, Christine Duffield, and their son was born in 1950. He built a larger studio in the Field, and bought a large, comfortable and convenient caravan, but eventually also bought a cottage in nearby Ilfracombe. And he began in earnest to write *A Chronicle of Ancient Sunlight*, publishing one volume almost every year between 1951 and 1969. His second marriage could not withstand the pressure of his difficult personality and this tremendous workload, and he and Christine were divorced in 1964.

Despite the attentions of friends and family Henry was then permanently lonely. His last book *The Scandaroon*, the story of a racing pigeon, was published in 1972. Many years previously he had drawn up plans to build a large house in the Field and he now achieved that ambition although he never lived in it. He finally gave permission for a film to be made of *Tarka the Otter*. With his life's purpose over he was now tired and ill and eventually was taken into a nursing home on the outskirts of London run by Alexian monks. The filming of *Tarka* went ahead unknown to him. He died aged nearly eighty-two years old on 13 August 1977 on the very same day that the death scene of Tarka was being filmed in the exact spot that he had placed it over fifty years previously, and a few days later he was buried in a simple grave in the church-yard at Georgeham, in a plot he had bought many years before.

ANNE WILLIAMSON
Summer 1994

Readers who are interested in the life and work of Henry Williamson might like to know that there is a Henry Williamson Society. Meetings are held twice a year and the Society's *Journal*, with a wide range of articles on his life and work, is published in the spring and autumn of each year. For further information please contact the Membership Secretary:

Mrs Margaret Murphy, 16 Doran Drive, Redhill, Surrey,
RH1 6AX.

Further Reading: *Henry Williamson: Dreamer of Devon*, an illustrated biography, written by Anne Williamson, was published by Alan Sutton Publishing Limited in August 1995.

A Chronicle of Ancient Sunlight

Part One

"LEYTONSTONE LOUTS"

Chapter 1

INTO THE LINE

In the first week of December 1914 the King Emperor George V arrived at St. Omer in Northern France, headquarters of the British Expeditionary Force. Orders were given immediately to all units, in rest and refitting after the battle of Ypres, to prepare for a Royal inspection.

Among them was a territorial battalion, the London Highlanders. Boots and short puttees had already replaced worn-out shoes and spats in which members of the original battalion had left England nearly three months previously; but only in some cases had new rifles been issued in place of those defective Mark 1 Lee-Metfords which, in action, had been used as single-loaders with the new, pointed ammunition. That was in the past, a memory of Hallo'e'en and the fighting beside the Menin road.

New faces, inter-company football matches, parcels and letters from home, estaminet nights, had reduced the war to a rumour beyond the eastern horizon of flat, tree-lined arable fields gleaming with wintry water in cart-rut and furrow.

The day before the King was to arrive there was a battalion route march led by pipers along dull *pavé* roads leading to nowhere and back again, before dismissal by the new Commanding Officer, a regular soldier from the Coldstream, for the great clean-up.

His Britannic Majesty in the service uniform of a Field-Marshal, brown-gloved, brown-booted with gold spurs, brown-bearded, pouches prominent under blue eyes, passed with Field-Marshal Sir John French, Aides-de-camp, and various General Staff Officers down the ranks of silent, staring-ahead, depersonalised faces of No. 1 Company, in whose ranks, one of the survivors of Messines and Ypres, stood Phillip Maddison, thinking that the gruff tones in which the King spoke to Sir John French and the Colonel were of that other world infinitely far away from what really happened.

Behind the King walked the Prince of Wales, seeming somehow detached from the massive power of red and gold, the big moustaches and faces and belts and boots and spurs all so shining and immaculate between the open ranks of the troops in kilts of hodden grey. The slight figure of the Prince, in the uniform of the Grenadiers, appeared to be looking for something beyond the immediate scene—a small white-faced boy in the shadow of Father.

The London Highlanders were looking forward to spending Christmas in billets. The battalion was still 500 under strength, having received a draft of only 300 officers and men to replace the wastage of fourteen days of fighting. There was to be a Christmas tree, and company dinners with turkey and plum pudding. Football teams were practising daily; and a match was being played between No. 1 and No. 3 Companies in a field outside the town when a motor-cycle dispatch-rider arrived with a message for the Adjutant. Many eyes watched him open and read it, and pass it to the Colonel.

Immediately the match was stopped. Laughing talk and banter behind the goal-posts ceased. Everyone back to billets immediately; the battalion had orders to move at once. The misty dampness of the December afternoon seemed suddenly to be hanging chill. Nobody took a last kick at the football. It was picked up, by orders of the regimental sergeant-major, and carried off the field.

Feelings of dread—thoughts of imminent dereliction in cold and wet, and worse, of sleeplessness—possessed the survivors of the recent battles walking to their billets among the slightly excited and inexperienced men of the new draft.

Phillip Maddison, accompanied by four of the new draft in his billet in the *Rue de Calais*, walked in silence among them, all in step with him, kilts swinging in unison. He was thinking what a fool he had been for not having applied, during the four weeks the battalion had been out at rest, to join the transport. What more wonderful life could there be, with just enough excitement near the front line at night to give the feeling that one was really in the war—unlike the base-wallahs of the A.S.C., the Ordnance Corps, and others too far back to see the flares over the battlefield at night? He envied the transport drivers, not so much for the safety of their jobs—the horse wagons taking up rations and ammunition stopped at least half a mile from the firing line—but because they could *sleep* after their work was done, in hay or straw in a barn, *out of the rain and mud.*

For Phillip the terror of battle, of attacking into the loud cracking of bullets fired from a few hundred yards away, from behind uncut barbed-wire, was the same terror of having to face cane-strokes at school in the past: when it was over, it was over; but sleeplessness at night, without shelter in rain and frost, life achingly unendurable from one long hopeless moment to another in chilly darkness, was the worse thing. Oh, to be with the transport—the excitement of bringing up rations and letters at night to the battalion dump, handing over the 20 per cent over-proof rum in earthenware jars, ammunition and rolls of barbed-wire—then round went the horses' heads, back jolted the four-wheeled wagons, faster than they had come because the horses were thinking of nose-bags of oats awaiting them in stable or on picket-line, the drivers thinking of hot tea or soup, of snuggling into dry straw *under a roof.*

Oh, why had he not applied, when the remnants of the battalion had first come out to rest, for a transfer? Several of the Bleak Hill chaps—including cousin Bertie, the transport sergeant—were then going back to England, to take up commissions, and there had been vacancies.

Some had been filled from the new draft. What an idiot he had been, deciding to stay in the company, to be with the four new fellows with whom he had chummed up! They had attached themselves to him, marvelling at the horizontal bullet-rip across his greatcoat, souvenir of sentry-go in Bellewaarde Wood in early November. One of the four, Glass, had actually asked him for tips of what to avoid doing in a battle! Phillip had pronounced the old soldier's philosophy.

"If your number is already scratched on a bullet, or your name painted on a shell, then it will find you. There's nothing you can do about it." And later, one particularly cheery evening, "Keep by me when we go in, it isn't so bad, really." This after several rounds of *café-rhum* in the *Au Rossignol*, when he was thinking of the way the bearded Grenadier Guards had looked after them when they had first gone into the Brown Wood line. Cranmer! He drank a toast to Cranmer, his eyes averted from the others. Cranmer, a Boy Scout with him in the Bloodhound patrol—those faraway days of cricketing hats and linen haversacks dyed in tea to look like khaki, of twopenny broomsticks and little pewter bugle, of scrapping between rival patrols and troops, Boer War tents of rotten canvas, and black-smelling wooden water-bottles!

In the billet there were three members of the original battalion, including Phillip, and nine of the new draft, mucking-in together —sharing food-parcels and rations at one table. Now the problem was what to take, and what to abandon—cakes, pots of jam, sardines, boxes of sweet biscuits, even the best part of a tinned ham. The men of the new draft spoke quietly among themselves; but the three survivors of the old battalion were, in different ways, visibly agitated. Lance-corporal Collins, with sour face, was swearing as he threw aside one thing after another, muttering about the balls-up of Christmas; Church had a sardonic, to-hell-with-everything expression on his face; Phillip felt that his life was shattered, or on the point of being shattered, as he failed again and again to decide which of his mother's gifts he must leave behind, and so forsake and abandon part of her gentle face regarding him. The effect was one of irritability. Why had she sent such silly things, like that bottle of linctus? And the red flannel chest-protector, gift from Gran'pa?

Even so, he was deeply attached to, or loyal to, all thoughts from home which had prompted the sending—both had come from the old life that was now lost for ever. What about the linctus? He could see Mother buying the bottle at Leo the chemist's in the High Road, Leo's own special recipe. Every winter since he was little, especially when the yellow fogs had come before the frosts, Mother had given him teaspoonfuls of syrupy, sweet linctus to guard against a return of childhood croup. How could he betray her loving care? Or her cakes? Or any of the pairs of socks (not *sox*, as she spelled the word) she had knitted for him? Then there were the two woollen scarves, the two cholera or body belts, the woollen cardigan (worn with the chest protector, it made his tunic tight), the two pairs of woollen gloves, half a dozen tins of cocoa and *café-au-lait*, thick bars of chocolate, two extra shirts, a dozen boxes of matches, a pork pie, almonds and raisins——

The door opened. The company sergeant-major, no longer "Colours" of easy Bleak Hill days, stood there. Quietly he said, "Company parade outside in twenty minutes' time."

When the door was shut again, Phillip, while knowing that he was showing his own weakness, appealed to Lance-corporal Collins, despite Collins's dislike of him.

"I suppose you don't know where I can get a sandbag, Corporal, by any chance, to pack my extra clobber in?"

"If you weren't so bloody selfish, you'd have given some of that stuff to the Brigade Fund, when you had the chance," replied Lance-corporal Collins.

"I saw that they already had two G.S. wagon loads of our casualties' parcels, Corporal."

"Yes, and a fat lot you added to them," said Church, a crony of Collins's.

"Well, I was still alive."

The appeal for comforts had been made by Captain Ogilby when it was thought that the Brigade would be spending Christmas out at rest. Many of their comrades in the regular battalions of the Brigade, he said, had people at home who were not always in the position to send out parcels of food and clothing. Anything that could be spared, therefore, by the men of the London Highlanders would be most welcome among the splendid fellows whom they had lately had the honour of supporting in battle.

To the appeal Phillip had given a tin of French sardines and a large slab of Chocolat Menier, which he had bought for himself in a *magasin*, but found too coarse to his taste, together with a tin box of Brand's Meat Essence tablets sent by his father. This apparent stinginess at the time had caused Collins and Church to exchange slow and scornful winks: they had not forgiven Phillip for a thoughtless or rude term applied to them when they had occupied the next tent in the company lines at Bleak Hill, in the heather of Ashdown Forest during those far-away August days which by now seemed so idyllic—"the Leytonstone Louts".

As the other men of the billet thrust what they could into pack and haversack, Phillip stood indecisive, the thin wire of frustration drawing his entrails.

From almost his earliest feelings, thought of Father had been a shade, the presence of Father a wire-like fear. Entirely precious

therefore in the massed shade or wire-like fear of war was every
object sent by Mother; to be held as life itself.

"Come on, get on with it," said Lance-corporal Collins,
barging into him as he passed.

"All right, corporal."

In desperation he decided to give his surplus to the old woman
of the billet. She was grey-haired, like his mother. To alleviate
the strictures of Collins and Church, he began with an attempt
at humour. Holding out two pairs of socks,

"Pour monsieur, madame! Pour faire chaud ses petits, comment s'a appelle the word *toes*? Ses petits rouge ou pink toes,
en dedans ses sabots, madame, you comprennez, pour ses petits
cochons qui crient oui-oui-oui! tout la route chez lui."

The old woman was puzzled; she did not understand this
mixture of realism and nursery-rhyme.

"Lorsque vous reviendrez, m'sieu?"

"Non, pour votre mari! Moi, peut-être je serai tué, *crack!*,
le claque, comme ça, regardez!" He struck his hands together
sharply, then pointed to the furrow torn by the bullet across his
greatcoat while on sentry-go at Bellewaarde Farm.

"Merci, m'sieur!"

He put a scarf round her neck. "Aussi pour vous, madame!"

"For Christ's sake cut out that blather!" said Collins.

"These peasants make enough out of us as it is," grumbled
Church. Then, swinging round upon Phillip, "You make me
sick! You knew bloody well that half the regulars haven't got
any socks to their feet! Why the hell didn't you give those two
pairs to the Brigade Fund?"

"I didn't think we would be going into the line so soon."

"Else you'd have applied again to go on the transport, eh?"
Lance-corporal Collins said shortly, as he dropped the brass
cylindrical weight of the pull-through into the breech of his rifle.

"I was keeping those socks for Cranmer, a pal of mine in the
Grenadiers, in case he turned up, if you want to know!"

"So *you* say. In my opinion, you're a bloody little shyster,
and I'm not the only one who thinks it," said Church.

"Anyway, what's wrong with my giving them to the old boy
here? After all, he did lend me his sabots when we first arrived!"

"Oh, shove your socks where the monkey put the nuts!" cried
Church.

"Your habits are not mine," retorted Phillip.

"You say that again!" cried Church, turning on him.

"Well, you said it first, remember!"

"Oh, stuff your socks——" said Lance-corporal Collins. "We've got ten minutes before parade."

"Church started it, Corporal. I didn't."

"Bloody little tick," muttered Church. "You didn't even give your Bill Brown pal who got those Zeiss glasses for you a five franc note. Your 'pal' Cranmer!"

"Yes, he was my pal!" cried Phillip, in a rage. "And a damned sight better man than you, let me tell you!"

"Will you fight?" retorted Church, suddenly very quiet.

"Yes, I will!"

"Hell's bells, aren't there enough Germans left to satisfy you two coves?" said Collins. "Come on now, get a move on, it's nearly time for parade!"

"When will you fight?" demanded Phillip, looking at Church.

Church laughed shortly. "There'd be only two blows," he drawled. "One when I sloshed you, and the other when you hit the floor."

"All right, wait till we get up the line!" Phillip hesitated; then turning to Church he said, "Any old how, let's shake hands for now, shall we?"

Church knocked aside the hand contemptuously.

The men of the new draft had watched and listened to this petty wrangling between three heroes of the original battalion in silence, as though slightly puzzled.

Darkness had fallen when the battalion left behind warmth and security. A waning moon rode the sky, sad memento of estaminet nights, frost-silvered cobble-stones, colour-washed house-fronts of the Grand' Place. The decaying orb was ringed by scudding vapour; a wet wind flapped the edges of rubber ground-sheets fastened over packs and shoulders of the marching men: a wind from the south-west bringing rain to the brown, the flat, the tree-lined plain of Flanders.

It looked as though they were going back to Ypres, by now a prospect of stoical acceptance, since marching in the rain absorbed nearly all personal energy, leaving little for thought beyond the moment. They marched along a road lined with poplars towards a distant hazy pallor thrown on the low clouds

by the ringed lights around Ypres. The sky was tremulous
with flashes: the night burdened by reverberation of cannon
heard with the lisp of rainy wind in the bare branches above.
To Phillip the way was unfamiliar, though it was the route
by which the survivors of the battalion had come out of battle
a little more than three weeks previously, many of them barefoot,
ragged, bearded, and near-delirious.

Sergeant Douglas said that they were passing through West-
outre, and Phillip told his new friends of the draft that they were
for Ypres—the regulars' "Ee-priss"—all right.

The battalion turned off at a lesser lane about two kilometres
beyond the village, and they saw the wooded slopes of Mont
Kemmel rising dark against the hesitant paleness of the eastern
sky. The muddy lane led under the hill through Kemmel village
to cross-roads, and a wider tram-lined road leading to a distant
line of flares rising along the crest of the Wytschaete–Messines
ridge, of Hallo'e'en memory.

A little way on the *pavé* route they halted; and with relief
Phillip learned that No. 1 Company was to be billeted for the
night in some sheds and lofts around a farm. Here speculation
ceased, when Sergeant Douglas told them that they were taking
over part of the line the next day. The Germans, he said, had
attacked down south, and the battalion was to remain in support
while diversionary attacks were made to relieve the pressure.

This was cheerful news to Phillip, heard as he rested with
others staring at smoky coal flames behind the wall of a farm
outbuilding, where black-faced, sweating cooks stirred dixies
of skilly. While they stood there, enjoying drowsy warmth,
a great white flash followed by a double crack smote them. Some
of the draft flinched. Phillip was also startled, but he knew it
for a sixty-pounder gun firing down the road.

"Don't get the wind up," he said to Glass, one of his four
friends of the draft. "It's one of our naval guns, a Long Tom,
by the double report. They fire lyddite shells, which burst
with a sort of nitro-di-oxide smell, a brown-yellow smoke—
usually in our own trenches." He was quite the old soldier.

In the morning the villages of Wytschaete and Messines were
visible at the end of the tree-lined road, about a couple of miles
away, at the end of a long and gradual slope. Phillip stared at
the scene of the first acceptance, in battle, that life was become

nightmare. The remote skyline villages seemed to have an everlasting remoteness. Somewhere up there lay his friends of the old August days in Charterhouse Square and Bleak Hill, of the time on lines of communication outside Paris in September, and Orleans in October. Baldwin, Elliott, Costello, the Iron Colonel, the three Wallace brothers—all lay up there. He thought back to the day and the night of Hallo'e'en, reliving moments which in memory were without fear, only of deep sadness that they were gone.

But it was a sunny day; when he looked around him again, he felt hopeful. And with hope was curiosity; he wanted to see everything he could about the war. So down he walked to look at the long slender gun on straked iron wheels, half concealed in a cart-shed beside a cottage, that had fired while they were waiting for the skilly. The gunners told him that they fired only twice every twenty-four hours, usually in the evening, to catch the Alleyman horse transport coming along the road from Warneton. They were still limited to two rounds a day, a bombardier said.

From the gun he walked on down the lane to look at the lines of mules belonging to Indian soldiers in an orchard. The bark of the trees was gnawn away, with hundreds of tooth-marks nearly an inch wide. The bearded soldiers wore pale blue turbans. They looked, he thought, cold and disheartened, like the mules on the picket line. It seemed a bit of a shame to have brought the Indians to France, when they belonged to a hot country; and the mules too, that had Spanish blood. He decided to be affable to one of the pale Indians.

"You one-feller, you come from Orleans? Base wallahs, eh? Me help makee your camp, carry wood all day, knock knock wash-house up, savvy?"

"Yes, sir," said the Indian soldier, gravely. "We were at Orleans, but for a few days only."

"Oh, I see," said Phillip, and giving the grave one a little salute, he went back to his platoon.

The damp December dusk was closing down as they approached the dark, still mass of leafless tress; and filed towards the edge of a wood. Then a novel kind of path began, firm but nobbly to the feet, but so welcome after the mud of the preceding field. The path was like walking on an uneven and wide ladder. The rough rungs, laid close together, were made of little sawn-off branches, nailed to laid trunks of trees. As they went nearer the flares, bullets began to crack. He found that he, like the new draft, was ducking, as during the first time under fire. But soon he grew accustomed to the cracks, and walked on upright.

They came to a cross-ride in the wood and waited there, near some bunkers in which braziers glowed brightly. The sight was cheering. Figures in balaclavas stood about. "What's it like, mate?" he asked. "Cushy," came the reply, as a cigarette brightened. These were regulars; he felt happy again. Braziers, lovely crackling coke flames!

They filed on down the corduroy path, and came to the edge of the wood, beyond which the flares were clear and bright, like lilies. The trench was just inside the wood. There was no water in it; he saw sandbag dugouts behind the occupants standing-to for the relief. It was indeed cushy.

Thus began a period or cycle of eight days for No. 1 Company: two in the front line followed by two back in battalion reserve in billets, two in support in the wood, and two more again in the front line. It was not unenjoyable: the danger negligible— a shell arriving now and again—subject more of curiosity than of fear—news of someone getting sniped; work in the trench, digging by day, revetting the parapet and fatigues in the wood by night: for the weather was fine. One trench, called Birdcage Walk, had a beautifully made parapet with steel loop-holes built in; and was paved along a length of fifty yards entirely by unopened tins of bully beef, taken from some of the hundreds of boxes lying about in the wood. These boxes had been chucked away by former carrying parties, in the days before corduroy paths. The trench had been built by the Grenadiers, now no longer bearded, though some of their toes were showing through their boots; it was said among the London Highlanders that a cigarette-end, dropped anywhere in it, while the Bill Browns were in, was a "crime", heavily punished. Phillip said it seemed rather awful, to be treated like that. "It's the form," remarked Church, and he wondered what Church meant.

All form, and shape even, of the carefully-made trenches disappeared under the rains falling upon the yellow clay which retained them. Phillip was soaked all day and all night; the weight of his greatcoat was doubled with clay.

After the rain, mists lay over a countryside that had no soul, with its broken farmhouse roofs, dead cattle in No Man's Land, its daylight nihilism beyond the parapet, with never a movement of life, never a glimpse of a German; except those that were dead, and lying motionless, in varying attitudes of complete stillness, day after day upon the level brown field extending to the yellow subsoil parapet of the German trench behind its barbed-wire fence.

At night mists blurred the brightness of the light-balls, the Véry lights or flares as they were now generally called; the mists, hanging heavier in the woods, settled to hoar, which rimed trees and duck-boards and tiles of shed and barn and clarified a keener air in cheerful sunlight. Frost formed floating films of ice upon the clay-blue water in the shell-holes, which tipped when mess-tins were dipped for brewing the daily ration of tea mixed with sugar. It was pleasant in the wood, squatting by a little stick fire. Movement was laborious now upon the paths not yet laid with corduroy; boots became pattened with yellow clay. Still, it might be worse—memory of the tempest that had fallen on the last day of the battle for Ypres, of the misery of cold and wet, was still in the fore-front of Phillip's mind.

Chapter 2

REALITY AND APPEARANCES

One evening, when the company was in the half-finished support line, called Princes Street, a harder frost settled upon the battle-field. By midnight trees, bunkers, paths, sentries' balaclavas and greatcoat shoulders, were thickly rimed. From some of the new men in Phillip's bunker came suppressed whimpering sounds; only those older soldiers, who had scrounged sandbags and straw from Inniskilling Farm at one edge of the wood, and put their feet inside, lay still and sleeping. Lying with his unprotected boots outside the open end, Phillip endured the pain in his feet until the moment of final agony, when he got up and hobbled outside. He would make a fire, and boil his mess-tin for some Nestlé's *café-au-lait*. There were many shell-fractured oak branches lying about; they were heavy with frozen sap, but no matter. He passed the hours of painful sleeplessness in blowing and fanning the weak embers amidst the hiss of bubbling branch-ends. As soon as he sat still, or stood up to beat his arms, the weak red glow went dull. His eyes smarted with smoke; there was no flame, unless he fanned all the time. Move he must; his arms were heavy in the frozen greatcoat sleeves; while the skirts, mud-slabbed, were hard as boards. He set off upon a slow stumbling walk, his senseless feet like wooden props taking the shocks on the hard corrugated surface of the path. Hardly knowing where he was going (for the pain of the pierced nerves of his hands was multiplied with movement) suddenly he came across what seemed to be a little paradise, the glowing coke-brazier in the doorway of the signallers' bunker at Battalion Headquarters; and peering in, was told that he looked like Jack Frost. After twenty minutes' jumping about outside, the pains abated; and he crept in, the ice in his greatcoat creaking and crackling as he sat down.

After struggling against a desire to sleep as he warmed his hands at the pink-blue brazier flames before the gap in the blanket-hung entrance of the signallers' bunk—each company in the line had its morse buzzer—he saw what looked like a tobacconist's shop, at least along one wall, on shelves fixed into the sandbags. Surely the signallers weren't hoping to sell that tobacco, with so much already lying about in the wood?

From talk at the Ration Dump on the road outside the wood, where the battalion wagons unloaded and returned (lucky devils) to their farmhouse two miles back, Phillip had learned that A.S.C. lorry drivers were selling hundreds of thousands of packets of cigarettes of every description to Belgian and French civvies of the towns along the supply route. A great quantity of tobacco was being sent at this time duty-free from England to the British Expeditionary Force. Many Comfort Funds for the Troops had been started by newspapers. As Christmas approached, "Smokes for Tommy" arrived in such bulk that the daily ration for each man was said to be anything between two and five thousand cigarettes a day, or a pound of pipe tobacco, or both. Carrying parties on the icy corduroy paths cursed the extra weights of wooden boxes. Scores of such boxes containing cigarettes, or air-tight tins of leaf tobacco, were lying about in the wood.

"How about a cup of cocoa, old boy?" said Journend, one of the signallers. Journend was in the Guarantee Department at

Head Office. It seemed paradise to Phillip to be able to live, and sleep, in such a bunker. There was straw on the floor, a hanging hurricane lamp, and magazines which made it seem wonderfully home-like. If only he had volunteered for the section when at Bleak Hill! But in those days semaphore flag-wagging and heliograph signalling in the sun had seemed pretty dull.

He sipped the thick hot liquid, sweet with condensed milk, offered to him in an enamel mug, while listening to Journend telling him that the section was collecting tins and packets of tobacco, of which two kinds of each brand were ranged on the shelves put up against the wall, resting on German bayonets.

"Let me know if you come across any unusual brands."

"Yes, I will, certainly."

Phillip looked at them, remembering when he had bought his first pipe, a huge curved Artist's, under the arches of London Bridge Station; and how he had been unable to choose a tobacco, not knowing one from another. Here, in the bunk, were more kinds than he had ever seen or heard of before. Sweet Briar Flake, Black Bell Shag, Three Feathers, Walnut Plug, Juggler, Battle Axe Sliced Bar, Coral Flake, Winner Shag Blue Label, Tam o' Shanter, Castle Honeydew, Bulwark Cut Plug, Baby's Bottom—what a name to give it!—Bogie Roll, Heather Bell, Dandy—he had to fight to keep his eyes open—then the trade marks of various firms on the labels: tortoise of *Churchman*, two boars' heads for *Hignett Bros.*—dear old Hignett's Cavalier, Mr. Howlett the manager upstairs in his office smoking away, and Mr. Hollis the chief clerk once saying to him as he came down the lead stairs, pipe in mouth, "Hi, no smoking in office hours!"

He jerked his head upright again, rubbed his eyes. *Adkin & Son* had three tobacco leaves; *Wills* a capstan; *Mitchell* a lurcher dog under a tree; *Clarke & Son* a lark inside the letter *C* and a smaller *e* added.

His Civic pipe, what had happened to it? Was it still lying in l'Enfer wood, where he had flung it that morning, in panic as they advanced to the crest of Messines, clearing his pockets for cartridges? Had a German found it, and kept it as a souvenir of one of the "ladies from Hell"? It was a startling thought: that a German would want a souvenir of an Englishman.

"Hi! old boy, this isn't Wine Vaults Lane! You can't doss here! Maddison! Wake up! Don't fall asleep!"

"Who? Me? I wasn't asleep, honestly!"

"Well, you were snoring pretty loudly, old boy! I could hardly hear the buzzer. Sorry, but it's against orders to let anybody except the battalion runners in."

"Oh, I see. Well, thanks for the cocoa. I'll stand you a café-rhum in the Rossignol, next time. Honestly, though, I wasn't asleep."

He crawled out of the bunker, and was once again in frore air, bullets smacking through trees spicket and sparket with frost. Returning to the smouldering fire, he sat over it and fanned little flames from it, his eyes red and smarting with smoke, until the morning came. When at last he got up, his water-bottle was felt to be frozen solid. Later, when thawed out over a brazier, it leaked, being split; but there were many lying about in the wood, with rifles and other equipment.

The march back to reserve in the starry darkness of the next night, despite the fatigue of carrying R.E. duckboards all day, was made contentedly. They were going out! Their billets were in a village a mile behind the front line, in a row of cottages, each with a stove in its front room, and a dry brick floor. Oh blessed hour, candle-lit supper at a table, parcels and letters to open!

With others of his section in the billet, Phillip slept till mid-day; spent the afternoon cleaning up: puttees hung up to dry with greatcoats; shaving; and after pay-parade, when they received the usual five-franc note, marched to the brewery for a bath and change of small clothes. They undressed chirpily in a grain-drying loft, slats open to the wind; hopped naked down wooden steps to the ground floor where into big round mash tubs hot water gushed from pipes. It was rather fun to be ten in a tub at once, to run about afterwards, drying and playing jokes. Then into clean underwear, shirts and hose, their kilts and tunics meanwhile having been ironed, to kill lice.

Outside, the Belgian brewer scowled, beside the mayor wearing cocked hat and sash. The water had been heated, the tubs used without his permission. But a salvo of 5.9 shells bursting two hundred yards away made them retreat. And they needn't have worried; the brewery was rubble before very long.

Clean all over, No. 1 Company marched back, content with life, but no longer singing the songs of the old battalion, or any

songs at all; the old careless gaiety remained on the crest of
Messines, in the Brown Wood Line, in the woods near Gheluvelt.
But one thing helped the heart to open, the cheer to fly from
the throat—the sight of a slim and boyish figure in the Grenadier
uniform, looking the more slight in riding breeches, puttees, and
spurs, instead of the regulation knickerbockers. Service cap set
at a slight angle on his head, walking stick in hand, H.R.H. the
Prince of Wales took the salute at attention; a smile was on his
face as he was cheered by the marching London Highlanders
who had passed him unexpectedly in the street.

Some speculation—coming, as from most rumours among the
infantry, from indirect hope—arose in the platoon when knee-
length goat's-skin coats were issued. Did it mean that the battalion was to be turned into an Officers' Training Corps? That
there would be no more attacks until, at least, the Spring?
The jerkins had broad tapes which cross-bound the white and
yellow hairy skins against the chest and round the waist. Balaclava helmets of thick dark wool, folded well down over the ears,
were the thing to wear with the goat-skins; one could please
oneself. Officers and men looked alike, except for the expression
on an officer's face, and the fact that an officer appeared to
stand more upright, an effect given, perhaps, by the shoulder-
high thumb-sticks of ash many of them walked about with.

The senior officers now wore Norwegian-type knee-boots,
laced to the knee and then treble-strapped, Phillip noticed with
envy. He thought about asking his father to send him out a
pair, when a thaw came in the third week of December; and the
misery of mud returned. And then, with a jump of concealed
fear, orders were read out for an attack, on the 19th, two days
after the new moon. The company lay out at the edge of the
wood, shivering and beating aching hands and feet, in support
to a regular battalion's assault on a cottage in No Man's Land
called Sniper's House and a section of German trench that
enfiladed the dreaded and dangerous Diehard T-trench. The
assault of muttering and tense-faced bearded men took place
under a serried bank of bursting red stars of shrapnel, and supporting maxim-gun fire: figures floundering across the root-field,
with its sad decaying lumps that were dead cows and men. Hoarse
yells of fear become rage arose; while short of, into, and beyond
the British front line dropped shell after shell to burst with acrid

yellow fumes of lyddite—from the Long Toms of the Boer War, whose rifling was worn.

The survivors, coming back through the wood, wet through and covered with mud, their uniforms ripped by barbed-wire, were singing as they passed the London Highlanders. When they had gone—away from the line, death behind them—a clear baritone voice floated back through the trees, singing "Oh, for the wings, for the wings of a dove—far away, far would I rove". They were wonderful, remarked Sergeant Douglas, the rugger-playing Old Blue. Yes, because they were going out, thought Phillip; they were marching away from death, to warmth and sleep. The local attack had failed before the uncut German wire; but Sniper's House was taken.

The cold and the wet, and the greasy diet of salted bully beef turned Phillip's stomach sour, his thoughts with it. He had the yellow squitters. Men who went sick with this complaint got medicine and duty; so it was no good going sick. How could he get away from it all? The rain fell, the bunkers dripped with water. The trenches were now knee-deep in water. If only he could slip and break his leg, like one of the new draft—one of his four new friends—who had an ankle broken on the corduroy path, while carrying on his shoulder one of the heavy eighteen-inch-square bright-tinned boxes containing hard biscuits. Another followed him, but with doubtful good fortune, for he had, more for bravado than alcoholic desire, drunken from the glazed earthenware S.R.D. gallon jar, supposedly containing rum, which he had found in the wood, and brought with glee to the bunker. After one swallow he dropped the jar and gave a cry and doubled up, retching. The jar contained an oily, thick blackish liquid which some rear-area thief had substituted for the rum; it was concentrated carbolic acid. He was carried away unconscious.

Phillip hoped that his own squitters would continue: then he might get light duty for a few days, when next the battalion went back to rest.

Owing to the many casualties in the attack across No Man's Land, the London Highlanders had to extend their stay in the line. One night when Phillip was detailed by Sergeant Douglas for the midnight listening patrol under Lance-corporal Collins, he complained.

"I shan't be able to lie still for two hours, Sergeant. I can't help it, I'm not very well."

Sergeant Douglas paused. "Report sick when we get back to billets."

"Yes, Sergeant."

"Corporal Collins, take Church in Maddison's place."

When the sergeant had gone down the trench Church said, "You bloody leadswinger! There's damn-all the matter with you!"

"I don't want to give the show away, by getting up to go to the latrine."

"You'd only find yourself there, if you did!"

"Will you fight?"

"Yes! And this time you won't get out of it."

"Nor will you! Come on!" said Phillip, starting to climb over the clay-bagged parapet into No Man's Land.

There was nothing heroic about this. The line for the past two nights had been unusually quiet. Only an occasional bullet tore flatly through the darkness, an occasional flare shot up to quaver in green deathliness over No Man's Land. It was known that the Germans were working on their parapets, and putting up wire; and as the British were doing the same, the line was quiet during the early part of each night. According to rumour, the Prussian and Bavarian divisions had gone to the Russian front, leaving only Saxons of the Landwehr.

For some yards beyond the British parapet the ground was littered with empty bully beef and Maconochie tins. The latter, being wider, and round, were in general use as one-occasion latrines. Phillip led the way beyond this metallic riband of litter to an area of untouched level ground, dimly seen to be free of shell-holes in the faint light of a thin moon hanging pale brown upon the western horizon. Although the German trenches were about a hundred yards away, Phillip had no fear or thought of them; for one thing, it was night, and for another, his mind was taken with the problem of standing up to Church, who could box very well indeed, while he had had only four lessons at the School of Arms before the war. He took off his goat's-skin, then his greatcoat, while drawing deep breaths to steady his heart.

Six feet away, Church turned to face him, then advanced slowly. Phillip awaited him, squared up, left arm held out, right bent before his face as guard. He tried to force himself to look steadily at the dim blur of Church's face, as he waited, entirely on the defensive. Church came on slowly towards him, in a crouch, hands held low. How Church got near him so suddenly he did not know; he was conscious of an electric shock on the nose only the slightest instant before another seemed to break his lips on his front teeth, and thereafter very smoothly he felt himself going over backwards, and without any sensation of having fallen he was lying on his back, restfully upon the ground, and quite content to lie there for ever. Church's face was near his own, "Had enough?"

Phillip thought it best not to reply. It was peaceful to lie with all the sky above him. He would pretend he had been knocked out.

"Want any more?"

"No thanks."

When Church had given him a hand up, Phillip sought to explain the quick ending of the fight. His lips felt salty to his tongue, broken, out of shape. But Church ignored his stammered words.

"That'll teach you not to talk about 'Leytonstone louts' in future."

"Quite right," replied Phillip. Whereupon Church picked up Phillip's balaclava for him, and thrust it roughly on his head.

"Thanks, Church. You know I didn't really mean it when I said that of Martin and the others in the tent at Bleak Hill. I owe you an apology, quite apart from your winning the fight."

"That's all right, then. Shake!"

Their hands were still clasped when a terror of bullets fired by a machine-gun from the German trench made them drop down. Then came the sweat-breaking loud stutter shatter of another gun even nearer. Phillip could see the flashes, like an electric morse code. He pressed flat upon the wet earth, hands protecting the back of his head. Then as a flare hissed out of the low darkness of the German line, followed by another, and another, more machine-guns opened up with loud directness, accompanied by the cracking air-shear of rifle-fire. Was an attack starting? It seemed that the bullets were cracking only an inch or so above his back. Then the night was filled with swishing stalks of white light, all from the German lines, by which he knew that they would not be going to attack: remote comfort only, as he felt to be so large and visible, sweating with fear, while bullets thudded and whanged away in ricochet. The whole sky seemed to be lit up by the terrible hovering white flowers of the dead.

The incident had set off the phenomenon known as wind-up. As before a wind, fire swept with driven bright yellow-red stabs of thorn-flame up the line towards the light-ringed salient around Ypres; bullets in flights, hissing, clacking, or whining, crossed the lines of the hosts held in the continuous graves of the living above the hosts of the unburied dead slowly being absorbed into the earth. The wind of fear, the nightly wind of the battlefield of Western Europe, from the North Sea to the great barrier of the Alps, a fire travelling faster than any wind, was speckling the ridges above the drained marsh that surrounded Ypres, stabbing in wandering aimless design the darkness on the slopes of the Comines canal, running in thin crenellations upon the plateau of Wytschaete and Messines, thence sweeping down to the plain of Armentières, among the coal-mines and slag-heaps of Artois, across the chalk uplands of Picardy, the vine-yard heights of Champagne, and the plains of the rivers; the wind of fear rushed on, to die out, expended, beyond the dark forest of the Argonne, beyond the fears of massed men, where snow-field, ravine, torrent and crag ended in the peaks of the Alps rising in silence to the constellation of Orion, shaking gem-like above all human hope.

News of the fight spread up and down the trenches. Mr. Thorverton, the new platoon commander, hardly knew what to say about it; but Sergeant Douglas, calm, reliable, dutiful, had only this comment, "If you are well enough to scrap in your spare time, you are well enough for listening patrol, Maddison. You will go on the next patrol."

"Very good, Sergeant. "

A listening patrol was not a thing to go on if it could be avoided without showing the white feather. It meant creeping through the gap in your own wire and crawling or wriggling over mud to just before the German wire, twenty yards before the German parapet, and then listening for any extra talking which might mean massing of troops for an attack. It meant crawling back if this was so, and then the signallers in the shelter would buzz it to battalion H.Q., who would buzz it on to the field-gunners.

The story of the fight grew in passing from one man to another like the wind-up itself. It was said to have continued, round after round, in the light of flares while the entire German army fired at the antagonists. The story was taken back by the returning Royal Engineers to Brigade H.Q. There the Brigadier heard it from his staff-captain, and said, "Stout fellows, those London Highlanders". The brigade-major's report to Division at midnight contained the phrase *the morale of the troops is excellent.*

In due course the story got to St. Omer, and inspired a newspaper article sent back by "Eye Witness", which implied that so little did a famous kilted battalion of Territorials, which must of necessity remain nameless, regard the presence of the low-spirited Huns, that a level area of land in No Man's Land, less than a hundred yards from the enemy's wire, had been selected, after careful survey, as the only fit and proper place to form a ring, in which to settle with fisticuffs, in the time-honoured British way, a point of difference. Another account appeared in *The Daily Trident*, duly to be read in the Town Department of the Moon Fire Office in Haybundle Street, where the name of one of "the bold exponents of the noble art" was known, through a letter from the battalion signaller to his father, a fellow clerk of Richard Maddison's, called Journend.

At first Richard felt unqualified pride for his son. Later, when the details were reprinted in *The Kentish Mercury* and *The Borough News*, he considered that too much was being made of it. Had "Hetty's best boy" spoofed a bit? He said "Pouff!" when Hetty told him how Mrs. Neville had said to her, meeting her in Randiswell, that she had always known that Phillip would do splendidly, given the chance. Still, he was secretly pleased.

Of course Mrs. Bigge, next door, had to have her say, too. "Hurray for Phillip, Mr. Maddison!" Then Mr. Pye up the road, passing Mr. Turney in the shelter on the Hill, had apparently made a point of telling him that his grandson was a credit to the district, according to Hetty, a day or two later. Richard did not like Mr. Pye. Nor did he care for the remark in the Randiswell Police Station made by Mr. Jenkins when they met at 8 p.m. one night the following week for a 4-hour spell of special constabulary duty, "It only goes to show that a father can never tell how a youngster will turn out, doesn't it, Sergeant?" —a remark that increased Richard's reserve towards the neigh-

bour he had disliked ever since, in a moment of stress, the younger
man had confessed to him, *à propos* of nothing, that his wife was
not of his class. "After all, she came from a back-street." During
his 4-hour patrol of dark streets he wondered if the fellow had
meant to imply that he, the boy's father, had misjudged his son
in the past? On what authority had Jenkins made his criticism?
He, the father, had never spoken a word outside the house about
his son's lies and deceits, and cowardly ways, except in confidence
to his sister, Victoria, as well as the boy's mother, of course.
What then did Jenkins' remark imply? Why couldn't the fellow
keep his distance?

In his lonely thoughts Richard wondered about the incident
of the fisticuffs in No Man's Land. Somehow it did not ring true
of Hetty's "best boy". Still, one never knew—the boy had
always been inclined to wildness, and perhaps that had been disguised adventurousness. Anyway, there it was, in *The Daily
Trident*. The *Trident* had always "printed the facts"; and almost
alone had revealed the German menace for many years before the
war. Richard had a high opinion of Lord Castleton, the proprietor.

The newspaper accounts had different effects on Phillip's two
sisters. They made Mavis feel important—away from the house
in Hillside Road where, particularly in the depth of winter, life
often seemed hopeless, since Father was always so beastly to
Mother. Mavis depended almost entirely on her mother. She
had had no chum since leaving the convent at the outbreak of
war: as for a "boy in khaki", no jolly fear, none of that sort of
vulgarity for her! Besides, men were more or less awful, young
and old. Mavis was a little ashamed of her father, whose bearded
presence behind his reserve in the Town Department of the Moon
Fire Office, where she now worked, was a cause of nervous de-
pletion, whenever she saw him, or heard his name. Why could
he not be like the other older men, Mr. Howlett, for example,
who was always jolly, or little Mr. Journend?

Doris, the younger girl, still at school, had no nervous qualms
about her father. She was adamant towards him in her thoughts;
she felt a blankness in his presence. She was set against him.
Hers was a simple attitude of aversion, of frigidity, an attitude
based on her mother's distress from her earliest years, when she
had defended her mother, in tears because of his complaining
irritability, so often, in those days before Richard had decided

to sleep alone. From loyalty to her mother Doris had never shifted from that rigid attitude of devoted love. She loved no-one else on earth; but her affection was given to Phillip, a steady and unwavering affection that had survived his early snubbings and occasional Richard-like contempt of her feelings. Both sisters knew that Phillip was Mother's favourite; but Doris felt no jealousy, as Mavis did. Doris wanted him to be her friend, so, when one afternoon she went to practise a new song, *Keep the Home Fires Burning*, with Muriel Todd down the road, and saw a photograph of Helena Rolls in Muriel's brother's new slip-in book of snapshots, Doris promptly sneaked it when Muriel was out of the room, and hid it above the elastic band of one leg of her rough blue serge bloomers. Phillip deserved it; she knew how much he had longed to be invited to the Rolls' Christmas parties, but had never been, because of his reputation for bad behaviour, for which Father had so often caned him. Dear old Phil! She understood him. What a pity he did not want cousin Polly for his sweetheart! In the old days he and Polly had been sweethearts; it was all Helena Rolls' fault that he had changed——

Thus the desperate attempt of Phillip to show some sort of courage in his own eyes led indirectly to a letter from his younger sister, with a snapshot of his Ideal (as he thought of her) in white tennis coat and skirt, smiling serenely, silhouetted against the summer sky upon the Hill. O joy, O beauty, O dear, dear England! He saw beyond the photograph to the core of his life, the woods and fields of Kent, the nesting birds and the nightingale, and the spirit which he had found away from his home, which had turned early to shadow, even as the war was now the wide reality of all shade.

During the night following the day of the letter's delivery, after a carrying fatigue ending in the small hours, he went off alone into the wood, and made himself a fire; and crouching over it, fanning slowly with the red chest-protector, was suspended in his dream of summer's beauty, in a drowse of half-sleep, before realising that the toe-caps of his boots were hot and brittle, so near had they been to the fire. He got up to swing his arms, and while on his feet thought to place the photograph in the fork of a small chestnut tree, so that the slanting green whiteness of the flares swept across it, giving the illusion of Helena smiling out of successive waves of darkness. He felt strangely happy; cold was defeated by fire; the rising and falling notes of ricochet bullets spinning away from No Man's Land in front were like the notes of whimbrel and golden plover passing in the night, while Helena smiled upon him, with eternal renewal, every time a new calcium light rose dazzling through the bare trees. There he sat until it was near the time of stand-to, an hour before the dawn.

Phillip reported sick when they went out of the line, and to his astonishment he saw Lance-corporal Collins waiting in the line before him. The Medical Officer, Major Willibald, was known to be a terror, a regular who wore both the South African War ribbons; he had a grim, curt sort of expression, as though accustomed to deal with criminals, or, at any rate, sharpers. Phillip was astonished to observe that Collins, a pained, quiet expression on his face, spoke almost pathetically of the agony of bleeding piles. Collins was very roughly examined, almost curtly, by the M.O., Phillip thought. He noticed that Collins's jaw-muscles were working rapidly when Major Willibald said sharply to the R.A.M.C. corporal, "This case to the field hospital." Shakily Collins pulled up his trousers; his face had sagged, as though he had gone limp, in order to keep down his joy. To Phillip's further surprise, he received a wink from Collins.

When his turn came, Phillip was given a large pill, out of a box numbered 9, said to be nearly as explosive as a shrapnel shell. He was also given two days' light duty, which covered the period in billets until the company was due to return to the trenches. It meant he was excused working parties, both by day and night. It was wonderful to be able to sit by the stove in the estaminet, and to sleep in the billet until the others returned. He threw the pill away—it was for constipation, anyway—and wrote several letters, in none of which was mentioned the so-called fight, as the newspaper story was all rot. He had not fought at all; he had fallen, pretending to be knocked out, in order not to have to go on with it.

What Phillip did not know was that he had been knocked out.

Chapter 3

HEILIGE NACHT

THE Diehard T-trench, of "unsavoury reputation" as the current phrase went, was a bad, water-logged trench on the left of the battalion front. Before the October fighting, it had been a draining ditch of the arable field now part of No Man's Land. It lay parallel to, and just behind a quick-hedge bordering a lane fifty or sixty yards away from the eastern edge of the wood. Not only was it a natural drain, but as it projected into a salient in the German lines, it was enfiladed both down the stem and along the cross of the T. Everywhere it could be shot straight down from various points in the opposing trench. A fixed rifle dominated one part of it; at least two snipers had two other places "set". The Diehard T-trench had a bad reputation with the London Highlanders ever since two men had been shot, one behind the other, one shorter than the other, by the same bullet, apparently, passing through the head of the first and the neck of the second. It was said to be an explosive bullet, for it broke a two-inch hole in the back of the skull of the first man, and, passing out, severed the neck and wind-pipe of the taller man standing behind.

On Christmas Eve the platoon commander, Mr. Thorverton, said to his men standing around him in Prince's Street, as the reserve line in the wood was called,

"We have a special task tonight, and I thought I would tell you what I know about it before we start. In the event of having to reinforce the Diehard T-trench during a daylight attack, supports will have to go across open ground from the edge of the wood, since the communication trench is flooded too deep for use. Tonight the brigadier has entrusted the battalion with the special task of making a wire fence from the wood to the trench itself, or rather two fences, about six feet apart. Against the wire, on either side, the idea is to lay hurdles, to give cover from view. Thus reinforcements will be able to get to the firing trench on more or less dry ground. The brigadier considers that, at first, the enemy will fire through the hurdles, hoping to catch an occasional runner by chance, but they will soon get tired of it. There are a fair quantity of hurdles, used for tobacco drying, in the tarred wooden shed near the Château. The task has been specially entrusted to the battalion; and Number Three Platoon has been given the honour of carrying out this task tonight. I need not tell you that we must all work as quietly as possible."

Mr. Thorverton, fresh from Cambridge University O.T.C., delivered this description of the work to be undertaken in a quiet and amiable voice, the very quietness of which sent some hearts, including Phillip's, bootwards; for the Germans were only eighty yards from the T-trench at the farthest point, and less than fifty at the nearest.

"We must of course be as quiet as possible, in order not to draw the enemy's fire. Before Sergeant Douglas details the wire-carriers, and those who will knock in posts with the wooden betels provided, would any man care to ask a question?"

This was so unexpected from an officer that complete silence followed. Then Phillip said, more to continue the feeling of part-intimacy with the officer than for information, "Sir! If you please, why is it called the Diehard trench, when it is so easy to get sniped there?"

Sergeant Douglas looked sharply at the speaker, as though suspecting impertinence.

"The regimental nickname of the Middlesex Regiment is 'The Diehards', and I suppose the trench was dug by them originally," replied the new officer, courteously. "But that is only my idea—I am, of course, a newcomer among you all."

"Thank you, sir," said Phillip.

"Any further questions?"

Feeling grateful to Mr. Thorverton, Phillip uttered his thoughts, without lesser thought that he was betraying his fear, "Sir! If the posts are driven in by big wooden betels, won't the noise be heard by the Germans?"

Mr. Thorverton turned to Sergeant Douglas.

Sergeant Douglas had a restrained, near-impatient look on his face. Fearing that Douglas despised him, almost desperately Phillip went on, "I once watched posts being put in yellow clay, rather similar to this, sir. The navvies dug the holes first with spades, sir. Then they tumped the clay around the posts, with tumpers, sir, thus making sure that the posts were quite firm. It made little noise. It was when they were putting up scaffolding, before building in the field behind my house, at home, sir."

Mr. Thorverton stood as though undecided; then he said in the same easy tones, "I quite appreciate what you, as one of the original members of the battalion, have just said; but the ground is frozen fairly hard, and I doubt if digging will make much impression. And in any case we have to carry out implicit directions from Brigade. Now Sergeant Douglas will detail the various carrying parties."

Phillip felt sympathy with the new officer for the way he had spoken to him. All the same, the orders were wrong. He knew the proper way to put posts into clayey ground. He saw again the navvies in the Backfield, a pail of water between two, each dipping his spade before a thrust, each with a wooden scraper tucked into the leather strap holding up his corduroy trousers below the knee, to clean the spade off when the yellow clay clung to the bright steel. When Father had dug out the garden to make the lawn, when they had first come to Hillside Road, he was three years old; but he remembered Father making a similar little wooden scraper for his spade.

The platoon filed away singly. With a stab of fear he thought of knocking in posts, into frozen ground, a stone's-throw from the Germans, and in moonlight! It was like sending the battalion into action for the first time on Hallowe'en, never having fired their rifles, and dishing out pointed Mark Seven ammunition that would not feed into the breech of the Mark One Lee-Mitfords.

"No talking!" whispered Mr. Thorverton, to the silent men.

It was most strangely quiet when, with posts, rolls of wire, hammers and staples, and R.E. wooden betels, they picked their way on the path of frost-cobbled mud leading to the open grey blankness beyond the wood. No flares were to be seen anywhere in the silent night. Not a shot was to be heard over the frozen battlefield. Did the silence mean that they were to be trapped? Were the Germans waiting until they were all out in front of the wood, before mowing them down with machine-guns? Yet, despite the thought, Phillip rejoiced that he was not afraid; he did not think beyond the moment; he was walking quietly through the silence of a night sparkling gently with stars and frost, walking easily into the whiteness of the moon.

Their breath hung in the still air as they crept over the hard silver ground to their tasks, rifles slung, free of all equipment save a cloth bandolier across the front of their goat's-skin jerkins. Soon they were used to the open moonlight, in which all life and movement seemed unreal. Men were laying down posts, arranging themselves into parties to hold and knock; others preparing to unwind the rolls of wire. Phillip went with Mr. Thorverton and three men to a tarred wooden barn or shed, to fetch and carry hurdles, hung with long dry tobacco leaves, which they brought out and laid on the site of the fence.

Not a shot was fired; not a sound came from the Germans. The unbelievable soon became the ordinary, so that they talked as they worked, without caution, while the night passed as in a dream. The moon moved down to the top of the wood behind them; always, it seemed, they had been moving bodylessly with their own shadows.

Sometime in the night Phillip saw what looked like a light on top of a pole put up in the German lines. It was a strange sort of light. It burned almost white, and was absolutely steady. What sort of lantern was it? He did not think much about it; it was part of the strange unreality of the silence of the night, of the silence of the moon in the sky, of the silence of the frost mist. He was warm with the work, all his body was in glow, not so much with warmth, but with moonlight.

Suddenly there was a short quick cheer from the German lines, *Hoch! Hoch! Hoch!*, and with the others he flinched and crouched, ready to fling himself flat; but no shot came from the enemy lines.

They talked about it, for other cheers were coming across the blank space of No Man's Land. Then they saw dim figures on the German parapet, about more lights; and with amazement he saw that it was a Christmas tree being set there, and around it were Germans talking and laughing together. *Hoch! Hoch! Hoch!* They were cheering.

Mr. Thorverton, who had gone from group to group during the making of the twin fences, looked at his wristlet watch and said, "It's eleven o'clock. One more hour, men, then we go back. By Berlin time, it is midnight. A merry Christmas to everyone! I say, that's rather fine, isn't it?" for from the German parapet a rich baritone voice had begun to sing a song Phillip remembered from his nurse Minny singing it to him. *Stille Nacht! Heilige Nacht—Tranquil Night! Holy Night!*

The grave and tender voice rose out of the frosty mist; it was

all so strange; it was like being in another world, to which he
had come through a nightmare; a world finer than the one he
had left behind, except for beautiful things like music, and
springtime on his bicycle in the country.

It was so strange that they had not been fired upon; it was
wonderful that the mud was gone: wonderful to walk easily on
the paths; wonderful to be dry, to be able to sleep. The wonder
remained in the low golden light of a white-rimed Christmas
morning. Phillip could hardly realise it; but his chronic, hopeless longing for his home was gone.

The longing for home returned with the loss of warmth, while
lying in the bunker; so he got up and went for a walk down
Prince's Street. Here by day were visible some of the officers'
bunkers, some with trellis-work doorways, and tables inside,
taken from the Château beside the road. One had a stove in it,
a white enamelled affair; smoke went straight up from the pipe
sticking out of the sandbag roof. Phillip had often seen one
of the officers who lived here: he was red-haired, red-bearded,
and his tunic sleeves showed where sergeant's stripes had been.
On each cuff was marked, in indelible pencil, the braid and
star of a second-lieutenant. He looked to be a sort of Canadian
backwoodsman. What was rather nice in the wood was that
you did not have to salute officers, and no officer ever spoke
as though on parade. These regular officers seemed to be very
decent to their men.

He went on down the ride, coming to a clearance which
seemed almost of a fairy world, until he saw wooden crosses in
rows. There was not a sound, as he stood there. It was as though
all the soldiers had gone, except the dead. He remained still,
his eyes closed, feeling himself to be a ghost inside his body.
Then the quirking pains started again, and going among the trees,
where ice gleamed on the shell-craters, he squatted, wondering
if the scalding looseness, so thin and slight despite the pain, was
due to the everlasting bully-beef.

He felt weak, and grey like the frozen wood, and went back
the way he had come. He got his valise, and collecting dead
leaves and grasses, re-entered the bunker and, taking off his
boots, put his feet into the pack and after a while was asleep.

In the morning his boots were white, and frozen hard. It
was agony putting them on, worse trying to walk in them. How-

ever, the sun was shining, it was Christmas morning, the post had come. He sat on an unopened box of 28 pounds of 2-ounce Capstan tins, and read his letters—two from Mother, one from Doris, another from Desmond; a parcel from home as well, including a present from Father of a 2-ounce air-tight tin of Capstan. Poor old Father, and he didn't know. There were no parades, so after making a fire and frying and eating his break-fast bacon, he sat down again and drank his tea, while opening the Gift Package from Princess Mary—a brass box containing a packet of cigarettes, another of tobacco, and a small Christmas card. These he decided to send home to his mother; and as it was Christmas Day, why not walk to the village, and have lunch in one of the estaminets there?

The only sound in the wood, as he walked down the corduroy path, was the *kee-kee-kee* of a kestrel being chased by two carrion crows above the treetops. The kestrel's wing-feathers looked redly brown against the blue sky as the bird turned, just as they did in England; but the sight held little interest. This was not England.

The sun was shining as he walked stealthily out of the wood, opposite the Château. This red-brick building had its roofs broken, ragged holes in its walls and a lot of fallen masonry about what once were lawns, now pitted with ice-craters. He had never before seen it by day. All was quiet, no-one was about, so he decided to explore.

He crossed the road, almost expecting to be fired at; but the quietness everywhere remained. He walked round to the back, picking his way through heaps of fallen bricks. In some of the walls, low down, were loop-holes. He came to a splintered door, half-open; he crept through, to find himself in a small room, with ceiling plaster on the floor, and signs that it had been used in all four corners as a latrine. A door led into a kitchen, a mess of upturned tables, pots, bashed pewter dishes and jugs, broken china, the whole littered with ceiling plaster. An open door at the farther end led up some wooden stairs; and after listening, while the hair on his neck seemed to twitch, he started to go up, on tip-toe. It was all rather eerie: only the sounds of his foot-falls, and his beating heart.

At the top was a landing, the wooden floor showing signs of polishing at the edges, where plaster flakes had not been trodden upon. The corridor was bare, with very wide boards. One board, he saw, was gouged for about a foot in one place, the gouge being half-an-inch deep: could it have been made by a goat-moth caterpillar? Many dead bees lay shrunken on the planks. Walking softly down the passage, he came to an open bedroom door. The lath-and-plaster of the wall beside the door-jamb was broken where bullets had burst through. Looking round the splintered door, he saw a dried brown splosh of blood, with hair stuck to it, on the wallpaper around the bullet holes. On the floor lay a dead German, with thighs and arms and body tight in the grey uniform. The back of his head was broken open. Obviously he had been standing by the door when he had been shot.

Walking into the room, he saw another dead German lying on a bed, also swelled. The pocket-linings of his tunic, and trousers, like the one on the floor, were pulled out. Letters were scattered about. He picked one up. It was written in queer German lettering; he put it in his breast pocket. Then, noticing the buttons on the tunic, he opened his knife and cut some off. They had a crown and a W on them. The tunic thus open, with wonder he saw that instead of the ordinary single trouser buttons to hold up the braces, the German trouser buttons were sewn on in pairs, side-by-side. The other German's trousers also had a complete spare set; the buttons were of aluminium, obviously for lightness. How even tiny details had been thought out!

He cut two off, to add to his souvenirs. Then, instinctively smelling his fingers, he realised with nausea that the corruption of the bodies had saturated the grey cloth.

The Germans must have been dead at least six or seven weeks, since the battle of Ypres. Cranmer would look like that now, and Baldwin, Elliott, the Wallace brothers—the Earl of Find-horn and the Adjutant, and all the other faces which he had known. Their faces and hands, too, would be the colour of whitish-pink wax. How still the dead lay; and these two in the Château had lain exactly in the same position every moment of the days and nights since they had been surprised up there. Then, after racing heart-beats, a long fixed moment, then a flash . . . and ever afterwards, complete stillness. He could feel the idea of death creeping into him, like an invisible fungus. Without thinking, he made the sign of the Cross.

The German on the bed looked as though he had been sleeping, or waking up at the time of death: one knee was raised as he lay on his back, an arm flung sideways, the hand loose over the edge of the bed. He must have been shot in his sleep. Perhaps he had been drunk; or very, very tired. Was the other his friend, and looking after him? Did the German soldiers have friends, or was all that brutalised out of them?

He went into another room, with open tattered roof timbers, and creeping across the floor joists, looked through a window towards the German lines. They must have a full view of the place, from a little hill only a few hundred yards in front. Supposing he were sniped? Suddenly he wanted to leave the place; not for any possible danger, but because an extra chillness of death hung about the whole ruin. On the way down another staircase he saw a cage hanging up, near a torn-open desk, all papers thrown about. A canary was lying on the bottom of the cage, withered and flat.

The dreadful smell on his fingers remained after he had rubbed them in mortar, then mud and water, then with a dock leaf. It was more than a smell; it was a deadly black essence, almost spectral, on his fingers. He lit a Robin cigarette to try and clear his nostrils. Then finding an outside lavatory, he sat on it, after inspection of the seat and pan, and for several minutes enjoyed a reverie of pure aloneness, despite the scalding and the straining.

His feet were now aching again in the partly-frozen leather, and the thought of sitting in an estaminet, and thawing them out by the stove became urgent. He would run part of the way, and restore the circulation; but the sight of a bicycle in an outhouse made him change his mind. There was a bowler hat hanging on a peg in the shed; and putting this over his balaclava, he thought how funny it would be if he cycled down the road like that. The tyres were almost flat, but what did that matter? Wheeling it past the rubble heaps, he mounted, and wobbled down the grassy carriage sweep between iron fencing and so to the narrow cobbled road, scarcely wider than a Belgian farm wagon. It was great fun riding up and down over the frozen humps, and round the iced pot-holes. If only Desmond, his great friend at home, were with him!

He had never seen this road by daylight, and was surprised that the farmhouses on either side were still occupied by civvies. They were less than a mile from the front line. He waved at them; but they only stared. Louts! He waved the bowler; then pushed it hard on his head, so that it sat down on his ear-stubs; the saddle was low, and he had to be careful not to knock his kneecaps on the handlebars, while pressing the pedals with his insteps.

The sight of the tall thin soldier, in bowler and kilt, coming unsteadily towards them, caused some gunners to stare at the approaching apparition, then to make various remarks as it raised the bowler to them as he went past, calling out, "Cheer-ho! Merry Christmas!" so glad was he to be approaching the village again.

But as the church, with the big shell-hole through it, grew near enough for the grey stones of its coigns and arches to be seen among the red bricks, caution overcame his sense of fun. It would be advisable to discard the bowler before reaching the village, just in case any officers were about. He left it with the bicycle behind a clamp of mangold-wurzels.

He called at his billet, where as usual the three grown sons of the little wizened woman were lounging, in sabots and cloth caps, smoking and spitting around the kitchen stove. These young men, red-faced Flamands, with large tawny moustaches, were considered to be a lot of slackers by the Highlanders, *smeerloops* (a word picked up) who lounged about all day, having no work to do. They were farm labourers, who had fled with their parents from a small holding now behind the German lines; and the question Phillip and others of the billet often asked themselves was, why hadn't the slackers joined up? Why didn't they do their bit to save Gallant Little Belgium, instead of doing damn-all except loaf around, eating pinched bully beef and smoking ditto British tobacco?

In former days Collins had taught these "Flamandische", as he called them, with insult to their supposed half-German origin, what he said was the polite English greeting; so that now, when he entered, Phillip was met with the words:

"'Allo, you bloodie vool! 'Ow izzit, you foogpeeg? Bullocks to yoo!"

To which, with an attitude of extreme politeness, he replied:

"Comment vous portez vous, madame et messieurs? You scroungers, skrimshankers, and dirty dogs dodging the column, bon jour!"

"Si, si," said the old woman, beaming upon him.

"Ah, oui, madame, you've rumbled them too, I see!"

These great louts, he thought, had a low sense of humour. Once when he had asked one if he were married he had replied, and before his mother, too, "Non, m'sieu! Pour moi, la main la fiancée!" and all had roared with laughter. Tom Ching, who had spat in his eye coming home from school one day, would be at home with them. They used filthy expressions as a joke, too, such as a word that sounded like estomachcloit, though what it meant exactly he did not know—something to do with *stomach* and *cloth*. Did they too wear belly-bands, or cholera belts? No wonder everyone in the billet was lousy.

"Au revoir," he said aloud; but under his breath he gave them the soldier's farewell.

Chapter 4

A BICYCLE RIDE

In the estaminet he warmed and greased his boots by the stove, put them on again, with cleaned puttees, and sat down to an omelette, with white wine, having remembered that Lance-corporal Mortimore of Bleak Hill days had said this was the right drink. After café and cognac, it was time to think of getting back, before he was missed.

Arriving at the root-clamp, he decided not to put on the bowler hat; he was worrying a little lest his absence had been noticed. However, anyone could ride a bike.

He was thinking of hiding it somewhere in the grounds of the Red Château, for possible use another time, when a passing soldier told him that everyone was out in No Man's Land, talking to the Alleymans.

"There's bloody hundreds on'm, Jock!"

This extraordinary news sent Phillip off at once; and cycling on past the Château, he saw what at first sight looked like a crowd on a football field during the interval of a match. With mixed feelings of trepidation, eagerness, apprehension and bewilderment, he pedalled on past the trees and arrived, with the most extraordinary feeling of loneliness and self-exposure, at the front line trench, at the sandbag barricade across the road.

It was like seeing it all in a dream, to be standing up in that strange daylit place. How small the barricade looked, how thin and puny, seen from beside it; how narrow the road, and how clean-looking, unused, with the grass growing on it. He saw too, almost with a start, the large brick building of the Hôspice, where the German machine-guns fired from, a couple of hundred yards on the right of the road in front. How large it looked now, though the bottom part of it was still hidden by the rise in the ground. This side of it another barricade stood across the road—the German front line.

All this Phillip perceived in a dream-like glance as, leaning the bicycle against the British barricade, he walked into No Man's Land and found himself face to face with living Germans, men in grey uniforms and leather knee-boots—a fact which was as yet almost unbelievable. Moreover, the Germans were actually, some of them, smiling as they talked in English. He hurried to be among them, and saw one writing his name and home address, to exchange it with an English name and address. They had agreed to write to one another after the war.

Most of the Germans were small men, rather pale of face. Many wore spectacles, and had thin little goatee beards. He did not see a *pickelhaube*. They were either bare-headed, or had on small grey porkpie hats, with red bands, each with two metal buttons, ringed with white, black, and red, rather like tiny archery targets.

"They are Saxons," a bearded soldier told him. "They watched some of the London 'Ighlanders—your lot, mate— putting up a fence last night, but they wouldn't fire, he told me, even if they was ordered to. Or if they was forced to, like, they said they'd fire 'igh."

"I saw the Christmas tree they put up, after singing carols."

"Not a bad lot o' bleeders, if you arst me, mate."

Among the smaller Saxons were tall, sturdy men, taking no part in the talking, but moving about singly, regarding the general scene with detachment. They were red-faced men, and Phillip noticed that their tunics and trousers above the leather knee-boots showed dried mud-marks.

Looking in the direction of the mass of Germans, Phillip could see, judging by the rows of figures standing there, at least three positions or trench-lines behind their front line, at intervals of about two hundred yards.

"It only shows," he said to Glass, one of his friends of the new draft, "what a lot of men they have, compared to ourselves. We've got only one line, really—our reserve lines are mere scratches."

"I was thinking the same thing. I say, Maddison, do you see those green lanyards and tassels on those big fellows' shoulders? They're sniper's cords. They're Prussians." Phillip thought that they did not look at all friendly. Their heads looked strong, big and round, compared with the Saxons'.

"That's what the Saxons told me what they are," continued Glass. "They don't like the Prussians."

"Yes, my father always told me that."

One of the small Saxons was contentedly standing by himself smoking a new and large meerschaum pipe. He wore large spectacles, and looked just like a comic-paper "Hun". Phillip noticed that the white bowl of the pipe had the face and high-peaked cap of Little Willie painted on it. The Saxon saw him looking at his pipe, and taking it out of his mouth, he said with quiet satisfaction, "Kronprinz! Prächtig Kerl!" as he looked at the portrait and wagged his thin black little goat's beard in approval, before putting the mouthpiece back carefully between his teeth, and puffing to keep the tobacco alight. This done, he removed the pipe, examined the bowl, rubbed it against his nose, and went on smoking.

"He's trying to colour it," said Phillip. "I had a curved pipe like that, only it was wood—the Artist's pipe. I got fed up with trying to season it. Cheer-ho!" he said to the man with the meerschaum.

Another Saxon came forward to explain in English. "'Prächtig Kerl' means 'Good Chap', or 'Decent Fellow'. What you would call a 'Proper Toff' in Piccadilly. The Kronprinz Wilhelm gave us all a pipe. Jolly fine Christmas box, eh?"

"Jolly fine," said Phillip. "You speak very good English."

"I have been in London. I was waiter at the Regent Palace Hotel for two years. You know it?"

"No," said Phillip, "but I know London, or bits of it."

"Do you know Germany, sir?"

"No, but I have German cousins in Bavaria."

"So?"

"So," said Phillip. "Prächtig Kerl—your Crown Prince."

Church, who had been amused by this conversation, said

amiably to Phillip, "Fancy thinking like that about Little Willie! But I suppose they don't realise what an absolute ass the fellow really is!"

"They're told nothing," said someone. "They're driven on from behind by their officers. You see the Germans standing by their support and reserve trenches? They daren't come over."

Church said to Phillip, in a confidential voice, "That's rot, in my opinion—he got it out of that rag *The Daily Trident*. But did you notice that Saxon called you 'sir'? They think we are officer-cadets in these goat-skins. Incidentally, I heard from one of the Germans this morning that the London Highlanders are supposed to be going back to St. Omer, and start an Officers' School for Kitchener's Army."

"I know how they got that," said a man that Phillip recognised from No. 3 Company. "The Germans listen to what our chaps signal on their buzzers. When about a fortnight ago Harvey-Lowther, in our company, was ordered to report to H.Q., his commission having come through, they knew somehow; and put a board in their trenches, saying, 'Congratulations Mr. Harvey-Lowther'. They've got an electric device which picks up our Morse messages."

"Good lord!"

"They're damned efficient," said Church. "Did you hear that the Mayor of Armentières was shot as a spy? They found a secret telephone in his cellar, going underground to the German lines."

"Then there is the case of a farmer plowing with grey horses in a field next to a battery of our heavies near our transport lines. His furrows were in the shape of an arrow pointing straight at the battery. A Taube overhead saw it, and soon afterwards the guns were shelled, and blown to hell. The farmer was shot as a spy. Yes, the Germans were well prepared for this war," said a man of the Black Watch.

"Well, I know one thing," replied Phillip. "Their trouser buttons are duplicated, in case of one coming off. They thought even of that detail! For the long march through Belgium!"

"Not like us, bunged out by the War Office to the Low Country in shoes and spats!" observed Church, sardonically.

"And the wrong rifles, don't forget!"

"Oh well, it's all in the game."

"Hear, hear," said Phillip, wanting to please Church.

Church and Glass and Phillip moved on to watch some Germans digging with great energy with pick and shovel, the spades ringing on the frozen field. A tall rather stout officer with a brown fur collar to his long greatcoat stood by, bareheaded. When the hard lumps had been shifted, the grave was soon two feet deep. Then a dead German, stiff as a statue that had been lying out in No Man's Land for weeks, was put on a hurdle, brought to the shallow grave, and put in, still a statue, and covered by a red-white-black German flag.

While the officer read from a prayer-book, and the Saxons stood to attention with round grey hats clutched in left hands, the three London Highlanders stood to attention with the others. It was during the shovelling back of the lumps that Phillip thought of his friend Baldwin, shot during the advance from l'Enfer Wood to the crest of Messines. Was he being buried, at that moment, by Germans with their hats off? Would it be possible to find out, somehow?

When the grave was filled up, the Germans put on it a cross made of ration-box wood, marked in indelible pencil

HIER RÜHT IN GOTT EIN UNBEKANNTE DEUTSCHER HELD

"Here rests in God an unknown German hero," said Church.

It was just like the English crosses in the cemetery in the clearing within the wood, thought Phillip. The three moved on. Two Germans came up to them, smiling, offering cigars. "Please accept, sir."

Not to be out-done, Phillip pulled a tin of cigarettes out of his pocket.

"Thank you, sir. Please have these cigarettes."

Other Germans seemed pleased even with the tins of bully beef given them. One explained that the meerschaum pipe in his hand was the Christmas gift from the Kronprinz.

"Ja! Prächtig Kerl!" said Phillip, trying out his new German. The German replied eagerly in his own language. Phillip remembered the saying of his old nurse Minnie, *Mittagsessen ist fertig!* and pointing to the bully beef tin one carried, repeated the words, adding "Nein, nein!" shaking his head, making a wry face, clutching his middle. "Pas bon, bully beef."

"Bully beef's a cad," said Church.

"Please? You speak German, mein Herr?" to Phillip.

"Nein, nein, mein hairy one," retorted Phillip, for the German had a deep black beard. Then, lest the German feel he was being made a joke of, Phillip said, "I'm afraid I know only a few words of your language. Regardez, Englischer Princess Mary, her Gift Box to us," as he showed the brass box, opening it to reveal Princess Mary's photograph. "Deutscher, Kronprinz Wilhelm! Englischer, Princess Mary! Cousins! *Yes!*" for Church had laughed. "The Kaiser is a grandson of Queen Victoria, and she was very fond of him, and he of her. I think I like these Germans!"

"Prinzessin! Schön!" said the German, puffing his meerschaum pipe.

"What is 'schön', Church?"

"Beautiful?"

"She is beautiful, Princess Mary, I think." To himself he said, She is rather like Helena Rolls, as he touched the envelope in his breast pocket.

Church moved away; Phillip wandered on, seeking other interesting sights. In the course of turning here and there, he overheard some Highlanders talking about the London Rifles. Immediately he thought of cousin Willie. The battalion, he heard, was holding the line just south of Messines in a large wood the other side of Wulverghem. An idea came to him: why not walk down and try and find Willie? And look for Baldwin's grave on the way? Why not? Was it not Christmas Day, and the war stopped still? But dare he? How far away was it? He stared towards the east.

Wytschaete, called White Sheet, was fairly close: that dark brown broken crab-shell cluster on the sky-line had been stared at for weeks, part of the lifeless, dangerous horizon. Messines, so far as he could remember, or recall from the fragmentary impressions of marching there under fire for the first time on Hallo'e'en, must be some distance away, behind Wytschaete. Wasn't it rather a risk, to try and go all that way in No Man's Land? What was the time? He asked a German, who was looking at a watch with spidery hands. The German replied, "Half-past twelve, mister." Glass, coming up at that moment, looked at his watch, and said, "I make it half-past eleven." The German showed the face of his watch, a French one. "It keeps good time."

Phillip remembered how Sir Edward Grey's ultimatum expiring at midnight had been one o'clock in the morning, Berlin time.

"You are an hour before us," he said.

"Yes," said the German, with a smile. "That is our proper place in the sun." Phillip wondered what he meant. Hadn't the Kaiser said something like that?

There was shortly afterwards another surprise in this day of surprises, when a football was kicked into the air, and several men ran after it. The upshot was a match proposed between the two armies, to be held in a field behind the German lines. If a footer match was allowed, why not a bike ride? In some excitement he went back for his bicycle, and wheeled it among others walking, laughing and talking, to the German barricade. They moved round it, and made for a field on the left, just beyond the part-shelled Hospice; and a German smilingly helped him. The flat tyres were objects of amusement; so Phillip mounted, and rode on the road, past a cottage which had sandbags inside the windows, while pretending to be very nervous of falling off. Laughter met his antics. He rode on. The field-grey and khaki crowd was making for the field. Trying to feel nonchalant, like the heroes in magazine stories, he rode on up the rise and turned to the left, seeing before him the massed houses of Wytschaete. Nobody was about, so he rode on, entering a wide cobbled square, with a church rising above it, and trees; and cycling on slowly, he went down a narrow street between cottages and arrived at right angles to a long straight road lined with poplars; and seeing rusty steam-tram lines laid in the sett-stones, regarded them with a shock of near-sickness: this must be the ridge itself, and this was the road from Ypres to Messines.

He pedalled beside one rail, between rows of cottages with white-painted German numbers on their doors, obviously billet-numbers. He got another shock when he saw what hitherto had been seen only in a photograph: the menacing words painted large on a barn door:

GOTT STRAFE ENGLAND!

Near the barn was an estaminet, and outside the estaminet a bearded German was standing, smoking a new meerschaum pipe. Feeling white about the gills, Phillip gave a salute, which nearly caused a fatal wobble. "Ja! Ja!" he cried out. "Kronprinz. Prächtig Kerl! Auf wiedersehen," and wondering if he would hear a shot any moment, he rode on, while the tune of *O, for the wings, for the wings of a dove! Far, far away would I rove!* ground like broken shells in his mind, accompanied by his teeth grinding out the time. Then, half-turning to wave at the German, he said to himself, incoherent with an upsurge of tremendous joy, "I bloody well am roving, too!"

There was no-one else in sight; he was alone on the Wytschaete-Messines crest.

Whatever he did, he must keep on cycling. He felt inside out, he felt unreal, he was on the wings of a dove, and if he kept on cycling, no-one would think of stopping him. After all, it was Christmas Day, which everyone was celebrating. The whole countryside was quiet: only the rattling of the bicycle, with its queer high handlebars, on the *pavé* surface of the long, tree-lined road. He hoped that the spokes wouldn't start going through the rims, so that the wheels collapsed, and he was forced to walk. He told himself that his luck would hold so long as he rode on. No harm would come to him, if he rode on, and kept his thoughts to himself—he must not look about him, lest he give the idea that he was trying to find out about the German defences. There were, he could see by taking half-squeezed glances to the left with his eyes, some trenches with knife-rest wire in front of them. When he got back, he must say nothing about them; it would be rather mean to do that.

The weak sun, free of clouds in the deep part of the year, cast a long shadow of himself across the rimed grasses growing above the ditch on the left of the road. Then he thought that he must, to attract the least attention, should he meet anyone, ride on the right of the road in the Continental manner. But no-one was in sight.

What a wonderful adventure it was! The whole thing was a miracle!

How the people at home would be utterly astounded, when they heard that the Germans were not just brutes, as hitherto everyone had imagined!

He must have been going for the best part of two miles, he reckoned, when with a shock he recognised the place where the company had come up in extended order on the morning of

Hallo'e'en. He felt a chill strike into him when he saw the farm buildings on the right, down the cart-track, where, during that awful night just before the Bavarians' bayonet-charge he and Martin had failed to bring up the boxes of ammunition to the firing pits. Martin, one of the Leytonstone tent, had lain down and been unable to get up, ill with pneumonia. His heart beat so rapidly that he felt faint when he came to where the Bavarians had poured over the road, and down the track to behind the farm, and the M.O., Captain McTaggart, had been bayoneted, and Peter Wallace too, going to his rescue. He began to feel very cold and frightened. What should he do? He must go on, keep on, he must go through with it now. Was he really alive, was he *really* there, was it all happening, had it all happened? He felt like a ghost.

In places where shell-holes in the *pavé* had been filled in with brick rubble, the ice was opaque. The steam-tram lines were gashed where splinters had torn them. Soon, now, somewhere on the right, should be the stump of the windmill, and the site of the corn-stack where the Iron Colonel had lain until the Earl of Findhorn came and ordered his body to be carried back. Over the field on the left the Bavarians had advanced as the moon rose up, cheering, shouting, bands playing. Ah, there were the old trenches, how small and forsaken, how *insignificant* they looked among the shell-holes. No sign of the windmill, but there was the red barn, or the walls of it, on which they had advanced, out of l'Enfer Wood. Suddenly he saw a burial ground, beside the road, with white-and-black painted wooden crosses. Before he could stop to think, he had dismounted, thrown down the machine, and was walking to the graves, many with crosses stencilled with the Iron Cross above the lettering *Hier rüht in Gott*. They all rested in God, German and Englishman buried side by side. With a pang he saw that some crosses were hung with the glengarry. Some had no names. He dared not be there too long. Many were nameless: *Unbekannt* after *Unbekannt*, resting. All of the *Engländers* were resting; but the Germans were resting in God. Why was that? Both German and Englishman shared the same deep deep sleep, side by side.

It was cold. He must go on. He must get back to the British lines. He began to feel desperately alone. The flat-tyred, high-handled machine rattled on over the sett-stones, following the rusty steam-tram rails. Messines now awe-fully near: a terrible place of machine-guns. With relief he saw a peasant in a black suit and peaked cap walking, with a pail in his hand, near the cross-roads. He had a huge moustache. He stopped and stared. Phillip waved; he must keep on pedalling, for if he stopped, he might be asked awkward questions, even be taken prisoner.

"Bon jour, m'sieu! Santé!"

The man stared, his peak-capped moustache-faced head moving round slowly, like a dummy's, as Phillip passed him.

Which way? Straight over the cross-roads was best. He went straight on, leaving the half-broken church behind. Going through the square, he tried to look as careless as possible, riding with one hand on the handlebars only, the other on his bare knee. He was now enclosed between houses on both sides, with white billet-numbers on them. Where did the road in front lead to? It was the wrong way to Wulverghem, judging by the direction of the sun: for Wulverghem, to where they had retreated, had been west of Messines, and the sun was in front, more or less south.

If any German sentry stopped him he would be able to tell them the truth: he had gone to watch the football match, and then thought he would look for his dead friend. How lucky he had come at just the right time, when everyone was eating, or sleeping after, Christmas dinner!

It would end all right, if only the wheels held out. The front wheel was twanging a bit, with a wonky spoke or two. He must go on slowly, and all would be well. To an imaginary hard-eyed German officer he heard himself saying, I saw your unbeknown German heroes being buried; and I came to pay my respects to my dead comrades.

When the road forked, or rather the tram lines turned to the left, he found he could not decide which way to go, so he followed the lines. Whatever he did, he must not stop, it would break the luck.

The road sloped down; he could free-wheel. Where did it lead? He must think. The sun would be west of south now, as it was about half an hour since he left White Sheet, round about twelve thirty. So it must now be one o'clock. O, what was he trying to think? Start again. If the sun was sou'-sou'-west, and on his back, as it was, then he was heading nor'-nor'-east, *which was straight behind the German lines*. Where did the steam-tram go to—Lille?

It was an alarming thought. Then he saw, not very far away
and below, the dim suggestion of a fairly big wood. This must
be the one south of Wulverghem, where the London Rifles were.
Yes, as the road curved, so that the sun was on his right cheek
once more, he could see that it led down to level ground extending to the distant wood. There was a little bridge in front,
slightly hump-backed; he rattled over it, seeing a narrow stream
below.

Phillip's misgivings had made of the ride an ordeal; but the
worst was to come. His mouth went dry when he saw in front,
where the road went through a small cutting that gave cover
from view, some field-grey figures standing; and pedalling nearer,
he saw wheels, spade-trails, the barrels of field guns, under
wooden shelters roofed with faggots. A German battery!

He felt himself going white. He thought of the story of the
plowman and the grey horses, plowing furrows to point at a
British battery. Shot as a spy!

He was being stared at. They were all smoking new meerschaum pipes. Feeling a little French beard on his chin, he
sliced a hand upwards from the elbow, and cried out, in a voice
thin and throaty, "Bon jour, messieurs! Kronprinz prächtig
Kerl! Hoch der Kaiser!" and rode on past one gun, then,
another, and another, hoping that, as obviously they didn't
know what to make of him, bare-headed in a goat-skin, kilt and
khaki puttees, he would be out of their way before anyone of
them might think to stop him. To extend the period of their
wonder, he curved his arm over his head and scratched exagger-
atedly. He could feel their eyes like potential bullets, directed
towards his shoulder blades.

There were some ruined cottages in front. The narrow lane
was very rough; shell-holes grey with ice. He must be just
behind the German support trench. Yes, there before him, a
hundred yards away, was the barricade. He had to walk now,
his legs were weak, but he managed to wheel the bike forward,
trying not to have a strained expression on his face He was
trembling, he looked straight ahead, deliberately avoiding a
glance at the German trench. The grasses on the road looked
very fresh and green, the metalling clean, washed by rains,
untrodden. Eyes on the road before him, he pushed on towards
the last sandbag barricade beside a roadside cottage.

So near and yet so far. Fear rose out of the ground, all about him, as though of the exhalations of the spirits of the hatless British dead lying on the ground.

Perhaps they had been killed in the attack of 19 December, one of many made all along the line in order to hold down the German divisions which otherwise would have been sent to Russia. Living German faces were looking at him, as he could see from his retinae as he moved through a thousand dragging threads of fear, his face feeling transparent, his glance upon the ground. Slowly the big barricade of the German front trench became larger in its fixedness across the lane, beside a white estaminet stabbed all over with bullet marks in its plaster. A thin ragged hedge, clipped and cut by bullets, stood on the other side of the lane. How could he get past that solid-looking barricade? It was frizzed with coils of wire above and around it. He must leave the bike there, and try and find a gap. Ah, there was a way between the sandbag'd door of the estaminet and the barricade. Now he was walking on an area, unrecognised as a field, torn up by circular shell-holes in places; and fifty yards away stood a group of mixed and mud-stained soldiers in khaki greatcoats, goat-skins, and *feld-grau* jackets. He was safe; he was in No Man's Land.

"Can you tell me the name of this place, please?"

"St. Yves. 'Oo are yer?"

"London Highlanders. Who are you?"

"Warwicks."

"I'm looking for the London Rifles."

Thumbs jerked—"Down there."

Through the fraternising soldiers, on the frozen level field, he walked towards some cottages seen in the near distance. He asked again.

"East Lancs, mate."

He went on, past Somersets, and Hampshires. He saw a peasant in the usual black suit being led away to behind the British lines. He had come up to look at his property—the white estaminet stabbed all over with bullets.

"I say, can you tell me where the London Rifles——?"

"We are the London Rifles!"

"Oh, good!"

"I say—who are you?"

"London Highlanders."

"London Highlanders? Are they here?"

"No, up north—near White Sheet."

"Have you just come down from there?"

More men of the Rifles were now gathering round him.

"Didn't you come from behind the German lines?"

"Yes. I came along the Messines crest, on a bike."

"A bike? From behind the German lines?"

"Where did you leave it?"

"Leaning against their barricade over there."

"Good God!"

"Were you with the London Highlanders at the battle of Messines?"

Questions followed in quick succession. He looked from one face to another.

"Give him a chance to speak, you fellows," said someone, who thereupon in the silence began to ask his own questions. "You did say you were with the original battalion at Messines?"

"Yes."

The questioner looked at him intently. "Mean to say you've been a prisoner ever since the bayonet charge?"

"Good lord, no! I wasn't taken prisoner."

"Then how did you come to be wandering free behind the German lines?"

"I just went there for a bike ride."

"What, right behind their lines?"

"Yes. Some of our fellows went behind them to have a football match, so I thought I'd have a look round. Then I came on here, on the off-chance of finding one of your chaps, called Maddison."

"Maddison? What company?"

"I don't exactly know."

"Maddison? Anyone know Maddison? Sure he's with the first battalion, and not with the second at home?" No-one knew Maddison. "He may be down in front of the convent."

Phillip was now the centre of about a hundred men, in khaki and grey. One of the Germans listening to him was a tall officer, who looked steadily at him when he had finished speaking. Phillip felt he was thinking about the battery he had passed in the sunken lane; and this feeling was confirmed when the German officer approached him and said in a quiet voice, "May I have a word with you? Shall we walk this way, and see the prie Dieu at the Cross-Roads—we 'huns' have not yet succeeded in shooting it down, you will be able to observe, to the satisfaction of some of your newspapers," as he indicated the several new crosses of ration-box wood set up over various new graves in No Man's Land that day.

The tall German officer went on, "May I count on the word of a London Highlander, that you will regard your recent visit behind our lines as, shall we say, never for a moment approximating to that of an agent?"

"An agent, sir?"

"A spy."

"Oh no, I wasn't for a moment spying, sir."

Phillip saw that they were closely followed by a German soldier wearing a green shoulder cord. He looked from the officer's orderly to the officer himself, at the big pink face, the expressionless grey eyes, the clean-shaven lips which had hardly moved during the speaking of the words.

"I am glad to hear it," the voice went on, "otherwise you would be my prisoner, do you understand. We are still at war."

"Yes, sir."

"Then you give me your word?"

"Yes, sir."

"Good. Now may I ask you some questions of purely personal interest to myself. How did your government manage to supply you with so many Maxim guns at the battle for Yper, or as you call it—Ypres?"

"Maxim guns? We had none."

"No Maxim guns? But everywhere our troops met with withering fire, both frontally, and across—no machine-guns?"

"It was the 'fifteen rounds rapid' that did it, sir."

"And your overwhelming reinforcements."

"But we hadn't any, sir. We had no reserves, other than local, of course," he said. "We've got a great many now!"

"I see. Would it amuse you to know that our High Command broke off the battle because your woods were supposedly full of hidden reserves, while we had no more regiments—we were putting in students, with one rifle among three—— War is full of surprises." He paused. "Well—auf wiedersehen, my English, or should I say Scottish friend? This war will not last for ever. Perhaps we may meet again when it is over. Until then, goodbye, I am happy to rely on your word." The German clicked his heels, and bowed.

Phillip came to attention, and bowed. What an extraordinary thing for the Germans at Ypres to be as exhausted as the British had been—and to think that the machine-guns were all on the British side——

Having asked the way to the convent, Phillip walked on. He was approaching a group of cottages about a cross-roads when he came upon a burial party. They had evidently just finished; for as he drew near, a German officer gave a sharp command, at which a German soldier came forward smartly, carrying an armful of ration-box wooden crosses. The officer pointed to one of the new graves. The soldier snatched off his round grey cap, with its red band, and knelt to put one of the crosses upon the loose earth.

Phillip was reading, *Für Vaterland und Freiheit* in purple indelible pencil, when he felt his arm touched.

"Hullo, Phil!"

"Willie!"

They stared at one another delightedly. Phillip felt warmth spreading over his body. They shook hands, while he thought how very young his cousin looked, his brown eyes large and eager like a child's, with his badgeless cap, his greatcoat with the skirt roughly cut off, his face pale and wan. He was only seventeen, too young to have come out. The friend of his boyhood had recently been killed, one of the first casualties in the battalion.

Willie was full of the strangeness of the Christmas Day.

"I've been talking to a Saxon, Phil, all night. We went out to the wire, at the same time. It's most extraordinary, but the Germans think exactly about the war as we do! They can't lose, they say, because God is on their side. And they say they are fighting for civilisation, just as we are! Surely, if all the Germans and all the English knew this, at home, then this ghastly war would end. If we started to walk back, and they did, too, it would be over!"

"I wish it were as easy as that, Willie."

"But it is true, Phillip!"

"It would be a miracle if it could happen."

"But this is a miracle now, Phil! Look, 'For Fatherland and Freedom'! Isn't that just the same as our side's 'For God, King,

and Country'. They *are* the same things! Both sides are fighting
with identical ideas to drive them on. Why then, when everyone
wants it to stop, should it have to go on? I'll tell you. Because
the people at home do not know the whole truth! They think
that the whole truth is one-sided, like Uncle Dick, who says,
'Look what they've done to Belgium, raping, Uhlans cutting
off children's hands, the burning of Louvain——.' Well, they
did burn Louvain, I suppose, out of what they call 'Frightful-
ness', to strike terror into the civilian population, like freezing
a gum before pulling out a tooth. But, so far as I can make out,
most of the newspaper atrocities never really happened.''

"Oh, none of us believe all that stuff in the papers," said
Phillip. "We know that they shot Belgian franc-tireurs, civvies
who killed some of their scouts when they found them camping,
or bivouacking. We'd have to do the same if we were in German
territory. Everyone knows that."

"My Saxon friend told me that a lot of bad things were done
by the gaol-birds in their ranks, who did rape and murder, but
hundreds were court-martialled for it," said Willie.

"Well, I can vouch for one thing," said Phillip. "A German
confirmed just now that some of their mass attacks on Ypres
were made by students having only one rifle among three of
them. That was a rumour at the time, with us. Christ knows
we were untrained enough, but some of the Germans were
absolute school kids. They even came over singing. The newspapers talk about German efficiency, but I don't believe it, at
least, not as regards preparing for this war. Why, I've talked
to dozens of regulars who were at Mons on that Sunday! They
said some of our fellows were bathing in the canal, when suddenly they saw horsemen on the skyline above them. They
turned out to be Uhlans, as surprised as themselves, as they
realised when the Uhlans turned round and bunked! Mons
was then being made into our advance base; the staff thought the
Germans were a hundred miles away! The Germans thought
we were still at Boulogne! In fact, one German this morning,
up our way, told one of our chaps that their General Staff didn't
know that the British Expeditionary Force had landed in
France until they read of it ten days afterwards in a Dutch newspaper! Then the Germans thought that we had many more
troops at Ypres than they had, and machine-guns, too—so they
broke off the attacks, being out-numbered. It was our 'fifteen

rounds rapid' that seemed to them to be machine-guns! Shows how even the highest authorities can blunder, doesn't it?"

"I think it is all very simple really, Phil. It's like the wind-up, both sides firing away, thinking the other is going to attack. Yet no-one does attack."

"Not now, perhaps!—but six weeks ago, I can tell you, it was quite a different story! When I look back, I can't think how I lived through it. Most of our chaps copped it, you know."

"Yes, we read about it, Phil, at Bleak Hill. We went there after you'd left. Is it terrible, being in a bayonet charge?"

"The thought is terrible before, and after, when you think about it. But when it is happening, it all seems to be like in a bad dream, all the movement, I mean. I don't think anyone can feel anything but awfully queer, but some feel less fear than others. Like Peter Wallace—you know, one of the original Bloodhounds. He really was brave. He went to save the M.O., who continued to kneel to attend the wounded when the Bavarians broke through at Messines, and lost his glasses, and couldn't see. So he got hold of a German and went for him with his fists, and was bayoneted. His two brothers went to his aid, and were bayoneted too. Peter would have got the V.C., if it hadn't been a defeat, our chaps say."

"Yes, Aunt Hetty told me. I went there for my twenty-four hours' embarkation leave, the day after the news about Messines came. The rumour was that we were going out at once to help you; but we did a fortnight's training, near St. Omer, before coming up here."

"You weren't at an unfinished convent, were you, by any chance?"

"At Wisques, yes! We got there a week after you'd left."

There was a pause; then Phillip asked how Jack Temperley was killed.

"He fired through a steel loop-hole, without putting his rifle through the hole, but standing back in the trench. His bullet hit the plate, and came straight back at him."

"Yes, I saw a chap get killed like that. Poor old Jack."

"Aunt Hetty told me about your friend Cranmer, Phil. He is 'missing', isn't he? At least it means a chance of being a prisoner."

"It's unlikely. Both our Guards and the Prussians don't take prisoners if they can help it."

"The Saxons told us this morning that the Prussians are relieving them next week. 'Shoot the lot of them,' they said, 'and the war will be over.' They hate the Prussians. I heard that long before the war."

"So did I."

The talk had taken place under the broken crucifix at the cross-roads of Le Gheer, about a hundred yards behind the British front line. They decided to take a look inside one of the cottages of the hamlet. German dead lay in the first cottage, surprised in a counter-attack of the Inniskillings the previous October; one whiff was enough. Outside in the flooded ditch, just under the ice, lay a British soldier, on his back, his blue eyes open as though staring at the sky, arms extended, fingers spread. A look of terror was still visible through the ice.

"I wonder what he thought as he was killed, Phil. Perhaps he saw himself going farther and farther away, and then he was looking down at his body, left behind."

"I don't know, Willie, I think one thing one moment, and another the next. By the way, did you see what looked like a round, glowing light, on a pole, behind the German lines last night, by any chance?"

"Yes, the Morning Star!"

"But doesn't that rise just before the dawn?"

"Not always. Do you know, Phil, I have been wondering if it was the same star that the Wise Men saw in the East, at the birth of Christ."

The frost was settling again in little crystals upon post and wire, new mound and icy shell-hole. It was time to think of getting back.

Having said goodbye to cousin Willie, Phillip set off at a vigorous pace down the road beside the wood into Ploegsteert, with its broken church, and from there to Romarin, and the road to Neuve Eglise. There he had the luck to find an A.S.C. lorry going to Poperinghe. After some discussion, and five francs changing pockets, the driver agreed to go through Kemmel, instead of his usual way through Dranoutre. From Kemmel it was a couple of miles to Vierstraat, he said, on parting; and thanking him, Phillip jumped down and, walking with a rapid, loping stride, got back to the line of bunkers just after sunset. Fires gleamed through the trees as he approached the reserve line, his boots ringing on the frozen cross-pieces of the corduroy path. No-one had noticed his absence.

He set about collecting wood for the night's fire, in the light of the moon tarnishing the iced shell-holes. Soon smoke was arising, turning the moon's horns brown. There he would return, after the carrying party that evening.

Much work was done during the next two nights, in the pale hard air. British and German working-parties put up wire, repaired parapets, carried up trench boards and other material, talking normally. No shot was fired. Then on New Year's Eve a messenger came over with a note addressed to the Officer-in-Command, saying that a staff-inspection was taking place at midnight along the Corps front; the "automatic pistolen" would be fired in accordance with orders; but they would be fired high. And at half past ten o'clock, as Phillip was knocking a staple into a post, he and others with him heard German voices calling out, "Go back, Tommee! Go back! It is nearly midnight!" Sergeant Douglas decided to take the party back, realising that Berlin time was an hour before Greenwich time. At eleven o'clock the machine-guns opened up all along the line, and from the British trenches the up-slanting flashes were seen. Flights of bullets sissed overhead, much to the alarm, it was said, of the Quartermaster, who had decided to ride up with the ration wagons from Bardenbrug Farm, three miles back, as there was a truce—only to find himself under fire.

One afternoon Phillip watched some of Headquarters Staff making a sling to throw jam-tin bombs. Two little trees were shorn of their side branches, roped together, and wound down on a block and tackle. A leather sling was then tied to the rope between their tops, a blue Tickler's plum-and-apple bomb put in, and the fuse lit. The onlookers hurried back behind thick trunks of standard oaks, while Staff-sergeant Lyon pulled the release cord. The saplings jerked up, but the bomb remained in the sling. It went off with a sharp flash and crack. The catapult, Phillip learned from Journend, was made from a sketch supplied by Colonel Cust, of the Third Battalion in London. Colonel Cust, before the war, was said to have been an Oxford professor of history, and the catapult to be based on one used by the Romans.

Chapter 5

THE DIEHARD T-TRENCH

THE frost broke, the rains came, the truce ended. No more wavings, like children saying goodbye, no more heads above parapets. The Saxon Corps left; Prussians took over the front. The sniper's rifle cracked, the lyddite shell spread its yellow fumes; but more deadly than nickel bullet and copper-banded shell was the cold and the wet.

Rains drove through the bare woods; diggings, which had cut through many of the tile-drains of that land of clay, led sub-soil springs into the trenches. The water rose to ankle height, to knees, to thighs. Frost winds made little crackling glaciers of goat-skins; greatcoats were slabbed stiff and hard as boards. In such weather it was Phillip's turn to go out on listening patrol with Glass, under Lance-corporal Blunden. Glass was fair-haired, and slight; the breath of his sighs was soon white on the wool of his balaclava. The three froze to the ground by woollen glove and kilt of hodden grey under the rise and fall of the calcium flares, the hammering hiss of machine-guns traversing through the iron tangles of the German wire. Glass whimpered, and cried; tears glazed upon all their cheeks. They lay for two hours and then, tearing themselves piece by piece from the ground, managed to get to their knees, and on all fours got back somehow.

It took a dose of rum, and an hour's agonised jumping and swinging of arms before there was some relief from frost-pain, despite the coke braziers, some of which flickered with ration biscuits added to eke out the scarce issue of coke; biscuits more valuable as fuel than food.

No braziers could be lit in the Diehard T-trench. One rainy January night it was the turn of Mr. Thorverton's platoon to occupy this dreaded sector. In file the men, led by the officer, slid and picked their way out of the wood. Phillip hopefully carried a fire-bucket he had scrounged together with a sack of charcoal. Floundering, sweating-hot with the weight of equipment and wet woollen clothes, he approached in the darkness made more absolute the moment a flare had died hissing in the mud and wire of No Man's Land. Staggering past shell-holes, suddenly before him, at foot-level, were the familiar red stabs and thuddings of rifles, fired to keep down the heads of the enemy opposite. Sliding down the parados, bottom naked to the mud, he found himself in water to the base of the belly.

So began a period in which time moved irregularly with human movement through swilling yellow marn, movement made step by step, with ponderous suck and pull upon each boot sunken into thicker bottom clay. Some of the darkness and all of the daylight was endured in the canal of the T-trench, often shrouded in mist and rain. What was beyond his twenty yards of trench, Phillip did not know.

Parapet there was none, unless it was a low ragged thorn-hedge, its stub-line piled with mud and straw. Peering through this as dawn came, he could see, in the mist, the low, uneven German parapet less than eighty yards away. In No Man's Land were lying the shrunken bodies of dead cows, and one black sow. Farther off were the crosses of ration-box wood, souvenirs of the Christmas truce. He lowered his head after two seconds' stare, because of snipers.

The Diehard T-trench was in fact a ditch widened and deepened under fire during the October fighting. Lean-to shelters, leading off it, had been made by former occupants. They were rough frames of sticks resting on the stub of the hedge, and thinly thatched with brown tobacco leaves and straw laid on cross-sticks. The thatch had in part sagged, in places collapsed; even so, the shelters were preferable to the trench, their floors being only a foot or so deep in water.

To avoid being sniped, Phillip and his three companions had to enter their shelter—Swamp Villa—on hands and knees, through the water. To squat in Swamp Villa meant that he had to sit in the water; and when this became unendurable, he crawled out to stand in the trench below the thin black stems of the hedge. Any movement was preferable to standing cold in the marn which shook with creamy ripples around the pockets of his greatcoat.

Intense weariness went with the cold; so when Phillip, Glass and another man were detailed to fill sand-bags, with which to build up the decayed parados, the trio made little progress. They took turns to hold the hessian bags, to fill them with a shovel from which most of the marn ran off, tying their slopping necks and hoisting them to the crumbling lip behind. The skin of their hands became white and corrugated; the entire body was chilled; and one bag became too much for the three to hoist up. Anyway, most of the bags laid into position had slidden back underwater. They were too dejected to swear. But helping to keep Glass and the other man from giving way to despair (for the horizon of life was lost) kept Phillip from sinking into himself. Also he took a swig of his linctus bottle, nearly gone now, every time he felt deathly cold. And he had his talismanic photograph. There were many times, though, when the thought of the photograph meant nothing.

He discovered a pump half-submerged at a point in the trench where the T was crossed, and appointed himself pumper when the sandbag fatigue ended. Working the double-handed pump alone was something to do, as with shut eyes he tried to think of nothing. But progress was slow, so he waded to Swamp Villa and asked Glass to give him a hand. They pumped for an hour or so, during which time Glass often lowered his head and cried with exhaustion. Phillip went on pumping, the action lifting up Glass' hand which weakly held the other end.

"I know how you feel, Glass. We all felt pretty awful when we first came out here. But if we go on, we will keep some of the cold out, and lower the level a bit. Have a sip of my linctus, it keeps you warm. Don't take too much—it's got to last out."

Either the pump was not working properly, or the water was rising quicker than it flowed away in the canvas pipe which disappeared through the hedge bottom. Perhaps it was running back into the trench lower down, since the ground sloped imperceptibly up to the German lines. Whatever the cause, the smooth yellow marn continued to conceal about eighteen inches of the skirts of their greatcoats and twelve inches of their kilts from the knees up. Phillip persisted that it was worth going on with the pumping. It was better to do anything rather than nothing.

"Thinking can paralyse you, sometimes. I used to call it 'the battle of the brain'. So let's keep going, Glass, old man."

Sergeant Douglas came to visit his men, moving at the rate of four yards a minute. He praised the work on the pump, and said that soon it would be dark enough to get out of the trench, when rations would be fetched from the advanced carrying party at the Château. Phillip wanted neither food nor drink. Smoking, too, was rejected as an idea; and apart from distaste, all matches were sodden.

In the night was hope, for warmth was life and life was hope; and the brazier outside the signallers' bunker was all warmth and hope and beauty. He sat on a box of tobacco and, taking the photograph from his brown pay-book, held it to dry in the crown of flames rising from the bucket rim. Then back to the T-trench, and the slide into life without horizon.

Private Church, the last of the Leytonstone tent in the old "P" Company's lines at Bleak Hill, was moving slowly along the T-trench to Swamp Villa. Sometimes to pull a boot out against the suction of the clay below the liquid marn took several minutes in the deeper places. In the shallower places, while trying to free one foot, he had to keep himself upright under weights of clay slabbing his greatcoat—weights added by touching the trickling sides of the trench. Church was making the journey along the trench from one wing to the other, in order to apologise for an accident with the mail that had come up with his fatigue party of the previous night. The six-foot Church made the journey with his head held as low as possible, since the trench was enfiladed from both north and south in some places. He passed the junction with the impassable communication trench (the hurdles put up on Christmas Eve had been blown askew by the stormy winds) and saw the pump lying there, handles half covered by water, and yellowish traces in the water suggesting that someone had recently been working it, and had gone away down the trench. About ten minutes later he arrived at Swamp Villa.

"I'm awfully sorry, Maddison," he said in his best public-school voice, "but the sandbag containing the platoon's mixed ration of sugar, tea, and letters, was inadvertently dropped somewhere in this trench in the darkness, and we haven't managed so far to fish it up. There were two letters for you, and I can only apologise for the fact that they are lost."

Church had recently been told that he was to appear in battalion orders, promoted to lance-corporal.

"That's all right, Church. I suppose you didn't notice the post-mark?"

"Afraid I didn't. But the hand-writing was familiar—I

think you've had several from the same source before, according to my recollection."

Phillip felt that part of his mother had been drowned in the mud. "Well, thanks for coming to tell me, Church. I think I'll do some more pumping—one way to keep warm. Any rumours of when we are being relieved?"

"I haven't heard. But for what it's worth, Mr. Thorverton doesn't look very well. He's got a flushed face, and a 'nasty 'acking cough'."

"Good thing I brought that bottle of linctus with me. I nearly left it behind at Hazebrouck, but thought it might come in handy."

Phillip decided to go along the trench to see Mr. Thorverton. He had been along the trench so far only once before, to the latrine, a sump-hole in a sap dug for the purpose. That was before the water had risen into the sump, foetid and yellow with the effects of dysentery. Now the sap was fallen in: a dangerous place, registered by a fixed rifle firing at intervals through a gap in the hedge torn by a shell.

Pushing slowly along the trench behind Church, he found Mr. Thorverton in a shelter made of three fire-buckets in a row supporting a plank of wood an inch or so above the level of the water. There was a mud-covered sheet of corrugated iron as roof, bent in the middle. A torn blanket, yellow with clay-marks, hung awry over the edge of the iron sheet. Mr. Thorverton was sitting with his legs before him on the plank, his neck bent owing to the short space between plank and roof. The officer looked fearfully cold and sallow, he was breathing quickly and harshly.

"Are you all right, sir?"

"Yes, thank you, Maddison. Sergeant Douglas tells me you have done good work on the pump."

"One way to keep warm, sir. Would you care to have some of this cough linctus, sir? It's a wonderful health restorative. I don't really need it."

"That's most kind of you, Maddison, but I have only a slight chill, I think. But thank you for coming to offer it to me."

"Well, do take care of yourself, sir."

He wrung out the edge of Mr. Thorverton's greatcoat which was trailing in the water, and tucked it under his legs on the plank. Mr. Thorverton thanked him again, and after a little bow, Phillip returned along the trench, a small warmth of satisfaction within him.

The misty day grew darker. It was near the time of clambering out, to spend the night on the comparatively solid ground behind the trench. The effort of getting out, dragging sodden coat-tails, was too much; so Phillip, like the others, cut his off with his jack-knife. Flares and stray bullets were heedless things, he never thought about them. What he longed for in the night was freedom to crouch on solid ground and, hidden and alone, relieve the pain of hot thin squitters, a dozen times in the comforting darkness. By day in the trench, he must wade as far from anyone as possible, always mindful of keeping bent, head well down: for all the T-trench was commanded by snipers.

"Remember, don't raise your heads. You must not raise your heads," said that faithful shepherd of sheep, Sergeant Douglas, visiting his men. Church did, while working at one end of the pump; he was explaining to Phillip that, although the bloody thing was allegedly fool-proof, it was obvious now, on looking at it closely (he was standing up, holding the body of the pump out of the water) that the intake end had been fixed by the sappers to the delivery end. "If this isn't the bloody limit——" he was saying, when there was a loud crack and a slight thud: a small blue puncture in his cheek: glassy-eyed he stared a moment at Phillip as though in surprise, then his head drooped and he slid down, snoring, one arm over the pump handle, blood-bubbles blown from his nostrils. He fluttered his arms feebly, they beat the water as he sank under, and when Phillip pulled him up he was dead. The back of his skull had a large hole in it. It was too dangerous to try and push his body over the crumbling parados, so Phillip laid him across the pump and left him there, his face with the small bluish puncture out of water, and the blood coagulating on nose, lips and chin.

So the pumping at that dangerous three-way place came to be abandoned. Sitting in the ruins of Swamp Villa, Phillip thought of the hot days of August during the march into Surrey and Sussex: O, why had he not appreciated them properly at the time. Never again would he complain of blisters on his feet, thirst, or aching shoulders.

Life was one shivering moment to another shivering moment,

awaiting relief: long moment after long moment of deadly cold, in a world of glissading yellow clay below black thin twigs of ragged hedge dripping its drops mournfully upon a little row of collapsed roofs of straw and tobacco-leaves.

The grey day spread greyer upon the almost level sameness of a landscape of skeleton farmhouses fringed with bare trees, diminishing figures of dead animals, the fragile crosses in No Man's Land; the little dying world of men waiting in water to their bellies, head sunken on chins, beyond speaking, waiting for night.

At last the dead weight and inertia of life in the T-trench yielded to the hopes of relief. The sniper could not see you as you got out of the trench, which was low after many cavings-in, and now perilously shallow; but if you lost your balance as you struggled to climb up the collapsing back wall in the quarter-light, and fell back into the marn, and were not seen and pulled out, you could at the worst drown in voiceless feebleness; while at the best you would have to stand on the ground above and drain off, shuddering and heavy with mud up your sleeves, your hands and arms and face thick with clay, icy cold on your spine and upon your stomach.

This minor calamity happened to Lance-corporal Blunden when the order came to leave the trench, on the fifth night. The prolonged spell in the front line was due to the casualties in the brigade, in the local attacks of 19 December. There was no relieving platoon; the T-trench was now to be held, until breastworks of sandbags could be built behind it, by machine-guns posted on the flanks, to give cross-fire. Two Maxims had just been issued to the London Highlanders, to replace the lost pride of Vickers guns which had been bought privately out of battalion funds before the war: the only two Vickers guns in the British Expeditionary Force in 1914.

Lance-corporal Blunden, disinterred troglodyte, was lugged into the wood by Sergeant Douglas holding the arms and two men each holding a leg of that living weight of wool and flesh, seemingly the heavier for being unconscious. Before he went away, Sergeant Douglas left Phillip, as the oldest soldier, in charge of the rest of the half-platoon left to cover the withdrawal.

"Do not fire unless there is an attack," were his orders. "I will send a runner to tell you when to bring the men to the rendezvous on the road by the Château. Is that clear?"

"Very good, Sergeant."

After twenty minutes waiting, the runner came; and Phillip, with a little reserve energy from his nerves, helped to push others up, while those already out pulled from above. It was a long, slow affair, amidst gasps and cramps and collapsings of men and clay into the water. Phillip, his life feeling wider with responsibility, was last in the trench. Searing pains transfixed him. He must be alone when he squittered; have one last peaceful moment alone.

"Lead on you fellows. I'll follow in a moment. I can get out by myself."

The hot stream relieved his pain; and feeling now content, he gave himself two minutes rest, before the effort of climbing out. Closing his eyes, he sank into the desired moment of nothing-ness, which soon enclosed him.

When he opened his eyes again it was to an awareness of a face staring down at him. He saw the face quite clearly to be that of Tommy Atkins, the stretcher-bearer. Tommy's voice said that he must get out, he must not go to sleep there. The voice urged him to try again when he slipped back. He wanted to be alone, but the face was so insistent that he began to push with deadened fingers at his web belt, to lighten himself of equipment that was carrying only mud. Then it began to rain heavily. Somehow he got out of the trench, and was staggering among watery boot-impressions gleaming in the mud of the field behind. He sat down to rest, indifferent to the wind-up beginning to move down from Ypres. He was quite clear as to what was happening; everything around him was distinct in the light of flares popping up from the German trenches, making bright the rain hissing all around him. He saw drops spirting up from watery boot-holes, miniature craters of heel and sole sharply outlined by greenish light above the musketry crackle. He lay down, in-different to rain, bullets, flares. He sank from it all in thoughts of sleep, sleep, sleep.

When the firing had gone away down the line, he heard again the voice of Tommy Atkins telling him to get up. It was all he could do to get on elbows and knees to empty the pouches of ammunition. He heard Tommy Atkins saying that he must not go to sleep.

When he reached the road by the Château he was warmer, and more sure of his balance. Mr. Thorverton told him that

Sergeant Douglas and Glass had gone back to look for him. The officer stood by the wagon waiting behind the wall of an out-building. Figures were lying in the wagon.

When Sergeant Douglas returned, he was furious; but in a level voice said:

"Why didn't you come with your party?"

"I couldn't get out, Sergeant."

"Why did you wait behind, instead of accepting their help?"

"I wasn't very well, Sergeant. It's this gastritis."

"All the more reason why you should have been helped out."

"I was, Sergeant, by Tommy Atkins."

"Who?"

"Tommy Atkins, Sergeant."

The reply confirmed Douglas' doubts about Maddison. Mr. Thorverton, since the good example set by the voluntary pumping effort, had spoken to him about giving Maddison a stripe. He was now the oldest soldier, and Lance-corporal Blunden was due for promotion to corporal. Sergeant Douglas had demurred. Now he thought that Maddison was a stupid liar, as well as being irresponsible: for less than half an hour ago he had heard, from the driver of the wagon, that Tommy Atkins had died of pleuro-pneumonia in hospital at Kemmel that morning.

"Very well, get up in the wagon."

"I'd rather walk, and get warm, Sergeant."

Sergeant Douglas turned away abruptly and reported all present to Mr. Thorverton.

"Thank you," replied the voice of Mr. Thorverton. "Lead on, men."

Chapter 6

HOSPITAL

THE transport wagon followed the lurching figures along the road to rest billets, leaving behind the line of flares diminishing with the crackle of musketry. It was not a march back, but a slouch; nobody spoke, nobody kept step. They entered billets dazed by oil-light, buffeted by heat of pot-belled stove. To Phillip the faces of the old woman with her sons and daughters standing by the open back-kitchen door were flat like an old painting.

Potage ? After the hot cabbage soup he floated in warm thoughts of sleep, sleep, sleep. His goat-skin was a drowned object on the floor; buttons of greatcoat thick, thick in hard shrunken cotton-holes. With fingers of pale canvas he took his little packet of letters, and sat down again, but could not read them, and flopping down with clenched eyes sank into a wave of contentment that he could sleep, sleep, sleep. The others were getting down on the straw, too, and the oil-lamp disappeared with the kitchen door closing to the old woman's "C'est triste, si si! Quel pauvres!" while in the darkness of the room the top of the stove began to glow dull red.

The next thing he knew was that it was morning, and his body was achingly comfortable in half-dry clothes. He lay for some time enjoying the thought that he could lie there all day, and it was after noon before he sat up, with others, to remove tunic, unwind puttees, and take off boots. This last act was done with difficulty, for his feet hurt sharply. When the socks were peeled off, he saw that they were puffy from toes to ankles. Within half an hour they had swelled red, while the little toes remained greenish-grey.

After dinner, wearing borrowed *sabots*, he hobbled along to sick parade. Iodine was painted on his feet, a No. 9 pill for bowel disorder was dropped into his hand. He had to swallow the fearsome thing while the R.A.M.C. corporal watched; and spent the afternoon and evening, when he was not lying down, straining in the *cabinet* at the bottom of the cottage garden. He ate only a little soup, between periods of delicious drowsiness. Glass had a thermometer, and by it he saw that his temperature was 101. Happiness filled him; he floated deliciously in the straw.

When the company paraded for the trenches again, three days later, he remained behind in the billet, well content that his feet, still swelled and painful with frost-bite, would keep him on light duty in his billet.

It was quiet and peaceful, alone in the cottage. About noon he clobbled woodenly to the estaminet for a *café-rhum* and omelette. At night he looked away east over the fields, thinking that the low rising parabolas of the flares were the lilies of the dead. Night after night it was going on, the misery and the sadness; night after night the pale horizon quivering as with a thousand, thousand sighs. It was a *spotted* horizon. The line of lights stretched away south along the crest of Messines, ever pale, ever sad. How long would it all last? The Russian steam-roller had apparently failed; the Wolff Wireless, or Liarless as *The Daily Trident* called it, claimed a great German victory at Tannenberg, with hundreds of thousands of prisoners and hundreds of guns. Why call it the *Wolff Liarless*, when liarless meant you were less a liar? Rather like the Corps Bulletin, which had claimed that the local attacks of 19 December were successful, in that they had held down German reinforcements to Russia. But, according to the Saxons on Christmas Day, the Prussians had already gone by then.

He thought about the brigadier's parting message to the colonel, which Sergeant Douglas had read to them in the billet. After the usual compliments, it had said that, "when hard fighting comes, your men will stick it out both in attack and defence with the tenacity and courage that your battalion has displayed unfailingly in every phase of its service in the field". The brigadier was going away, to command a division. *When hard fighting comes . . .* was there no end to what they would have to go through? But putting away his thoughts, he wrote a letter to the Magister of his school. Dare he address him as Dear Magister?

Dear Sir,

I hope you are well, and that the Old School flourishes. Indisposition enables me to rest in my billet and send you my news. We have had rather a stiff time at the front. The chief trouble is the mud. We sleep on mud, we freeze on mud, we get mud on our rifles, on our clothes, in our hair, in our food. We have been holding trenches in front of a wood in Flanders. Pumping had to be done day and night, also baling, but it availed little. The parapets of the trenches slipped down, the sides fell in, the trench got dangerously shallow. It was impossible to dig, and we were compelled to crouch down in the daytime and wait for the night. When night came we worked in the trenches, put up barbed wire in front (the Germans were about eighty yards off), went and fetched water and rations, and exercised ourselves a bit. All this, remember, under intermittent rifle and maxim-gun fire, and a continuous shower of white rockets that lit up the country for two or three miles around.

Then, when work was done, sentries were posted. Each man did one hour off and one hour on all the night. When wet and freezing up to one's thighs in mud and water the game is apt to get a bit trying at times; but, when the relief comes, oh, blessed hour! We troop back indescribably muddy but cheerful. Woollen caps on most of our heads, some with equipment over goat-skin coat, others with helmets and other souvenirs, we reach our billets (peasants' cottages) about 1½ miles away, take our soup and then lie down on the floor.

The stove is burning brightly, we are warm and well filled. A good post of letters and parcels awaits us, "grub" is not scarce. We are men who live in the moment only; we cannot tell when a bullet will find us or a shell hasten our end, but for the moment the room is warm, the roof over our heads keeps out the rain, we are happy and contented. Three days later, another week of wet and mud. Thus our little life goes on. The past appears to have belonged to another world. We hope and pray that it will come again, and hope inwardly that, if we are spared, the day is not so very far away when, having done our duty to our country, we shall look back on the days of fighting as but a memory, and not a very pleasant one.

The recent Xmas Day was a curious one. The Saxons opposite us wanted a truce and we exchanged souvenirs and gifts. They promised not to fire until we did. This was kept up for a day or so when we sent over a note to the Germans saying our artillery was going to begin and would they please keep under cover. Before this, they had asked us the same, when their maxims were going to fire. So ended the truce.

Please give my kindest regards to all at the School, and accept,
  Sir,
     my respectful good wishes towards yourself,
      yours sincerely
        P. S. T. Maddison.

Having written this letter, Phillip had to hasten away to the closet in the garden. The usual scalding stream, which by now had made him so sore that only by gritting his teeth and holding his breath dare he wipe himself.

The next day, to his concealed delight, he was sent in the horse ambulance to the Field Hospital at Kemmel. His feet were examined by R.A.M.C. doctors in new uniforms who looked more kindly than those he had met so far. Then he had to provide a "specimen stool". *Severe enteritis and frostbite, suspected gangrene of little toes* was written on his chart. It was better than he had dared to hope. He must lie very still, as though he were really ill. It was wonderful to lie between army blankets again. The blankets were lousy, but what matter: so was he, so what were a few extra sharp itching pin-points? He kept telling himself that he was warm, he was under a roof, he was in a bed. Unfortunately his temperature was only 100. If only it would go up. Then his chart might be marked *Train*.

In the evening came the deciding inspection—the lieutenant, the captain, the colonel of the Field Hospital all together by his cot.

"How long have you been out?"

"Since September, sir."

"What were you in civil life?"

"Junior clerk, sir."

"How old are you?"

"Nineteen, sir."

He heard the R.A.M.C. captain say to the sergeant, as they moved to the next cot, "Base."

The Base! Never did bread and butter and cocoa for supper taste so good.

A motor-car ambulance took him and three others to the train next morning.

He had never imagined that there could be such a train. It had red crosses on its outside; and inside the big coaches were wide compartments of soft grey upholstery, electric lights over each seat (though they did not switch on) and thick grey carpets. *Wagon lits*, much better than the Belgian trains he had ridden in before the war, with Mother and Mavis, and cousin Petal. It was almost unbelievable, but the nurses on the train were actually English. One nurse came into the compartment with a basket of apples. She wore a grey and red uniform, with the letters *Queen Alexandra* and stars of rank on her shoulder. She was an officer nurse; and a little subduing as she smiled frostily when he said, before he could stop himself, "Oh, are you English, how wonderful!" Then she said, "You are the enteritis case, no fruit for you!" with a little warning wag of her finger and left the carriage as swiftly as she had entered it.

> *Somewhere in France*
> Date unknown

Dear Mother,

I write hurriedly to let you know that I am now on my way to the base, where I shall be in hospital. I am suffering from "enteritis". My insides have been rotten for 3 weeks. There is no cause for worry at all. I am thin and pale but I am not downcast. I am writing in the Red Cross train, which accounts for the uneven writing.

The arrangements for "malades" are ripping and the authorities are kindness itself. Will drop a card later.

> Yours affectionately,
> Phil.

Étretat,
19 February 1915

Dear Father,

I am in hospital now: writing in bed. The hospital is an hotel on the sea-front, with chalk cliffs below. Am weak and in slight pain occasionally. Hope you are all well at home. The sea is roaring on the beach about 50 yards away.

I received your most welcome letter last night, for which many thanks. If I were you, I should chuck the special constable work. It must be very fatiguing, especially as you are so busy in Haybundle Street. Also, the Defence Force you mention (composed of elderly men, I presume?) may be very nice as a sort of hobby, but, believe me, in case of invasion (by invasion I mean at least two corps landing) they would be of no use whatsoever, unless under the control of the Army Authorities.

Suppose a hostile army managed to establish itself in England. It would have to advance on London, the centre of all railways to the Channel. It might get to, say, Romford. The streets of London, would, perhaps, swarm with patriotic men armed with rifles and bandoliers eager to repel the Hun. The Huns have met our army at Romford, and the armed citizens are in reserve, waiting. Suddenly a most awful bombardment would begin. No sign of an enemy, yet huge shells would hurtle out of the heavens and with a terrific "womp" would explode. Houses would crumble up, huge holes appear in the road-ways, factories and warehouses burn furiously. We will *suppose* that our army before Romford is overcome: and the reserves are coming up, from the Midlands and South-west. Meanwhile London would be a smoking heap of ruins, dead women and civilians bestrewing the streets. Where would the patriotic but wholly useless men be, who are not in the regular army? Perhaps a day later the Germans would appear with field-guns and maxims, and another fearful carnage would ensue. A few might be killed by the citizens, but then no mercy would be shown to the rest, and an awful state would ensue.

Supposing the armed civilians have withstood the bombardment, the flames, the falling buildings, they would then have a chance to show their mettle: they would snipe the invaders. Result—all civilians ruthlessly slaughtered. That is what happened in Belgian towns. Civilians, otherwise francs-tireurs, are barred by the Hague Convention from taking part in military operations.

Believe me, if, IF, the Germans can land a force sufficiently strong (two army corps at least) to make any attack or advance on London possible, then the Defence Leaguers would not be the slightest good at all, unless taken over by the military to man trenches in fields, or positions that surround London; *and in uniform.*

Now I must end. The orderly is coming to put out the lights. With a final sip of my hot milk (my diet at present) I close this letter. With love to all at home,

Your affectionate son,

Phillip.

PS. Please send me a ten-shilling note at once. *This is very important.*

Phillip wanted the money as a present for the R.A.M.C. orderly, who might then recommend that the word *Bunk* be written on his chart by the doctor. *Bunk* meant that you were for home. He dreaded that, being more or less well after a fortnight in the hotel, he would be sent back to the battalion. The newspapers said that the mud at the front was drying up, and soon it would be the turn of the British Army to take the offensive.

The skin had come off his feet, but the little toes had not gone bad. The enteritis had stopped; he was on a light diet, milky foods and fish. He was weighed, in his coarse holland nightdress, by the medical orderly. "Blime, you're a lamp-post all right! Four pounds under nine stone."

At the evening round the doctor asked Phillip what he was before joining up.

"Junior clerk, sir."

"I mean, what weight?"

"About ten and a half stone, sir," replied Phillip, adding on a few pounds.

"Ever had a persistent cough?"

"A sort of persistent cough, sir, but it went away, when I took linctus."

"H'm, we'll sound your bellows."

After tapping, followed by the usual *ninety-nine* business, the M.O. folded his stethoscope. "You seem all right, my boy."

"Thank you, sir."

There were three beds in Phillip's room at the top of the house. One was vacant; the other held a young regular soldier of the East Surreys who had taught him Hindustani words as he told him about the old days in India, where each soldier, he said, had at least three native servants, or *wallahs*—one to clean his boots and equipment, another to make his bed and help keep the barrack room clean, a third to help cook and wait at table—each paid a few annas a week. An officer had anything up to a score of native servants, grooms or *syces*. In Hindustani porridge was *bergoo*, bread was *rooti*, jam was *pozzie*, tea was *char*, high-class was *posh*.

"You're posh, aren't you?" the other said to him suddenly, as though to surprise him into admission of a secret.

Phillip smiled modestly. He had an idea, all the same, that he was not really posh; as regular army officers were posh, for example. Most of the officers in the battalion had been partners or directors of firms in the City, if they had been in business; some were above business, and owned land. They went to Oxford University; perhaps to Cambridge; but not to London University. They were *really* posh. He was a sort of mongrel, a half-and-half person. All the same it was rather nice to be considered *posh*, in spite of the fact that the soldier could not really tell the difference. He was like Cranmer, who had believed that he was of another world.

The East Surrey man packed up one morning, for a base camp. Phillip felt very sorry for him. From the base camp he would go with a draft up the line. *When hard fighting comes——* The East Surrey man was bound to be killed. The regulars on 19 December had had to make attacks against uncut barbed-wire, as there were not enough high-explosive shells to cut it. The few lyddite shells of the British as often as not burst in their own trenches, or beyond the German; so the gunners used shrapnel to try and cut the thick belts of wire, with machine-gun bullets to help. As if a round lead shrapnel ball, or a pointed nickel bullet, could cut stretched or loose wire! It would in most cases ricochet off. So the regulars, cheering hoarsely, or rather uttering oaths and shouts of fear, were mown down before the enemy wire.

The East Surrey man looked worried all the time. He had far-staring dark eyes, and looked white about the face, and muttered a lot in his sleep, poor devil. He had no ten-shilling notes to spare; his wife lived in Bethnal Green, on a tiny little separation allowance. Phillip felt bad when he had gone away.

Alone in the room, shaded electric lamp by his bed, he lay and tried not to think of the truth of things. The truth was a sort of dry-rot, like there had been under the downstairs lavatory floor before Father had scattered carbolic about. He had gone down the trap-door with Father long ago, and seen the old 'cello standing there. Father had shaken the bottle, and a dollop had burned his leg. He hadn't cried, he remembered; and

Father had come up to his room when he was in bed, and looked at the blister with a candle, and then given him a bar of Callard and Bowser's cherry toffee, on condition that he ate it in the morning, since he had cleaned his teeth; and he had sucked it when Father had gone, then wrapped it in the silver paper again, in case Father came back, and said that he could not be trusted.

When the ten-shilling note arrived in a letter, with cigarettes and tobacco, Phillip said to the orderly, an amiable chap who sometimes sat on his bed and talked to him, "I say, could you get me marked 'bunk', before I get too well?"

"Why, d'you want to go home?"

"Yes, and I'll explain why. It's going to be a bloody long war. Have a Three Castles fag? Have several, go on, have a handful. You blokes don't get the issue that we get up the line. Honestly, we paved the trench with air-tight tins of Capstan."

"Go on!"

"It's a fact. I'll send you a hundred fags if I get home. I can send them duty-free, you know. Honestly, do you think I've got any chance to be marked 'bunk'?"

"I'll see the doctor. He says you are debilitated, and need a rest. Anyway, we are clearing out this place soon, getting ready for the spring offensive."

Phillip took the note out of the envelope.

"Anyway, here's a little present for looking after me so well."

That evening when the doctor appeared—he always entered the room suddenly and left abruptly—he pointed a stylo-pen at Phillip and said dramatically, "You are too pale, you are not getting well fast enough, you are debilitated, so I am going to send you home for a long convalescence!" Then seizing the chart on its wooden board, he scribbled the word BUNK on it.

Phillip hoped that his face would remain pale and debilitated at least until the door shut behind the doctor. He lay quiet and solemn while the doctor stared at him, before turning on his heel and departing. The orderly, as he went out of the door, smiled at him. As soon as the door was closed, he got out of bed much quicker than he had been practising of late, and danced a jig on the oil-cloth. Then, lest it give him a good colour, he got back sedately into bed again, where he simmered with suppressed delight.

"When do I go?" he asked the orderly, at lights-out.

"Next boat, laddie. Probably early tomorrow morning. You'll go from Lee 'arf."

"Well, thanks very much for all you've done."

"Don't mention it," said the orderly, in a mock-posh voice. "The pleasure is entirely mine. Now you get some kip, you mustn't run a temperature now, hor you'll have to stop 'ere— here. How's that for classy speakin'?"

"Very posh indeed."

In the night he grieved for the East Surrey soldier. He had been really sick, after a burst appendix. He had hoped to be marked *Bunk*, and get home to Bethnal Green, to see "the missus and kids". Phillip shivered as he thought of the East Surrey soldier having to go up the line again; then, as he hid his head under the warm blankets, thoughts of *Bunk* made him entirely happy for himself.

In the morning letters, pipe, matches, packet of toffees, pencil, writing paper and envelopes, Prussian Guard leather belt with other souvenirs—all his few, portable possessions went into the linen bag given him for the purpose; and holding it on his stomach, he was carried on a stretcher down flights of stairs and so to the hall of the hotel. It was a day bright with north-east wind. When the motor ambulance came, a nurse bent down and gave him a delicious drink of hot milk, honey, egg, and brandy. He thanked her, and was lifted up into the ambulance, which held three stretcher cases. The motor was driven by a civilian Englishman in sloppy khaki cap with a red-cross badge on the front, and a loose-fitting khaki tunic—volunteer driver from the Royal Automobile Club.

The back of the body was open, the canvas door strapped back. Phillip could see the Channel, grey with rocking white tips of waves, and low chalk cliffs, as the motor hummed along the coast road. He felt warm and contented. He was marked *Bunk*: he was going to England! No-one in the ambulance spoke. He could see only the man opposite, who had a yellow face, a dark look of extreme weakness about it.

Soon the journey was over. He saw an immense red cross painted on the white side of the hospital ship. On a stretcher he was carried past iron doors opened in the side of the ship. There were hundreds of beds with railed sides, like children's cots, filling the wide floor within. With a mild shock he heard from an orderly that it was one of the Mackarness Antipodean liners. Uncle Hilary's line! He lay all the morning in a cot, dozing and counting the number of port-holes converging along the walls. They were very crowded in the distance: he must count them before the ship left, otherwise he would be sent back to the front. Each counting gave a different number. He tried to scorn his superstitious dread; but returned to the counting. Then a slight vibration through everything told that it was heading for the open sea, and he gave it up. Why were not the port-holes covered? An orderly said the red-crosses were lit up by electricity on both sides, as warning marks for German submarines. Phillip hoped he would not be sick, as he had been going to Le Havre five months before. Five months! It was a lifetime.

He slept fitfully in the night; and lay awake in periods of calm reflection, picturing his home-coming. He would see Mother, Desmond, Mrs. Neville, Gran'pa, Aunt Marian, Father, his sisters and cousins. There would be his old white rat, Timmy, in the scullery. His birds' eggs in his corner cupboard, his model yacht *Dipper*, stationary steam-engine, his electrical apparatus, and best of all his saloon gun and fly-fishing rod! And thinking of the old life in a sweet dream, he fell asleep and awakened to realise that the ship was gliding, the engines hardly turning.

"We're in Southampton Water, lad," said the orderly, bringing him a mug of tea. It tasted so funny with milk, sort of white-fatty.

In the hospital train—of trucks white-painted inside and fitted with beds separated by a walking space down the middle—telegraph forms were given out, for messages to next-of-kin. Where were they going? A passing orderly told him. There were no windows in the truck, so he could not see what England looked like after all the long time.

> MADDISON LINDENHEIM WAKENHAM KENT
> PROCEEDING HOSPITAL BIRMINGHAM
> LOVE TO ALL PHILLIP

Kent sounded more countryfied than London, S.E., which was really the postal address. He imagined Mother running in to tell Gran'pa and Aunt Marian; then Mrs. Bigge, perhaps, and then Mrs. Neville, and Aunt Dorrie. Cousin Gerry was already at home, and with the Second Battalion, his wound having healed. Cousin Bertie was at Caterham, having been given a special reserve commission in the Lilywhites, his grandfather's regiment. Fancy having to salute old Bertie! He would make a good officer, being so calm and thorough.

The viewless journey became tedious. The electric lights were put out, except one. The orderly appeared now and again, on plimsolled feet, to bring or take a china bottle. Why was everything so noisy, rattles everywhere, the wheels thumping so loudly over the breaks in the rails? Why were pictures of the Menin Road and all that hell so persistent in his mind? Ah, how lovely was the hot milk, with sugar and beaten egg in it! Now he could feel snug.

When he awakened the train had stopped. He lay drowsing contentedly between rough sheets (so much more intimate, somehow, than the smooth ones at Étretat) while it crawled on; stopped; went on gradually, until voices outside told him that they had arrived. The doors were rolled back, revealing cold lilac lights of arc-lamps above a station platform.

"Manchester," said the orderly. "They couldn't take you little old lot at Brum."

He was put on a stretcher, his bullet-torn overcoat, tail slashed off, covering blanket, as, glengarry on head, he was carried past staring civilians.

"Good old Jock," said a man. "How are ye, laddie?"

"Arl recht the no', mon," replied Phillip, feeling like Harry Lauder. He hoped they would ask no more questions and find out that he was a fraud; so closed his eyes, pretending weariness.

The motor ambulance went to Ancoats Military Hospital as Phillip learned on entering the gloomy hall. He was put in a ward with fifty other patients.

In the morning, after inspection, he was given a hospital suit of bright-blue jacket and trousers lined with white flannel, carpet slippers, grey socks, and a red tie. Many of the men of his ward smoked clay cutty pipes and thick twist, which they cut up with knives, like the regulars in France. A whiff of smoke from one of them made his eyes smart, so he kept to the bulldog Vichand pipe Father had bought for him at the Stores, and Hignett's Cavalier.

There was a room guarded by a soldier with rifle and bayonet. A dozen German prisoners were inside, dimly seen through the lower frosted glass.

"Can't I go in and see them, sentry?"

"My orders are no-one's to enter, mate."

Phillip saw they had shaven heads. Some were on crutches.

"Does anyone visit them?"

"Only the Medical Officer."

"It wouldn't do any harm, would it?"

"None s'far's I know, but orders is orders."

He went away, after waving at the curious figures. Instantly they waved back, smiling.

The next day he was driven out, in hospital garb, to a convalescent home at Alderley Edge. He was in Cheshire. How he was seeing the world! The convalescent home was also an asylum, with a great many buildings. One of them was for soldiers; the others for civvies, mental cases and nervous disorders.

The soldiers' wing was almost empty, most of the patients having recently been sent back to their regiments after ten days' leave. *When hard fighting comes——* Only about two dozen soldiers, including three Belgians in civvy suits, remained.

He made friends with this trio first. They were from the flooded Yser district. One, with crutches, had a very sad face, and a shattered leg in plaster cast. The other two were stronger looking. The second was thickset, with blue eyes and reddish hair; the third, a corporal, was smaller, but well set up, with pale face rather like that of Georges Carpentier, the European heavyweight champion boxer.

The corporal, in an aside, explained that the man on crutches was a peasant, and could neither read nor write, being a foundling who had worked on a farm for his keep before being mobilised. He was worrying, he said, because after the war he would have to starve. His leg was very bad, the wound would not heal; but he would not have it off, lest he be unable to work on the farm after the war. He knew no other life except on the farm. He himself, explained the corporal, had his job to go back to, in a bank; so had Jacques, who worked in a bakery. But Jules—he had, how do you speak it, no prospects.

Phillip got from the corporal the full name of Jules; and in his first letter to his mother asked her to send Jules a "parcel of goodies", up to ten shillings in value, including postage, and "debit his a/c with this sum". She must on no account mention her name, as it must be an anonymous gift. "Just put a card in it, in French, 'To Jules, from a Soldier's Friend who knows and loves Belgium'. It is you who are the Soldier's Friend who loves Belgium, not me, but I will pay."

The doctor visited once every morning. He was a bluff old grey-moustached country doctor who wore a floppy tweed hat stuck with rusty trout-flies from which the gut had rotted. A straight wooden stethoscope always stuck out of his pocket. His visits were brief, his questions perfunctory.

"Everyone all right? No change? Everyone mending nicely? That's right! Hullo, you're new, aren't you? Feeling all right?"

"Quite all right, sir."

"What's your name? Regiment?"

"Maddison, sir. London Highlanders."

"Good fellow. No aches, no pains?"

"No, sir."

"Good! Keep warm. Like your food?"

"Yes, thank you, sir."

"Good. Well, I must be trottin'. See you all tomorrow. G'morning, Matron!" and out he went again, to his trap on the drive, where a red-faced groom in bowler hat held the striped hammer-cloth to wrap round the doctor's knees before jumping up behind, and away dashed the pony to a wave of the whip.

There were other visitors. The matron greeted them. She explained beforehand that the most important was the Countess of Cheshire, who should always be addressed as "m'lady". When she came, she spoke to each man, asking him one or two questions in a smiling, easy, Irish voice. She invited some to tea every afternoon, six at a time, taking turns. The six went for a motor-ride first in a large black Daimler, driven by a big, clean-shaven chauffeur, who spoke in a gentle, quiet voice. He saw that the dark-blue rugs, each with its coronet, were tucked neatly and solidly round their legs.

Phillip, when his turn came, sat in front, hardly daring to speak to the chauffeur of such a lordly equipage proceeding at a uniform rate of twelve miles an hour round the roads for half an hour before arrival at the Big House, where rugs were taken off knees, refolded correctly for the return journey, coronet upwards; and the six went hesitant and curious into a hall like a small church, where coat-armour stood with pikes and halberds, and old pictures hung on the walls.

Tea was served by a man-servant in a large room of inlaid furniture with spidery legs, glass cases holding china and other valuables, and a polished steel hearth wherein enormous logs blazed. There were lovely water-colour paintings on the walls. In another large room, which he heard mentioned as the Ball-room, were rows of beds, and men in civilian tweeds and officer uniforms sitting on them smoking. After one glance, Phillip fled. The beds, he learned, were occupied by sick and wounded officers; the châtelaine had turned her mansion into a private hospital, paying all the expenses herself. Two of the nurses were her daughters, others their friends. He had no feeling of being over-awed, as he had been when visiting Aunt Victoria at Epsom, for here everything seemed very free and easy. The countess was very natural, he thought, and just like any other old lady—except that she seemed more energetic, and to the point. She wore a floppy old blue hat with a riband round it, a man's upright starched linen collar, and a black sort of man's coat. He was not in the least afraid of her. Her husband, the earl, was at the front. She asked him where he lived; and remembering that Mr. Purley-Prout, the scoutmaster, had addressed the Countess of Mersea, when she had come to visit the camp, as "Mar'm", Phillip said "mar'm" now and again, instead of "m'lady". Then, on learning that she had known his first colonel, the Earl of Findhorn, Phillip lost his tongue.

"Do come and see us again before you go, won't you? And when you are stronger, you must tell me about Findhorn, a dear friend and schoolfellow of Cheshire."

Phillip said he would while thinking that he must avoid it by all means in his power, since the countess obviously believed that he was the *friend* of the Earl of Findhorn, and *posh*. When next his turn came to visit the Big House he pretended to have a headache; and went instead to visit the epileptics in their room where they played billiards and snooker. The soldiers were wel-come any time during the day.

Among the inmates he had made friends with a man who had misty blue eyes and fair hair. This man had already given him some lessons in billiards: how to hold a cue properly, resting your left hand on the table and making a bridge with your fingers, how to strike with the cue steadily, not jerkily, or you would tear the cloth and likely send the ball bouncing heavily over the cush onto the floor.

When he arrived at the epileptics' wing a concert was being given by the patients. A contralto was singing on the platform *When you come down the Vale, Lad*, clutching her music at arm's length before her, while another woman tried to keep time on the piano. The contralto was just singing the words *There's music in the air* when a third woman got up in the middle of the hall, gave a wailing cry and collapsed, and was carried off while the song proceeded. Two others followed the same way before the last verse, and then the singer herself had an attack, while the accompanist hastily beat out *God Save the King*.

"Funny," said Phillip's misty-eyed friend. "But When you come down the Vale, Lad often sets off the female patients. Do you notice that there is a similarity between the sort of cooing bellow of the contralto and the cooing or moaning of the patient before she goes down? There's a reason for it, to my way of thinking."

"Does it have to do with sympathetic vibrations? You know, Caruso was supposed to have shattered the chandelier once in Covent Garden?"

"You've said it!" cried the other, putting down his billiard cue. "You've got it! I advanced that theory to Dr. Shufflebotham, you know, the one who sees to you fellers, but he poohpoohed it. Ah, what does he know what we have to go through, in our minds, before we feel a fit coming on? In the old days, they used to pummel the patients, to get them out of it, to make them fight the attack. Some used to recommend dousin' 'em with water. Barbarous old times, weren't they? Can you imagine it?"

"I should think I can! Why, in our battalion, a chap . . ." and Phillip recounted the story of the man whose appendix was about to burst being given a No. 9 pill and duty. Only this time he varied the details. "He lies buried in the Brasserie cemetery, by the cross-roads between Vierstraat and Elzenwalle, at this very moment!"

"I know, you needn't tell me, the whole world's gone off its rocker. There's a soldier here now, who has fits. He was at Mons, and never had so much as a quaver before the war. He was blown up by a shell. 'Dusty' Miller, they call him. He lies in bed next to me, and often I hear him crying. He bites through his sheets, not in a fit, mark you, but just lying in bed. But the doctor says it is a variant of epilepsy. Can you beat that?"

Phillip wondered how he could beat it, while he tried to pot the red. Then he stood up. "I'll tell you one thing, old chap!" (He never knew his friend's name.) "And that is this! No-one who has not been out in France can possibly imagine what it is really like. If you read the papers, with their humorous descriptions of our chaps, and the 'humourless Hun' opposite, you'll get no idea at all!" He bent down to do the stroke. The red went wide. "Curse, I can't get the angle." He stood up. "I suppose, in the old days, cannon balls used to bounce off positions, like these balls. Nowadays they don't bounce off any more. They strike home, and the chips fly—chips of flesh and bone, I mean. And the worst feeling of all is not the fear, but the loneliness. I don't mean that we have no pals, but——"

"That's all right, old man, I understand. You've done your bit, so take it easy!"

Another interesting place to visit was the back-door of the boozer, as O'Casey called the village pub. They weren't allowed to sell drinks to soldiers in hospital blue, and it was war-time closing anyway, during the day, explained O'Casey, an old sweat of the Liverpool Regiment, who took Phillip. "Say nothing at all, at all." "Not a word," replied Phillip, paying for the drinks of hot Irish whiskey with water and sugar in the kitchen. It was a wry taste, he didn't really want it, but it was the thing to do. He didn't want the clay pipe he bought, either, on O'Casey's advice, with the twopenny roll of thick twist; but he smoked it, until he was sick. Then O'Casey got him some brandy, to cure the sickness, and had one himself to keep him company. "A rookie 'as allus to buy his way in the army, and you're with a real so'jer now, my lad," said O'Casey.

Phillip wondered how he could get rid of O'Casey, without hurting the old fellow's feelings. The Liverpool Irishman, who had long grey-black hair brushed back over a nobbly forehead, and a cunning rather lined but handsome face, one night in the dormitory did it himself. O'Casey was telling funny stories, chuckling as he spoke, of his adventures in Dublin and Liverpool, and stories of the army, too. One was about a soldier in India who got the "doolally tap", according to his mates. His madness took the form of crawling about on hands and knees, examining every little bit of paper he came across. He even pursued this peculiarity, said O'Casey, across the barrack square while the Commander-in-Chief of India and the Viceroy

themselves with their ladies had come a-visiting the Colonel.
"Put that pore feller in hospital," cried no less a man than the
Viceroy himself. In hospital the soldier continued to crawl
about on hands and knees, examining the most minute pieces
of paper. At last, as a harmless lunatic, he was discharged;
whereupon he walked upright, and passing the guard-room
on his way out, waved his discharge and said: "I've found that
little bit of paper I was looking for!"

O'Casey laughed ferociously, revealing teeth brown with
chewing quids of thick twist. "He was a clever sod, to think
that one out!" The word *sod* was frequently used among the
old soldiers in the dormitory, so, when the laughter had stopped,
Phillip called across, meaning it as a compliment, "You are a
clever old sod yourself, O'Casey!" whereupon without a
moment's hesitation the Liverpool Irishman leapt out of bed,
ran across the floor in nightshirt and bare feet, and bending over
Phillip's face, his clenched fists an inch off Phillip's nose, cried
harshly, all humour gone from his attitude, "I'll batter yer
head off if you insult me mother! How dare you call me a sod!
Me mother was an honest woman!" with such intense fury that
Phillip shut his eyes, awaiting blows on his face, after saying
that he was sorry. O'Casey went back to bed, just as the lights
went out, muttering and spluttering about rookies who had
not yet got their foreskins back daring to tell him, who had
gone through every campaign from Chitral and Oomdurman,
North-West Frontier, South Africa, and Mons, who his father
was.

Phillip went no more with this ferocious joker to drink Irish
whiskey in the kitchen of the little pub. He had already given
clay pipe and black twist to Jules, the Belgian *blessé*, who
seemed much more cheerful since he had had a parcel, containing socks, scarf, tin of *café-au-lait*, plum cake, chocolate,
raisins, figs, a book of the convent at Thildonck with pictures,
a pair of mittens, a red flannel chest-protector, and what he
liked best of all, a small crucifix, silver on ebony, of the kind
Phillip wore.

While he was at Alderley Edge, Phillip had letters from
Desmond, Mrs. Bigge, Mrs. Todd, and others, welcoming him
back. One was in the meticulously neat writing of Tom Ching,
on Admiralty writing paper. It might have been written, he

thought, by a tender male nurse. It described the wonderful times he, his dear old school chum, would give Phillip when he was safely home: the walks he would take him, holding his arm in memory of old days; the fatted ox that would be killed to welcome him home, etc. Tom Ching even wrote the last word on every page twice, as a carry-over word, to aid the eyesight, apparently.

This letter, slightly nauseating, told Phillip only that Tom Ching was still after his sister Mavis. And Phillip had never forgotten the occasion when Tom Ching had spat in his eye, and run away. Ugh! What a creature! He threw the letter in the fire.

At the end of a fortnight he was passed Fit for Light Duty after a brief listening-patrol by the old doctor with his brown wooden stethoscope. The examination was about as useful as a listening-patrol, because the doctor, whose white moustache was yellow with nicotine, was wheezing away all the time one end of the stethoscope was on Phillip's ribs and the other end in the doctor's ear. The next day he was driven into the town for a medical board, with several others, including O'Casey. Jules, Jacques and Pierre waved in the doorway, beside Matron and the nurses. In an ambulance they rode to Manchester, to the Ancoats Military Hospital. On the way they passed some of the new Kitchener's Army, in odd blue uniforms with red forage caps worn more or less flat and square on their heads. They marched with yellow Japanese rifles at the slope, and what a slope! That rag-tag-bob-tailed lot, remarked Phillip to O'Casey, what use would they be—rookies!

"Thank God for the Navy, O'Casey."

"Don't let me hear you take That Name in vain, my friend," replied O'Casey, grimly. "Me mother was a religious woman, and taught me at her knee."

Phillip noticed that O'Casey now had a walking-stick, and appeared to be, as he declared to Dr. Shufflebotham, a proper cripple from rheumatism. He had a rosary, and was telling his beads while he awaited his turn for the medical board. He went into the room for this before Phillip, his face all twisted up, like his walk; and came out scowling a minute or two later, saying with a hoarse laugh as he threw the stick on a table, "Anyone want this ould shillelagh? Only don't let anyone, for love of the Blessed Mother of God, take it in there wid him before that lot of ould sods! Bad 'cess to it, it brought me no luck at all, at all!"

He cackled with laughter as he held up a little paper bag. "Blime, the ould counthry's sound at heart, boys! An old geyser in there gimme this bag o' suckers, to keep me little tootsies warm all the way to Frisby Dyke!" Then with his old swagger O'Casey picked up his bundle of possessions, clapped his shapeless service cap on his head, and walked out, puffing a Woodbine.

Phillip was given three weeks' leave, a little bag of bull's-eye sweets ("This is from the Lancashire Methodists' Fund for Soldier Comforts") and a railway voucher to Randiswell. For some reason, after all the prolonged anticipation and hope, the sight of this name made his heart sink. Rather tremulously he wrote out a telegram in the sooty station: ARRIVING TONIGHT PHILLIP.

Chapter 7

HOMECOMING

IT felt strange to be wearing a tunic again, kilt and hose of hodden grey under the bullet-ripped greatcoat with nearly two feet of its length missing, and the old glengarry. He had been given a ten-shilling note on production of his pay-book, but no food; and since there was no dining-car on the London train, he sat in his corner seat in the empty carriage until the arrival at St. Pancras. Then, in what seemed to be a very lonely and uncaring London, by Underground to Charing Cross and the train home. How drab and empty everything looked. At Randiswell he got out, and crossed over the wooden bridge. A new porter took his voucher without a word as he walked through the door into the waiting-room where the newspapers were still displayed on trestle tables by the coal fire in the grate. Ah, there sitting on the edge of the trestle table was the same old tom cat with the sulky bee-face and torn ears that he remembered when, for a change, he had caught the train to the office on the S.E. and C.R. line from Randiswell. The cat was a great dog-fighter, waiting on the corner of the trestle table to spring on the back of any dog, no matter how big, which dared to enter the waiting-room. Paws round dog's neck, the cat clung and bit and ripped with its hind claws as the dog rushed away with its unwanted jockey. Then, dog seen off, the cat dismounted and walked slowly back to its perch on the newspaper table.

"Hullo, Moggy, how are you? Remember me?"

The hunched-up object did not move so much as a flip of its ear. Phillip continued to rub its neck until his persistence drew a tiny, rusty purr. Ha, the cat remembered him after all! "Puss-puss, good old puss-puss!"

Randiswell looked dull. There was the flashy Railway Tavern at the corner of the High Road; Longstaff's the grocer's opposite, next to the sweet-stuff shop; then Hawkins the barber's, beside the boot shop; Soal the green grocer's, then a length of advertisement hoarding, stretching to the newsvendor's shop; Chamberlain's the butcher; Hern's the grocer's. All looking so much smaller than he had remembered them. He walked past them all, hoping not to be recognised; and saw no familiar faces. Then more hoardings—ah, there it was still, the great dark stare of Kitchener, black moustache much wider than the face, finger pointing. Your Country needs YOU. He hurried on, his gaze on the pavement. At the corner, the baker's; then the curve of Charlotte Road, with its chestnut trees, and houses leading up from steps, all nearly hidden behind unclipped privet hedges.

Charlotte Road seemed much shorter, somehow. Past Mr. Bolton's house; past Aunt Dorrie's; past, with furtive glances, the blind-drawn front of the Wallaces' house opposite. A glance, half uncertain, a little unsure, at the upper window of Mrs. Neville's flat. No-one sitting at the window; no large white face, no wave, no smile. With controlled agitation he turned the corner into Hillside Road. How short it was. The great mass of the red brick Modern School that had enclosed the poor little West Kent Grammar School looked very square and near and brick-heavy on the Hill. And how small, really, was the grassy slope below the sheep-fold, where once the toboggan runs had seemed so long in the snow-light of winter. With a start he thought that the School might be a larger Hospice on the Wytschaete Ridge. Soon the flares would be rising, twilight was coming, braziers would be showing red along the line of bunkers in the wood. O, why had he come back? something cried inside him, as he walked slowly past house after house. He was about to go by No. 6, when he saw Mrs. Todd was beckoning at the window. He waited reluctantly, then the door opened.

"Phillip, Phillip, welcome back! Here, give me a kiss, dear!" Mrs. Todd hugged him. He pushed slightly against the hug. "Now, Phillip, your mother will be waiting. She told us you were coming! We are all so proud of you! See the flag, dear? That's for you!" The big, kindly woman kissed him again, he felt the tears on his cheek, but pretended not to notice them. A printed Union Jack, about three feet by two, hung from its stick tied on the balcony. "We're all proud of you, Phillip."

"Goodbye, Mrs. Todd."

He saw a flag outside "Sailor" Jenkins' house, but, thankfully, no round small red face of Mrs. Jenkins behind the lace curtains. Blank as usual, almost grim, was the front of No. 9, the Groats, above the hearth-stoned steps. Mr. Groat, taciturn headmaster of the Deptford Council School, who had coached him for his scholarship: his boyish tears, he couldn't learn, while all Mr. Groat said, after long and ponderous silences, was "Think, boy! Think!" He passed by quickly; and saw two flags sticking out from under Mrs. Bigge's bedroom windows. One was the Royal Standard, as on the Rolls-Royce bonnet of the King at the Hazebrouck inspection, the other a Union Jack. And there was dear old Mother Bigge gesticulating at her downstairs window. Up it went, the same old window-cord squeal.

"Welcome home, Phillip! We're all so very very proud of you! Now mind you go straight in and give Mother a big hug! She's so excited. Be patient, I told her, Phillip'll come all in good time. You see, dear, I didn't want Mother to get one of her bilious attacks! Now go on in with you!" and down squealed the window.

He stopped a moment at his gate, seeing the letter-marks of its old name painted over, and the brass number 11 in their place. He hesitated before pushing open the gate, and having done so, was most careful, even anxious, to close it quietly, restraining the coiled black spring. On tip-toe he walked under the glassed-in porch; more hesitation, struggling with a destructive wish to go away, to remain cold within himself, and alone, for ever and ever.

Feeling wan, he sat down on the brick wall above Mrs. Bigge's alley-way. There was her dustbin down below, just the same. Why was it all so disappointing, so drab, so—colourless? Why had the neighbours put out those awful flags? Why, O why, had Mother told them that he was coming home?

Then, as with thud of a bullet, the idea struck him that he had no right to be home. Peter Wallace, and David, and Nimmo were the ones to be proud of. They were brave, they were heroes, they had stood by one another, by their friends; when the Bavarians had broken through they had died fighting, in that night of burning farm and windmill and cornstack at Messines.

As he sat there, he heard the gate bang, and stood up. It was Mother. She did not see him at first. When she did, she stopped, her mouth opened slightly, then she said, still standing still, "Is that Phillip? Is that you, dear?" as though for a moment she had seen a ghost.

"Hullo."

"Phillip, Phillip, how long have you been there? Didn't you ring the bell? Doris is in. You mustn't catch cold." She pressed the bell. "Well, dear, and how are you?"

"Oh, all right."

"We were expecting you later on, dear. Your telegram said tonight. Well, you're here now, that's all that matters!" she said with forced cheerfulness. He looked so thin, so lonely, so lost.

Doris came to the door. Her eyes opened wide, she smiled, showing her canine teeth slightly overlapping, then pink spread up her cheeks. "Good old Phil! Bravo, well done, say I! Have you just come? We were expecting you to arrive about the same time as Father. Gramps tried to work out the trains from Manchester on his time-table, only it was a Bradshaw, printed before the war. Well, how are you, old boy? Still feeling a little dickey?"

"Don't keep Phillip on the door-step, dear. He will be tired after his journey. Come in, dear, and sit by the fire."

He followed her on to the mat. There was really no need to wipe his boots, but he did so; then hanging greatcoat and glengarry on his peg of the hatstand—first removing a special constable's hat—he went down to the sitting-room. It seemed very small, somehow. The same old plush tablecloth, Father's green-leather armchair, the cane-bottom rocking chair, the pictures, roll-top desk, bookcase, gramophone, mantelpiece that Father would call chimney-piece, the same green roll-blinds, the darkling silhouette of the elm tree seen through french-windows, horse-hair sofa still broken at one place, crackling coke fire—ah, crackling like the braziers in the frost, before the floods. The same lilac-pink flames, like the charcoal Maconochie hand-braziers of the Lilywhites and the Bill Browns. Cranmer's lucky fire-bucket . . .

"Sit down, dear, and rest. I expect you're hungry. Have you had any tea?"

"I had a cup at London Bridge, thanks, and some bull's-eyes."

"Anything to eat?"

When he shook his head, Hetty said, "Doris dear, lay the cloth. I'll soon have something for you, Phillip." She went out to the kitchen.

"Well, Phil, what was it like out there?"

"Oh, I don't know."

When Doris had laid the cloth and set a silver-plated spoon and fork, he sat at the table. Every dent and scratch of the spoon was familiar to him, as was the ivory-handled knife part-blackened where many hot soda-water washings had seeped after cracking the ivory, Father's querulous complaining voice, *Very well then, if Mrs. Feeney doesn't know any better after all these years, all I can say is that it is time she did know better.*

"I say, Phil, you won't forget to kiss Mother, will you? She has been so looking forward to your return, old boy."

"Oh, *do* shut up."

Hetty came in with a tray, on which was a loaf of white bread, a knife with wooden handle cut in the pattern of a wheat-sheaf, salt and pepper castors, and a plate with two slices of cold mutton lying in its centre. She put them down.

"Now dear, try and eat, a little food will do you good."

He took up the knife with the cracked and blackened handle, the fork with the prongs straightened by himself after he had bent them using them as a harpoon on a stick. He looked at the cold mutton. Seeing with the eye's retina the two faces regarding him, he got up and without a word went out of the room, and up the stairs to his bedroom.

Hetty looked at her younger daughter. "I expect everything seems a bit strange to him, dear. Did you say anything to upset him, when I was out of the room?"

"No, Mum. Of course not."

"I expect he'll be all right soon. Perhaps, after his illness, the sight of cold mutton has put him off. I'll boil him an egg —put one on the gas, will you, dear, and make some toast—what a pity, I'd prepared some plaice for him, I expected your Father with Phillip, I don't know why, and imagined us all having dinner together, as Phillip likes it to be called. Anyway, you boil the egg, Doris, and make some toast. Phillip's stomach agrees with a boiled egg. I meant it the other way. Hush, Doris, it is no laughing matter, we mustn't laugh. Not just now, at any rate."

Upstairs, Phillip had taken one look in his corner cupboard; felt nothing for the boyhood "treasures" within; closed it; and was sitting on the bed when Hetty looked round the door.

"Are you all right, Phillip?"

As he did not look at her, she put her arm round his shoulder. He moved away from her; and turning his face to the wall, wept.

She felt swollen with sympathy withheld, as she sat there. He went on crying when she took his hand; still his head was turned from her. It had always been like that, ever since he was three years old; her little boy had not wanted her. Even so, he was still her son. She made another attempt to bring him to her.

"It's—it's all so different, Mother. My room—this house —you know—out there—I used to think of it—and every-thing——"

Hetty reached up and kissed his brow. "There now, don't you worry, Sonny. You *are* still my little son, you know——" and, her assumed cheerfulness gone, she broke into tears.

"Here, have my hanky, Mum." He pulled it out of his pocket with a piece of string and a bull's-eye sweet. "It's the khaki one that came in the St. Simon's Christmas packet. Not very clean, I'm afraid. And I saved you a bull's-eye, it should be rinsed before you eat it."

"How very kind and thoughtful of you, dear! Mrs. Feeney is coming tomorrow, and she can do all your washing. Now, come down with me, and warm yourself by the fire. You must not worry any more, now that you are home again. Father and I want you to be very happy. He is so proud of you, so are we all. Come along, Doris is very kindly boiling you an egg, and making some buttered toast."

Having eaten this, and drunk several cups of sugary tea, Phillip felt better. He showed them the crucifix on its leather bootlace round his neck with the *papier-mâché* identity disc; the Prussian Guard leather-belt, with the brass clasp *Gott Mit Uns*; six pieces of 5.9 shell, three leaden shrapnel balls; a tiny pair of wooden *sabots* found in the Château; and best of all, Princess Mary's Gift Box, with its contents and the cigar a German soldier had given him on Christmas Day.

"It's an odd thing, but all you fellows are the same, in so far as I can make out," said Richard, sitting in his armchair later that evening. "Not one of you wants to talk about the front. Why, bless my soul, each of you must have had enough experiences to fill a book. Yet you never speak about what goes on out there. Why is it, Phillip?"

"Oh, I don't know, Father."

"Well, tell me this, old chap, did you shoot any Germans?"

"I don't know, Father."

"Well, you beat the band!" laughed Richard. "Your cousin Gerry Cakebread was just the same when he came home. Hubert we have not seen yet, though I believe he went in to see his grandfather next door. A very soldierly figure Hubert is nowadays, what I believe is called a Guardee. A very decent fellow, he takes after his father, Sidney Cakebread."

"Is he or Gerry at home, Mother?"

"I don't think so, dear. Gerry is with the second battalion, and Bertie at Caterham still, so far as I know."

"Before I forget it, Phillip, no doubt Mother has told you about Timmy Rat—we were sorry to have to put him down, Phillip, but he had croup very badly, and the skin disease was spreading, and with all my Special Constabulary work, and late hours at the office——"

"Oh, that's all right, Father. Timmy's race was run."

"He had a reprieve, you know, old chap, on the day the news came about Messines—— Oh well, Hetty, have it your own way!" Richard laughed, seeing his wife's frown-signal. She went out of the room, ostensibly to look at the fish kept hot for Mavis' supper—the girl had gone straight from the office to a St. John of Jerusalem Ambulance Brigade meeting in St. Simon's Parish Hall. Doris was doing her homework.

"If you don't mind," said Phillip, "I think I'll just go in and say how d'you do to Gran'pa and Aunt Marian."

"Wrap up well, old chap! We don't want to lose you, now we've got you home, you know. By Jove, you had a narrow squeak, judging by your greatcoat!"

"Oh, I'll be all right, Father."

"Come back afterwards, and play the gramophone, Phillip, if you care to. I shall have to leave at seven-forty-five precisely, as I am on special constable's duty tonight."

"Well, thank you, Father, but I think I'll go and see Mrs. Neville, after I've been next door."

"Very well, just as you wish. You know, I suppose, that Desmond has joined up?"

"Desmond? But he's only sixteen!"

"Well, he's in uniform, and has left school, so I hear."

"He's in the London Electrical Engineers, and comes home every night," said Doris. "Didn't he write and tell you?"

"I had only two letters from him all the while I was out there."

"I expect he had a great deal to do, dear," said Hetty.

"Yes, I understand they have to do with searchlights," went on Richard. "Raids by Zeppelins, you know, old chap, can't be ruled out! The Prussians will stick at nothing to bring England down—you mark my words! It says here in the *Trident*——" and Richard read out part of a speech by Winston Churchill.

Phillip sat with his eyes on the tablecloth. After a while he said, "Well, I think I'll go and see Gran'pa now, Father. By the way, Mum, if Ching calls, tell him I've gone out, but don't say where. I did not want him to write his soppy letters to me, while I was in hospital."

"Very well, dear. But don't remain in the cold damp air too long, will you?"

Phillip did not stay long next door. Gran'pa was having supper. He refused a glass of wine, and also ideas about a spring offensive to the Scheldt. "You'll remember that river, at Antwerp, m'boy? Well, it says here in the *Telegraph* that the high land, or ridges, that would give command of it, now in German hands around the town of Ypres, if assaulted—in the spring—— Oh, must ye go? So soon? But you've only just come! I expect you'll want to talk to your mother. Tell her not to forget to come in for bezique, won't you? Keep well wrapped up. Goodness me, what's become of the rest of your overcoat?"

"I sold it, sir, to buy bread with."

"You're not serious, are ye——"

"The Belgian peasants, since the Cloth Hall was bombarded, can't get any material to patch the seats of the trousers of their grown-up sons who have dodged the call-up and are sitting about all day at home."

"Most reprehensible!" remarked Great-aunt Marian, with serious, attentive face.

"It was a joke, Aunt Marian. Well, I'm glad you're both keeping well. How is Mr. Bolton, Gran'pa?"

"Poor fellow, poor fellow," said Thomas Turney, sipping his claret. "His son's death has broken him. He's an old man now, before his time."

"Well, no-one can live for ever," said Phillip, eager to see Desmond. What luck, that Des was at home!

Outside the gate of "Wespaelar" he hesitated before tip-toeing up the road, to look at the house of Helena Rolls. He told himself that no flag would be hanging there; and saw that it was so. Chinks of light showed through the drawn curtains. Dare he call? No, they were probably at dinner. Mr. Rolls always dined at night, sometimes in a smoking jacket. Why did not Father wear his sometimes, with a white shirt? Turning away, he walked slowly down the road, to cross over and knock and wait while remembered footfalls came down the stairs. The door opened.

"Hullo, Desmond."

"Hullo, Phil. I was expecting you later. I've just come home, and am having my supper!"

As Desmond did not move at the open door, Phillip said, "Oh, I'll come back later then."

"Who is it, dear?" called out Mrs. Neville.

"It's Phillip, Mother."

"Well, aren't you going to ask him up, dear! Come on up, Phillip! Welcome back!"

He went up behind Desmond, feeling the floor shaking as Mrs. Neville came out of the drawing-room to kiss him— "Phillip, Phillip, dear boy——" He was hugged in her huge arms, led into the kitchen with a "Let's have a look at you, dear——" Then, to let Desmond finish his supper, Mrs. Neville told Phillip to make himself comfortable in the armchair by the fire, his old place.

Mrs. Neville asked no questions. Wide-eyed, with Mazeppa the large neuter cat at her feet, she looked at him, exuding sympathy, tragedy, acceptance. His thin, haunted look drew forth tears, which turned to gaiety very soon, as she gave him an account of the day when she had seen, from her window, Timmy Rat in his box being carried down the road by his mother, to the vet's; and then all the way up again. "Mazeppa knew there was something in the air, didn't you, Mazeppa? Oh yes, *he* knew! He was watching the box in your mother's hands, from Desmond's window, for Mazeppa remembered when you used to bring Timmy in his box here; and when Mr. Bolton came out of his house without his stick and gloves, to speak to your mother, we both knew there was something wrong. Yes, he'd had the War Office telegram——" Mrs. Neville dabbled her eyes again. "Mazeppa knew, cats do know, Phillip, I am sure. Yes, Mazeppa knew. He came and gave such a funny little howl when your mother went back with Timmy Rat up the road again. Ah, but it was no laughing matter, dear. Poor old Bolton, oh dear, what a day! Then the telegraph boy calling at Mrs. Wallace's, all three boys killed! Poor woman, she was distraught. When your Aunt Dorrie called to offer sympathy, she cried out, "It isn't right that you have two sons, while all mine are killed.""

"I did think of calling to see Mrs. Wallace, Mrs. Neville, but perhaps it would be better if I didn't."

Mrs. Neville knew about Phillip's past trouble with Peter Wallace, before Boy Scout days, when Peter had fought his battles for him.

"Well, it was a long time ago, Phillip, and that poor woman would be glad, I am sure, to hear anything about her boys." Mrs. Neville wiped away her tears. "What times we're living in! Well, you do what you think best, Phillip. There's no hurry, after all. Death is so—no, we must be cheerful! Now I expect you'll want to talk with Desmond. He'll want to take you down to 'Freddy's', if I know my son!" She called out to Desmond in the kitchen: "There's apple tart in the oven, dear!" To Phillip: "Don't say I told you, but Desmond wants to take you for a ride in his motorcar."

"A motorcar? Has Desmond got a motorcar?"

"Yes, but only lent to me for a week, by my uncle," said Desmond, holding a piece of tart as he came into the room.

"What is it?"

"Singer open two-seater."

"How wonderful. Where is it?"

"In Wetherley's garage. I'll take you for a drive when I get a day off."

"Desmond, what are you doing? Why don't you offer Phillip some of your apple tart?"

"He knows he can help himself, any time."

"No thanks, Mrs. Neville. I had enough Tickler's Apple and Plum in Belgium."

Phillip told them the story of the soldier who pretended to be mad, by crawling all over the barrack square picking up little bits of paper. This set Mrs. Neville quivering with laughter; and in happy mood, the two left for the High Street, on their way to Freddy's.

"Freddy is a most extraordinary man, in his way. Everyone calls him Freddy. He has a very good billiard table. I've learned to play since I joined up."

"I've played a bit, too, at Alderley Edge."

Freddy, in his warm, bright, saloon bar, politely lifted his yellow straw-hat. He was in shirt-sleeves, his cuffs kept back by nickel-silver bands. He smiled a Chinaman's smile, his eyes almost disappearing behind his gold-rimmed spectacles.

"Good evening, gentlemen! This is your friend we have had converse about, I take it? Welcome to my 'ouse, sir! May I have the pleasure of offering you one, as tribute to a hero? My word, you had a narrow escape!" The landlord stared at Phillip's greatcoat. "You need fortifying at once, if I may say so!"

"It will be a pleasure," said Phillip.

"The pleasure's mine," Freddy lifted the front of his hat again. "What is it, gentlemen?"

"I recommend Freddy's hot rum, Phil."

"That's the stuff to give the troops!"

After the half quartern of rum, Phillip began to feel that life was good. Then it was his turn to stand a round. Freddy politely tilted his hat again, and let down a half quartern of water from one of the bottles hanging upside down from a shelf behind the bar. "I'll take a drop of gin, gentlemen!" he said with his tittery laugh, his eyes almost disappearing. "Well, your very good health!"

They played a game of billiards. Phillip could neither pot nor go in off; only strike the ball hard in the hope that something would happen. Desmond reached fifty when Phillip's score was still thirteen. They put back the cues, and went through the stained-glass door to the saloon bar again.

More gas-mantles had been lit. The evening trade was beginning. Behind the mahogany counter stood a young woman, with a sweet childish smile on her face. It was a sly-eyed pretty face, with the dark hair drawn back tightly from her forehead. She carried a baby, rocking it. She looked about fourteen years old. Phillip ordered two more hot rums.

It was much nicer, taken hot with lemon and sugar, than the Belgian *rhum*, which had made him swirl. They sat on the horsehair settee, and Desmond began to tell Phillip about the extraordinary adventures of Freddy. He had been all over the world, according to his yarns to Desmond: Australia cattle-droving, New Zealand sheep-farming, diamond-mining in Africa, silver-mining in the United States, gun-running in Cuba, gold in Alaska. "Freddy's motto, he told me, in all those places," sniggered Desmond behind his hand, "was 'frig and run!'"

The way Desmond said this seemed to Phillip to be so fright-fully funny that he nearly spilled his drink with silent laughter. He pictured Freddy, in shirtsleeves kept up with nickel-silver bands, running, straw-hat on head, from one vast open space to another, a little cloud of dust behind him; then after a pause, and some polite hat-lifting and square-pushing as Cranmer would say, on again! Desmond was grunting with laughter beside him; several people turned to look at them on the settee, Phillip also grunting as he bent sideways with his backwards-in-throat laughter that he had "patented" at school, presenting expressionless face while jerky groan-like noises were stifled upon indrawn breath. Desmond, who had copied the patent, sat groaning beside him; while the child-wife behind the bar regarded them with the look of a small ferret on her white-and-pink face.

"Hi, you two!" she said. "What's the joke?" as she bobbed the baby. Their laughter burst its constriction, they leaned on one another, half-empty glasses shaking in hands. Tears came into Phillip's eyes; with a gasp he sat up, ribs aching, his eyes avoiding the challenge of Mrs. Freddy.

"Oh dear!" gasped Desmond.

"'And that's the bit of paper I've been looking for!' said the soldier, as he walked past the guard room," said Phillip, winking rapidly. "Well, how about another rum?"

"It's my treat, Phil."

"No jolly fear! I don't suppose your pay'll run to many of these in a week. And I've got three weeks' leave, and a lot of back-pay to come."

"I said, 'What's the joke?'" repeated the girl-wife.

"Sorry; I didn't hear you," said Phillip.

"Then wash yer ears out! D'you think I don't know your friend was talking about me?"

"I was telling my friend about a soldier in India named O'Casey who successfully swung the lead with the Doolally Tap."

"I don't think! See any green in my eye? You made that up, I know by your face. Tell the truth, and shame the devil. You were talking about me. Doolally Tap! I'll Doolally Tap you! What you want, the same again?"

She poured them, her face sweet and childlike once more.

"How much, please?"

"One and a kick to you. Ta!" She took the half-crown he put down. As she shut the till with a bang she turned round, and said, hard-faced, "I'll give you and your friend talk about me, if you take away my character, you bleeder! Who d'you think you are?"

"I'm Sergeant Haggis, didn't you know?" said Phillip, picking up the shilling change, and smiling amiably at her.

"Gerr'rr't yer!" she cried, making as though to give him a back-hander. Her face looked pretty again. "I'm glad you can take a joke."

Freddy came up from the four-ale bar, raising his hat to his wife. "My dear, I want to introduce you to a friend of a friend of mine, I would like to say also a friend of mine, who 'as just come back from the trenches. Am I right, sir?" he beamed.

"Well, actually, I've just come out of hospital."

"I think your name is Maddison. I once had the pleasure of serving your father. Meet my wife—the missus," said Freddy, sipping his pseudo gin.

Phillip saluted her, and shook her hand. "How d'you do!" Then gently he wiggled the lobe of the ear of the sleeping infant. "And how d'you do, too!"

This put her into a happy mood. Sucking a tooth familiarly, she said to Freddy, "I knew his name wasn't Haggis. Wonder you didn't say Harry Lauder. I'm not a fool you know! What'r'-you thinking now? Come on, out with it, a penny for them!"

"I was thinking how nice everyone is."

She studied his face; decided he was not being sarcastic, and said suddenly, "Here, kiss the baby for luck." Phillip touched its delicate little wrinkled brow with his mouth. Then, while Freddy beamed with his slits of eyes, she turned to the till, and took out a half-crown. "Go on, shove it in your pocket! 'Ave those two on the old man. He's got plenty, the mean old devil."

"Te-he," tittered Freddy. "Every Englishman's home is his castle, I don't think."

"Well, thanks," said Phillip. "You know, I keep thinking I've seen your wife's face before, somewhere."

This was obviously not a tactful remark; for she looked at him with half-angry sullenness, half bright-eyed challenge.

"What do you think I am, a four-penny pick-up?"

Keeping a straight face to this extraordinary person, he said, "I know—you're Mona Lisa!" Fancy a woman, young and pretty, talking like that! he thought.

"None o' your sauce!" she retorted, her free hand going to the handle of the water jug. Phillip thought it was time to go back to the settee. "How about another game o' billiards, Des?"

In the billiards-room, as they chalked their cues, Desmond said, "Freddy told me something about the acoustics of the saloon. When it isn't too full, he can hear what people say on the settee, by listening beside the water-jug. I suppose the sound-waves reflect off the ceiling, and down into the jug. Perhaps that's why his wife stands there, to hear what people are saying about her."

"Rather like the listening apparatus the Germans put up in No Man's Land, Des, to pick up our morse from the signaller's dugout in our trenches."

"Yes, we had a lecture about that the other day. The Germans gave away their invention, when the news came over to our buzzer, for a Lieutenant Smith to proceed on leave, they put up a notice on their parapet saying, 'Enjoy your leave, Mr. Smith'."

"Yes, but the name wasn't Smith. He was an officer in our brigade," said Phillip, crouching over his cue. He would aim carefully this time. But he could not get the angles, and it ended in the same old sloshing strokes, 9–50.

Back in the bar, he told Desmond that it was the finest place he had ever been in. It beat the Rossignol hollow! By God, he

was not afraid to go in and see Mrs. Wallace! Even when he saw
Tom Ching entering, bowler-hatted and carrying a rolled
umbrella, he greeted him with an "Och aye!" Ching shook
him by the hand and held it so long that Phillip had to pull it
away, ostensibly to scratch.

"I'm itchy-koo, you know, so look out."

"I called at your house, hoping I'd see you. Your mother said
you were out, so I guessed you were down at Desmond's, and
calling there, found out from his mother where you had gone."
Ching's cold damp hand pressed Phillip's again. "I understand
what you've been through, old pal." The pressure came again.
Phillip put his hand in his jacket pocket, before more sympathy
could exude from the lip-licking Ching. "Now I want to hear
all about it. Let's have a drink first. What'r you drinking?
Rum? That's my drink. Two rums, please, miss. Oh, I forgot
your friend Desmond. Three, please."

"Singles or doubles? They're drinking doubles."

Ching hesitated, then, "All right. After all, it is a special
occasion."

Mrs. Freddy winked at Phillip. "Mine's a Johnny Walker.
The baby likes that best," she said to Ching.

"All right," said Phillip. "I'll stand that."

"No, no," said Ching. "It won't break me." All the same, he
looked unhappy, as though tricked. He lifted his glass. "Here's
to the wishes of your heart, Phil. You've done your bit." They
sat on the settee.

"Good gracious, is this your overcoat?" Ching spread it
and whistled. "You have a merciful providence looking after
you, Phil. Have the others seen it? I say——"

"Oh, put my coat down!"

But Ching's reflection of his supposed glory had had its effect.
Others in the bar came to look. A stranger asked Phillip if
he might shake him by the hand. The London Highlanders?
Indeed! He was honoured to shake the hand of——

The embarrassing pressing forward of faces was interrupted
by Freddy leaning over the counter and saying to Phillip that
two old friends of his were in the snug next door, and would
like to see his coat, too, if he could spare the time.

"They don't think it's right for ladies to come this side," he
whispered in Phillip's ear. "You know them, I think, Mrs.
Birkett and Mrs. Cummings, where your parents lodged before

you were born." And tipping his straw delicately, Freddy moved to another customer.

Leaving the greatcoat behind, Phillip went into the mahogany-panelled snug next door. He saluted the pair. Optimistically he replied to their questions. He was very well, the war would end after a break-through in the spring, over the Scheldt in June, over the Rhine in July, Berlin by September. After some talk, to most of which he did not listen, he learned that his father's beat, as a Special, included the High Street outside, from eight o'clock until midnight.

"He comes so regularly that anyone could set their clocks by Mr. Maddison's punctuality! He was always so in the old days—punctual, never miss a train, or the date of a payment——"

"Fancy remembering all that time ago, Mrs. Cummings."

"We remember more of the past as we grow older, dear. You don't mind me calling you dear, do you?"

"Good lord, no!"

He accepted a hot rum and lemon from them, swallowed it, shook hands, gave a bow to each; and hastened back to the saloon.

There he saw a face that he welcomed. Good old Cundall, fellow bagman of the last term at school, faithful old Cundall of the Old Heathians fourth football team! Cundall, in the Artist's Rifles, was waiting to be gazetted into the Royal West Kents.

"You lucky devil!" said Phillip.

"Heavens, haven't you applied for a commission yet, Phillip? They want thousands of officers for the new Service battalions."

"What is a Service battalion?"

"All the county regiments are taking on a dozen and more service battalions, for Kitchener's New Armies. You'd get your pip tomorrow, if you applied. Get a blue form from the War Office at once, man! Then get your Colonel to sign it. Simple!"

"The trouble is, the C.O. of our battalion in France won't let any more applications go in."

"Then get posted to your second battalion, and apply from there!"

Desmond said he would be on searchlight duty the following night, in Hyde Park, and have to sleep at headquarters. This would mean the next day off. Would Phillip like to drive down to the second battalion in Sussex, in the Singer?

"Topping!" cried Phillip. This was the life!

"By the way, Phil, if you see the motor in Wetherley's, don't let on that it belongs to my uncle. I told Wetherley, you see, that my uncle had given it to me. I'm hoping he will, as a present for joining up."

Cundall told Phillip that nearly fifty old boys from the school had got commissions already. Milton was there the other day, sword and all, calling on the Magister. "He's with the Middlesex. Remember 'Snouter' Greenall? He's in the Berkshires. Practically all the Swelling Belles of the Sixth of our time—Cruttenden, Latymer, Fysh, Keble, Grounds, Howard—have got their pips. You'll get yours! Hullo, what's happened to your greatcoat? Somebody tried to knife you in Paree? Seriously, I'm damned glad you got through all right, Phil."

"Hear, hear!" said Ching, adding that he wished he were free to join up, but the Admiralty would not allow it.

"Not allow it? Why, in heaven's name?" asked Cundall.

"I'm reserved."

"Reserved in the Admiralty? What for? The immemorial sport of all sailors?"

"I'm a writer, if you want to know."

"What do you write, besides rude things on lavatory walls, O Ching?"

"I can't give away official secrets."

"I can. There are no 'writers' in the Admiralty, not permanently anyway. 'Writers' go to sea in ships. But perhaps you mean you're a typewriter, O son of China?"

"Certainly not! We don't have such things in the Admiralty."

"Then you're a human typewriter?"

"Well, that's one way of putting it. Except that a typewriter cannot think."

"Can you think, O son of the Orient?"

"All God's higher creatures can think."

Cundall gazed around with wonder. "The man's gone religious! Are you one of God's higher creatures, Ching?"

"If you'd studied Theosophy, you wouldn't be so ready to scoff, Cundall."

"I am merely, like Alexander Pope, a humble student of mankind. I am wondering about your real motives for studying Theosophy, Ching."

"What's all this leading up to?"

"Your bowler hat!" said Cundall, blandly. "Your umbrella! Your gloves! Your natty gents' serge suiting! Put them in moth balls for the Duration, my son! Your King and Country need you! Pro Patria Mori, Ching!"

"I would if I could but I'm not free, as I told you."

This conversation, held close to the counter, had apparently been listened to with absorption by Mrs. Freddy, to judge by the detached expression as she stared at the floor, her ear near the water-jug. When Cundall invited Phillip to have a drink, she poured two rums, filled the glasses with lemon and sugar and hot water from the copper kettle simmering on the gas ring, and put them on the counter. A port in lemonade for Ching followed, and a tot of neat whiskey for herself.

"You gents can have yours with me," she said, to Phillip and Cundall, as she raised her glass. "Cheerio."

Tom Ching held up his port and lemon. "Cheero," he said, to her.

"Whatjer looking at me like that for?" demanded Mrs. Freddy.

"I wasn't looking at you like anything."

"Yes you was! You was oggling me! I've seen a sight too many of your sort. Soppy date!"

"I was drinking your health, the usual custom when one is stood a drink."

"Who stood you one? Me? I never! Who d'you think you are, Oliver Twiss?"

"I understood that you asked me to have a drink with you."

The small pink face, made for charm and innocence, scowled at Ching. "Not in these trousers! Oo'y'r trying to spruce? I asked these two gents, not you! Port'n'lemon, sevenpence, come on, cough up!" She held out a hand.

"Anyway, my friend here asked me to have a drink. It's his turn."

"What abaht your turn to put on khaki? You look healthy enough."

"I'm in the Admiralty."

"Where's that, next door to the Lavatory?"

"I can show you my pass. Look here!"

"You know where you can put that, don't you? Come on, don't let me ask again, sevenpence!"

Freddy had listened to the last few words. Standing behind

his wife and baby, he tittered silently towards Ching, then leaning across the bar, said in a confidential voice, "Are you married, sir? Then take my advice—don't!"

"Ger't'yer!" cried his wife, kicking his bottom.

"Married life doesn't suit her," said Freddy, to the company at large. "Marry in haste, and repent at leisure."

"Freddy's caused it now," chuckled Desmond, in Phillip's ear. "I bet he gets the jug treatment."

In an edgy voice Mrs. Freddy declared that Freddy had insulted her baby, despite the fact that the infant was still sound asleep. "Yes, you can stand there, smug and amused, thinking you're his dad, but only I know the right answer, see?" As Freddy tittered with amusement, Phillip wondered where he had heard that hard, aggrieved voice before. Ah, the people in Mill Lane, locally known as Botany Bay, through which he had walked on his way to and from school. Mrs. Freddy's face, too—she looked now exactly like the pretty little doll-like girl in an old woman's hat and pinafore he had once seen, proudly wearing a new pair of boots and splashing through puddles, one winter morning as he was going to school. It must have been six years ago, far away in the remote past.

"Don't you think you can oggle me you bag of haggis, you!" she cried, catching Phillip's eye.

"Ha, ha!" laughed Phillip, thinking it was all terrific fun.

"You shut your big mouth, or I'll shut it for you!" shouted Mrs. Freddy.

"No-one would believe that she learned the Licensed Victualling Trade at the Ritz," murmured Cundall. "Ah, watch the maître d'hôtel!"

Freddy turned round slowly and said to his wife, "This is a respectable house, this is! Up to bed you go, both of you!"

"He means the baby, not Ching," whispered Cundall.

Mrs. Freddy, thin-lipped now, took a proper kick at her husband. Freddy dodged nimbly, and with a titter, explained to the roomful, "The missus is nursing the baby, you see, I told her to drink only lemon with the customers. Yes, my girl, take more water with it next time."

"That's more'n you could do, you old river-rat, you!" cried his wife. "But in case I'm mistaken, here's some to be goin' on with!" and, picking up the water-jug, she jerked the contents over him.

Freddy appeared to take it all in high good humour, as he shook his straw hat before putting it on again and remarking: "Now you know, ladies and gentlemen, why I always wear it!" Having wiped his spectacles, he placed them carefully on nose and ears again; then, going to a door, opened it, bowed to his wife, and said, "I think it is now the baby's turn, my dear."

"You wait till I get you alone!" she called out, as he was closing the door behind her.

"It will be my turn then," said Freddy, smoothly. "Now customers all, last orders, please!"

For Phillip the room began to shift about. He had to fix his eyes on the lights to keep it steady. He was wondering if he was going to be sick when he saw "Sailor" Jenkins coming in the door. Mr. Jenkins wore a special·constable's arm-band, with the yachting cap he affected before the war when cutting his front hedge.

"Hullo, Phillip. I heard from your father only a moment ago that you were back. He's outside."

"'Struth!"

"He's on the other side of the road. He never comes in here, so you're quite safe."

"Oh, I wasn't thinking of that, Mr. Jenkins."

"He can't very well object to your being here now, surely," went on Mr. Jenkins. "You're not a boy any longer. Still, I realise that he can't be exactly popular with you. He was always very strict, wasn't he? Too rigid. The usual half-quartern, landlord! Too rigid by half—in fact, narrow-minded. And he tries the same game on us, between you, me, and the gatepost. No, the sergeant is certainly not very popular among the Randiswell Specials."

"Fancy, Father a sergeant!"

"Yes, he's the senior, and has had some experience, when was it, on Bloody Sunday, nearly thirty years ago. He appoints us to our beats, every month, and comes round to see us without notice. Hardly the neighbourly thing, you know, after all, we're volunteers. Well, to illustrate his attitude, just now I said to him, when he met me over the road, 'Sergeant, you won't mind if I slip in over there to have a quick one, as it's a cold night, will you? It doesn't look as though any Zeppelins will be over.' 'You never can tell,' he replied, 'and in any case a sworn constable should know better than to ask his superior such a question when he is on duty.' You see what I mean, Phillip."

"Very regimental, Mr. Jenkins, very regimental!"

"What does that mean, Phillip?"

"Well, Mr. Jenkins, if you knew he was like that, why did you ask him?"

"Well, how shall I put it—out of a sense of decency, Phillip. I could have slipped in, of course, and said nothing about it, and no-one been any the wiser. Your father is too pettyfogging in my opinion, he's set rigid, Phillip. Never get like that. After all, we are fighting against a rigid system that would enslave us all if it could, aren't we?" Taking a gulp of his whiskey, Mr. Jenkins said, in a lower voice, "I suppose you noticed that the name of your house is no longer on the gate?"

Phillip nodded. Mr. Jenkins nodded too.

"Still, you've done your bit for your country, Phillip, I'll say that for you. And you cannot help having a German for a grandmother, can you? Still, there are lots of them about, you know—full-blooded Germans. I think myself they ought to be rounded up. Well, how d'you feel about the war? When's it going to end? It's ruining trade, you know. We can't get any more silks from Lille and Brussels, as we used to. I used to go over there twice a year, as buyer for our firm. Freightage on Japanese silks is rising every day. Still, we must carry on, and try not to grumble. Food prices are up enormously, you know. This won't interest you, not being married. Take my advice, Phillip, and think very very hard before you marry. Look at me—can I take my wife to meet my business friends? She wouldn't have a word to say to them. Yet once I thought she was like Lorna Doone! A mistake for a man to marry beneath him, Phillip. A woman can. Oh yes, a man can learn, he can adapt himself: but a woman—never! Well, we must meet again sometime, and have another little talk. I've enjoyed meeting you again, Phillip. Cheerio!"

"Hur'r," said Phillip when Mr. Jenkins had gone. "P'r'r!"

Freddy cried out once more, "Time gentlemen, *please*!" To Phillip he raised his straw-yard. "It isn't every day we have a fellow home from the front in this 'ouse. I regard it as an honour, if I may say so."

"Thanks," said Phillip.

"I'd like to ask both you gentlemen up to share some tripe

and onions for supper, but another time perhaps—you understand?" And Freddy tittered.

"Phillip," said Desmond, on the pavement. "You haven't told me what I've often thought about—what is it really like out there?"

"It's hell, Desmond."

Half an hour later they were sitting on a seat in the Recreation Ground beside the Randisbourne. Phillip lay back, fighting swirl and giddiness. He lost the fight, and staggered away to an old willow tree in the reclaimed meadow, now a level football pitch, and vomited. It did nothing to take away the swirl. Stars slid up the sky. He picked himself up and got back to Desmond. They sat together on the seat, Phillip head between hands. Feet crunched on gravel, a policeman's helmet stopped, a voice asked if everything was all right, the footfalls went steadily on again. Phillip fet very cold. He tottered several times to the willow tree before he felt well enough to walk home.

The thin black hands on the white face of the clock at the top of the stairs pointed to half past eleven when he got in. Hetty had waited up for him. She saw his pinched wan face; smelled his breath; and thinking of her dead brother, Hugh, said as cheerfully as she could, "Well, here you are at last! Oh, your hand is icy! Go and sit by the fire dear, while I heat some milk."

She asked no questions. As he sipped the milk, she said, "Father will be in at ten past twelve, Phillip, and he likes everyone to be in bed and asleep when he comes home. He has had a hard day at the office. I've put a hot-water bottle in your bed. Are you sure you are all right?"

"Yes, this milk has put me right. I had some hot rum with Des, and a game of billiards. Then Ching came in, and Cundall, and others, and we all paid for a round. Desmond wasn't sick, but I was. I don't think my stomach is quite right, yet."

Hetty was relieved. Billiards, bad companions—for a while she had dreaded lest it be poor Hughie all over again.

"Well, Phillip, you'll know next time what not to do, won't you. Now we must go upstairs, I think. Don't make a noise, the girls are asleep. Mavis was disappointed not to see you, but never mind now. Of course you wanted to see your friends again, after so long away from home."

When she had tucked him, up she bent down to kiss him.

"Say your prayers, dear, won't you? I felt all the time that God was looking after you, and would bring you home safe again."

Phillip thought of the ten-shilling bribe to the hospital orderly at Etretat, of other parents who had prayed for their sons, including Germans. *Für Gott, Vaterland und Freiheit*. When mother had gone, he hid his head under the bedclothes. In three weeks' time, would he be sent back? He would never be able to face it again. He began to sweat. He clenched his hands, wincing from imagined shell-bursts.

The next morning at breakfast, while Phillip was still in bed, Richard said nothing to Hetty about his son's whereabouts of the night before. From across the High Street he had seen him come out of the public house. Nor did he make any remark on the following night when Phillip arrived home, at a quarter to eleven, obviously from the same place. Richard had to wait up for him this time.

To Richard's thoughts about this were added others that his son did not seem to want to confide in him. He remembered the almost derisive criticisms written by the boy in hospital, on the subject of himself joining the Defence Force. He told himself that he was a back-number, that was it: a back-number.

Chapter 8

TENSION

IT was wonderful to be sitting beside Desmond, in the little brown open car. It was a fine morning. They were on the way to Crowborough, by way of Westerham Hill of famous memory.

As they passed the new London General Omnibus depôt on the right of the road past Fordesmill, now occupied by the Army Service Corps, a sergeant called his squad to attention, saluted, and gave Phillip an "Eyes Right!" Gravely Phillip, with brown leather glove, returned the salute. He felt cool and firm; that somehow he was entitled to the salute, though it had been given by mistake.

"The second battalion is at Bleak Hill, in hutments, Cundall said the other night. It's a fairly long way to Crowborough, about fifteen miles past Westerham; thirty in all. Will she do it, d'you think?"

"Easily! My uncle took me to Brighton and back last Sunday, about a hundred miles. We did forty on the level."

The Singer buzzed up Brumley Hill. Soon they were through the market town, and on to Shooting Common, scene of old nesting expeditions. At the end of the Squire's estate they turned up the long incline to the Fish Ponds, Phillip eagerly gazing at remembered landmarks—the Two Doves Inn on the left—orchards and distant woods, tarred keeper's cottage—over the cross-roads and so to the cleft-oak fence of the Lake Woods, and Knollyswood Park. It was really only a short distance from home, after all.

They stopped by the gate-stile, leading into the Park, and Phillip walked a little way among the silver birches, hollies, and oaks by himself. Soon he returned, realising that his old feelings for the place had gone.

It was a strange, almost obliterating, experience to be driven over roads where he and Des had so often biked in the old days. A new excitement replaced the old feelings—the road rushing towards him and hedges streaming past his eyes. Soon they were at Leaves Green, where once they had stopped, and gone into an inn, quite an adventure in those days, to ask for ginger beer; and had been puzzled by a printed notice of *Well-known Horse* calling at various villages on certain dates, *with plenty of bone.* They had wondered what the bone was; could it have been——? The landlord had explained: cannon bone, the straight lower part of the front leg. "From fetlock to just below the knee, young gents." Ever afterwards they had called the pub *The Cannon Bone.* Once, in his last summer at school, father had accused him of having drunk beer there when he got home; he had seen their bikes outside as he passed. *I can smell your breath, it is of no use your denying it. You will go the way of your grandfather, I can see that, my boy. I hope you are not leading that young boy Desmond astray!* One glass of stone ginger each!

Would the little bus get down Westerham Hill safely? What about the brakes? And going down in low gear. Phillip remembered himself, "a bony skeleton out of the chalk", out of control on his bicycle, years ago. After some horrible metallic jarring

Desmond managed to get it into bottom gear before the bend. White dust arose behind them. The engine vibrated. A hot, burnt smell arose from the floor-board.

"It wants some more grease in the gear-box, I think." The bus seemed to be bucking a bit, too.

"I think it may be the cardan shaft, Phil."

"The universal joints may be worn." Phillip had read a lot about motorcars in *The Automotor Journal* in the Free Library, in the past.

They got down safely, and stopped in Westerham opposite the red-brick brewery by the roadside pond, where the mythical monster pike, rusty treble-hooks and brass gimps hanging from its jaws, was supposed to live. The excitement of the journey had stirred old feelings.

"Wonderful to see it all again, Des, simply wonderful!"

They went into a pub for some beer; and with large ha'penny arrowroot biscuits in their pockets, decided not to visit Squerryes Park, where Phillip's permit to study wild birds still held good, but to carry on to Bleak Hill. He felt a stir of fear at the thought of what would happen if the Colonel would not recommend him.

Off and on he felt nervous all the way to Crowborough. Memory was powerful. As they passed the Beacon Hotel, he breathed faster, remembering the luncheon that September day when Mother and Father had come down; the dull, almost whispering visit to the dining-room, the presence of officers at other tables.

From the driver of a Maltese mess cart in the village he learned that the second battalion was near the old tent lines on Bleak Hill. Shades of Baldwin, Church, Martin—the grey tents, the Leytonstone tent below his own, which he had called, to his shame, the "Leytonstone Louts".

The little brown motor car bumped along the track of black sand and pebbles through the frayed heather. Now he was for it: he got out, leaving Desmond on the track; walked up to the Orderly Room. Pausing to let his heart slow down, he forced himself to open the sergeant's door of the long hut.

"Good morning, Sergeant. I was wondering——"

The sergeant, a rather fat youngish man, took particulars, but said he didn't think there was much chance of the C.O. recommending any more applicants.

"You ought to fill in the Application Form, and send it to the first battalion. The C.O. has refused many like yours, already. Still, I'll tell the Adjutant you're here."

"Is he, Sergeant, by any chance from the first battalion?"

"No, we have no 'first' officers here."

That was a relief! Phillip waited, breathing deeply and slowly to calm himself, until the sergeant returned.

"The Adjutant will see you."

Phillip gave him a Guardsman salute, and stood stiff as a rifle.

The Adjutant, smoking a pipe, told him to stand easy. Then he repeated what the sergeant had said.

"What you had better do is to wait until you report here, after your leave, and then to apply again. But I can hold out little hope of it going through. What is it, Sergeant?"

The sergeant presented a file of papers, murmured something to the adjutant. Phillip was amazed to hear that he had been promoted to the rank of lance-corporal.

"So you can put up your stripe immediately, Maddison."

"Thank you, sir."

"How did you get your coat torn like that?"

"Bullet in the Menin Road scrap, sir."

"Lucky escape!"

"Yes, sir."

"I'll tell you what you might do," went on the Adjutant, conversationally. "You might try the third battalion in London, and get Colonel Cust to sign your papers. Some of the returned first battalion men have done that."

At the end of the interview the adjutant told Phillip that if he wanted any lunch would he tell the orderly room sergeant? Giving him another stamping Guardsman salute, Phillip departed. He considered that Desmond was included in the invitation; and the two sat down to a hot meal of roast beef and vegetables, drenched in brown gravy, followed by prunes, custard, and a cup of tea. Shades of uncooked boiled mutton and skilly of the old tent lines!

And yet, in a way it seemed somehow wrong to be sitting indoors at a long wooden table among all new faces except one: pale little Kirk, who had been invalided before him, and now, passed fit again, was on the roster for the next draft to France. So soon! Kirk, with his rimless *pince-nez* spectacles, looked too frail to be going out to that hell again. He should be on the orderly-room staff. Phillip felt that he ought to be going out in Kirk's place, he could stand it if he had to, to save little Kirk, who hadn't a hope of a commission.

"Goodbye, Kirky, old boy, and the best of luck. I hope we'll meet again, one day."

Prophetic words; though spoken at the time lightly, carelessly. In a little over six months Phillip was to come across Kirk again, in very different circumstances——

The run back was the more pleasant that Bleak Hill was being left farther and farther behind, and more than two weeks leave lay ahead. Before he had left that morning, mother had suggested a visit to Beau Brickhill. "Where the country air, especially from the pine-woods, is so very health-giving in spring." It would be nice to see cousin Percy again, though it would mean not seeing dear old Des for a bit; and this time he really would get even with Polly.

The Singer ground its way up Westerham Hill without stopping, despite the smell of burning oil and a radiator boiling at the top. After a wait to let it cool down, Desmond let Phillip drive. He had never held the wheel of a car before, but soon got into it, though changing gear was a bit of a problem. Desmond kept his hand on the hand brake at first, but after passing the Salt Box by Biggin Hill, Phillip was all right on his own.

For the sake of old times they stopped at the Cannon Bone of Leaves Green, for beer; the same fly-spotted *Horse at Stud* notice was on the wall. This led to another stop at the Greyhound, below the windmill on Reynard's Common. After that Desmond took the wheel. They stopped for more beer at a pub in Brumley Market Place, where Phillip bought an evening newspaper, with headlines of an attack that morning at Neuve Chapelle.

So the "hard fighting" had begun! That night in Freddy's was an especially hilarious one.

He could read between the lines of the *communiqué* from G.H.Q., printed in *The Daily Trident*. Time was everything. By an early train next morning he went to the War Office in Whitehall. Entering by a sidestreet, the pavement of which was vague with the trodden chalk pictures of a vapid Crown Prince and corpse-like Kaiser, he waited among others in a narrow corridor. All were after commissions; some in civilian suits, others in khaki. A Boy Scout gave him a blue form to fill in, with particulars of name, education, service, etc., what branch of the Service a temporary commission was applied for, and what qualifications. He wrote *Army Service Corps*, the qualification being *Knowledge and experience of internal combustion engines*, and thereafter waited in another corridor until his name was called by another Boy Scout, who led him upstairs to a room where at a desk sat a quiet captain, without a Sam Brown belt, and wearing slacks. Phillip's salute was ignored, he was told to sit down.

"Army Service Corps is full up," said the captain, in the quiet voice of one who had been repeating the same remarks hundreds of times every day for weeks, "There are vacancies in the Infantry, for the New Armies. Sappers, Gunners, all require some experience."

"I'd like the infantry, sir."

The quiet captain looked up, and saw without comment the bullet-rip across the greatcoat.

"That was a near shave."

"All in the game, sir."

"Where was it?"

"Bellewaarde Farm, sir."

"I know it. Let me have your form, will you. Any special regiment?"

Phillip frowned, to think the quicker. Devon? It was rather far away. Where else? He could think only of Polly, and Beau Brickhill. Damn Polly. He must not keep the officer waiting. Beau Brickhill, and Polly's misty grey eyes in candle-light, the four-poster bed, the glass dome over the stuffed woodpecker on the chest-of-drawers.

"I have relations in Gaultshire, sir."

"'The Mediators'," mused the officer. "Very well, bring this back to me with your present Colonel's recommendation, and I'll pass it through for you at once. Good morning."

In some excitement Phillip strode towards the City. His boots were blacked, his cutaway tunic under the foreshortened greatcoat sponged and ironed, his cap-badge polished. Mother had sewn lance-jack's stripes on both sleeves, one a little higher than the other; but by holding the shoulder lower, it might not be noticed.

He hoped that his arrival at the third battalion would be

welcomed as that of a veteran of the first; but in the large Drill Hall he found himself unknown, one of hundreds in uniform. At last he was before the adjutant. His heart sank as he was told that Colonel Cust could make no recommendation, at least until a man had served with the third battalion. Phillip saluted and went out.

Cust—Cust—what did the name convey? He thought hard, then remembered that it belonged to the retired officer of the regiment, the Oxford don who had sent out the plans of the Roman catapult he had seen tried out in the wood. They had cussed too, when the jam-pot bomb had exploded while still in the sling!

While he hung about in the hall, wondering what to do and where to go, a face recognised from Bleak Hill days passed him in a civilian suit, and raised a bowler hat to an old officer with gentle face and four rings on his sleeves, with a crown and two stars, whom Phillip thought must be Colonel Cust.

"Ah, Sparks, we are expecting you," said the C.O. "Come up and meet the adjutant." As he passed, Phillip gave him a salute like that of the R.S.M. who had been killed in the Nun's Wood. The old colonel smiled, and said, "Are you waiting to see me?"

"Sir! 9689 Lance-corporal Maddison. I had the honour of seeing your catapult used in action against the Germans before Wytschaete, sir."

"Oh, really? I hope it proved to be of some use."

"It had a wide range, or throw, sir, and livened everyone up."

"I am most glad to hear it. You are reporting here for duty?"

"I am still on sick leave, and am offered a commission by the War Office, sir, if I can obtain a Commanding Officer's recommendation."

"You were at Messines?" The colonel was looking at the greatcoat.

"Yes, sir."

"Come with me to the orderly room, and I will see what I can do."

"Thank you, sir," said Phillip, giving him another R.S.M. salute.

To his relief the adjutant was not in the room. The courteous, gentle face peered at the application form.

"You are on sick leave, I see. How do you feel?"

"I'm quite fit, sir!"

The C.O. signed the paper and shook hands with him. After another vibrating salute, Phillip departed down the stairs two at a time; and lest anyone be sent to recall him, he took a taxicab.

"Drive likes blazes!"

"Where to, sir?"

"The War Office!"

"Yes, sir!"

Seeing the cloud of blue smoke behind him from the little window in the back of the cab, Phillip, from past studies of motoring journals, imagined the engine, probably old when Blériot flew the Channel in 1910, thumping on its worn big ends, slapping its cast-iron pistons, their rings acting as oil-pumps in the "pots" as the ex-horse-cabby jigged his wheel about and zigzagged in and out of traffic at twenty miles an hour. He gave the driver a shilling tip as they stopped in Whitehall, then turned away and strode down the side-street he had left barely an hour previously. A pavement artist was now there, touching up the drawings of the day before. The Crown Prince and the Kaiser now had scarlet tips to their noses.

The captain with the Sam Brown slung on a peg with his cap, gloves, and cane, told him it would be between ten days and a fortnight before the posting appeared in the *London Gazette*. He left in great glee, and gave half-a-crown to the pavement artist who promptly added to both Kaiser and Little Willie devils' horns, and tails sticking out of their uniforms.

Phillip and his mother arrived at Beau Brickhill from London the next afternoon. Polly was out to tea with a little friend, said Aunt Liz.

"Oh dear, what a pity. She will be so disappointed when she knows you have arrived, we expected you a bit later, but never mind now. We were also looking forward to seeing you in your kilts, Phillip—what's happened to them?"

"Oh, I was only too glad to get into mufti."

"Phillip has been given a commission," said Hetty proudly. "Yes dear, Aunt Liz is right, we shall all miss you in kilts."

"Oh, Mother, *do* be quiet."

"We are all proud of you, Phillip, I am sure," said Aunt Liz.

"I think I'd like to go for a walk, if you don't mind, and look at the old places. When will Percy be coming home, Aunt Liz?"

"Uncle Jim and Percy will be late this evening, as it's market day, Phillip, and what with the increased plowing-up, the seed-trade is very busy nowadays. Have some tea first—I've got some of your favourite sausage rolls—then we'll go down and tell Polly. She went to fetch a cockerel for supper, and would never forgive me if I did not tell her you'd come."

After tea they went down to the house where Polly was with her school-friend. At once Polly announced in her forthright way that she would have to leave. She took her small fur hat and muff, and putting them on, went with Phillip for a walk down to the Satchville brook, running through the Duke's moors.

"I wonder if those oak-apple sprays we put in last Whitsun will have petrified yet, Polly. D'you remember when I got that stoat, or clobster?"

"Yes, they're still there, and turning grey, Phil. I often look at them."

Wild duck were nesting in the hollow pollard oaks, and snipe were drumming over the rush-clumps; but he had none of the old feeling of spring; rather a feeling that this time he must really do what he had failed last time to do with Polly.

Polly carried a basket with some ribstone-pippins in it, a gift from her friends at the farm. She tied two on the brass-wire, after removing the oak-apple sprays, and dropped the wire again into the water under the little arched road-bridge. The brook petrified everything—apples, nuts, even dead frogs or sticks, it was the lime in the water. She took his hand on the way back.

"You mustn't get a chill, you know, Phil. You don't look very well. It must have been awful, all that fighting."

"When you're out there, you're done for, unless you can get into hospital. I was lucky to get dysentery."

"Never mind," said Polly, putting her arm in his. "You're back now, and you've done your bit."

"Everyone talks about a 'bit'! What 'bit'?"

"Anyway, I can't imagine you fighting, somehow."

He shook off her arm. "What made you say, just now, 'I can't imagine you fighting, somehow'?"

"Well, you never were a quarrelsome sort of person." She seized his arm again.

"Let go my arm!"

"I shan't, if I don't want to, so there!"

"Oh, yes you will! Who d'you think you are?"

They faced one another. She looked at him stubbornly, the fur hat perched on her dark curls, her grey eyes challenging him—Polly in a black serge school dress reaching to her knees, her lace-up boots half-way to her calves, which were fuller than when he had seen them last. So was her bosom.

"You're a cheeky kid, always were."

"What about yourself?"

"Well, what about me?"

"I think you are extremely comical."

"That's right, laugh at me—everyone does."

"*I* don't laugh at you, so there!" She took his arm again.

"I'm hungry. What time's supper?"

"Seven o'clock."

"What is it?"

"A White Wyandotte, which I've got in this bag." She swung the cockerel against his leg. "Are you feeling in better temper now?"

"If I am, it's not due to you!" as he threw off her arm again.

"What does that mean, pray?"

"You ought to know."

"Well, I don't, so there!" Tossing her curls, she walked on alone.

Exasperated within himself, he walked beside her unspeaking, hoping she would take his arm again. Polly did so, while little trills of temptation ran through his nerves.

He gave the stone oak-apples to his mother as a present when they arrived back. The warm brightness of the farmhouse kitchen made him feel suddenly glad. It was like old times—the fowl sizzling on the spit, turned by the jack that clicked inside the tinned-copper cowl in front of the oak-log blaze on the open hearth; the fat falling on potatoes roasting below; and Grannie Thacker's gooseberry wine glowing on the table. He helped himself, at Uncle Jim's request. Percy came in, his face and large ears red with washing under the pump in the yard. They all drank wine, even Mother. It was better than old times—until Uncle Jim proposed a toast to the "great victory at Neuve Chapelle."

After supper, the three younger people went into the music room to sing the old duets, Polly at the candle-lit piano; but somehow the words and music were not the same—*In a tavern in the Town, Polly-wolly-ooly,* and *Fleur-de-lys.* Afterwards Percy went out on his motor-cycle to see a friend about some seed barley. Polly and Phillip were left alone.

"Where am I sleeping tonight, same old room?"

"Yes."

"Same old four-poster bed?"

"That's right."

"Where's Mother?"

"In the room opposite to you. Do you want the gas?"

"I don't like too much light. I'm used to candles." He thought of the bunkers in the wood. "Thank God for a warm fire." He picked up the poker, and began to shift the logs. Warm and safe; he could hardly realise it. The tree-shadows would be slanting in the flares now. Ration parties hobbling on the corduroy paths; shrapnel whistling and cracking suddenly; white *paa-aangs* of detonating light followed by red spark of burning fuse as one of our eighteen-pounder shells screamed towards the Alleyman lines. It would be cushy in the wood compared with what the poor devils were undergoing down at Neuve Chapelle. "A great victory": what did Uncle Jim or any other civvy know about out there? It was obvious from the *communiqués* that the attack had been held up on the wire, before enfilading machine-guns. There weren't enough high-explosive shells in France to cut the wire properly; but it was no use saying that to these people at home. Even the eighteen-pounders were allowed only five rounds a day each, and shrapnel at that, which would not cut wire, although all the gunners asked for H.E. He had seen on the bike-ride on Christmas Day what a lot of lines the Germans had behind their front trench; and thick tangles of rusty wire in front of each one. Our wire was galvanised; theirs was plain iron, much thicker. How could shrapnel cut that?

"Why didn't you come in your uniform, Phil?"

"Oh, I prefer mufti. Do you remember this herring-bone suit? I wore it when I came down last time. By God, I was ticked off when I got back to Wine Vaults Lane! I overslept, remember?" His throat felt a bit dry.

"You're cold," said Polly. "Here, let me make up the fire."

"Don't touch it!"

"You're very particular all at once, aren't you?"

"These logs aren't dry. Sappy oak is very hard to burn. Out there—oh, you wouldn't understand."

"Tell me, Phil. I'd like to hear."

He could not say what was in his mind: Polly coming into his bed. Curious that she should say, almost in the next breath:

"Have you seen Helena Rolls since you came home?"

"Good lord, no. I hardly know them."

At once something seemed to click dully inside him, almost like the jack in the kitchen. The click became an ache.

"How is Mavis getting on with Lieutenant Wilkins?"

"Lieutenant Wilkins? I've never heard of him. Who the hell is he?"

"Someone she met in the train. She's sweet on him. I thought you knew."

"Someone sweet on *Mavis*? Good lord!"

"Well, don't say I told you, will you? I think Aunt Hetty is rather worried about it. Now would you like a game of billiards?"

"No, I like the feeling of the darkness. Blow out the candles."

He thought of braziers crackling in the new breastworks behind the Diehard T-trench. Or had the breastworks been shelled to bits?

There was a knock on the door. Mother giving "the young people" due warning? The door opened, and her voice said, "Cocoa in the kitchen, children." Then she came in, followed by Aunt Liz and old Grannie Thacker, who said in a gentle, quavery voice:

"Well, Phillip, your mother has been telling me all about your doings, dear. So you are going to be an officer! Well, I must say I think you have deserved it."

"Percy wants to join up soon in the county regiment," said Aunt Liz. "How nice if you two can be together."

"He can be my batman," said Phillip.

"Batman! Oh! How nice to get some cricket," said Grannie Thacker. "Don't you want the gas lit? What are you about, Polly?" as she held to her thin bodice a copper hot-water bottle in its red-flannel jacket.

Aunt Liz said, "We are all going in the warm kitchen now, Mother. Now up to bed you go, it's past your bed-time."

Cocoa and sausage rolls on the kitchen table, half a faggot blazing in the hearth, warmth, warmth! For a special treat a tot of peach brandy, as a night-cap. Stuff to give the troops, thought Phillip, emptying his glass. To get another glass, he proposed Percy's health.

Percy was now a big youth of eighteen, who had been left slightly deaf from pneumonia in childhood. He was a simple person, thought Phillip, who liked his Dad, and was always happy and smiling. Uncle Jim was a sort of chum to Percy—unlike his own niggling, grumpy Father.

Uncle Jim, puffing his calabash carved in the shape of a negro's head, soon got round to his favourite bugbear, the Duke. His yellow-green eyes glared as he held forth, and his pipe went out. While he relit it, Hetty, seeing that Phillip was about to argue with him, said, "Well, dear, I think we ought to be thinking of making tracks for bed. You must be tired after your journey."

"You mark my words!" said Uncle Jim, puffing furiously. "Lloyd George will make the Duke and his like sit up after this war!"

"Well, I don't think I'll sit up any later now," said Phillip. He avoided looking at Polly as he said good night all round. Then, thinking that perhaps his omission of Polly was too obvious, he shook hands solemnly with her. Aunt Liz gave him and Mother a lighted candlestick each.

"Ah," cried Uncle Jim. "I had almost forgotten the bed-warmer!"

Phillip went up to his cold bedroom, waiting there until Uncle Jim brought up embers in the copper pan, and slid it about in the bed. Then Polly came in with a brass can of hot water, and wrapped the towel around it in the basin. He began to feel that the room was friendly, and as he had always remembered it.

"Good night, Polly."

"Good night, Phil."

Would she come in later on? Why had he not asked her when he had had the chance?

He waited impatiently while Mother came in to tuck him up, and to say that if he felt ill in the night, she was only just across the landing.

Both Hetty and Richard had heard shouts and cries from him during his sleep, every night at home; but they had said nothing to him.

"I'm absolutely all right now, Mum, please don't treat me like a kid any longer." If only she knew that he was a secret Don Juan!

Time went by in the shiny darkness. The candle at the bed-head burned with occasional slight flickers. Why were the heavy curtains drawn across the window, suffocatingly? He lay, hands behind head, still in the soft feather mattress, which was too soft, almost horribly soft, for one used to the bare earth, to the billet floor. There was no sleep like billet sleep, on a firm, hard floor. Anyway, the question was, would Polly come?

The patchwork quilt, of all shapes and sizes and colours em-broidered together, arose, a hill of many soils and pastures, over his knees. There were curtains around the bed-posts, tied back with blue ribands. In one corner, on a table, a dome of glass protected two stuffed woodpeckers, one a green or galleypot, and a smaller, spotted one, the rattler. They had always been there, shot by dead-and-gone Grandpa Thacker when a boy, with muzzle-loader and dust-shot. They must have been wonderful days, soon after the coming of the railway.

Was Polly coming? Had she taken his hand-shake as final? He must go and get her, if she wasn't coming. Why didn't she come? The last time he had been no good; this time he must —he would—— And lying in a mixture of doubt and longing, revulsion and uncertainty, he waited until he could wait no longer; and getting out of bed, opened the door and crept down the passage, cursing the creaking board that he had forgotten.

From Grandma Thacker's room came regular soft snores. If Mother opened her door now, he would pretend to be walking in his sleep. He had done it once before, after scarlet fever, at Brighton. Thank God Polly's door was ajar. He pushed it open enough to whisper:

"Are you asleep, Polly?"

"No."

"Are you all right?"

"Yes, are you? You mustn't catch cold."

Why did she let him stand there, clenching teeth against chattering? A white ghost arose before him.

"You're cold," breathed the ghost, dark curls over neck and shoulders. "Come in to my room," he whispered, shuddering. The ghost followed, the board creaked twice.

A ghost no more to lie beside him, but one strangely soft, grey eyes the colour of smoke in candlelight, while the eye of the woodpecker gleamed behind the dome of glass. There was softness, there was warmth, but it was not within Phillip; he remained cold within the spirit, and the more he tried to release the coldness with Polly's help, freely offered, the more he felt he was like the spray of oak-apples he had taken from the brook, petrified.

Across the landing, Hetty lay unsleeping, worried by a succession of her own failures, foolish acts, humiliations, all of her own making, all of the past which now seemed to envelop the present with greater darkness, which was the war. Why had she drunk cocoa so late at night, when she knew it did not agree with her?

Behind the wall Jemima Thacker lay awake, after her first short doze, thinking of how she might have helped her husband Charley more when he was worried by business, had she but known; of her dead son, little Charley, who had died of lockjaw at the age of forty; and many other griefs arising from her own failings in so many ways in the past.

At the other end of the house Jim and his wife Liza slept back to back, in warm relaxation as one being, as they had slept ever since marriage two years before the Diamond Jubilee of the old Queen, whose oleograph portrait from a bygone *Pears Annual* hung on the wall above them, with various texts from the Holy Bible worked in silk and wool.

Fifty miles south, across fields of gravel and heavy gault clay—the blue lias—beyond the dimmed lights of London and the gleaming serpentine coils of Thames, Richard lay in the iron bedstead with brass fittings which he had occupied alone for several years now, his knees drawn up like an embryo in the womb. His early-morning glass of water was on the bed-head table beside his nickel-plated revolver, his constable's whistle, and the truncheon ready for duty at any moment in the night. He was alone in the house; his daughters, one working at Head Office, the other still at school, were sleeping next door: a matter for relief, since he was the less perturbed when alone, and always had been since the break-up of his old home in the West Country thirty-five years before, when his father had deserted his mother. For this ageing man, in the rushing black spaces of the night, it was now harder to live with the dead than with the living.

"It's no good," groaned Phillip, finally, as the grandfather clock downstairs struck one. "The truth is, I keep thinking I am a chap called Church, a friend of mine out there, Polly, and I can't do anything."

So Polly went back to her room, the board creaking again as, pulling bedclothes round neck, Phillip drew up his knees for warmth and companionship, and clasping himself, tried not to think of "out there", until he went to sleep.

Part Two

TEMPORARY GENTLEMAN

Chapter 9

IN CLOVER

RICHARD had repaired the bird boxes in the elm at the bottom of the garden while Phillip was in hospital, and refastened them with brass gimp to the trunk; they had been nailed before, and the nails had rusted. Now, as April approached, he went every morning down to the sitting-room, to watch the pairs of blue and great titmice which had evidently decided to use them again this year. He hoped his son would approve of what he had done, and make some mention of it when he returned from Beau Brickhill; but when Phillip did come home with his mother before the week was up, he was so full of his commission— Richard had telegraphed immediately he had seen the announcement in the *London Gazette*, in the Town Department copy of *The Times*—that he had no desire apparently to hear about the birds.

"Well, Phillip, I have some further news for you, about your bird boxes which I repaired, as best as I could—I don't say I am as expert in the matter as you are—but at any rate both boxes seem to have acquired tenants."

"Oh, good. By the way, Father, might I have the money you are keeping for me? I have an account now, at Cox's the Army Agents, and should like to pay it in."

"Certainly, Phillip. There is a sum of thirty-four pounds odd due to you."

"Oh, thank you, Father."

Phillip calculated. £50 kit allowance, plus £34, plus about £8 back-pay as a ranker totalled over £90! He was flush. His pay from the Moon Fire Office was now £70 a year, since the annual Lady Day rise jumped from £10 to £20 at the commencement of the third year. He, Second-lieutenant P. S. T. Maddison, 10th Battalion the Gaultshire Regiment, with a private income! How suddenly life could change!

"And while I remember, Phillip—I saw your Uncle Hilary

the other day, and he asked me to tell you that he and Aunt
Beatrice would be delighted if you cared to pay them a visit.
Just send a telegram, he said, to announce your coming. They
live in Hampshire, as you may remember, and Uncle says he
can offer you some salmon fishing. Perhaps you will write to
your Aunt? I'll give you the address."

"Oh, thank you, Father."

But fishing, like watching birds, was a thing of the past now.
Full of visions of himself in officer's uniform, he went up to
Town in a first-class carriage, as befitted his rank. He had
decided to get his uniform made at the Stores (which was, apart
from his old tailors in Fenchurch Street, the only place he knew
of. Father dealt there). So to Queen Victoria Street went
Phillip, where he was duly measured. The tunic cost £3 10s.;
the khaki breeches were £1 7s. 6d.; Sam Brown belt, £2 2s.;
cap, 15s. 6d.; Fox's puttees, 15s. 6d.; two khaki shirts, £1 1s.; a
silk tie, 3s. 10d. He saw for the first time a gilt button of his
new regiment; it seemed to glow in his hand, a star of many
rays embossed with a wild ox with big horns in the centre. Buttons were included in the tunic price, said the shop-assistant,
but the bronze lapel badges were extra, at 6s. 6d. the pair.
Phillip scarcely heard the figures; prices were nothing to him;
all that mattered was, would the uniform be ready by Saturday,
so that on Sunday morning, after church on the Hill, Helena
Rolls and her parents could see him in it. When would it be
ready?

"In five or six days, we hope, sir."

It was then Tuesday.

"Can't you possibly let me have it by Saturday?"

"Well, I'll try, sir, but cannot promise. Our stitchers are going
day and night. But I'll do my best. Now, how about a valise,
sir? You will find it an absolute necessity; it can be turned into
a sleeping-bag by night, and accommodation can be on the
rough-and-ready side, so I hear, in the new encampments.
You will need a canvas wash-basin at 27s. 6d., but perhaps you
would like to see the list for yourself, sir?"

Phillip's eye moved down the list, scarcely seeing the items:
green canvas mattress 7s. 6d., pillow 3s., camp-bed 15s., water
bottle 8s. 9d., haversack 10s. 6d., holdall for sponge, soap, and
toothbrush 2s., whistle 1s. 7d. including lanyard.

"Are the straps for the holdall extra?"

"Yes, sir, six shillings and sixpence."

"Oh, I want a British warm, instead of a greatcoat. How much is that?"

"Three pounds five shillings, sir. Shall I order them to be sent to your residence, sir?"

The shop-assistant, who was forty years old, with a wife and two children, was paid commission on his sales, in addition to his weekly wage of thirty shillings; so the war was, as he often told his wife, a God-send to him. Nowadays he made as much as seventy shillings a week.

"There is likely to be a shortage, sir, you know. The new armies are expanding very fast, almost faster than the equipment makers can cope with. You are the fifth gentleman since we opened this morning, sir."

"Well, I don't think I'll need the camp-bed. I'm used to sleeping on any old floor, in fact a bed is too soft."

"You'll find this camp-bed redolent of the rigours of the campaign, sir. It's the standard bed for the officers of the Army in France. And a sword, sir, for ceremonial drill, best Wilkinson, two guineas, engraving with regimental crest or coat-armour and name, extra of course. Prices are liable to rise, too, that is a consideration. I would suggest that you acquire your kit and equipment while you can, sir."

"I shan't need a sword. Nor a washing-basin. We usually wash in a shell-hole. As for a whistle, we don't use them at all out there. What I would like, is a patent collapsible coke-bucket——"

"Ha, ha, I see you have a sense of humour, sir. No doubt you've seen the new Bairnsfather pictures in *The Bystander*? They depict, truly, I think, the essential humour of our Tommies in contrast to their humourless opponents. Let me see now, have we got all your requirements?"

Phillip said he would take the bed, mattress and pillow; but shook his head at wash-basin, sword and field-glasses.

"I had a fine pair of Zeiss glasses, but they were pinched in my billet by one of those skrimshanking Belgians."

"Oh dear, dear, what a state of affairs, sir! You will want some boots, of course? And shoes, for wearing with slacks for mess dinner."

The shop-assistant accompanied him to the boot department, where Phillip bought the first pair of shoes he saw, with rubber stubs coming through the soles. "I see you play golf, sir. All right for clubs and balls?"

"I'll need a tennis racket for No Man's Land."

"Quite a joker, I see, sir! Now may I interest you in a brooch, in gold, or gold and platinum, of your regimental badge, for a lady friend?"

"Yes, that's a good idea!"

Phillip decided to take the haversack he had bought, with the holdall containing shaving kit, and towel; and his new pair of poplin pyjamas. Then he wrote his first cheque for the total, and was assured that the goods would be delivered by Carter Paterson as soon as the uniform was made; while the badge in nine-carat gold, costing three guineas, would be sent later on, by registered post, to Lindenheim, Wakenham, Kent. "It will have to be specially cast, sir, by our goldsmiths."

"Oh, good!"

He would ask Helena Rolls to accept the brooch! Having shaken hands with the shop-assistant, he left the Stores in elation, and decided to call on his father in Haybundle Street. There the idea came to him that, to fill in the time until Saturday, and also to pique Helena—whom he had not yet met since his return—he would go down to Hampshire to visit Uncle Hilary.

When he told his father this, into Richard's mind came the thought that his brother Hilary was on the way to becoming a wealthy man: that his wife Beatrice was turned forty, and it was unlikely that she would give Hilary any children of his own: moreover, Hilary had been buying back some of the family land at Rookhurst—— But of this he said nothing to Phillip: it was not his affair, anyway: but if Phillip did well in the Army, as he had begun, there was every likelihood—— "Well, be sure to give them both my kind regards, won't you?"

After saying au revoir to his father, Phillip shook hands with several of the older men in the Town Department, including Mr. Journend, and then went on to Gracechurch Street, through Leadenhall Market, and so to Wine Vaults Lane. Mr. Howlett received him with smiling face; Mr. Hollis cried, "Bless my soul, we thought we'd got rid of you, you Pugilistic Scotsman, you!"; while Edgar grinned as he sat in his corner now adorned with high officers of the Allies, the Grand Duke Nicolas, Sir John French, "Papa" Joffre, the Kings of Belgium, Servia, Montenegro; and several V.C.s. Phillip pretended interest in them, to please the messenger; and when Edgar asked him for a photograph, Mr. Hollis said, "But I thought you had discontinued your famous boxer series, my lad?" with a wink at Phillip, who gave a forcedly comic account of the supposed bout in No Man's Land, to comply with what was evidently expected of him.

"You should have been a clown," said Mr. Hollis, "for your gifts certainly do not run in the direction of accountancy! My word, your stamp book was in a mess when you left last August!"

This startled Phillip, for he did not remember ever having pinched any stamps. Ashtrays, yes, and a packet of Pear's soap now and then; but no stamps.

"Don't let it worry you, my boy," said Mr. Howlett, seeing his face. "By the way, Downham is commissioned with the Surrey Sharpshooters, did you know?"

"Third battalion, home service, commands a company," said Mr. Hollis. "A full-blown captain, paid twelve shillings and sixpence a day, plus allowances, while I have to stay here and earn his damned salary for him. I suppose I ought to include you in that remark, young fellow, for you never did any work while you were here, did you? But I don't, all things considered, you ugly duckling. Seriously, Maddison, you're a credit to the branch, apart from your taxidermatical—if that's the right word—aberrations, young fellow-me-lad."

Both Mr. Howlett and Mr. Hollis were beaming at him, so Phillip felt bold enough to say, "I suppose, gentlemen, you would not care to lunch with me at the London Tavern today? I have to catch a train to Hampshire at half-past two."

"That's very civil of you, Maddison," replied Mr. Howlett. "But I shall have to go to Head Office, having some business there. However, thank you for the invitation."

"And I have an appointment, young fellow, otherwise I would avail myself of your most kind invitation," said Mr. Hollis, glancing at the clock. "By Jove, I must get on with this new clothing-factory survey. You remember Roy Cohen? His father, Moses Cohen, now has contracts to supply the new armies with uniforms, made up of old police uniforms, the value of which is about quadrupled. Through him we've got his wife's people's furniture factory, old Morris Hartmann, you know, running into fifty thousand pounds and more! Then there is the house the Moses Cohens have built in Hampstead. If this

war runs the three years that Kitchener forecasts, you'll see a
lot of the Jews will be out of the Whitechapel ghetto. Remember
Rothschild in the Napoleonic wars? So you see, Maddison,
young Roy Cohen looks like becoming one of our most valuable
agents. I needn't remind you whose initiative got him for
Wine Vaults Lane!"

Phillip was just going, when Little Freddy Fanlight came into
the office. He looked just as dapper and airy as before the war.
In the old days, Little Freddy had not noticed him very much,
if at all; now he said, "Hullo, aren't you the chap who challenged
Carpentier or somebody in the trenches?" Without waiting for
a reply, Little Freddy went on to explain, as he flipped a violet
cachou into his mouth, that he was not fit. "Otherwise I'd
have gone long ago. Well, Hollis, I've got a proposal for
you——"

Uneasy in the presence of Little Freddy, Phillip raised his
bowler and departed, remembering just in time to give a wave
of the hand to Edgar as he went through the glass door.

At Breamore Station a chauffeur in a long coat touched his
cap, and having enquired his name, smilingly asked if there was
a portmanteau to be collected. Phillip explained as he sat
behind him in an open green Sunbeam motor-car, with an A.A.
registration, that he did not need pyjamas or anything like that;
a toothbrush was all he had brought with him. At which the
driver grinned, showing irregular teeth.

"You haven't been to us before, have you, sir?"

"No. What's the fishing like?"

"Very good this season. Mr. Maddison killed two fish yesterday morning from Martin's Pool, twenty-one pun' and
eighteen pun'. On a prawn, both on'm. He's had to go to
London this mornin', and told me to take you down his beat.
It's fly water, except in Martin's Pool, where he used them
prawns. Don't hold wi' prawns misself."

Phillip kept silent, guarding his ignorance. Then he asked
when his uncle was coming back.

"No idea, sir. Somethin' to do with ships, to the Mediterranean,
he said. He's with the Admiralty now, you know."

"Who's at home, then?"

"Only Mrs. Maddison, and her sister-in-law, Mrs. Lemon."

"Oh lor'. Is she called Viccy?"

"That's the one, sir. The children's away at school, they'll be home for Easter."

"What children?"

"Master John and Miss Pamela, name of Murgatroyd, of Mrs. Maddison's first marriage. Master John's at Winchester, Miss Pam's at Eastbourne. You've lived abroad, I take it, sir?"

"More or less, yes," replied Phillip, hurriedly, dreading further questions. They turned into a drive, going what seemed a long way along a gravelly lane, with tarred railings on either side, and cattle standing near rows of straw and hay spread on thin grass under oaks. In the middle of the enclosed area was a circular plantation of tall blue firs.

"We never shoot that plantation, it's the Sanctuary. We holds the pheasants there, away from the poachers. There's another on the south side o' the park, same purpose."

"Is all this my Uncle's, then?"

"What, the park? That's right. He bought the 'ouse with nigh on four hundred acres, when it was in the market, let me see, twelve year come next Michaelmas. He farms it, under the steward."

"I knew he had a farm in Australia, in fact, I nearly went there."

"Go on," said the driver, adding, "I thought I'd never seen you come here before, I never forgets a face. Well, here we are, sir," he said, with a return to his original manner, as a red brick Queen Anne house came into sight.

The thought of its bigness made Phillip nervous. Why hadn't he pressed his trousers? Oh, hell, would they expect him to dress for dinner? And his tall starched collar was frayed a bit at the top. What a fool he had been to put it on, trying to look like Mr. Hollis, instead of one of his narrow pale-blue Hope Bros. collars. And no gloves. His hands were grimy, the nails wanted cutting. He must keep them hidden as much as possible. The motor stopped. He got out.

On the top of the steps, by the open door, stood a woman in a plum-coloured bodice and skirt. Could it be Aunt Beatrice? Her hair was grey, her hands folded in front. "Good afternoon, Mr. Maddison," she said with a smile, and slight inclination of her head. Behind her, in the hall, stood a maid-servant in blue with a white starched cap. "No luggage, Mrs. Coles," said the driver.

"Just come back from France, you know," explained Phillip jauntily, as though he had left his luggage there. Ought he to tip the driver? He felt in his pocket, touched a milled edge among the coppers, wondered if half-a-crown would seem paltry; and was about to turn back to give it to the driver, when the housekeeper said, "I expect you would like to see your room, sir? You can go, Parkins," whereupon the maid in blue gave a little bob and went away. "Will you come with me?"

The hall had a floor of black and white tiles, with an open hearth and polished steel fire-dogs almost embedded in a mass of grey wood-ash. He vaguely noticed glass cabinets with china in them as he followed the housekeeper up wide polished oak stairs and pale green walls on which water-colours and other pictures were hanging, and pedestals in the corners with statues, the whole place being lit by a wide skylight in the roof. He was shown into what seemed to him to be a very large bedroom.

"Your bathroom is here," said the housekeeper, opening a gleaming white door, to reveal a bath encased in mahogany, silver rails with thick towels hanging on them with mathematical neatness. "Mrs. Maddison and Mrs. Lemon are in the morning-room, and if you ring this bell when you are ready to come down, sir, I will be in the hall, to announce you." She smiled and went away, turning at the door to give him a slight bow before she went out.

"'Strewth," said Phillip to an imagined Desmond. "It's all too damned posh for me." He cracked his fingers, and did a jig, before going round his bedroom examining it in detail.

The room had big windows looking out on a garden and lawn. It had a soft carpet that was like walking on sand, a four-poster bed with gold satin coverlet, bookcase, table with leather-bound pad, blotter, and tray with writing paper and envelopes and pens on it, with a tiny matchbox in a silver case, with an unused stick of blue sealing-wax. "All very posh, Desmond, my boy." Through an open window he heard the remote double-crow of a cock pheasant. Uncle Hilary must be very rich.

The plum-coloured housekeeper was in the hall arranging flowers in a bowl when he went down. Opening a tall door, she said pleasantly, "Mr. Maddison, ma'm!" and he was walking forward to shake Aunt Beatrice by the hand. Then Aunt Viccy, thin and pale as ever, sitting beside a log and coal fire in a polished steel hearth, gave him her hand, and a slight smile.

"Well, Phillip, so you've come back from the war. Let me look at you. Are you quite recovered?"

Aunt Victoria's voice was gentle, but he could not feel at ease. He stuttered when he spoke, sitting on the edge of a chair by the fire, conscious of the smoothed-out skin around Aunt Beatrice's eyes—white, very soft skin and frightening china-blue eyes—frightening because their rare blue, like the eyes of Helena Rolls, seemed to hold the secret of the inscrutable mystery of Woman. Aunt Beatrice's skin was very white and smooth, especially the skin of her slender wrist and forearm. He felt small, almost guilty, as she looked at him, with her brilliant smile; he felt, in a way, less afraid of Aunt Viccy, who was not affectionate in her regard, but remote in an unwarmed way. Between the feelings of the two women he felt rigid; he spoke jerkily, trying to overcome his uneasiness. Was it because the room, and everything about the house, was too comfortable?

Aunt Bee asked him if he would like some beer, after his journey; and when it came, he was surprised to see that the man bringing it, in dark trousers, wasp-striped waistcoat, and black vicuna jacket, was the driver. The bottle of beer and glass, on a little round silver tray, with corkscrew also of silver, was put on a low table by his side, then the man went away. Was he supposed to draw the cork, or wait to be invited? In his nervousness, because he had forgotten to say "Thank you"—in the magazine stories he had read, servants were never thanked when they served at table—ought he to have thanked him, anyway?—in his uneasiness he found, to his horror, that he was telling lies about himself. Aunt Viccy had never liked him: she had lectured him as a boy, she knew his real self. So he found himself giving a false account of the "boxing match" in No Man's Land, and unable to stop talking rot.

"Yes, the Germans sent up flares specially to light the ring, which was made of posts and telephone wire. Of course I didn't stand a chance against Church, who was the company runner-up at the School of Arms before the war. Anyway, the Germans cheered as round after round ended with the bell. What bell? Oh, someone had taken one of those old wire-pull bells from the Red Château, you know, perhaps it was a door-bell, anyway, it ended each round, until I got a biff that sent me down for the

count. I learned to box more or less before the war, you know,"
he ended up lamely, avoiding both pairs of eyes upon him,
feeling that Aunt Viccy was thinking of the time Father had
taken him to her Epsom house in disgrace, after Peter Wallace
had called him a coward for getting him to fight Alfred Hawkins
for him in the Backfield.

"Do help yourself," said Aunt Bee; and too quickly he drew
the cork, and spilled froth on the carpet.

Dinner that night, served by the driver now in evening dress,
was just as awkward for him. That night he could not sleep.
The mattress was too soft, Uncle Hilary's silk pyjamas too large,
the bedroom curtains suffocatingly heavy. He selected some
books to read, and was wondering if he dared light his pipe—
or would it stink out the room afterwards—when there came a
soft knock on the door and before he could leap out to switch
off the electric light, the glass handle turned and Aunt Beatrice
came in with a tray with a tiny teapot and sugar jug on it, and
two small cups, almost transparent, they were so thin. She said
she always had China tea at night, and would he take a dish
with her?

She wore a silvery kind of dressing-gown, which made her
rather like a fish; she did not look so old as she had looked
downstairs, she looked almost girlish, with her fair hair brushed
down her back, but nevertheless with the very smooth skin of
her face and the large china-blue eyes she was quite frightening.

"I could not talk to you as I wanted to 'Mr. Cornflower',
before Viccy. That woman freezes me. Do you remember
when you called yourself 'Mr. Cornflower', when you ran
away with that old dog Joey, to see the races, the Derby wasn't
it, or was it the Oaks, at Epsom? You were such a sweet little
boy, Phillip. My heart ached for you, you were such an unhappy little pet. How old are you now, twenty?"

"Nearly twenty, Aunty Bee."

"Don't call me 'Aunty', there's a dear boy. 'Aunty' has
always reminded me of a dressmaker's dummy, for some reason.
Would you prefer some hot milk, instead of tea? You look so
thin, my pet. Do say. I want you to be well again."

"No, really, thanks ever so much. I like tea."

He tried to conceal his quivering hand as he took the saucer
and cup with the grinning mandarin figure and dragons in gold
and black. She took his hand between hers, and warmed it on

her lap. "What slender fingers you have, Phillip. An artist's hand." She turned it over. "Shall I read your fate? Do you believe in palmistry? I do. I must cast your horoscope, too. Hilary laughs at all occult things, but he's an old materialist, with no imagination. You don't like him, do you? Tell the truth, and shame the devil!"

"Yes, I do. He's been really very kind to me."

"Yes, I know, in his way. But he wants everyone to be like him." She sighed. "Are you shocked at my frankness, Phillip? I've always said exactly what I think—it's got me into hot water more than once. 'The Cornish urchin', they called me at home when I was a child. We're Celts, you and I, you know. We know things by intuition, don't we?" She looked into his eyes, still holding his hand.

Phillip thought that he must hide his intuition; he must pretend that he did not know what she meant. And when, after some more talk, she asked him to kiss her, his pretence broke down, and he felt ashamed that he could not. When she looked at him with another expression, a much older one, he felt sorry for her: and managed to kiss her on the cheek, slightly.

"Dear 'Mr. Cornflower', do you know that you have the most beautiful eyes? No, do not look away from me," she sighed. "God, isn't life hell? We all have to dissemble most of the time. I knew you were dissembling before Viccy. What a cold woman she is! Are you shocked, dear boy, at my frankness?"

"No. I think I know what you mean."

"Of course you do. Well, I must not keep you from your beauty sleep. Kiss me again, 'Mr. Cornflower'. Is my skin soft? Don't you feel that it is kind to you?" She sighed again, looking very tired.

"Yes, it is very soft. Is that why they call you Honey Bee?" he managed to say.

"'Honey Bee', my God! 'O Bee, where is thy sting?' I've shocked you, haven't I?"

"No, of course not, really you haven't!"

"I suppose I'm an old woman to you, Phillip?"

"You look very young, Bee."

"Do I *really*," she said, looking at him, with a sad, resigned expression. "You won't tell anyone I came to 'drink a dish of tay' will you, my pet? I came really because you looked so lost, so lonely. I am lonely, too—everyone is lonely in this world, I think. Don't you?"

He was not so afraid now that she sat back, away from him. He told her about Helena Rolls. She listened sympathetically.

"She sounds a lovely creature, my pet. You keep your ideals, Phillip! Don't sell the pass. And thank you for your confidence, dear boy. She must have a heart of stone if she can resist those eyes of yours, and those long dark lashes! She loves you, Phillip, of course she does! Well, I must go now. May I come with you by the river in the morning? I'm quite a good ghilly, you know! An expert with the gaff!" Her voice was ironic. She bowed her head, and to his dismay he saw she was crying. "Now you'll see what an old hag I am!" she said, smiling at him.

He stroked her head. She took his hand and held it against her bosom. She kissed his hand. She stroked her cheek with it. "Slender fingers, my pet, they should hold a painter's brush. Did you ever paint?"

"No. I can't draw."

"You're a poet, I think. Is my cheek soft?"

"Yes, it is. Sort of creamy." He was alarmed by what she might do next. "Do you wash it in special soap?"

"I've not used soap since I was a 'Cornish urchin'. I wash my face in milk."

"Didn't Queen Victoria always have a bath in milk?"

"Vinegar, I should think, more like it! You're very sweet, Phil. Don't let anyone change you, my pet."

Then leaning over, she took his face between her hands, and kissed him lightly on the lips. He could not help drawing back slightly. She stroked his hair, got up from the bed, smiled tenderly, fluttering her eyelids at him, and whispered, "Now you must sleep, my child! I've ordered your breakfast to be brought up on a tray. Come down any time you like. It's fun, isn't it, our little midnight party? Till tomorrow, then, 'Mr. Cornflower'."

With a last tender glance, she was gone.

"Well," said Richard on Phillip's unexpected return next day from Hampshire, "this is a surprise! But no doubt you are keen to get into your new uniform, to show yourself to a certain goddess——"

Phillip was sitting in the front room. He had just opened a large envelope, seen that it was his commission scroll, glanced at his name and regiment, and was skipping the copperplate engraved words, to dwell upon the signature of *George R.I.*, when his father, on the way upstairs, looked round the door.

"What's the matter, are you feeling under the weather?" Had the boy been drinking? "Well, tell me about the place down in Hampshire? How did you find your Uncle Hilary?"

"I didn't see him, Father. He had gone to London on business, Aunt Bee said."

Richard waited for his son to say more, but Phillip remained silent. "What did you think of Uncle's place? I've not been there yet, you know."

"It was all right, Father."

"Oh, I see." Another pause. "Did you have any fishing?"

"No, Father."

"I see. Was there anyone else staying there?"

"Aunt Viccy, Father."

"How was she?"

"All right, I think."

"Did she send any message?"

"She asked after you, Father."

Richard remembered that his son had left unexpectedly—run away, in fact—when staying with his sister Victoria at Epsom, years before. Well, he was a funny chap: he didn't understand him, or his moods when he closed up like an oyster. Phillip held out the commission script.

"What is that, something for me to see? Oh, the patent of your commission. My spectacles are in the other room—I'll read it when I come down."

Later, in the sitting-room, Richard said, "Well, you will have a lot to live up to now, old chap. I suppose you have read it carefully?"

"To tell the truth I haven't, Father."

"Well, I hope you will, because it is a declaration of what is expected of you. It implies a solemn undertaking on your part."

Seeing Phillip's frown, and trying to avoid anything that might lead to an abrupt departure for Mrs. Neville's, Hetty said, "You have done very well, Phillip; promotion in the field is something to be very proud of."

"Oh, Mother! I wish you wouldn't talk like that! Besides, I wasn't 'promoted in the field'."

"Well, dear, you were made lance-corporal, weren't you?"

Phillip sighed. "I think I'll go for a walk, Mother."

"Very well, dear. Don't be late, will you?"

He made no reply. They heard the front door close.

Hetty was worried by Phillip's visits to the public house in the High Street, sometimes with Desmond, sometimes alone. She was worried, too, about Mavis, who also came home much later than Hetty felt was quite safe. Mavis, she knew, was seeing a strange officer she had met in the train. All Hetty knew about him was that his name was Wilkins, he was at the War Office, and wore a red band round his hat. He must have an important position, since, according to Mavis, he had just been promoted from lieutenant to major. She would have to trust Mavis, who was seventeen and very young for her age, and hope that everything would be all right; all the same, she could not help worrying.

"Why not ask him home, dear?" she had said once. At this Mavis's face had expressed dread. What would Father say? Oh, she would die of shame if Father said anything at all grumpy.

"Mother, *please* don't say a word to Father! Promise me!" The girl had become so agitated that Hetty had given her promise.

She sighed as she thought of the barrier between Dickie and herself. She had to be so careful, always, in what she said; the least little thing was liable to upset him. His reserve was growing deeper; he was indeed a lonely man. She knew that he felt hurt because Phillip never wanted to talk to him; he was longing to hear about his son's doings in France; and seemed to have no idea that the barrier between them was due, in part at least, to his own intolerance, and lack of sympathy in the past.

While Richard read *The Daily Trident*, sometimes snorting to himself at "that old woman Asquith", Hetty read the wording of her son's commission.

GEORGE by the Grace of God, of the United Kingdom of Great Britain and Ireland, and of the British Dominions beyond the Seas, King, Defender of the Faith, Emperor of India, &c.

To Our Trusty and well beloved Phillip Sidney Thomas Maddison Greeting.

Trusty and well-beloved Phillip! O, I am so proud, she thought. And they have spelled his name correctly, with two l's, her original mistake in registering his birth!

We, reposing especial Trust and Confidence in your Loyalty, Courage, and good Conduct, do by these Presents Constitute and Appoint you to be an Officer in Our Land Forces from the Twentieth day of March 1915. You are therefore carefully and diligently to discharge your Duty as such in the rank of 2nd Lieutenant or in such higher rank as We may from time to time hereafter be pleased to promote or appoint you to, of which a notification will be made in the *London Gazette.*

O Sonny, Sonny how proud I am of you, dear! I knew in my heart all the time that you were a good boy, and only needed a chance to show your true self! Fancy, the King himself had read and signed this wonderful document!

You are at all times to exercise and well discipline in Arms both the inferior Officers and Men serving under you and use your best endeavours to keep them in good Order and Discipline. And We do hereby Command them to Obey you as their superior Officer and you to observe and follow such Orders and Directions as from time to time you shall receive from Us, or any from your superior Officer, according to the Rules and Discipline of War, in pursuance of the Trust hereby reposed in you.

GIVEN at Our Court, at Saint James's, the Twenty second day of March 1915 in the Fifth Year of Our Reign,

BY HIS MAJESTY'S COMMAND
Henry Sclater A.G.
R. W. Brade.

All the same, Hetty could not help feeling uneasy at what had occurred that afternoon, when Phillip had gone on the Hill, after returning home from Hampshire. He seemed so dejected that it had worried her.

On impulse, leaving the house in charge of Mrs. Feeney, Hetty had put on hat and coat and followed him, coming upon him outside the shelter, his gloved hands bending short whangee cane behind back as he held forth upon the situation in France to the old men sitting in a row within.

"Yes," he was saying. "It is a fact that the Mayor of Armentières was shot as a spy, after it had been discovered that a buried telephone wire led from the cellar of the Mairie to the German lines. The whole of Belgium is riddled with spies."

Whereupon a pale-faced man with woeful dark eyes, dark clothes, and black hat had almost hissed at Phillip, "Zat is not true! I and my wife and family are from Belgique, let me inform you! Further, let me inform you that my wife's cousin was ze Maire of Armentières before ze war, and he is still ze Maire of Armentières, and has not been shot as a spy at no time at all!"

"Anyway," said Phillip, rather lamely, "apart from the fact that two negatives make a positive, that is what we heard."

"What you heard is not what is fact, sir! Let me tell you that Burgomaster Max of Bruxelles was himself followed by Boy Scouts in the streets of Bruxelles last August, until he, the supposed spy, was forced to seek shelter in someone's house, for fear of the mob!"

"Oh."

"Let this be a lesson to you, Phillip," said Thomas Turney. "'Guard well thy tongue'."

"Anyway, Gran'pa, it is all rot about the atrocities, or most of it, anyway."

"What atrocities?" cried the pale-faced refugee. "Are you denying that the reports from my suffering country are untrue, or fabricated? The massacres at Tirlemond, Louvain, Dinant——!!"

At this, Mr. Krebs, the big pink-faced German, who had hardly spoken all the morning, got up, and raising his hat to all, said good morning in his guttural voice and walked slowly away, one hand behind his bowed back.

"A lot of them are," said Phillip.

"How do you know?"

"The boy doesn't know," said Thomas Turney. "He is only repeating what he has heard. It is like the story of the Russian soldiers coming through Scotland at the outbreak of war, who turned out to be a consignment of Russian eggs, he-he-he."

"I would suggest, sir," said the Belgian, "that until you are sure of your facts, you do not contribute to the untruths about my country!"

"The boy has only just come home from playing his part in the trenches," said Thomas Turney. "All the same, Phillip m'boy, let this be a warning to you. 'Guard well thy tongue'."

Whereupon Phillip had gone away; and when Hetty saw him

again, he was holding forth to half-a-dozen ragged boys near the bandstand; but moved on when he caught sight of her.

The order came to report the next Monday morning at 9 a.m. to the Officers' Instruction Course at Sevenoaks, at the Regina Hotel. It was fortunate that Gerry and Bertie came to see Phillip during the morning of Sunday, for then, with two splendid cousins by his side, he could go on the Hill, and join the after-Church parade.

All three were in uniform, Hubert Cakebread wearing the Lilywhites chequered band round his cap, with the gold-braided peak of the Guards.

"No smoking outdoors, young Phillip," he said by the gate. "And why aren't your shoes properly cleaned? You mustn't let down the side, you know."

The two brothers waited while Phillip took his father's Wren polish, and put on so much that it took some time to polish it off again. Then he had to wash his hands, having brown-polished his nails; and ran out to join his cousins walking up the gully before him.

Gerry had got into the gunners, the R.F.A., and was at what he called the Shop, at Woolwich. On the Hill they walked up and down, Phillip looking anxiously for sight of the Rolls family. They passed two of Peter Wallace's sisters, in black: they gave him the barest acknowledgement to his salute. Had they got to know about his past in the night of Hallo'e'en? He was relieved when they turned off, to go down the gully.

It was a sunny morning; khaki mingled with Sunday best clothes, there were still many toppers showing with broad silk lapels of frock and morning coat. "Business as usual" was the slogan, held in scorn by some of the khaki boys, unaware of the tragedies caused among poor people at the outbreak of war, when their means of livelihood went overnight. Here were no signs of war, beyond the clay-coloured uniforms, and bunches of pale-faced Belgian refugees, of whom various stories were told. Phillip told Bertie how his Uncle Hilary's wife had opened her house in Hampshire to some of them soon after the war had started: how they, of an industrial class from the north, had shown surprise and resentment when Aunt Bee had suggested they visit their poorer countrymen billeted in cottages in the village.

"'But they are common people! We do not know them in our own country', they said. Aunt Bee didn't half tick them off. 'Then it is time you began to do so in this country', she told them."

"Well, if they were anything like the lot we saw out there, I don't blame them—or your respected aunt," remarked Hubert. Then, "My word, here's a peach, if ever I saw one!" Twenty yards away, Helena Rolls was coming towards them, her face fresh and smiling.

Phillip felt a glow of pride when the entire Rolls family stopped and congratulated them all, as they stood on the grass. In the centre of the lovely people stood Helena, looking straight at him, so eagerly it seemed, as though the Spring were rushing through her in beauty, to fulfil the golden moment of his life. She did look eagerly at him, she did! Her face was glowing; then he saw her beautiful eyes lift to Bertie, and a faint flush spread up from her neck, like hawthorn petals faintly pink when they were dying, and the nightingale was no longer singing in the day and the night. Then they were gone, and he was no longer walking, but borne forward effortlessly in the stream of life flowing from the sun.

"She's a peach, that girl of yours," said Gerry, to Phillip.

"My word, yes," said Bertie. "If ever there was a peach, it is that girl," and Phillip's face shone with joy.

Phillip sat on his bed, gazing at the photograph of Helena. He would have a coloured miniature made of it, enclosed within a gold locket, and wear it on a gold chain round his neck, where once he had worn his Mother's crucifix, which now lay with his old identity disc in his cupboard.

This plan, of course, had to be confided at once in Mrs. Neville, in whose sympathy Phillip's real life found such constant nourishment.

Chapter 10

"HELENA"

HE was still living in the golden moment of that Sunday morning when after tea Desmond drove up Hillside Road with the Singer, to take him to his course at Sevenoaks. At the last moment, during leave-taking on the pavement, now beginning to show green bines of convolvulus through its asphalt cracks, he decided to leave his kit behind, as an excuse to get leave to collect it. So the valise was taken in again; and with another glance at the house at the top of the road, hoping that his departure by motor car would be noticed, he got in beside the driver, and with a muttered, "No more farewells, for heaven's sake," gave the assembled family a salute, and with relief turned the corner, took salutes in Randiswell, and so down to the High Street and out into Kent. Soon they were opening up along Shooting Common.

"How's Eugene?"

"He's left school," said Desmond, "and wants to join the Public Schools Battalion of the Royal Fusiliers. He's coming to stay next week-end, so if you can get off, you'll see him."

"Good. But do you think they'd have a Brazilian?"

"His father's given permission."

Soon, too soon, they reached the top of River Hill, below which lay the wooded Weald, and the smoke of Sevenoaks spreading into the calm spring evening.

In the Regina Hotel a tall dark captain, beltless and in slacks, left a newspaper and armchair and came forward to greet him, and enquire his name.

"I see you have brought your servant with you," said the commandant, seeing Desmond sitting at the wheel of the car. "No official accommodation is provided for officers' batmen, so no doubt you will make your own arrangements."

"Yes, sir," said Phillip.

"There's the office," said the captain. "I expect they can fix you both up."

Phillip was told that a single bed in a double room was all that they had left. Would he mind sharing with another officer? As for his servant, there was the harness room vacant.

"I'll be back in a moment," he said, not knowing what else to reply.

"Fixed up all right?" said the commandant, back in the armchair with his paper.

"Yes thank you, sir." Outside he said, "'Struth, they think you are my servant! They want to put you in the harness room! Play the part, until you go. Cave! Porter coming." In a louder voice, "Well, James, take the car back to Town and get the cardan shaft seen to, will you?—Drive slowly. That universal joint is distinctly rocky."

"Very good, sir."

"Begging your pardon, sir, but there's a good garage in the town, it might save your man a journey," suggested the porter.

"Thank you, but we have our own little stable, with mechanics. No, I haven't any bags for my bedroom."

At that moment the gong sounded inside the hotel. "Hell, I shall have to leave you now. If I hadn't pretended you were my batman, we could have had supper together elsewhere. Damn, I don't like this place. I'll write. I'll get a motor-bike as soon as I can."

The subaltern of the shared bedroom was elderly, almost portly. He occupied the double bed, while Phillip had the small one against the wall. The first night was an agony of sleeplessness, since the elderly subaltern snored loudly. A score of times Phillip sat up meaning to wake him; but each time he could not screw himself up to do it. Screw was the right word: the snores seemed to arise from the other bed like thick fat corkscrews until, feeling himself to be a cork breaking under the strain, Phillip reached under the bed, pulled out a boot, and hurled it with a wild cry at the farther wall. Then he hid under the bedclothes.

At once the sleeper awakened, sat up, and said, "What was that?" Ashamed of what he had done, Phillip pretended to be muttering in a nightmare. "Look out, Johnson coming!" came the muffled voice from under the bedclothes. "Keep down, chaps!"

He listened while the other seemed to be getting out of bed. Then a voice enquired huskily, "I say, old man, are you all right?" He pretended to be asleep; listened while the other moved about the room; heard the rattle of a glass, then the squeak of a cork, and liquid being poured, followed by the sound of a sucking sort of drinking. Peeping from under the sheet, he saw in the light of an electric torch on the white marble mantelpiece that the other had what looked like a bottle of whiskey in his hand.

"What's the time?" said Phillip in a weary voice, appearing from under the bedclothes. "When's Number One up?"

"I beg your pardon?"

Phillip sat up, pretending to be awakening as he rubbed his eyes.

"Oh, thank God it was a dream! I thought I was back in Birdcage Walk, and we were being crumped. I could hear them droning down."

"Would you care for a pull?" said the other, offering the bottle. "I always keep a little drop for an emergency."

"Thanks."

"You were asleep when I came in late last night, and muttering then, and grinding your teeth."

"Was I? I hope I wasn't snoring."

"No, but you were bathed in sweat. Have you been in France?"

"Yes."

"In the infantry?"

"I was with the London Highlanders."

"My dear chap, help yourself to a good stiff peg! And may I shake you by the hand?"

Phillip shook the older man's hand, which was shaking enough already, he thought. Had he met a real drunkard at last? What fun!

"Cheer-ho! Ah, that's the stuff for the troops!"

"Take another pull, my dear fellow! It will feed your nerves."

In the morning, as he watched the other shaving, Phillip remembered he had left all his kit at home, including his cut-throat razor. "Do you think I need a shave?" he said, playing a rather helpless rôle.

The other examined his face through spectacles. "Hardly. Have you used a razor yet? You can borrow mine, if you care to, only do be careful. Perhaps I had better shave you? It is just as you like."

Seeing the shaking hand, Phillip said no thanks. He was confirmed in his belief of the newcomer being a drunkard when, having washed off his lather, Kenyon drank the half-glass of whiskey he had poured the night before. Then he saw that some false teeth were left in the glass.

"Whiskey is the best disinfectant. Did you think I was giving my teeth a drink last night?"

All the same, thought Phillip, he must be careful: this man

was possibly one of the bad companions Mother had often warned him about.

"This must be your boot," said the bad companion. "Look, where it struck the wall! Didn't you know you had thrown it?"

"It must have been in my dream, I think. I was hurling a a jam-pot bomb."

"It's a damned good thing you didn't hit me, old man!"

"You can write home and say you've been in a bombardment," laughed Phillip.

The next night, Kenyon, the elderly subaltern, had moved to another room, his place being taken by a newcomer, a younger red-faced man with almost white hair and eye-lashes, named Cox, in the Middlesex Regiment.

The commandant was a pre-war crammer for Sandhurst, recalled from the Reserve of Officers. He wore the General List badge on his lapels, with leather buttons on his tunic. His aides were a quiet lieutenant of the Royal West Kents named White, who had the D.S.O., and a merry second-lieutenant with an acorn-shaped face crowned with golden curls, from the King's Liverpool Regiment, called Porritt, who rode a Red Indian motor-cycle. It was an easy course, so far as Phillip was concerned: he took the minimum of notes, and listened to little of what was said during lectures.

Outdoor work was done in a park of rolling grassy chalkland set with old oaks and beeches around a great house, or cluster of houses enclosed within a walled rectangle. It was the historic home of the Sackvilles, said Kenyon, who added that he was a writer. The mansion contained as many staircases and rooms as there were weeks and days in the year respectively.

In the park, on rising grassland in front of Knole, the young officers took turns to drill their own squads. There was a King's Sergeant of Foot Guards who put them through it, teaching them how to salute on parade, after halting with stamping feet— "One—one two!"—rather like a horse, Phillip thought. Then the semaphore of the right arm, the quiver of the flat hand: the sergeant did it as though his hand at any moment might fly off his wrist. Terrible howled sounds of command tore out of his throat, echoing back from the grey stonework of Lord Sackville's historic mansion.

After drill, they practised advancing in extended order by sign and whistle, and to give fire direction on targets on the landscape to be regarded as a clock face, its centre a given mark.

"All the old stuff, in fact," Phillip told Kenyon. "At the clump at nine o'clock, fifteen rounds rapid, Fire! Out run all the hares and pheasants! Honestly, a fat lot of good this sort of thing is out there!"

The R.W.K. lieutenant with the D.S.O., wearing mackintosh however warm the weather, and leaning on an ash-plant, seldom speaking, remarked conversationally: "It had its use for fire control before the war became static, you know"; and since he had commanded his battalion, though wounded, on the Aisne, where he won his D.S.O., Phillip made no more criticisms. Both the commandant and his lieutenant were invariably very quiet in manner, never raising their voices. They were real gentlemen, he could see.

At half-past eleven every morning the commandant gave the class a map-reference.

"We will meet there at noon precisely, gentlemen; each officer will find his own way there, in so far as is possible, independently. Any questions?"

On the second morning Phillip asked if they must walk, or might they ride to the map-reference?

"You can get there how you like, on foot or by bicycle or motor car, as you wish."

Thereupon, after dismissal, he went to one of the garages in the town, and asked to be allowed to try out a second-hand motor-cycle for sale. It was a Fafnir, with poppet inlet valve, very old, priced five pounds. He took it back afterwards, saying it was not fast enough. The next day he took out a Triumph, but this too had a defect, he explained upon returning: it whistled loudly through the belt pulley.

"But that is the design of the 1911 model, sir. It's the crankcase relief valve."

"I suppose you haven't a later model? This one sounds too much like a starling to me. I want a machine as soon as possible, so I think I'll just have another look around."

A third garage had what Phillip thought looked like a Stick Insect on Wheels: a four-cylinder shaft-driven Belgian F.N. "I would like to try this one."

"Certainly, sir!"

The F.N. was duly returned, with the criticism that the handlebars were too far back.

"They are rather like a huge hairpin, aren't they? You have to sit too far back, causing a tendency to skid in the dust round corners. Well, I'll come back later, when I've had a look around. Maybe you'll have some others in by then."

In this way the first week was passed, six machines in all being "tested"; and so Phillip learned more or less how to ride a motor-cycle. His conscience told him that he was a bit of a swindler, getting the machines out on false pretences, thus raising false hopes. Perhaps one of the little tin-roof-shanty proprietors had hoped for a better livelihood, after a sale.

Thus condemning himself, almost by habit, Phillip deceived himself: for he did want a motor-cycle, but did not know what kind to buy. This ignorance of what he was and what he wanted led to him falling an easy victim to an astute amateur business-man, a qualified electrical engineer who happened to overhear what he was saying to a garage man on the Friday morning.

"This 10 h.p. twin-engined N.U.T. is really too powerful, and far too costly, for me. I think I'll buy a two-stroke after all. What about a Levis? Oh, what a pity you haven't got one. I must have a bike by tomorrow, for a very special occasion."

As he walked back to the Regina for luncheon, he noticed a rather nice-looking two-stroke with red and green tank coming towards him, making a fine buzzing noise. The rider drew up.

"If you are looking for a reliable machine that can't go wrong, never let you down, how about a Connaught? The engine has no valves to break, none to grind in, no springs to lose temper, no oil to pump into the crankcase. Like to try it? Much more economical to run than a four-stroke. Of course, it's no use pretending you can blind about on it."

"I don't want to blind," said Phillip. "How much is it?"

The fellow seemed to be thinking. Then he looked up side-ways and said quickly, "Thirty-five pounds. Why not have a ride?"

Phillip got astride, and paddled off as directed. When the engine fired, he wobbled, it seemed to be going very fast. He fumbled throttle and brake, and went diagonally across the road, helplessly into a lamp-post.

"I say, I'm awfully sorry," he said, picking himself up,

then the machine. If he had damaged it, he would have to buy it.

The other soon straightened the handlebars, holding front wheel between knees.

"You'll be all right when you get the hang of it. There are two gears, as you see."

"What year is it?"

"Nineteen twelve."

"How fast will it go?"

"Forty on the level; tuned up, probably forty-five. I'll tell you what I'll do: knock off a pound. There! Thirty-four pounds."

"Well, I haven't got any money on me," said Phillip, entranced with the idea of riding up Hillside Road on it the next afternoon. "My cheque book is at the Regina."

"Then it's a deal at thirty-four pounds?"

Phillip shook hands on it. Following the rider to the hotel, he was given a registered packet at the office. His gold brooch from the Stores! He would ask Helena Rolls to accept it on the morrow! He ran upstairs for his cheque-book, and five minutes later was the proud possessor of the Connaught.

Later that day he realised he had been done, when he saw, in the only garage he had not so far visited, a new 1915-model Connaught for £29 10s.

"Why didn't you come to me first?" said the garage owner. "You could have had the machine you've got now for fifteen pounds. That's the price I got for it, from the fellow who took it out the day you tried it. It's got a cracked crankcase, you know, that's why there's little compression. I told him that when he come back here after he had seen you, and bought it off of me."

"Then," cried Phillip, "that's fraud! He sold what wasn't his!"

"Too late now," said the other.

Phillip did not mind about the little oily crack, or the price: he had a motor-bike, that was the main thing. He thought about the coming weekend all the rest of the afternoon and evening, his new life symbolised by a gleaming, golden brooch.

Yet the fear of returning to the front sometimes recurred. One of the officers in the Green Howards had already received orders to go overseas before the end of the course. At night, in the room which now had been set aside as the ante-room, he asked Phillip if he could suggest anything, outside the prescribed officer's kit, essential for the trenches. "Bearing in mind, of course, that one's kit must not exceed thirty-five pounds in weight. You're the only one of the class who has been out, so I wonder if you would advise me?"

The others gathered round the veteran.

"Well, yes, now you come to mention it. Take plenty of newspapers."

"Newspapers? I'm afraid I don't quite follow you."

"Well, you know," replied Phillip, "they are very scarce at the front. For going to the latrine."

"But why not take the real thing?"

Phillip was puzzled. "I don't know what you mean by the real thing."

"Well, a box of Bronco."

Phillip felt that he had shown himself to be rather a simpleton; and after a while left the circle of polite port-sippers. He went out into the street, seeing Cox his room-mate standing there with an undecided air, a monocle fixed in one eye.

Cox's face looked as though it had been so scorched by the Chinese sun that the skin had peeled off and never grown again. Cox's boiled red look seemed to be in his very nature, for he was always restless, seldom able to sit still. He had a hoarse voice, and every evening so far he had walked about the town, looking for what he called a bird.

"They hunt in couples in this town," he said to Phillip. "How about coming with me?"

"Right ho!" replied Phillip, not really wanting to meet any girls, but at the same time he did not want to appear to be a greenhorn. Cox had an extraordinary method of attracting their attention. He carried a whangee walking stick, full length, and when they passed a girl half way down the hill, he turned round and rattled it on the pavement, a grin on his face. "Will that fetch her?" he said to Phillip. The girl went on up the hill without looking back.

"No," said Cox, "that one doesn't rattle!"

Nor did any of the girls in Sevenoaks rattle, apparently; for after hanging about outside the Picture House at the bottom, they returned up the hill on the other side of the street, Cox's rattles having no result.

"I think your presence is putting the birds off," said Cox, with sudden red-faced irascibility.

"Where did you get the idea of the rattle?" asked Phillip.

"Shanghai," said Cox, shortly.

Then, gnawing his lower lip, he swung on his heel and barked, "I must write some letters to my fiancée! And I'm damned if I remain at the Regina with you, muttering and groaning to yourself all through every bloody night, especially as they won't reduce their scale of charges! Damme, how can one live on seven-and-six a day, and pay eight-and-six at a hotel? I gave up a good job to come home and join up."

"What were you in, Cox?"

"That's my bloody business! I suppose you've got private means?"

"Well, sort of. I'm sorry I mutter and groan, but you snore like a barn owl, don't forget! Well, cheer-ho!"

Cox abruptly left Phillip, and strode away. Phillip saw the red round face turn again at the corner, as a girl went past. There came the rattle of the whangee cane, again without response. Cox threw up his hands in a hopeless gesture before disappearing round the corner. Well, thought Phillip with glee, he had learned something about customs in the Far East. He was seeing life. He went back to the Regina, hopeful of seeing more.

The next day, Saturday, was fine; work ceased at 12.30 p.m. After a hurried luncheon, he set out for the journey home. It was most pleasurable. The Connaught ran with a pleasing purr, and he soon mastered the way to change gear without clashing the teeth, with de-compressor valve lifted.

He enjoyed the shape and colour of the red and green tank, long aluminium foot-boards, on which he tried to stand up and drive as though it were a circus bike. He tried hands-off, too, but an alarming stagger showed that the weight was not properly distributed. Soon he was buzzing along Shooting Common, then through Brumley, down the hill to Cutler's Pond—and then he was going up Charlotte Road, seeing above him the sticky brown chestnut buds broken into green, and with a brief glance at Mrs. Neville's window, up Hillside Road.

That afternoon, hearing that Helena Rolls was going to visit her grandparents in Twistleton Road, Phillip waited until she left her house to walk over the Hill, then mounted the Connaught and went along Charlotte Road to meet her the other way. He wore his light fawn British warm because it looked so nice on other officers, with the gilt star on either shoulder-strap— the wonderful yellow star with red and green enamelling in the centre. He waited near St. Simon's Church; watched her turn the corner from Foxfield into Twistleton, waited with drying mouth for her to get fifty yards down before starting up and passing her. Fifty yards on, he stopped, got off, and feeling in his velvet-lined pocket for the blue case, opened it with slightly shaking hands; and clutching the brooch in his left palm, walked forward and gave her a salute.

"Hullo, Phillip!"

Panic held him; but he managed to say, as he had rehearsed, "Hullo. I say, would you like to have this brooch? It's my regimental badge, the Mediators."

He had never before been so close to her, to see the beautiful moulding of her cheeks and forehead, her lips, her chin. Then calmly and pleasantly she was saying,

"I don't think I could take it, Phillip, but thank you very much for offering it."

"You—you aren't offended?"

"No, of course not! It is a beautiful brooch. But I couldn't possibly accept it."

"I see. I hope everyone is well at home?"

"Yes, thank you."

"Well, goodbye."

"Goodbye."

Ten minutes later Phillip had told Mrs. Neville all about it, having asked, several times, if she thought from Helena's frank manner that it might after all mean something; and heard Mrs. Neville's reply that she was very young, but, of course, in her heart a woman would be pleased to think that a man thought so much of her that he would want to give her of his very best——

"I don't know, Phillip, I can't say dear——" went on the fat woman, hoping she would not cry. He was so young, so inexperienced, she knew how he worshipped that girl; the more, she sometimes thought, because his early life had been so un-happy. Oh dear, these boys and girls, how they were growing up. There was Phillip's sister, Mavis, only seventeen, but already she had got an officer—a staff-major in the War Office, of all things!

She was glad that Phillip and Desmond and Eugene, the Brazilian boy, were together that evening; it was almost like old times, Bloodhound Patrol pram-wheel wagon camping days, to see the three of them setting off for Freddy's—Phillip driving, Desmond on the carrier, and Eugene sitting on the tank, his legs over the handlebars. Let them be happy while they could, bless them.

Mavis, a slim dark girl with large brown eyes that glistened with a strange light when she was happy or animated, had fallen in love with an officer she had met in the train, when, during the rush-hour, she had, with considerable nervousness, got into a first-class carriage at London Bridge Station. He was sitting alone in a carriage, and he wore a very new uniform with red tabs on his lapels and a red band round his hat. From the three pips on his shoulders she knew he was a captain. When she got out at Wakenham station, he saluted her, and said that he hoped he would be allowed to see her again.

On the second occasion of their meeting, Mavis' new friend was in ordinary clothes, what Phillip had called mufti; and he invited her to the Hippodrome. She went with him, determined to go straight home afterwards, since strange men were not to be trusted. It was with some apprehension that she had a cup of coffee with him in a teashop, with two chocolate *éclairs*; then he walked with her part of the way home, saying goodbye outside St. Mary's Church, and adding that he hoped to see her again soon. In some excitement that he was so gentlemanly, Mavis hurried home, telling her mother that she had been out with her friend Nina, having first found out that Nina had not called for her that evening. Nina was a fair girl with rather fat legs who lived in Rushy Green.

Hitherto Mavis and Nina had been inseparables. Their friendship was one of spiritual intimacy, based on Nina's regard for the porcelain-delicate dark-eyed Mavis; and on Mavis' acceptance of her friend's devotion.

Mavis felt that she was now leading more than a double life. In order to be with her officer, she told Nina that she was going out with her mother, and her mother that she was going out with Nina. She felt herself to be living a very strange life indeed, when, in addition to playing off Mother and Nina, she became involved in a conspiracy with Phillip. An envelope marked

Strictly Confidential and Private arrived one morning, with the Seven-oaks post-mark. Mavis responded at once to the contents: for it would give her an additional safeguard, or excuse, should Nina find out that she had not been out with Mother.

> Dear Mavis,
>   How are you, alright I hope. Now listen. I want you to meet Helena Rolls accidentally on purpose, and invite her to come with you next Saturday at 3 p.m. to go to the National Gallery in London near Charing Cross station to look at the Old Masters there. As you know, Mrs. Rolls is an artist, and very much interested in paintings, etc. She has done some very fine paintings herself, and once told me that Helena was interested in Art also. DON'T SAY I AM COMING TOO. I will meet you at Charing Cross station, about 3.22 p.m. on Saturday, as though by chance. I will of course offer to accompany you, and will needless to add pay all expenses. TELL NO ONE, not even mother. It is to be a surprise. I have had my photo taken, and when we are going home (I am coming by train, as my crankcase is being soldered up, they can't weld it or braze it, you see), I shall offer it to her. Write by return, on the enclosed stamped addressed postcard, as soon as you have seen Helena. *Don't say I am coming.* Life is fairly hectic down here, though the actual work is boring and unnecessary, being for open warfare, which won't be for a long time yet, in my opinion. No more now, love to all,
>
>   Your scheming brother
>   Phillip 2-lt.

The meeting took place as Phillip had planned. Although it was a warm sunny day, he wore his fawn-coloured British warm, carrying gloves and whangee cane, and punctiliously returned all salutes. He wandered in a dream within the tall cool rooms of the National Gallery, between Mavis and Helena. He took a taxicab to the Trocadero afterwards, having heard that this was a place where officers took ladies. He gave the waiter a half-crown, and bought a packet of gold-tipped de Reszke Turkish cigarettes, the fat ones, remembering it was not done to smoke in the streets. Then home again, buying first-class tickets to Randiswell, as he could not bear the idea of drab Wakenham station. They walked up Hillside Road together, watched by Mrs. Neville, who was in the secret, from her flat window. Outside No. 11 they said goodbye, Helena thanking him before she went on to her home, carrying the photograph.

The next day, after Evensong at St. Simon's, he got a report from Alwyn Todd, a friend of Helena's, about the happenings of the day before, and entered notes, "for later cogitation and analysis", in his old 1914 diary, in a space between records of birds' nests found, and the holiday on Exmoor, just before the war. He wrote partly in code, based on the little Latin he had bothered to learn at school, and "let the truth rip", as he said to himself.

National Gallery Business, Results of

1. Mrs. R. told A.T., "Why can't young people enjoy themselves sans faciendum stultus ipsi."
2. H.R. told A.T., (a) Didn't accept brooch because she "didn't like me, and it wasn't fair".
   (b) P.M. "runs" after me, and uses M. to further "suit".
   (c) Mavis did not say until very end that I was coming, and then bunked before Helena could say if she minded.
   (d) What would she do if I joined the Tennis Club and ran after her "like a two-year-old"?
   (e) I was alright as a "chum", but she felt young and skittish.
   (f) Bertie asked her to go with him to the old Alleynian Dance, but her mother said she was too young. He took a hint, and I wouldn't.
   (g) The photo was "ripping". A pity I could not be just an ordinary friend.
   (h) Alwyn could consider ipse privileged person: can go out with H. sans faciens ipse stultus sanguineus.
3. Mrs. R. told A.T., "I was 'morbid as a boy, and the corners of my mouth were always turned down, not up'."

Conclusion, at first impression of above :

I understand. My own fault. Finish!
At second thought: Considering (e) and (g):—I shall join the Tennis Club!

Hope kept the dream alive. He practised, in the mirror, turning the corners of his mouth upwards. Then a bold idea struck him. It came when, during the third and final weekend before the closing of the course, he stopped at a little garage in the High Street for petrol and saw in the workshop a racing motorcycle, the sporting lines of which immediately took his fancy. If only he could roar up Hillside Road on it! It had racing handle-bars, small rubber-padded foot-rests, a single-cylinder engine with big cooling fins, a straight-through exhaust pipe of large diameter. As he stared at it the proprietor, a short stocky man with a face like an old boxer's, smeared with oil and carbon, his dark suit shapeless and gleaming with grease, took an oil-soaked briar pipe from his mouth and said, pointing with bitten-through stem, "Nice job, ain't it?"

"By Jove, yes!"

"Made by a bloke like you what 'ad to leave sudden for France. Left it 'ere to be sold. It can 'op it. Racing cams. He built it 'isself."

"I wish I'd known, before I bought this piffling little two-stroke!"

"What's up with it?"

"It loses speed when it gets hot."

"Rings gummed up?"

"They were, but I've had new ones fitted. I've only had it a fortnight. I was swindled." He told the man his story, not concealing the crack in the crankcase. "But I've had it welded up now, with solder."

"You can't solder aluminium. I've got a spare crankcase, as it happens. I'll tell you—what about a straight swop? You'll find this bus all right. Go on, take 'er out. She starts very easy. It's a Binks three-jet carburettor, she fires at once on the pilot jet."

Phillip had already learned to push and vault into the saddle, awkward as it had been with the back-extending handlebars of Triumph and F.N.; but with these bars the start was a dream, especially as the engine fired at once, with the least opening of the lever. The saddle was comfortable, too. He lay forward, body-weight on wrists, knees gripping the leather pads strapped round the tank, feet well back on the rests. His body felt like an arrow into the wind. And what a fine drum-like beat of the exhaust! He was entranced. A straight swop! But would he be doing the old chap?

He went as far as the Hippodrome, then swung round in the road and returned sitting upright, left hand just touching rubber grip, right hand in trouser pocket. He could balance by sitting on part of the saddle, body slightly slewed round, while the engine barely ticked over, the exhaust uttering a resonant *pun-pun-pun*.

"'Ow d'yer like 'er?"

"Absolutely spiffing! Did you really mean I could exchange mine for it?"

"If you're satisfied, I am."

"Right!"

Phillip returned with his beautiful bike an hour later, Desmond on the carrier.

"I wonder if I could have it painted, and call for it next week? In case you think I'm dishonest, I'll leave a cheque with you, for its value, and take away the Connaught, as I've got to get back to Sevenoaks tomorrow night. Then next week I'll come for this. Can you paint it in a week?"

"Easy. Painter next door."

The frame to be black enamelled; tank to be pearl grey, lined out with thin red, and the name *Helena* to be painted in small letters on the left-hand front end of the tank, in black. The tank then to be clear-varnished.

"Oh, and I want a plate on the front mudguard, above the number-plate—no, I'll have it broadside on, across the front forks, just here, see, with the letters in white on black enamel, O.H.M.S."

"On His Majesty's Service. What are you, despatch rider section?"

"No, I'm just on His Majesty's service. How much will that cost?"

"Is this your own bike, or do the Government pay, mister?"

"I pay, of course."

"Look 'ere, I'll tell you what I'll do. You leave me a bradbury for the painting, and I'll be satisfied. Then if you don't come back, that'll cover the painting, and no 'arm done."

"But I will come back."

"'Ow d'you know? What about the gas attack at Wipers? 'Ave you seen the evening papers? The 'Uns let loose a lot o' chlorine. You might get recalled."

"I've been out."

"Well, you can go agen, can't you?"

There was a wonderful party in Freddy's that night—until the rum proved too much for both Desmond and Phillip.

When the course ended the commandant read out where each officer was to report. As name after name was read, so many for France, Phillip felt shaky. The newspapers had been filled with details of the second Ypres battle, with appeals for emergency gas-masks to be made by women at home, with accounts of retching French Colonial and Canadian troops dying with liquescent lungs. His name, however, was not among the B.E.F. replacements.

He was ordered to report to a Territorial unit in Suffolk, for training and duty. "I cannot give officers any leave, but if you apply to the commanding officers of the home-service units where you have to report——"

Chapter 11

LIFE IS FUN

Most County Regiments in the British Army had two Regular battalions, a third Special Reserve battalion, perhaps a fourth Militia Reserve, and a fifth battalion—the Territorial unit. There were exceptions. The London Regiment was composed of twenty-eight Territorial, with no Regular, battalions; the London Highlanders and the London Rifles were two of them. Their traditions before the war were those of the old Volunteers, their battle honours gained by small detachments sent to the South African War.

The County Regiment to which Phillip had been ordered to report for training and duty was composed before the war of one territorial battalion only. Soon after the outbreak of war a second-line battalion had been formed, on a cadre of old retired officers and those of the first battalion who had not volunteered for active service. The first battalion had gone to France a few weeks before Phillip was ordered to report for duty to the second battalion, which was stationed in a market town famous for its training stables.

The officers of the second battalion, none of whom had experience of war, either in the past or in the present campaign, were drawn from occupations and professions long established upon the flat, largely agricultural county, famous for its university and fruit farms, and its smooth rolling heaths, part tilled for oats and hay of fine quality—a perfect country for breeding and training bloodstock.

The colonel of the second battalion wore the riband of the Territorial Decoration given for long service—equivalent to what in the Regular Army was known as the Rooti, or Bread-eating Medal. He was a university don, an old man with white hair, thin gold spectacles, and nicotine-stained moustache that he had now clipped short, as befitted military efficiency. He was known among the officers, many of whom he had tutored in college, by the nickname of Strawballs, derived from his real name.

The adjutant had a nickname, also based upon his real name. He was tall and stalky of leg, with a curved middle or elongated paunch, rising to sloping shoulders supporting an egg-shaped Nordic head. Captain Whale, partner in a family firm of County Estate Agents and Auctioneers, having their main office in the university town, was known as Jonah.

To the peace-time officers of the battalion, mobilisation had come as a tonic, an affirmation of real values, a stimulating change from routine living, most of it at desks. The company commanders and subalterns, with two exceptions, were drawn from members of the established provincial middle-class—lawyers, doctors, schoolmasters, yeoman farmers, wholesale merchants connected with agriculture (the main industry of the county) such as iron foundrymen and implement makers—who, to improve their own family standing, had sent their sons to public school and university.

The battalion, with three other territorial battalions of adjacent counties, formed a brigade commanded by an old soldier of the Regular Army, who had retired sometime during the reign of Queen Victoria. This "dugout" was reputed to have survived the Charge of the Light Brigade as a cornet of horse in the Crimean War, and was generally known as "Crasher".

The colonel of the battalion, whose tutorial background was classical-historical-archaeological, sometimes spoke, with donnish wit, of his command as "The Cantuvellaunians", a name which went back at least to the time of the Roman Occupation of Britain. All his junior officers had been approved by him for what he called their autochthonous associations with the county; and it was therefore with some slight dismay that this regional patriot heard from his adjutant that half a dozen young temporary officers from "band-box" establishments of the New Armies were to come to the battalion: for temporary duty and training only, he heard with relief from "Jonah" his adjutant.

Five of these officers of the New Armies had duly reported for duty on the Saturday morning at 9.0 a.m. in the Orderly Room on the ground floor of a house fronting the High Street; the sixth had not appeared just before noon, the hour when the colonel usually went into the Pigskin Club, of which he and all the other officers of the regiment had been made temporary honorary members, for his midday Hollands gin and water.

The adjutant had gone into the colonel's room, which gave a view of the High Street beyond its bow windows, exactly at noon, when a loud noise like that of a shot-gun came from outside. At once a string of race-horses, being walked down the broad street opposite, began to rear and plunge under their stable-boys.

"What the devil can that be?" asked the colonel. "It sounded like a ten-bore." The adjutant, seeming the more bow-fronted because of his height and the thinness of his legs from the knees downwards tightly encased in new grey canvas leggings, said from his stance by the window:

"It looks like the missing subaltern, Colonel, on what appears to be a racer motor-cycle."

"Horrible things," said the colonel, shortly. "Why were they ever invented?"

A few minutes later the orderly-room sergeant knocked on the door, opened it immediately, and said that there was an officer reporting for duty. The adjutant moved towards his orderly room, but stopped when the colonel said:

"Ask him to come in here, Jonah."

"Yes, Colonel."

The seated colonel looked over his glasses at the new officer, noting, during the time that he came to attention with what he considered was a totally unnecessary series of stamps upon the parquet flooring, and saluted, that his service cap, set at a townee angle, was without the wire which usually kept the top flat. The appearance was therefore sloppy. The colonel observed, furthermore, that the button of one tunic pocket was undone, and that an oily mark disfigured one of his puttees.

"Sir! Second-lieutenant Maddison reporting——"

The adjutant, also critical of the newcomer's appearance,

said sharply, "You report to the adjutant, not to the Commanding Officer! Didn't they teach you that at your course?"

"Sir! I was saluting the senior officer present."

There was a pause. Then the colonel said in a guttural voice of slight nasal harshness, aggravated by his Adam's apple being compressed against his starched light khaki collar, "What is your name, did you say?"

"Maddison, sir."

"Where were you at school, Mr. Maddison?"

"Heath's, sir."

The colonel said "O-oh," as though he were none the wiser.

After a few moments, still standing stiffly to attention, Phillip said, "Sir! Permission to report my arrival to the adjutant!"

"What do you want my permission for, Mr.-er-Maddison?" enquired the colonel, peering over his gold-wired glasses, as though at some strange wading bird.

Phillip hesitated; then with a "Sir!" he turned away to face the adjutant with a one-one-two stamp; saluted; and said, "Sir! Second-lieutenant Maddison——"

"Come come, Mr. Maddison, we are both well acquainted with your name by this time," remarked the colonel.

"Why are you late?" said the adjutant.

"Sir! The belt of my motor-cycle broke. I had to push the machine several miles to get a spare link."

The colonel listened to his voice, trying to place the young officer with the glistening blue eyes in the face of a small boy. Was there a hint of Kent, or was it Cockney, in some of his vowels? After a few moments he said:

"Where do you come from?"

"Wakenham, sir."

The colonel seemed to be considering this reply. By long habit a placer of persons, he could not be quite sure about the youth before him.

"Where is that?"

"In a part of Kent now blackened by London, sir."

"Oh." After a pause, "Jonah, will you attend to this officer."

"Yes, Colonel." To Phillip he said, "Come with me and I'll take your particulars."

"Sir!"

Phillip gave the colonel his guardsman salute, without the stamp this time, and followed the adjutant out. In the next room he recited details of address, next-of-kin, religion, age, service, etc. He was about to leave when the adjutant, looking him up and down, remarked sternly, "It is quite out of order that you are wearing your service cap without the wire within. Don't you know that?"

"Without the wire within, sir?"

"That's what I said, dammit!" replied the adjutant, with some testiness. "And stand to attention when I speak to you!"

"Sir! I was thinking for the moment you meant 'without' in the sense of 'outside', sir. Well, sir, we all removed the inside wires in the trenches, because of snipers."

"Well, you are not in the trenches here, so get the wire put back before Church Parade tomorrow."

"Sir! May I have the honour to apply for leave, to get the wire?"

"Where is the wire?"

"Sir! With my kit."

"Do you mean to say that you have reported here without your kit?"

"Sir!"

"Why?"

"Sir! I hoped to be given leave to get it. The commandant of the course——"

"Well, I'm damned if you haven't got a nerve! Now stand at ease, for heaven's sake. Have you got a camp-bed? You'll be in an unfurnished house, and will need one. You will draw half-a-crown a day field allowance, in lieu of a furnished room. Messing is three shillings a day——"

"I see, sir."

"Don't interrupt, I haven't finished yet. I was about to say that you'd better go and see your room——Godolphin House is on the corner, on the left towards the Heath, at the bottom of the hill. The mess sergeant will show you. Did you bring *no* kit at all?"

"Only a walking stick, sir."

"Good God, is that all you had in the trenches?"

"Yes, sir."

"Very well, you are given leave until midnight tomorrow, Sunday. On Monday morning you will parade at 6.30 a.m. under the regimental sergeant major, for arms drill, followed by half an hour's Swedish drill with your platoon. Your posting to 'C' company will be in orders tonight."

"Thank you, sir."

Phillip saluted and went out, delighted that he would have another Saturday night with Desmond and Eugene at Freddy's, and the Guild Hall over the road, where, at little tables round a fountain and fish-pond, lots of interesting girls went every night.

His bedroom in Godolphin House was in one of the attics, three stories up back-stairs of stone. It was a fairly large house, the main staircase being in the centre, where in larger rooms other officers had their canvas beds, each with hired chests of drawers, wash-hand-stands, and bedroom china.

Phillip shared his attic with a short, rosy-faced youth called by the others "Chick", so named from his small stature. He was also of Kitchener's army, attached for duty. Chick said the set of furniture could be hired for 2s. 6d. a week, so Phillip ordered his from the shop named by Chick.

The routine was much the same every day—6.30 a.m. under the R.S.M., parade, after breakfast, at 9 a.m., march away to the great stretches of grassland sloping to woods and the sky, practice advances in extended order, signs by hand and whistle, rush and lie down to give covering fire—in fact the old useless Bleak Hill routine over again—a matter of expressed scorn by Phillip.

"They never do it out there like this."

He went on to say that the yellow obsolescent Japanese rifles the battalion was armed with were "ridiculous". What was the point of cleaning them, when they would never be used? When the wag of his platoon, a man called Bellamy, showed his rifle on inspection, to be full of dust, Phillip did not report him. The C.Q.M.S. mentioned this to the junior captain, an eighteen-year-old, who told Phillip that such cases in future must be reported to his company orderly room.

"A rifle is a soldier's best friend, sir," added the C.Q.M.S.

"I always heard it was a Blighty one, Sergeant-major."

Phillip's company commander was an elderly major, with a cast of mind, and face reflecting that cast, entirely different from the other officers of the battalion. It was a remotely reserved face, as though withdrawn from the hurly-burly of life: the life of the market place.

Major Wayland spoke with a manner of extreme reserved politeness, which made him appear, in Phillip's eyes, to be unaware of what was happening about him. He had *The Honourable* before his name. He seldom came out with the company, which marched away from its parade ground every day under the eighteen-year-old captain, known to everyone, except Phillip, as "the Infant Hercules". He had left school at Christmas, and seemed to be a favourite of the colonel, because he wrote sonnets and read Greek poets in the original, as well as having been captain of his school, the rugger fifteen and the cricket eleven. He was fair, blue-eyed, with a pink and white complexion. His poems had been published by the firm of which the second-in-command, an elderly university bookseller, was the senior partner. From the same man in the mess, O'Connor, Phillip learned that "Strawballs" had been a friend of the poet who had recently died in the Aegean, soon after the Gallipoli landings. It was for this poet, Rupert Brooke, the colonel wore the black crêpe band on his arm. Phillip felt a slight importance that his Aunt Theodora, in her last letter, had mentioned that she had known Rupert Brooke. The letter had warned Phillip about "treading the primrose path", a phrase which he did not understand, unless it meant drinking. Anyway, old people were always giving warning of this and that. The only one of his Maddison aunts who had never criticised him was not really a Maddison—only by marriage—and she had tried to get into his bed. Phew, that was a situation! He had been too ashamed even to tell Desmond.

Phillip thought that "Hercules" was lucky to have three pips. It was probably because his company commander, the old major, was a dugout, with a poor word of command. Major Wayland was an uncle of the Earl of Mersea, a fact that made Phillip realise how small the world was: for Major Wayland must be the brother-in-law of the Dowager Countess, who owned Knollyswood. He did not live in Godolphin House, or come into the mess, except once a week, on guest-nights.

These weekly guest-nights, Phillip thought, were rather fun. After dinner, they had high-jinks in the ante-room. One of the games was called *Kruger*. Two officers were blindfolded, and lay on the floor, rolled newspapers in their right hands, and holding each other's left hand. One cried, "Who goes there?" the other replied "Kruger!" and then had to move his head away from where he had spoken, or be sloshed by the rolled newspaper. Another game was to put two armchairs together, back to back, and taking a run at one, turn a somersault and land sitting down in the other chair. Then to do it blindfold.

Phillip had heard about this trick from Bertie, who had had it done on him. The joke with a newcomer was to remove a chair while he was being blindfolded, others talking round him to muffle the sound of the castors, and when, having learnt to do it with open eyes, he tried to somersault over the back of one chair blindfold, he went wallop on to the floor.

Phillip could not see the fun of it; indeed, remembering how he had hurt his spine years before when Gerry had pulled his chair away, at Gran'pa's supper party, as he was about to sit down, he thought it was positively dangerous. Knowing what was in store for him, he shook his head and slipped away when Baldersly, the senior subaltern, flushed and smoking a cigar, called out with it between his teeth and his long yellow moustache, "Come on, you new wart, now do it blindfold!"; and waited in the lavatory until he thought Baldersby would have forgotten. There was a lot of clapping and cheering, and unlocking the door, Phillip darted back, in time to see the "Infant Hercules", resplendent with three new pips, hair ruffled, do the somersault blindfold, to land upright on his feet. The Colonel looked very pleased, and patted "Hercules" on the shoulder. "Hercules", of course, already knew the trick.

At ten o'clock the following night the officers went up to the wide gallops of the Heath, for compass reading. Pairs had to advance through darkness on imaginary trenches by given bearings. As Phillip did not have a luminous compass, the officer in charge, Major Howes, the bookseller in private life, kindly lent him his. When all was over, they re-assembled for a brief talk by the senior company commander, known to Phillip merely as the captain who had a Rover motor-cycle with a three-speed Sturmey-Archer gear in its huge rear-wheel hub.

"In finding your way at night in hostile territory, as any country would be, of course, occupied by the Germans in retreat, the question of silence is all-important. I heard one officer's voice as I stood out in front, moreover, he was smoking a cigarette. That, of course, would be fatal if done at the front, for he would immediately call down retribution on his head, in the shape of machine-gun fire."

"Another point I would like to make, sir!" the captain went on, turning respectfully to the rather stumpy form of Major Howes, the bookseller. "At present progress in the dark on compass bearings is necessarily limited by the length between the compass-bearer and his partner who goes out before him, to mark the direction, and to remain the starting-point for the next advance. It occurs to me that if the marker carried a ball of string in his hand, he could pay it out as he advances, and when the compass-bearer sees he has gone far enough forward, that is to say, well before the point of invisibility, he could give the string a jerk, and stop the marker, without the necessity of any further notice."

"An awful good idea," said Major Howes. "Awful good," he repeated. Phillip had heard the colonel use this expression: it seemed to be rather the fashion among those officers who were "'vars'ty m'n". Another expression was "awful bore", the opposite of anything "awful good".

"Chick" had been to the "Vars'ty", though, Phillip understood, not as an actual member. He had been at Fitzwilliam Hall, a sort of extra college, which didn't quite count. Some of the real colleges had strange nicknames, like Pemmy or Pemmer, Pothouse, and Keys.

"Anyone like to say anything?" asked the captain with the Rover motor-bike.

No-one spoke for a moment; then Phillip said, "Sir! Were we supposed to be going into trenches tonight?"

"Well, not exactly into our own trenches, but advancing on a position where the Germans would be entrenched. Why do you ask?"

"Well, sir, it isn't done like that out there."

"Oh, really." After a pause the senior captain said, "Perhaps you will tell us how it is done, then?"

"Well, sir, if it was at night, the German lines would be lit by flares, making a compass unnecessary. Anyway, the luminous paint would not be visible in the bright lights."

"But supposing the Germans were not sending up flares?"

"Well, sir, the Germans do send them up, all night."

"At present, yes. But present conditions of stalemate will not hold when the time comes for open warfare. It has already begun, at Neuve Chapelle and elsewhere. Any more questions? No-one else has anything to say?" He turned and saluted Major Howes, who said, "Thank you, Captain Rhodes. I think that is all, gentlemen. Will you make your own way back?"

Phillip, on returning to Godolphin House, went upstairs to get his pipe; and on coming downstairs was about to enter the ante-room, when he paused by the half-open door, hearing the somewhat thick voice of Baldersby, the senior subaltern, saying something which at once he thought must refer to himself.

"Damned cheek! Bloody rude, contradicting Rhodes! 'It isn't done like that out there!' Just because he's been out for a week or two as a Tommy! Abominable manners! Blasted little Cockney! Look how he helped himself to half the trout mayonnaise the other day at luncheon! By God, we'll take him down a peg or two—show him what isn't done here, what?"

Phillip was about to creep away from this unpleasant revelation of his effect upon others, when he saw that the mess-sergeant, bearing a tray of drinks, had come silently on his rubber-soled shoes. "By your leave, sir," said the sergeant, gravely, with a slight inclination of his head. Before the war he had been junior butler to one of the noble members of the Pigskin Club, Phillip had been told by "Chick".

Phillip waited to hear no more; he felt shame about the incident mentioned by Baldersby. It had occurred three days before, when eight of them, including Baldersby, had had an early luncheon, at noon, as they were going out with an advance party on brigade manœuvres. The mess-sergeant had brought in a large silver two-handled tray, of salad and pink fish, said to be trout presented to the mess by Colonel Baldersby, father of the senior subaltern, who was often referred to, among the junior subalterns, as "Bertram Baldersby, of Baldersby Towers, Baldersby, Berkshire". Phillip had been the second officer at table to be offered the dish, over his left shoulder; he had been helping himself liberally, while saying to the mess-sergeant, "I like this, Sergeant," when the ex-butler said, slowly and gravely, "Yes, sir; but there are other gentlemen present."

Hastily Phillip put most of it back on the dish, amidst a silence that had ended only when the sergeant had gone away; then O'Connor, also an attached officer, and an Irish barrister, had remarked, "I have not yet visited the Pigskin Club, after the colonel's awful warnings to us about minding our pees and queues in the matter of not sitting down in the favourite arm-chair of any of the venerable and noble members of that historic gaming house. Has anyone?"

"Of course I have, my uncle is one of the stewards," replied Baldersby, shortly.

Phillip put on belt and cap, and wheeling out *Helena*, pushed and ran and vaulted and sped away up the street with loud drum-beats of the open exhaust to the large and famous red-brick Belvoir Hotel. The entrance was under an arch, through which in the old days coaches had driven. He had been through the arch twice before, the first time to the bar, where the bar-maid was the girl he had seen several times on the flapper-bracket of a Douglas motor-cycle belonging to a dark, pale-faced A.S.C. subaltern; on the second occasion, to listen outside a small room, lit by a pink-shaded electric light, through the open door of which had come the gramophone strains of *They'd Never Believe Me*, which "Hercules" sometimes played and sang with others in the ante-room, around the piano. It came from the George Grossmith musical comedy, *Tonight's the Night*, according to the sheet-music.

Phillip, walking under the arch, heard the gramophone playing; and as before, stopped by the open door to listen. Several Royal Naval Air Service fellows were sitting in the room. Phillip knew that the Belvoir Hotel was the headquarters of the anti-Zeppelin gun-crews who drove the Rolls-Royce tenders, one with search-light, the other with a pom-pom gun, about the countryside at night, whenever one of the German gas-bags was supposed to be over; but he had no idea that this little room was the Petty Officers' mess.

"Jolly good little gramophone," said Phillip, after a while entering the room, and sitting down.

"Yes," said one of the petty officers. He had rather a cultured voice Phillip thought. "We find it sufficient for our limited circle."

"Had any air-raid warnings recently?" asked Phillip, his voice assuming the tone of the older man's voice.

"I am really not in a position to say," replied the other, going out of the room.

Phillip took up a *Tatler* and looked at it. When the record of *They'd never Believe Me* ended, one of the R.N.A.S. took it off and closed the Decca gramophone, making of it a black cube. Then he, too, went out.

Phillip thought he would go into the adjoining bar for a glass of beer. The R.N.A.S. men were there, but feeling that they did not want him to speak with them, he sat by himself. If the barmaid rode on the flapper-bracket of a Douglas, perhaps she might care for a ride on his 'bus? But she went off duty before he could ask her, and a cellar-man in a green baize apron took her place.

When he went outside a policeman with notebook and a long piece of iron wire was standing by *Helena*. He said it was his duty to report Phillip for offences contravening the law. He put the wire up the exhaust pipe, and said: "Have you any baffle plates in the pipe, sir?"

"If I had, they are all blown out by now, Officer."

"Then would you agree that you have no silencer?"

"Yes, of course. This is an open exhaust."

"Thank you, sir," said the policeman, shutting his book.

"Your perfect witness, officer."

Phillip liked O'Connor, the barrister from Trinity College, Dublin; and when he was summoned to appear before the Magistrates' Court on two counts—(a) for exceeding the speed limit of 10 miles per hour through the High Street, and (b) riding a machine powered by an internal-combustion engine fitted with an insufficient silencer or alternatively the said machine not being fitted with a sufficient silencing box in accordance with the Motor Car Act of 1896 and subsequent Acts, he sought his advice. O'Connor advised him upon the wording of the letter pleading guilty to both charges and "unreservedly placing himself in the hands of the Bench".

"We might dispute the legality of the ten miles an hour speed limit, which was imposed by local bodies, as it happens, without authority from the County Council, the duly elected and legally constituted body which alone can make such a speed limit enforceable by law; but that would be unwise under the circumstances, my boy. This is a town famous for bloodstock, and trainers have an established right to lead their strings through the High Street, and the burgesses to insist on protection for the valuable animals on whom the prosperity of the district largely depends—you follow me?"

"Yes," said Phillip, "I'll plead guilty as you say, and place myself in their hands."

"And get a silencer fitted to that exhaust pipe, my boy, or they'll get you again."

The letter as advised by O'Connor was written and sent; with apologies that urgent military duties prevented the writer from being present in court to pay his respects and offer his regrets to the Bench in person. He was fined £1, and there were six inches of single column in the local weekly newspaper headed WARNING TO YOUNG BLOODS IN ARMY RUSHING ABOUT ON MOTOR-CYCLES.

Alone in the ante-room just before half-past twelve, Phillip cut the report out of the paper, pinned it upon the green-baize board, and sat in a chair with *The Times*. Officers came in to read it, before going into the mess. When, a few minutes later, he followed in, the Mess President, Major Fridkin, sitting at the top table, said out loud to the senior subaltern beside him,

"Who stuck it up there? 'Young bloods in the Army', what? I see the report says the 'young blood' was a member of this regiment, Baldersby. A bit inaccurate that bit, don't you know."

"It ought to have said 'Young ticks attached'," snorted Baldersby, his small deep-set eyes glaring. "Damn it all, a hoss might get foot-fever, or swelled pasterns, bangin' 'em on those cobbles! Damn beastly things, motor-cycles. *Bikes*, little ticks call 'em! Young ticks on what they call 'bikes'. Faugh!"

Phillip feeling Major Fridkin's sleepy-lidded gaze on him, kept his eyes on his plate. He had never meant to agitate the race-horses as Baldersby seemed to think.

He saw the very thing for a silencer after parade the next morning, on one of the market-day stalls in the cobbled gutters beside the broad main street. It was lying amidst odds and ends of old junk on a shallow. A coffee pot, the very thing! The percolator would muffle most of the gasses, and he might even fit a whistle on the spout, as a cut-out! It seemed to him to be frightfully funny, a coffee pot on the end of the pipe, on his bike displaying in large white letters O.H.M.S. There was a garage half up the hill leading to the Heath, and thither Phillip went, pushing his machine, coffee-pot tied to handlebars. A dark young man with a handsome face, sharp of profile, wearing a bright red and blue striped tie, came out of the little glassed-in office.

"Hullo-a-lo!" he said. "I've often see you go by. You are a lad! The young blood pinched by the beaks. Crikey, what's that you're riding, a new kind of thrashing machine? What's the make?" He bent down. "*Helena*. Sounds like an advertisement for shampoo. What an assembly of oddments! The mag. looks like the Tower Bridge; you could almost fly under it. Don't you get the rain in? Perhaps it's meant to be water-cooled? Well, at least you've got a decent carburettor. The engine is French, square bore and stroke, I suppose. My, what an Old Iron never Rust, Solid Tyres never Bust! Now you want to complete it with a coffee-pot silencer! You *are* a lad!"

Flattered by the older man's admiring laughter, Phillip explained what he wanted. The manager, to whom he had taken an instant liking, said that it could be brazed on.

"You're the fool of the family, I can see that! I like fools of the family. What d'you do with yourself in the evenings?"

"Oh, I just muck about."

"Well, let's go out together one night in the Studebaker, shall we, when my boss is away in London? I have to see a few potential customers, farmers who're making piles of dough nowadays, so come along with me one evening, and we'll look for birds. You never know your luck! Well, tata for the time being. Your old thump-thump will be ready at six o'clock. I'll put a mechanic on it right away. Call me Monty. My name's Jarvey, my old man invented Jarveyised steel. I know your name already from the local rag, you 'young blood'! Righty-ho, Phil, Gran'ma Helena will be done by tea-time."

Immediately after dismissal at four o'clock Phillip went to the garage. An officer was there, standing negligently by a long, Metallurgique open four-seater, into which cans of petrol were being poured. He belonged to another territorial battalion in the brigade. When he had thundered away up the hill, Phillip learned from Monty that he and his brother were rich. Monty was now elegantly dressed in a grey-green suit, with a white silk shirt and low starched collar with pointed peaks; on his black brilliantined hair, at a jaunty angle, was a new straw-boater with the same colours as his tie. The brother of the Metallurgique owner, he went on to say, had a Harley-Davidson, a Yankee 'bus, that could do over seventy miles an hour on the straight.

"The brother's a mad devil like you," he said. "He scorches

like hell, and won't allow anything to pass him on the road, so don't try and race him on that old rattle-trap of yours."

"Rattle-trap? It didn't rattle before it came in here!"

"Well, now you've got some sort of a silencer, you may be able to hear its cries of agony."

"What's wrong with it?"

"What's right with it? Why, it's falling to pieces!" He lifted it up by the handlebars. "The head's loose! Look out for a speed wobble, my lad! The wheels want rebuilding, half the spokes are loose. Listen!" He ran a pencil round them. "Hear that twanging?" He squeezed the horn. "Moo-cow! When d'you milk the old girl?" He laughed with a gurgle in his throat. "You don't need a speedometer, old boy! At twenty miles an hour the spokes rattle, at thirty your ribs rattle, at forty a red light glows, and at forty-five a gramophone record plays *Down Among the Dead Men*! Ha, ha, ha! What you want, my boy, is a nice little light car—like that two-cylinder monobloc Swift over there, going for only sixty quid. I'll let you have it cheap for sixty-five! Or how about this Sizaire? A spiffing car! The spiffs come out of the radiator when the dam' thing boils. Then there's this White's steam car—roast your kippers and chestnuts while you drive! Only a mere bag o'shell—one hundred and fifty quid, sixty per cent discount for cash!

Phillip was fascinated by the easy way his new friend spoke; all the same he felt a little wary of him. Possibly Monty was a bad companion. He went out, to try *Helena* across the long straight stretch across the heath. At the top by the fountain and horse-trough he stopped to examine the new silencer. It looked quite a neat job, joined to the end of the exhaust pipe by brass wire annealed to the iron by the oxy-acetylene blow-pipe. He pushed and vaulted into the saddle, opening the throttle. The spout made a pleasant, high-whistling sound when the engine was running, and when he opened up it sounded rather like a cock-pheasant rocketing out of a spinney. As he pushed the lever farther, the hedge rushed by with a blur, and the machine began to wobble. He was holding the bars straight when with a clattering roar it seemed that the engine was breaking up; then he saw a Harley-Davidson passing him, the driver's head bent low over his handlebars, so that he appeared not to be looking where he was going. Phillip pulled the valve-lifter lever, and with a series of muffled pops in the coffee-pot

Helena slowed up. The Harley-Davidson was now small in the distance. Phew!

He decided to go to Cambridge, a town he had not visited before, for the ride. He did not remain there long; having bought a new pipe at a shop in one of the narrow streets, he returned, arriving at Godolphin House in time to wash and change into slacks, as it was Guest Night.

Chapter 12

LIFE IS A SPREE

On the occasion of this weekly ceremony all officers were expected to dine in. This was a courtesy to the guests. Phillip had already observed that guests, whether dinner or day-time callers, left two visiting cards which were put under one of the criss-cross green tapes on the baize board in the ante-room. One card would be inscribed to the Officer Commanding, the other to the Mess President and Officers. He had observed this; without any comprehension of the spirit that had directed the convention.

The guests sat at the top end of the long mess table, which "Strawballs" referred to as High Table, in line with the senior officers, including Baldersby; the rest of the subalterns sat at the lower tables, below the seniors. It was like a large family party, Phillip thought, as a champagne cork popped on his right side and the mess-sergeant poured from the napkin-covered bottle into the shallow glass, one to each officer all along the snow-white tablecloth. Brown belts shone; brass buttons gleamed; a dozen half-a-crown-a-week batmen had seen to that. Black, brown, and yellow heads were smooth with brilliantine. Cheer-ho, he said, to black-haired O'Connor on his right, and curly-yellow "Chick" on his left. They were sharing the bottle of bubbly, or fizz, as some of them called it. The name on the label was Veuve Cliquot, 1906.

He had already sipped his soup and swallowed three glasses of sherry at table, following three dry martinis in the ante-room. He felt himself to be a lad, a mad devil.

"By God," he said to O'Connor, "I am enjoying this base-wallah's life."

"Not so loud, my boy."

"Was I speaking loudly?"

"You were, and you are, my boy."

The fish was more pink trout from the paternal estate of Baldersby of Baldersby Towers, Baldersby, Berkshire, sent by train in ice. Second-lieutenant Brendon, almost an elderly subaltern, since he wore the Boer War ribbons, had remarked in Phillip's hearing recently that Baldersby's father was in effect a fishmonger, trying to buy his son a third pip. Baldersby, Phillip realised, was generally regarded as a fool, a joke, without any brains whatever; and that was why he had not been promoted although he had been commissioned since 1910.

Phillip thought the fish was the best he had ever tasted; much nicer than plaice. It was served luke-warm and eaten with thin cucumber slices. "Strawballs", he noticed, did not use his fish-knife, but a fork only. So he did the same. The colonel's guests were "Crasher" the brigadier, and "Little Willie", his brigade major, the latter so-called owing to a facial resemblance to the German Crown Prince. He had thin straight fair hair, a longish nose, and pale greenish eyes rather close together. The brigadier, alleged veteran of the famous charge, sat on the colonel's right, wearing a tunic with small round brass buttons which went up to his neck enclosed in a turn-down collar on which were red gorget patches and gold oak-leaves. His trousers were pulled down tight under Wellington boots by elastic bands under the arch, and swan-neck spurs jingled on his heels when he walked. He had a face deeply tanned and lined, his white hair was grizzled into tight curls upon the corners of a large round head. Seeing the stare of his round pale-blue eyes as he drank his soup with loud noises, sucking it down through thick mulberry lips while holding up the spoon-handle, Phillip imagined him to be a pretty fierce character.

The colonel had explained to the junior officers in the ante-room that morning that the brigadier after drinking a toast always dashed his glass upon the floor, so that no other toasts could be drunk from it. It was an ancient custom, said "Straw-balls", but—ah—with a glance in the direction of Phillip—no junior subalterns were required to emulate the brigadier's customs.

"How about another bottle of Veuve Cliquot? It's my turn," he said, after the fish. He raised a finger, and a waiter came forward.

"No, no, my boy, hold your horses," said O'Connor. "One bottle's enough. Your pay will not run to such extravagance."

"I jolly well like that! Why, you paid for the other bottle, so now it's my turn. Another bottle, waiter."

"You should not have done this, my boy," said O'Connor, raising his glass. "Here's to us all."

Before the capon, as the *menu* called it, was finished, Phillip's bottle was empty. "Chick" offered to stand another one; but O'Connor said no, they had had enough. The mess-room was now merry with voices and laughter. Looking round, Phillip thought what a wonderful thing it was he was there; less than three months ago he had been in the Diehard T-trench. He wanted more to drink, to keep the fun going. Who cared for the morrow? Eat, drink, and be merry, and to hell with everything else.

"I'm damned thirsty, O'Connor."

"The very thing," said O'Connor, pouring him a glass of water, then one for himself. "The normal healthy human liver objects to more than two, at the most three, fluid ounces of alcohol. The Widow Cliquot laces her wine with liqueur cognac. Hock is the best drink for food with company, in my opinion, or a dry wine from the Moselle. For that, we must wait till we get to Berlin."

The dinner went on timelessly. No table-cloth was ever so white or silver in gleam with candle and glass and leather; the table seemed to float in laughter and happiness.

The waiters, having served caramel, and then cheese, cleared the table. A decanter of port wine was placed in front of the colonel. He removed the stopper, and put the crystal jug by the left hand of the brigadier, who poured himself a glass and passed on the decanter until it had gone all round the table and come back to the colonel, who thereupon filled a glass for himself; and after a pause the Mess president, Major Fridkin, rose to his feet and said to the subaltern who was orderly dog for the day, sitting at the far end of the table, "Mr. Vice, the King!" Whereupon a new second-lieutenant got up and called out in a voice firm and much rehearsed mentally, "Gentlemen, the King!" And they all stood up saying, "The King!", followed by a diminishing muttering chorus of "God bless him", then drinking the toast, while from the brigadier known as "Crasher" came a belated deep grumble of "God bless 'er".

He always drank the toast to Queen Victoria. There followed a brittle crash as the brigadier turned and flung his glass into the marble fireplace.

Then they sat down, and the colonel said, "Gentlemen, you may smoke."

Phillip was interested in what O'Connor told him about the brigadier. His nickname had come from the Galway Blazers, in which country all the stone walls had to be flown as though they were fences.

"Why is that?" asked Phillip.

"*You* wouldn't know!" said Baldersby shortly.

"He was a wild man in a country of many wild men in an age of wildness. In the hunting field, I have heard my father say, he was a top-sawyer all the time, stone, bank, or black-thorn bull-fence. They still tell stories about him in the Shelbourne in Dublin. Have you done any huntin', my boy?"

"A little."

"In whose country?" enquired Baldersby.

"Oh, ours."

Baldersby, pulling a yellow moustache, leaned across the table. "May I enquire where *your* country is?"

Phillip thought he might be going to say something about him being part-German. "I—I don't quite understand what you mean."

"Do you have the button of any particular hunt?"

Not knowing what this meant, he replied, "Well, not exactly."

In a spreading silence Baldersby went on, "When you said just now, '*Our* country', what country did you mean?"

"I don't quite follow you."

"Well, then, whose pack did you follow?"

"With what pack did you hunt, he means, my boy," said O'Connor, as the port decanter reached him on its second coasting. Refilling his glass slowly, while feeling hot and entangled, Phillip tried to recall some of the fox hunts in *The Field*, but all he could think of was Mr. Facey Romford's Hounds in the novel by Surtees.

He must say something. Then having passed on the decanter he raised his glass to the glowering Baldersby across the table, and said:

"Here's to all sportsmen, including Mr. Facey Romford, the immortal Jorrocks and 'them stinking violets', coupled with the name of Crasher, the broth av a bhoy among the Galway Blazers!" and drained his glass as if it were beer.

"Steady on, my boy, or you'll find you have the drink taken," said O'Connor. "What you need is black coffee."

O'Connor could see that Phillip was attracting more than immediate attention. The room was not a large one, Godolphin House being of moderate size, similar to a score facing the High Street.

"Some more black coffee for Mr. Maddison," whispered O'Connor to his servant, who with other batmen was waiting at table.

When the Colonel rose they all stood up. In decorous silence the senior officers followed the jingling rowels of "Crasher" into the ante-room. Then the subalterns trooped in. They had been warned to behave quietly in the presence of the brigadier, as a mark of respect to both his rank and his great age; he would not, the adjutant said, stay very long.

Phillip found himself near the brigadier and his brigade major, "Little Willie". He wondered where he had seen the brigadier's face before. Then he remembered: in old pages of *Punch*, and cartoons of Bismarck. "Crasher" looked just like Bismarck. He heard him say to Major Fridkin, polite and smiling by his side, "In my day we had a crackin' good spree after guest night, the faster the better. Damme, time flies like a duck-hawk."

"Yes, indeed, General," said Major Fridkin, raising his eyebrows, as he puffed at a long, fat cigar between his fat lips.

When the brigadier and "Little Willie" had departed, the fun began. There was a competition to see who could pick a coin off the carpet, bending down while the heels of your feet placed closed together against the wainscoting did not shift. Phillip fell over. Then couples were matched to stand with arms stretched sideways, to press with chest and flat hands in an attempt to shift the other backwards. This was Baldersby's special trick: he was short, Saxon and stocky, and tall, Celtic Phillip could not force him back. On the contrary, Baldersby pushed Phillip into an armchair and bent him over until Phillip felt his back about to break, so he yelled, "Let go, oh, you're hurting!" Then Baldersby, stooping, got him round the knees and tossed him feet over head into the chair; and jerking out Phillip's tie, pulled the ends tight.

"Steady there," exclaimed O'Connor, seeing that the other could not breathe. He worked the tie free, and Phillip sat down to recover.

While he was in the armchair, the others started cock-fighting: a couple sat on the floor, broomstick behind knees held by elbows, hands clasping knees, the idea being to tip an opponent off balance with toes. Meanwhile, at the far end of the ante-room a small group had gathered around the piano, singing *They'd Never Believe Me*.

When the colonel returned with Captain Whale, the adjutant, there was a sudden break in the noise, and all officers got to their feet, except Phillip, who was struggling against a swirling feeling, through which he heard the colonel saying, "Continue as before, gentlemen, let the fun be fast and furious. I do hope you are going to give us your awful good 'Stonecracker' song, Jonah?" at which there were cries from the far-away piano of "Yes, come on, Jonah! Give us *The Orderly Room Song*, sir!"

Thus encouraged, Jonah the Whale stood by the piano, ready to let his rich baritone voice fill him and others with sentiment.

> *O, I sits here and cracks 'em*
> *With great regularity*
> *Yes I taps 'em and whacks 'em*
> *For Highway Authority*

The colonel picked up *The Times*, which he read usually after mess-dinner in his room, and sat down in a wicker upholstered armchair, paper across knees, spectacles pushed up over bushy brows while he relaxed.

> *Yes I do now, yes I do now*
> *I earns all my pay*
> *Yes I do now, sure I do now*
> *'Tis but ninepence a day.*

> *With a ripfoll, a riddle oll*
> *A riddle ole-a-ray*
> *All for ninepence a day.*

Phillip, when the swirling feeling had partly subsided, began to giggle, as he visualised the adjutant in the orderly room, cracking nuts, and eating them, for ninepence a day. Then he became aware of the colonel's brown shoe on a knee-slung leg revolving at the ankle. This turning movement continued clockwise until the end of *The Stonecracker*; and was resumed anti-clockwise, to his distress, when Father O'Flynn rolled out like very neat brown rich cigars from the corner by the piano, gleaming cigar-shapes of sound.

"Awful good song, Jonah, awful good," said the colonel, and opening *The Times*, covered all of himself from view except part of his fingers, trouser'd thighs and knees, sock'd and shoe'd feet.

Hoping to dispel the swirl about him, Phillip sat up in the armchair opposite the figure reading the spread newspaper. Thank God the swirling was now entirely gone. When Captain Whale sang again, a new and very beautiful song, he got up and started to go to the piano; but he felt safer in the armchair, and sat down again, quietly, to avoid any creaking of wicker-work, and attention to himself.

> *O, the clang of the wooden shoon*
> *O, the dance and the merry tune*
> *Happy sound of a by-gone day*
> *It rings in my heart for aye.*
> *When the boats came in,*
> *And the decks were all a-glow*
> *As the moon shone down*
> *On the rippling tide below.*

He watched with fascination the toe of the shoe opposite revolving on the ankle, just as his own foot turned at times, working off energy. He began to laugh to himself, the indrawn breath laugh, imagining Desmond beside him at the Hippo, when Fred Karno's Mumming Birds had jumped high off the elastic billiard table, turning somersaults, and then, while one rested in an armchair reading a newspaper the other somehow lighting the methylated spirit on his boot-cap, lifted his foot and set fire to the newspaper. It would be terribly funny if "Straw-balls" suddenly saw his paper on fire from the bottom upwards! Act of a "mad devil"! Feeling that the joke would set everyone roaring with laughter he took a box from his pocket, struck a match, and creeping to the other chair put the flame at the bottom of the page in the centre. The flame started small, but ran up quickly, and a harsh throaty voice behind the paper exclaimed, "What the devil?" before the paper was crunched up, and through smoke and pounding hands Phillip saw the open-mouthed face of "Strawballs". "Oh, it's Mr. Maddison!" said the colonel's voice, changing its tone to one of mingled exasperation and resignation. Before he could say any more, Phillip left the ante-room, and hurried up the stone steps, with their curving iron rail, to his attic, not quite certain what had happened to his frightfully funny joke; but after all, the colonel had said, Let the fun be fast and furious.

He decided to go to bed, having a feeling that he was going to spew. In pyjamas, he went into what Baldersby called The Throne. This ancient lavatory outside his door consisted of a mahogany box enclosing an old-fashioned pan patterned with purple ferns. He waited; tried to accelerate matters with a finger; went back and got into camel-hair sleeping sack, flap turned down by batman all ready on green canvas camp-bed, and left the candle burning just in case. His forethought was justified; and ten minutes later he crept back again, cold and shivering, vowing that never again would he drink champagne or port.

He was aware of Chick coming in; then the candle going out; then a dancing light by the door, voices, and someone saying quietly, "Chick, a telegram has come for you, and you're wanted downstairs to sign for it," then Chick's drowsy grumbling voice saying, "Why can't the damned thing be brought up?" It was urgent, said the voice, and the special messenger was waiting. Chick got up, rubbing his eyes, and putting on slippers and British Warm went away down the stone steps, leaving the door wide open.

Phillip raised himself on an elbow, listening. The telegram was a ruse to get Chick away. Was he going to be arrested? He lay down again. He saw his life in ruins, as so often in the past. "Strawballs'" paper on fire, the Backfield grass on fire, also for a spree, then lying under his bed, saying to Mother, *Ought I to kill myself*, in terror of the police, as the whole field crackled and rose in yellow-brown smoke behind the wooden garden fences. His jokes had never really gone well. As Mother always said, he was his own worst enemy. He had always known

that they were idiotic, before he acted; it was always as though
someone inside him prompted him. Why was he such a fool,
why, why, why?

He pulled the soft fawn flap of the sleeping sack tight round
his neck when he heard a remote shuffling of feet coming from
far below the stone steps: the shuffling of many feet came nearer,
then light and shadow waggled in the open door-space and
peering through eyelashes he saw someone with a tent candle-
lantern and forms behind entering to move Chick's bed and
valise against the wall. Then after more shufflings and whis-
perings, Baldersby's voice said, "One at a time, go steady,
and don't miss the cad," and he saw they carried the black-painted
leather fire-buckets which hung on the wall of the hall with their
red coat-armour and then *swish!* all over him, water and
carbolic acid. *Swish!* again, and again, continuing while more
subalterns came through the door now carrying green canvas
buckets. Colder and colder the sluicings became, as they
penetrated all the sleeping sack, and his pillow, under which lay
the gold locket containing the coloured miniature of Helena.
Water gushed upon him, as he lay unmoving; and when the light
was gone, and footfalls had clattered down the stone staircase, he
drew out the locket, and felt that it was ruined.

In silence, after a few minutes lying still, he began to cry.
He stopped when the undulating notes of Baldersby's hunting
horn floated up, thinking of the last time he had heard such notes,
when General Fitzclarence was leading the charge of the Guards
brigade against the Prussian Guard in Nonne Bosschen, the
Nuns' Wood. Then, laughing to himself (hollowly, he said
to an imagined Desmond in Freddy's bar) he pulled and
writhed himself out of the sopping, weighted sack, and stood up,
shivering in pyjamas clinging to his skin. All the same, the locket
must be ruined, the carbolic acid was very strong, it burned his
eyes and lips, and stank horribly.

He looked for matches in his tunic, but it was sopped through,
so was the box. Footfalls came up the stairs, with light; he
waited, wondering if more was coming; but it was O'Connor
with his Orlix electric lamp, bringing his own British warm, and
a laundered pair of pyjamas.

"Here, my boy, put on these," he said. "Then come downstairs with me, and sleep in my room. I have managed to get
a spare camp-bed for you." Seeing his face, and shudders,

O'Connor said, "The thing for you is a hot bath, but the bath-room is in the colonel's suite, so come down in the coat and I'll give you a rub down with a stiff Turkish towel."

Phillip stuttered his thanks, and putting his new Loewe pipe in his mouth, he followed O'Connor down to a larger room on the second floor, which O'Connor shared with Brendon, the elderly subaltern, who had been a volunteer in the South African War. Brendon often referred to two things in the mess: that his wife, a cousin of the colonel's wife, had not been able to join him owing to the lowness of a second-lieutenant's pay, seven-and-six a day; and that he could not afford a whiskey-and-soda. He was rather stout, with ginger hair, a large moustache; he walked with a bit of a swagger.

Brendon came into the room while O'Connor was vigorously towelling Phillip, who now felt better. Conscious of his military superiority, Brendon began to hold forth with his usual con-descending air of amusement when regarding Phillip.

"A soldier is not a soldier, as Napoleon might have remarked in parenthesis, until he has learned to regard himself as the lowest thing on God's earth, something that crawls on its belly. Until then, he will merely be something that is chucking its weight about. Before he can advance, he must first learn that his centre of gravity has to be lowered, like that of water, to the lowest level."

"Oh, I don't mind a cold tub," said Phillip with assumed nonchalance. "One way to keep fit!"

"In other words," went on Brendon, ignoring the interruption, "the tyro who chucks his weight about by speaking out of turn has to be taken down a considerable number of pegs. Or to change the metaphor: while remaining the newest entry, he must not assume for himself the prerogatives of a stallion hound, *if* you can follow my meaning. Until then," continued Brendon, fixing Phillip with his eyes, "Until then, a mere puppy in the pack, in the old phrase of the classical side, he simply remains, as a soldier, simply *non est*."

"May I offer you two gentlemen a drink?" said Phillip. He had seen that the locket was not spoiled.

"No, thank you," said Brendon.

Pyjamas on, Phillip felt more cheerful. He flicked the water from his new pipe, and, offered O'Connor's big glazed jar, filled his pipe, and was about to put it in his mouth when

Silas B. Ramshott, another elderly subaltern, looked in from his room next door. Ramshott was a short, rather puffy pale-faced American actor, always talking about the plays of Pinero, Winchell Smith, Somerset Maugham, and others in which his Broadway successes had been made. Now he cried out:

"Well, I'm darned, if you're not gum-sucking my noo pipe! Jeese, that's my Loewe you've got, I bought it King's Parade, Cambridge, last weekend. I missed it three days ago!"

"I bought this one in Cambridge, too, really I did!"

"The hell you did! That's my pipe! I left it on the ante-room table, by the noos-papers."

"Well, I bought this pipe in Cambridge."

"What was the name of the shop?"

"I didn't notice."

"Where was it?"

"In the High Street."

"There isn't a High Street in Cambridge!"

"Anyway, I bought it there. However, if you think it's yours, by all means have it," and Phillip held out the pipe.

"D'you think I want the darned thing now, after you've been gum-sucking it?" cried the other, his putty-coloured face showing disgust.

"Well, then, what's all the fuss about?"

"You wouldn't know," said the voice of Baldersby, as the yellow moustache came round the door. "The sooner you clear out of our regiment, the better everyone will be pleased. You're nothing but a damned outsider!"

"Come, now," said O'Connor. "Maddison, as an anomaly in our midst, may be out of place for the time being, but there is a possibility of misunderstanding in this matter of the pipe. Maddison said he bought the pipe in the High Street of Cambridge. Admittedly he does not know the town, and quite possibly the tobacconist where he says he bought it has sold others of that make and pattern. As for tonight, he has the drink taken, and I suggest that an apology to the colonel in the morning is due for his act of misplaced humour. Now, as we have an early parade, I for one have a wish for m' bed."

When the others had gone, O'Connor said that he would suggest to Phillip that he wrote out an apology immediately after breakfast, and took it to the colonel personally. He appealed tactfully to Brendon, who was getting undressed, revealing a bulky body almost covered in long woollen combinations. "What do you say, Brendon?"

"Well, since you ask my opinion, I should say that my cousin, being a good sportsman, will appreciate that it will take some effort on Maddison's part to ask to see him, after his attempt to cremate him in his own ante-room."

"I am sure that is very good advice, Brendon; and courage is always its own reward. But go aisy in future, my boy, or you may find yourself in the wars again."

"Yes, I will, certainly. And thank you for your kindness, O'Connor. And also for your good advice, Brendon."

Brendon turned in his bed and looked at Phillip. He said nothing; for O'Connor was kneeling by his bed, head bowed, touching the beads of his rosary.

In the morning when Phillip went down to breakfast, he stopped at the letter-rack in the ante-room. There was a foolscap envelope addressed to him, without a stamp, obviously just put there, for the gum on the label still felt slightly damp. He took it to the lavatory to open it.

> To (T) Sec.-lieut. P. S. T. Maddison,
>   Gaultshire Regt.
> Sir,
>   We, the undersigned subaltern officers of the Cantuvellaunian Mess, hereby request you to apply immediately to return to your Regiment, alternatively to resign your Commission, which in our unanimous opinion you are not in any way fitted to hold——

Phillip ran his eye down the list, headed by Bertram E. St. George Baldersby, and followed by a score of names. He did not examine them; but tearing the round-robin into little pieces, went out and dropped them in a trickle across the ante-room floor, as though for a miniature paper-chase. After this gesture of defiance he went into the mess, where a dozen officers, including Major Fridkin, were sitting, eating fried bacon, kidneys, mushrooms, and scrambled eggs.

"Good morning, gentlemen," said Phillip: to which there was no reply. Helping himself to a plateful from the silver dishes over the spirit flames on the sideboard, he ate his breakfast, with feigned unconcern that he had obviously been sent to Coventry.

Sir,

I have the honour to submit this Apology to you for my unwarranted act of incendiarism upon your person last night, after which my person was rendered sparkless by a great many gallons of water——

He scrumpled this up, and began again,

Sir,

I have the honour to offer you, with my most sincere regret for my conduct last night in the ante-room, this Apology for my effrontery and ill-timed "joke" upon your Person. I can only plead the heat of the wine in my head, which was, shortly afterwards, duly cooled by a great many gallons of water——

This joined the first draft in the waste-paper basket.

Sir,

I have the honour to submit this Apology for my outrageous behaviour last night, for which there is no excuse. I can only say with sincerity that I realize my place in a Regiment of such Traditions is an anomaly, that I am unworthy of remaining here, and therefore request that my name be put down for immediate return to the Front.

I have the honour to be,

Sir, Your most obedient Servant,

P. S. T. Maddison, 2-lt.

After this momentary submission to the idea of resurrection through death, Phillip put the letter under the blotting pad, meaning not to send it. He would think it over. It was time to go on parade.

The mess-sergeant found it later, and put it in a plain envelope, and took it to the mess president, Major Fridkin; who gave it to Jonah, the adjutant; who showed it to the colonel. "Strawballs" read it, gold spectacles on nose; and later signed a chit, typed in the orderly room, recommending the application. Thence to brigade; and to Eastern Command, held by the white-haired General Sir Horace Smith-Dorrien, who had been relieved of his command in France; and so to the War Office in London.

"So I went in and apologised in person, Mrs. Neville. Well, the colonel, I won't tell you his nickname, looked at me over his glasses, and all he said after what seemed a long time was, "Very well, I shall accept your apology, Mr. Maddison," so I saluted and went out. My luck was in, in more ways than one, for that very afternoon after parade I bought an almost-new O.K. Junior motor-bike in a local garage for seventeen pounds ten, and sold it straight away to someone in the mess for twenty-two pounds ten. With the profit I bought a new set of tyres for my own bike, and here I am, on weekend leave!"

"I can see all as you describe it, Phillip; you ought to write a book, you know, you make it all so vivid. What times we're living in!" A sudden shriek punctured Mrs. Neville's words. "Have you heard about Mavis' officer on the staff? Oh, oh, that major on the staff!" She quivered helplessly. "Haven't you heard?" Another puncture, followed by subsidence into her chair; helpless flipping of hand; turning away, wiping eyes, gasping, "Oh dear! Oh dear!" Another shriek, "We haven't any money, but we do see life!"

When she was calmer Mrs. Neville became solemn. "Not a word of all this, Phillip! Your mother would never forgive me if she knew I had told you! Your Father must not know, you see, dear," she went on in a sweet, clear voice, as her mind took command of her feelings. "If you promise, Phillip, never to say a word about it, I will tell you—although I feel mean in saying anything at all."

"I promise, Mrs. Neville."

"Well, Phillip, how can I begin? First, let me say, there has been nothing wrong, you know what I mean, concerning Mavis! Oh no, all above board! She met him in the train, and he took her to the Hippo. Nothing more! I would never breathe a word of scandal, you know that, dear, don't you?"

"What happened, Mrs. Neville?"

"He was a fraud! He ordered a Review of Troops on Black-heath!" shrieked Mrs. Neville, flipping a hand at him. "On a horse! That he had hired from Soal the coalman, down here in Randiswell! What a nerve! You know, Phillip, I can't help admiring the fellow. Inspecting a whole battalion! All dressed up in staff major's uniform! And the horse found its own way back to Soal afterwards!" She quivered away once more into gasps, little groans, and watery eyes. She went on to tell him details, while Phillip began to feel it was very funny. What a cheek, for a civilian to dress up as a major and inspect a battalion, after writing to the C.O. on War Office paper!

"He did it very well, too, Phillip. Oh yes, nothing paltry about Mavis' major! He arrived on a horse, oh yes, very magnificent was Mavis' major from the War Office! Mavis and her mother were watching, and Gran'pa and Aunt Marian! There were thousands of others, on Blackheath, as it was Saturday afternoon. The rows of ribbons he had on his breast, everything from the V.C. to the Temperance Medal. Oh, it was all very smart, very smart indeed!"

"What happened? How did they know he was a fraud, Mrs. Neville?"

"He vanished into thin air, after he had led a recruiting march, still on the horse, beside the colonel. There the bands were playing, the flags flying, and lots of recruits following the procession. They signed on and he rode away down Belmont Hill and no-one has heard from him or seen him from that moment!" Another shriek. "Soal's horse arrived back without the saddle or bridle! What a nerve, Phillip, what a nerve! Of course," went on Mrs. Neville, now recovered, "enquiries were made by the colonel. The War Office said it knew nothing about him. There was no-one like him known there. They had sent no-one down to any inspection. The War Office paper he used had been stolen. No, he had not defrauded anyone; he had even paid in cash for his uniform, at a tailor's in Fordesmill! Obviously he did it all for a spoof. What a nerve, Phillip, what a nerve! You know, I jolly well admire a man like that!"

"I seem to remember a cobbler doing something like that, before the war, with the German Army—the cobbler of Zabern—no—Zabern was where the Prussian officer cut down a cripple in his path, wasn't it—oh, anyway, it was a spoof, as you say, Mrs. Neville."

"Such men have missed their vocations, obviously," said Mrs. Neville. "Well, dear, you won't say a word about what I have told you at home, will you? Your father must never know about it. Shall I tell you what I think he did it for, Phillip? For a spree! And now he's done his bit, he's retired!" she ended with another explodent shriek, which set off the laughter again.

Mrs. Neville in more sedate mood went on to say that Mother

was getting about nowadays quite a lot, going up to London with Gran'pa, riding in omnibuses, even going to the theatre for matinées. Sometimes they met Aunt Dora, who was still working in the East End.

"I do so admire your aunt, you know, dear. She is a brick, the way she has helped the poor mothers whose men have gone into the army. She is so good for your mother, too, who deserves her little bit of gallivanting. I often see her trotting down the road with Papa, usually they set off about eleven o'clock, and come back in time to give your father his dinner. She leaves the front-door key with me, so that Doris can call for it. Now don't you go mentioning this, will you, you know how strict your father is about such things. So don't breathe a word, dear. Well, Desmond will be home shortly, he is on night-duty every other night, on the searchlight in Hyde Park—they've got only two for London now, but more are coming, he says. You'll stay and have tea with him, won't you?"

Chapter 13

LUSITANIA

ON the following Tuesday Hetty and her father set out to visit Dora in the East End. Their way led over the Hill, and down through streets of houses and so to the electric tube station which ran under the Thames. It was a warm sunny day, but Thomas Turney wore his overcoat, as he had recently been in bed with bronchitis. They sat down on the wooden seat half-way up the gully, under a laburnum tree in flower, and rested, the old man supporting his chest on his hands clasping his lemon-wood walking-stick.

Hetty's mind wandered into the past, seeing Phillip as Sonny when he had run away from home, and she had found him sitting on that very seat, looking lost, pale, a mite whose world had collapsed under his father's anger. She had taken his hand, and led him home again, trembling, nervous, apprehensive.

"You would hardly think, would you, Hetty," said Thomas Turney, "that in this beautiful spring weather, such terrible things could be possible. Nearly two thousand poor souls in the deep water south of Ireland! What foolish people the Germans are! They have done their cause irreparable harm in the eyes of America. They gave notice in New York, it is true, but no-one apparently took it seriously. One thousand nine hundred and fifty-nine passengers and crew, and of that total ninety of them little children and thirty-nine infants in arms. Terrible, terrible."

The newspapers that morning had given details of the recent sinking of the Cunard liner *Lusitania* by submarine torpedoes off the Old Head of Kinsale in Southern Ireland.

In the light morning air, made brighter with clusters of white buds everywhere on the thorns growing above the gully, a faraway cuckoo's voice floated to where they sat. The cemetery behind the houses of Charlotte Road was, with its shrubs and bushes and flies breeding upon the heaps of wilting flowers, a sanctuary for small birds; to Hetty and her papa, a place of memory, of suspended acts and thoughts still arising from the past, still valid, still existing in their lives, for there lay mother and brother, wife and son, at rest, at rest.

"Well, Papa, how do you feel? Ready to go on?"

"Yes, my dear, there's life in the old dog yet! Ah, here's Bolton. Poor man, how he has aged!"

Mr. Bolton, led by his pug-dog, was coming slowly up the gully, one arm held behind his back, in his eyes a look of the dead. He lived until he could bring home the bones of his only son, killed with the London Highlanders six and a half months ago, and buried, as Phillip had told him, in the German cemetery east of the road along the Messines crest.

Phillip had also told Mr. and Mrs. Wallace that their sons were in the cemetery; and he had visited Baldwin's girl, in Bereshill, with the same tale. It was untrue that he had seen any names there that he recognised, in his brief and nervous stopping before the low wooden crosses, the few hanging glengarries; but they *could* have been there, he had told himself. Anyway, he had told the Wallace parents as a fact during his uneasy visit, eyes downheld out of nervousness from the feeling that Mrs. Wallace, in her withdrawn attitude, was despising him. He had mentioned Baldwin's name then; and so had to keep up the story when he went to see Baldwin's girl. The awful thing was, supposing David and Nimmo were prisoners, after all? Peter was dead; several had seen him bayoneted, and heard his screaming cries dying away, as he was stabbed again and again, rolling on the ground with the Bavarian whose head he had been pummelling.

On the crest of the Hill, within the first shelter, sat Mr. Krebs, a little less pink of neck and head and face nowadays, a little shrunken with the thoughts of a mind which saw the two sides of the war at once: a mind which had, until recently, aspired with almost every conscious breath that a synthesis of reconciliation might be found; yet had had to remain mute, not from fear, but because he regarded himself as a guest in the native country of his wife. News of the gas attack at Ypres had come as a partial asphyxiation of the spirit which yearned for compromise; again, he had been like a man drowning when the Cunarder from New York had been torpedoed; he had walked from curtain-dark room to curtain-dark room of his house, tears running down his satin-smooth Kropp-razor'd cheeks as he thought of children in mothers' arms stifling in the waves, mothers praying to God to be saved—yet knowing that the Fatherland was surrounded on all sides, blockaded by the power of the British Navy, which would in the end strangle his people, reduce them to destitution, destroy them as it had destroyed Napoleon dreaming of a self-sufficient Europa freed of the satrapies of usury, so that the "canaille might become the best educated in the world". The British Navy had swept the seas clear of all ships trading with the Fatherland; the Fatherland had replied with the submarine. So thought Mr. Krebs; while in his ears were the cries of lost little children, becoming feebler in the massive green drifts of ocean, *mutter, mutter*.

Pride and courage had brought Mr. Krebs upon the Hill that morning. His wife had accompanied him in ordinary loyalty of love, to reassure him, and to stand by him should what she dreaded, after reading *The Daily Trident's* call for all Germans to be interned, occur: that his acquaintances on the Hill show him the cold shoulder. To her great relief she heard Mr. Turney greeting him as genially as ever, while Mr. Bolton was his invariable courteous self.

As the Krebs were returning home later, on what was to be their last walk together across the Hill, the pink and almost hairless South German said to his greying English wife, "You know, my dear, the English are at heart a most kind people, taken all in all. We old fellows were so happy, to meet in the little Chalêt every day, until this bad vaw came."

"Yes, dearest," replied Mrs. Krebs, with sudden unconventionality taking his arm (since only children were near), "and we are the cousins of your people, never forget."

Having made her visitors a pot of tea, Dora sat down for a few minutes' rest. "A wonderful work you have achieved here," remarked Thomas Turney.

"Oh, I am but a very small cog, Mr. Turney. Sylvia is the originator, the dynamo. I am sorry she is not here just now, and she will be sorry too, when I tell her you have called. She has gone to see Herbert Samuel again about sweated-labour conditions, here in the East End. Yes, Hetty, Sylvia's is the inspiration, the will, and the intellect. She is Great-heart. Sylvia will go down in history, with Florence Nightingale."

They were visiting *The Mothers' Arms*, a clinic made out of what until recently had been an empty public house, *The Gunmakers' Arms*, a dirty dark place with floors encrusted with fish-bones, and walls stinking of thick-twist tobacco smoke and paraffin soot mingled with beer and foetid human breath. Now it was clean and fresh, painted white inside; pictures were on the walls; the rooms set with cribs and cots. *The Mothers' Arms* was scrubbed and soaped and polished.

The spirit of *The Mothers' Arms* was such that Hetty was like a girl again. If only she could help with the little ones! What a brave and beautiful spirit Dora had. Oh, the little children, so clean and happy, in the cots, or playing in the nursery! Yet what tragedy lay in some eyes: the fixed stare as of very old and sick people, the stare of fear, of fright fixed in the children's eyes: their thin little arms and legs, stalk-like necks; sharp features; bony, skull-like faces. And all the result of starvation, fathers away at the front, or "fallen down", as the widows said; and neither allowance nor pension sufficient to pay the rent and feed the mother and her children. Some of the mothers had had to pawn all their household goods, Dora said. Price of the staple food, bread, was nearly doubled: from $4\frac{1}{2}d$. to $7d$. the quartern. Sugar was $3\frac{1}{4}d$., instead of $1\frac{3}{4}d$. before the war; skimmed milk $7d$. a tin, from $3\frac{3}{4}d$. Meat had doubled in price, and the cheapest cuts, scrag and shin, almost thrice the peace-time prices.

"One woman's baby at fifteen months weighed seven pounds six ounces, instead of the normal eighteen, Hetty. The coroner's jury returned a verdict of 'Death from natural causes'. It had been fed, from necessity, on water in which white bread had been boiled. There were six other children in the family; and all that was coming in was twelve shillings and sixpence. That, I ought to add, was before the scale of allowances for a soldier's wife and family."

"Poor things," murmured Hetty, thinking of Phillip as a baby, so thin, starving, while his father sat with him all night.

"One unhappy mother came here crying, 'I haven't had any food in the house for four days, and I have strangled my little boy!' She was tried for murder, and was sentenced to ten years' penal servitude."

Hetty broke into tears.

"Now, now," said Thomas Turney, blowing his nose. "You're upsetting Hetty with such tales, Dora."

"Very well, I shall generalise, Mr. Turney. The War Office, until recently, refused allowances for children born less than nine months after their parents' marriage."

"But what about a seven-months child, Dora? Surely——"

"'There hain't no sich hanimal', legitimately, in the eyes of the authorities, apparently, Hetty."

"What is the soldier's widow's allowance?" asked Thomas Turney.

"It has been raised now, Mr. Turney, to seven shillings and sixpence a week, which allows a shilling for food, clothes, gas, and coal, after the average rent of six and six is paid. The first child gets five shillings; the second, third, and fourth half-a-crown, and two shillings for any others."

"But the mothers go out to work, surely?"

"It is a little better, Mr. Turney, now that the factories are going again. Even so, the prices paid are very small indeed. Let me give some examples. A clothing factory near us, on army contracts, works every day until eight o'clock, including Sundays, paying wages less than those before the war—there is so much unemployment, you see, the old question of supply and demand. The wages work out at twopence farthing an hour. There are several firms giving out piece-work, you may judge for yourself when I tell you that officers' khaki shirts, all the sewing together, all the buttons and ribbed button-holes, are paid for at the rate of two shillings and a penny, less twopence farthing for the reel of cotton——"

"Well, that sounds very good to me, Dora—just under two shillings for a shirt——"

"That's for a dozen, Mr. Turney! The dark material tries their eyes, and they cannot make more than a dozen in a long day of sixteen or eighteen hours."

"This sounds like the times of Dickens come again, Dora! Are you sure of your facts?"

"They are confirmed by the figures of the Amalgamated Society of Tailors and Tailoresses, sir. Complete khaki uniforms, jacket and trousers, for private soldiers, are taken for eighteen-pence. But that is not the worst. Contracts are often sub-let as many as four times——"

"Ah, that's the reason! The sub-contractors are making the money! Many are Jews, of course."

"Yes, Mr. Turney; with the result that soldiers' trousers are being finished for as low as a penny farthing the pair. Soldiers' kit-bags, of stiff white canvas, take four hours to finish seven, the sempstress receives under sixpence; while the eyelet holes, to be bound with stiff thread, are paid ten for a penny. A mother of three children and a six-month babe told me she received five shillings and sevenpence for the work of forty-two hours. We have written and complained to the Home Office, and to the Director of Contracts at the War Office; we have taken deputations to both places, and been put off, if not actually snubbed. Recently the Army Clothing Stores at Pimlico sold one and a half million Indian body-belts at four shillings a dozen, which were bought up at eighteen shillings, and sold again at a still higher price, to the soldiers."

"Well, as I told you before, there is bound to be a muddle until we change over to war-time economy, Dora. First every-thing was at a stand-still; now it is confusion; but things will get better, ye'll see. Meanwhile you and your friends here are doing a fine job of work, a fine job of work. Well, Hetty, we must not keep Dora any longer from her work. Come and see us when you can spare an hour or two, Dora, won't you?"

"I shall be delighted, Mr. Turney. Oh, thank you, thank you!" for he had slipped a five-pound note into her hand at parting.

"Now," said Thomas Turney, at the turning out of Old Ford, "I want to see my broker in Lothbury. D'you think you can walk so far? It's a fine day, we could go by bus to Liverpool Street Station if you wish, Hetty."

"Are you sure you will be all right, Papa?"

"Right as rain, Hetty. Now we can go down here as far as Whitechapel, or cross over and go down the Bethnal Green road. What d'you say?"

For Hetty the walk was of great interest; all she saw was new to her, the Yiddish lettering on coloured posters outside little picture theatres which were slightly wider than the shop-fronts; orthodox Jews, who she thought must be rabbis, dressed in long black robes, wearing hats of astrakhan and other furs, all black like their own long beards and whiskers, hair looking as though it had never been cut, but left to grow naturally. Their faces had the yellowness of old candles, skin unsunned, as though they cared only for righteousness within, fortified by truths revealed to the prophets who still lived in their minds though they had died thousands of years before. Other Jews passed, some desperately poor, in tatters. One had half a dozen hats on his head, one fitted neatly into the other, while two bulging sacks, one of waste paper and the other of cloth trimmings, were slung over his shoulder, as his broken boots shuffled in the gutter. A few soldiers were about, many ragged children; one little girl was hastening along with a pig's trotter held tightly in one fist, a look of suppressed excitement in her face. It was all so dreadfully sad, how the poor lived.

"You don't see any cats round here," chuckled Thomas Turney. "They have long ago gone into the pot."

A boy ran past with a loaf under an arm, swiftly, dodging in and out on bare feet. Farther down the street they passed a woman wheeling a battered pram with several loaves hidden under two grimy babies wrapped in bits and pieces of cloth, old stockinet and brown paper wound round them and fastened with string. Other people came by, clutching bundles under coats and aprons.

Farther on they saw the reason: a shop front was shattered, glass lying on pavement and in gutter, a crowd jeering. "Germans! Boo, Germans!" The name painted above the shop was STRACHAN. As a policeman approached the crowd scattered.

"It's happened to other shops as well, sir. Over a hundred so far, and more being reported. This man is Scotch all right, but the name looks German."

"Poor fellow," said Thomas Turney. "No compensation, I suppose, is payable?"

"I could not tell you, sir. In some cases, of course, it's done to rob. It's housebreaking within the meaning of the law."

"Have a cigar," said Thomas Turney. Thanking him, the constable put it inside his helmet.

"The sooner we leave this neighbourhood, the better, Hetty. We come into the extension of Bishopsgate at the end, and then to Liverpool Street. This place is a rookery, you know. You'll never get these people to change their ways, I'm afraid, despite what Dora and her friends say. 'The poor are always with us.' I had an idea that I would sell some of my paper shares, and find out about iron and steel. The sinkings of our tonnage will increase, I think, for Germany is still very strong, and imports of pulp and newsprint will have to make way for more necessary raw materials, and manufactured armaments from America. This is the time, I fancy, to buy shipping shares, now slumped."

The neighbourhood of the Stock Exchange, narrow streets and tall stone buildings drab with smoke, was in some excitement, similar to that of the district of small factories and tenements they had just left. While Hetty waited below on the marble floor by the lift-cage, Thomas Turney went up to the fifth storey to his broker's office. There he learned that business in the House was virtually suspended; prices were so irregular, said his broker, as to be highly speculative; he advised waiting until they settled somewhat. He had a list of his client's securities, and promised to post a statement when some sort of stability re-established itself.

While they sat there, an office boy came in with a gleaming silk hat, explaining that he had had to wait his turn, for many others had been waiting before him, at the ironing basement.

"I am one of the Members of the House marching to the Palace of Westminster this afternoon, Mr. Turney, to demand the internment of all Germans in London for the duration. It is an open scandal how our war effort is being hamstrung in high places. The City is riddled with spies. Deputations are coming from the leading banks, from Lloyds, and other City Houses. The sinking of the *Lusitania* has brought matters to a head. I will write to you as soon as the market is more settled. Good day to you, sir."

Hetty and her father had brought sandwiches, as usual on their jaunt; and going into an A.B.C., ordered cups of coffee and ate while discussing how best they might see the forthcoming procession.

"History is in the making, my girl. What would not Samuel Pepys have made of our times? The pity is, life is so short; but you will read of it in due course, when the war is over; so will Phillip, and Bertie and Gerry—well, we must hope for the best. They are safe for the moment, thank goodness. This war will, as Kitchener said at the beginning, take a long time; and Europe will be devastated at the end of it. Did ye read of that fellow Bernard Shaw's pamphlet last autumn? I cut out a quotation from the *Telegraph*, and remember it well. 'There are only two flags in the world henceforth: the Red flag of democratic Socialism, and the Black flag of Capitalism.'"

"Yes, Papa, I remember Dickie reading out about it. I'm afraid it is all above my head."

"History tells us that there is usually a revolution in a country which loses a war, Hetty. 'Nothing succeeds like success', they say; and the converse is true. Come, eat up your food, my girl; you mustn't starve yourself, on account of the world's troubles, you know. It will be all the same in a hundred years time, so we must make the best of life as we have it."

"Of course, Papa," smiled Hetty, thinking that Phillip would be all right. Perhaps the war would be over before he would have to go out again.

They rode on top of an omnibus, open to the air and light of the spring day. Hetty felt happier away from the spiritless interior of the tea-shop. Passing Trafalgar Square with the pedestal of Nelson's memorial enclosed by hoardings advertising the new Government 4½% War Loan, £100 of stock being purchasable at £95, Thomas Turney pondered the advantages of gilt-edge over industrials. The bus ran down Whitehall, past the Horse Guards now in khaki, while Hetty looked at the varied uniforms of the officers to be seen there: Russian, French, Belgian, Italian, Montenegrin, among the top-hats and frock-coats of men whom she supposed to be members of the Government. How strong it all looked, the massive buildings, the calm of the people, the company of Royal Navy men marching by, spick and span, on the other side of the road, the gleaming wings of pigeons, white clouds sailing by in a sky of purest blue. O, things would come all right in the end!

They waited by the front of Westminster Abbey, opposite the Houses of Parliament, enjoying the sun. At last the procession appeared, top-hats gleaming and bobbing with here and there a straw-yard, umbrellas held under the left arm like shot-guns, and a patriotic stiffness about the marchers, the more noticeable as on either flank of the column hastened a straggling crowd of excited nondescripts and small boys.

"You know," said Thomas Turney, holding his daughter's arm, as she looked a little timid, he thought, "it is agin the law to march in procession within a mile of Parliament while it is in session, for the purpose of influencing its decisions or debates. I wonder how many policemen accompanying this lot know that?" as the head of the column actually passed through the iron gates, while the two constables on duty there stepped aside.

After hesitation, the two followed across the road, and into the Palace Yard. There seemed to be no objection to their following into the Central Hall with the deputation, so they went on, Thomas Turney holding his rolled umbrella under his left arm, as befitted the occasion, and the Chairman of Mallard, Carter & Turney Ltd., of Sparhawk Street, High Holborn.

"I hope," he chuckled, "that the chairman's head will not be found on one of the railing spikes after it is all over!"

The crowd pressed into the hall; the two managed to get into a free space by the side, at the back, beside a burly constable. There arose a chant, "We want Asquith! We want Asquith!——" while other sections began a counterpoint slogan, "We won't wait and see, we won't, we won't wait and see!" while the noise increased. The Prime Minister did not appear; but two Members of the Commons did, one instantly recognised as that grand old seadog, Lord Charles Beresford, bluff, broad-faced, frock-coated, with another, whom the constable said was Sir Henry Dalziel, a Liberal Member.

There was so much cheering and shouting or "Order! Order!" that the two speakers were heard only in snatches; but that they expressed the feelings of the assembly was obvious from the roar that went up with every sentence.

"I am convinced," shouted Admiral Lord Charles, "nay, I

can prove it! That if ever Zeppelins drop incendiary bombs on London, on this great city, heart of the Empire, then many of those Germans, our hated enemies, the destroyers of civilisation, of fair play, of God Himself—I am convinced that when that happens, as it will happen, my friends—that Germans now free among us will be out and about, to set fire to the City in twenty or thirty different places!"

When he could be heard again, "German barbers, German waiters, German bakers, they are potential dangers, I grant you, but the Germans who are the greatest threat to life and property are those in high social places! I would put them, one and all, behind barbed wire!"

Then his fellow parliamentarian spoke, "I have consulted with the chief of one of our Government Departments, and that authority confirmed what we all already knew: that there are many men of German origin holding high positions of confidence and responsibility in all departments. They are sons of naturalised Germans, born and brought up in England. I asked him if they were pro-German. 'Not necessarily,' he replied, 'but they are not exactly pro-British.' That was the gist of his reply. But what if, through only one case of treachery, arising from doubtful loyalty, some of your sons and brothers were lost in a troopship upon the High Seas? Is it not better to put them all out of harm's way, I mean by internment, rather than take such a risk?"

A messenger came in; passed a note to Lord Charles Beresford. "The Cabinet is at this very moment considering the position of naturalised Germans, so you may rest assured that the will of the people will prevail!" and to more cheering, and the National Anthem, the deputation broke up; and Hetty found she was trembling.

Two days later Richard was declaiming, from his armchair as he read *The Daily Trident*, that the Prime Minister was an Old Woman.

"He has not done enough, Hetty!"

Naturalised Germans were to be left at liberty, unless there were special reasons in individual cases.

"*The Trident* says, 'Intern the lot!'"

Male Germans of military age, between seventeen and fifty-five, were to be interned; over military age, including women and children to be repatriated. Hitherto they had been registered, and kept under observation.

"Well, we knew that," said Richard. "I've spent many an hour watching that fellow Krebs' windows, to see if he is signalling; and others, too, but that's a secret, Hetty. We are not asleep, you know, on our beats!"

He snorted.

"Asquith all over! What he gives with one hand, he takes away with the other! An advisory body is to be set up, if you please, to give some Germans a chance to claim exemption from both internment and repatriation! Most of the naturalised Germans, he says, he believes to be loyal British subjects! And would you believe it, Hetty, just listen to this! He goes on to say, 'Even the majority of the aliens who are not naturalised are, I believe, decent honest people! To initiate a vendetta against them would be, I contend, not only disgaceful from the moral point of view, but impolitic from the point of view of the country's best interests.' Good God, and that is the man whose wife visited the Prussian officers in their luxurious quarters in Donington Hall, whom she had known before the war as friends!"

Richard was about to say, as he had many times before, that the Prussians under Bismarck had destroyed his mother's family, killing her father and brothers, but he stopped himself in time: after all, half of him was *Bayerischer* blood, and the least said about that nowadays, the better. The thought calmed him down; and taking advantage of her husband's easier mood, Hetty said she was just going next door for half an hour or so, to play piquet with Papa.

The following night he was happier about the enemy in the midst. *The Daily Trident* congratulated its readers on their patriotism and common sense, which had led directly to the command of His Majesty, issued the previous day, that the names of the German Emperor, the Emperor of Austria, the King of Württemberg, the Crown Prince of Germany, and other German princes, including the Duke of Cumberland (who was the cousin of King George V) be struck off the Roll of the Knights of the Garter.

"Good," said Richard. "Listen to this, Hetty."

He proceeded to read an article on the Ancient Order of Chivalry to his wife. It declared that, in the seventeenth century a knight was publicly degraded in Westminster Hall, his spurs being hacked off his heels, his sword-belt cut and his sword broken across his head. The last expulsion had occurred exactly one hundred and one years before, in 1814, when Admiral Cochrane, M.P. was, despite his declaration of innocence, convicted and imprisoned for fraud on the Stock Exchange. He was expelled from the House of Commons, and his banner as a Knight of the Order of the Bath, hanging over his stall in the Chapel of Henry VII in Westminster Abbey, was torn down and kicked across the floors on to the sidewalk outside.

That, however, had been a mistake, Richard's voice repeated —unlike the present expulsions from the Roll of Garter Knights. In 1844, Cochrane, then Lord Dundonald, was proved innocent; he was restored to his Knighthood, but his banner was not put up in Windsor Chapel until he was dead. "'In these enlightened times, no such mistake could be made: Louvain, Dinant, Tirle-mont, and other Belgian towns, cry out the justification for the expulsion of the self-styled All-Highest from our most notable Order of Chivalry.'"

In the next house, Hetty, sitting opposite Thomas Turney, fortified by a steaming glass of Irish whiskey with lemon and honey in it, was given a less illiberal point of view. "You know, Hetty, for the King to have to accede to the cries of the mob is a bad thing, and in this case a significant thing, the consequences of which will be felt when the war is over, if not before. It is a sign of the times, of the dissolution of the old order. On a smaller scale, consider what has happened to Krebs——"

When Hetty returned to play chess with her husband, a game which she had lost consistently, with one exception, for the past twenty years, she wanted to tell him about Mr. Krebs, the German on the Hill; but dreading what he would say, she kept her thoughts to herself.

Mr. Krebs had been arrested during the previous night, and taken away, where, his wife did not know.

Chapter 14

SPREE—*continued*

THE flush of Irish rye-grass amidst the wild white clover of the open pastures was beginning to gleam in the wind; nightingales sang in the beechen spinneys, in solitary hawthorns along the verges of the open grassy gallops called the Severals, and in the shrubberies of large gardens of the horsey and prosperous. Phillip had little thought of wild birds now; life was full of new prospects. It seemed to him that he had never lived before.

There was his new friend the garage manager, the handsome Monty with the rich chuckling laugh, debonair manner, graceful figure, and dark, good-looking face. He took Phillip out in various motor cars in the long sunny evenings. Monty's idea was to have some sport, to get hold of two birds, as he put it. Phillip's idea was to learn to drive properly.

One night they drove through flat green pastures and cornfields, seeing in the distance a small town on a little hill, clustering round a cathedral looking as though all the walls had once been under water, and dried off again, very long ago. He mentioned this to Monty, who laughed and said, "Well, you're not far out, for Ely was surrounded by water in Hereward the Wake's time."

"Good lord, were these the Fens?"

"They still are. And what's more, here are two birds out for a walk on a nice spring evening. I'll drive past, and we can get a squint at their faces."

He set his gaily-ribboned boater at a slight angle, and cleared his throat. The black Studebaker went past; drew up; reversed, while Monty said, "Not bad at all. I bags the bird on the left," with a gurgling laugh. Phillip was slightly scared; he had no desire to talk to girls, and deeply within him was the fear of syphilis.

The Studebaker stopped. The girls walked on. Raising his hat, Monty said, "Is this the way to Manchester? My friend Major Dogsbody has an urgent appointment with General Nuisance."

Soon he was on easy terms with the girls. Phillip did not know what to say, so he said nothing.

"Dogsbody is shy," laughed Monty. "He's been doing too much drill. How about a ride, girls? Let me introduce myself, I'm Lord Helpus."

The girls were willing; Phillip was not. So Monty suggested that he went for a ride with his chosen girl, leaving Phillip with the other.

"We'll go around and see the sights, and be back in half an hour, old man, and pick you up here, how's that?" said Monty.

Phillip sat still. He did not know what to reply. He was not going to risk being left miles away from the battalion; besides, he did not want to be alone with the other girl.

After some attempts by Monty to get him to agree had failed, the driver put in the gear and drove off violently, his face contorted with rage, his words bitter. Through the tirade Phillip remained unspeaking. The words fell upon him like small explosions. There was nothing to do but wait until Monty had finished; when he too became silent, after a final remark, "Well, I thought you were a sport, now I know what you are, you'll never come with me again!"

A hare got up by the grassy wayside soon afterwards, and Monty accelerated, trying to run it down, as it sped along in front, kicking up a little dust and jumping from side to side as it stared backwards with terrified eyes. The chase seemed to restore Monty's good humour; then just as the speedometer needle reached forty-five and the brown animal was almost beneath the front axle it leapt sideways and got away.

After that Monty became his former self; and when Phillip had apologised, and told him what he had been frightened of, Monty slapped him on the knee and with a gurgle of laughter said, "You silly old ass, why didn't you tell me? I could have given you a fish skin, they are better than ordinary letters. Anyway, I had only one, and you never know, I might have got a dose. My girl comes next week, you must meet her, she's an actress. We're going to be married as soon as I can save enough dough."

On the way back he turned off to visit a farmer to whom he was trying to sell a Studebaker. The farmer was out—"They're making pots of money now, you know"—and Monty let Phillip take the wheel through the narrow lanes. Phillip drove carefully, still unable to change gear while in motion, but keeping in mind where the brake pedal was. They entered a village, and almost at once Monty was waving his boater, and saying, "Stop!", for three fair-haired young women were standing outside a cottage gate. Monty pulled the hand-brake tight, the Studebaker slid in the dust to a stop. "Hi, put the clutch out next time, you ass! I say, three fairies! Now don't bilk this time, Phil—just be your charming self."

He leaned out of the window and called out gaily, "Hullo-a-lo-a-lo! Didn't we meet at the Cesarovitch? Or was it the Polusky Brothers at the Tottenham Palace of Varieties? Seriously, do you know the Green House, it's somewhere here."

Phillip saw this name painted on the gate. "I've got a two-seater Swift for sale, cheap, I come from Freshwell's garage. My card," he held one out between two fingers, and then got out of the car.

"Well, this is the Green House, but we don't want a motor-car, thank you."

"Good," replied Monty. "Business is so boring, isn't it? Let me introduce myself." He twiddled his straw hat expertly like a top. "My friend—Sir Phillip Longshanks, generally known as Tubby."

To Phillip it was a marvellous adventure, as he sat on a sofa, drinking coffee, and listening to the gramophone. Then the eldest girl, with red-gold hair, played Chopin, after which her sister sang *Three Hundred and Sixty-five Days*, and other musical comedy songs. The odd thing was that Monty had guessed the place where they came from, Green Lanes, Tottenham, right first time. The eldest girl, who was twenty-one, had just married, and owing to their parents' fear of Zeppelin raids, her two sisters had come to stay at her cottage.

"Do you believe in fate?" asked the married girl, coming to sit by Phillip, while Monty and the other sisters were in the kitchen, making more coffee and sandwiches.

"Well, yes and no," replied Phillip, regarding the reply as a kind of insurance.

"I do," said Fairy, smiling.

"Oh."

"You are a funny boy. What is your name really?"

He told her, and where he lived, and other details of his life. She seemed greatly interested.

"You seem so young to have been to France, Phillip. May I call you that? Or is it cheek?"

"Good lord, no! I'm highly honoured. I'm sorry, I forgot your name."

"Everyone calls me Fairy. I suppose it is because I am so thin."

"I'm pretty thin, too, but I'm quite strong, you know. You don't look thin. *Petite*, yes—but sylph-like I would say suits you better."

She looked at him with a happy face. He could see a pulse in her neck beating. He thought she was quite different from any woman he had ever known. She was shy, but also frank and outspoken, in a nice way. The shape of her face was pleasing, she was quick, a sort of nice foxy face, red-gold hair and eye-lashes, a few freckles, very nice shaped ears (like Mavis') and a good little chin. The roast-beef sandwiches made him realise how hungry he was; and also that he had forgotten to sign-off for mess-dinner, having met Monty by chance outside Godolphin House as he had driven past, and jumped in beside him.

"Very nice wimps," remarked Monty, as they drove back. "I heard all about Fairy, your bird, when I was in the kitchen. She married to escape from her old man, who's a bit of a tartar, and jumped out of the frying pan into the fire. She can't bear the chap she married to touch her. He apparently did the cave-man stuff in the bridal chamber straight away, before even his coat was off. She's been married two months, and he's gone to Egypt with the Territorials. What more could you want, old horse? I like the sister, the fair one, I bet she's a casse-noisette, she quivered when I put my arm on her shoulder, friendly like. That cave-man stuff is no good, you know. Begin gently, make 'em laugh, leave 'em alone at first, that gives 'em confidence in you. Though my bird won't want much working on, if you ask me."

Phillip was repelled by this attitude towards what generally he regarded (except, of course, cousins like Petal and Polly, who didn't really count) as the holiness of love and female beauty. He did not know what to say: so once again sat silent beside Monty.

The Studebaker was the latest model, with electric headlights; and they were approaching the railway bridge by a big chalk quarry on the left when Phillip saw a figure on horseback in front of a column of marching soldiers coming over the bridge.

Immediately Monty turned down a lane to the right, drawing up as he switched off lights.

"Better not risk being told off for using headlamps," he said. "The military are getting hot now, since Zeppelins are about. I have thought of joining the R.N.A.S. They won't be sent abroad, or have any fighting to do. What do you think?"

"I think you're right, Monty."

"Their headquarters are in the Belvoir Hotel, you know."

"Yes, I've seen them there."

The head of the marching column halted opposite the turning. Three mounted officers moved about on the road, turning their horses. With a shock Phillip heard the voice of "Strawballs" growling, "Bloody rot! And why does 'Crasher' have to choose a guest-night to blow his own trumpet?" Major Fridkin replied something, but it was in too low a voice to be overheard.

"Good lord!" whispered Phillip to Monty. "It's our lot! And I've cut guest-night! I forgot all about it! My God, I ought to be with them!"

"I should worry. But if you hop off, farther on, you can slip back."

"Hell, I'm in their bad books enough already!"

Monty drove on, and stopped on the far side of the long bridge; Phillip got out, said good night, and walked back on the grass verge, then on past the rear company, walking now briskly, as though returning from a scouting mission. He found his company, and by listening to voices, his platoon. O'Connor saw him.

"Where have you been, my boy?"

"Scouting around. The flanks are not being turned. What is it, a night exercise?"

"Yes. We were in the ante-room, when the alarm rang out in the High Street, on a cavalry trumpet blown by 'Crasher' himself. 'Twas a fine rousing sound, despite some notes wavering and others misplaced, but it made the colonel swear, for he had to mount his charger wearing slacks."

"I suppose my absence at dinner was noticed?"

"It was, my boy. The senior subaltern keeps his eye on you as an earth-stopper watches the habits of a fox."

Phillip congratulated himself the next morning at the nine o'clock parade when nothing was said about his absence the night before; and again when his skipping guest-night was not mentioned by after dinner of that day. He forgot it in his next adventure, which was on the back of a horse.

The transport officer, an Australian, whose tutor at the 'varsity, Phillip heard, had been "Strawballs", said at breakfast the following day, that any subaltern who wanted a horse could have one for the afternoon by giving in his name. Seeing Baldersby regarding him, while pulling as usual at his yellow moustache, Phillip said at once that he would like a hack. That was the correct term, he had recently learned.

The horses were brought round to the entrance of Godolphin House at 2 p.m. By this time Phillip was in some apprehension, mixed with a determination that he would ride off very slowly until he got on the open grass beyond the town, when he would teach himself to ride, come what may. Trying to maintain his good resolutions, he mounted a horse for the first time in his life, after the groom had adjusted the stirrup leathers to the length of his arm from pit to fingertips.

There were four horses waiting; a dozen interested faces at the open door and others by the open mess windows as the four started off. Phillip was the last to mount, on a fat white horse that from the first determined to have its own way, and follow the others stringing up the High Street. It trotted: which, translated to the rider, meant an alarming and perpetual series of hard bumps on the base of the spine every one of which seemed about to topple him sideways despite muttered requests to the animal to whoa back, good horse, stop you brute, steady boy, curse you, you swine, walk WALK! Bump, bump, bump. The horse's ears were pricked high and forward; and only when it approached the tail of the bay, its neighbour on the picket line, did it slow up and the ears become flaccid thus giving its rider a chance to sort out the four reins into a pattern of which he was ignorant, and to wonder with alarm what would happen if the horse in front, when on grass, decided to gallop. Wasn't William Rufus killed that way, in the New Forest, his chin caught on a horizontal branch?

On grass, the horse broke into a canter.

"Sit down to it, sit down!" cried the Australian transport officer to Phillip, trying his best to sit down despite the fact that the horse was bouncing him up, once a second, what seemed to be at least a foot off the saddle.

"Sit down to it! I could jump between you and the horse! Sit down to it!"

"I'm trying to," gasped Phillip. "But it won't stop bumping me up again!" How he managed to remain on, he did not know.

"You want to go with your horse's motion. Yield to it, don't set up a counter-motion! Don't sit so stiff! Relax! Imagine you are in an armchair!"

Phillip had no more energy to explain to the transport officer, who wore enormous spurs. Thank goodness Baldersby was not there to see him. Gone was his former idea of riding over to the Green House in time for tea with Fairy and her sisters, and thus displaying his equestrian powers. It would be better to go in the open Humber motor-car which Monty said he could have out for ten shillings the afternoon.

Handing over the fat white horse to the groom, Phillip walked back feeling that the landscape had changed since he had left Godolphin House an hour before. His stiffness soon wore off, and he was jubilant again as he went down the High Street, wondering as he passed Tom Hill's if he would have a pair of grey canvas leggings made, like the adjutant's. Later on, perhaps. The immediate thing was to get the green Humber car. What luck, it was in. A mechanic swung the brass handle, the engine started, Phillip occupied the driver's seat, was told what the gears were, how many times to pump oil into the glass container on the dashboard to feed the engine, which pedals were for what; and drove out of the garage, and down the slope to Godolphin House. Leaving the motor outside, he went into the ante-room, glanced at a newspaper, dropped it, and went out again, hoping that he would be noticed. He was: Baldersby's face, teeth holding cigar stump, regarded him from the open mess window.

"Hullo, Baldersby. Nice weather, isn't it?"

"Hr-r-r," growled Baldersby, with a scowl. Phillip thought he was really harmless; he was a joke to the others—"Baldersby of Baldersby Towers, Baldersby, Berkshire". His bark was worse than his Berkshire!

In high good humour—he would take out a horse again, until he could ride properly—Phillip swung the handle, and got in. He started off full of confidence, and changing gear with only two clashes, was going up the High Street at about 25 m.p.h. when he saw the three other horses coming down on what he thought was the wrong side—they were on his left-hand side—and putting on the brakes, sat helplessly while the motor-car swung to the right, then to the left, before revolving completely on its own tracks and stopping, facing backwards. The polished steel-studded rear-tyres had skidded on the tarred surface.

He sat there while the horses went by, giving a little salute to each; then getting out, restarted the motor, and reversing without incident, went on and arrived at the Green House, to be welcomed by three sisters for tea—and supper, with songs, Chopin, and gramophone records while a nightingale sang in the garden.

The notes of other nightingales could be heard in the silence of the High Street after the ten o'clock closing of pubs, when the touts, who spied through big black binoculars, stop-watches in hand, from the beech-clumps of the Severals upon race-horses by day, and the stable boys, who might be any age between fourteen and eighty years, had gone to out-house, loft, harness-room, and stable. A peaceful country town, in the fullness of May; and nobody enjoyed the ups of life there more than Phillip despite the downs, from which he arose again with the buoyancy of ignorance, unaware of the reasons of his being disliked, a herdless youth having little or no percipience of the feelings of those older men who were to him merely faces whose critical gaze was to be evaded or disregarded.

Laughing to himself as he thought of the terrific spree in the Belvoir Arms, he walked back to Godolphin House in the moonlight, and stopped to listen to a nightingale. It was a calm and beautiful late evening in the third week of May. The old feeling for birds and woods and spring was overlaid by the excitements and adventures of his new life. He chuckled, imagining Desmond beside him, enjoying his account of the adventure; and continued on his way, now and then deviating a little from his course, which added to his sense of the evening's fun. His head was wet, so were the shoulders of his tunic, his tie, and his collar. What a rag it had been! In this mood he went in by the side door of the mess, and pulled himself up by the rail beside the stone steps to his attic room, where his camp-bed stood by itself.

Lying within his sleeping-sack, he reviewed the evening's details. When he had gone under the brick arch into the courtyard, the gramophone was playing *They'd Never Believe Me*. He was standing by the open door, listening, when an R.N.A.S. man said to him, "I say, would you mind not using our mess? This is the C.P.O.s' mess, you know." Phillip said, "Oh, I didn't know," and going away, walked out of the courtyard and up to the clock-tower at the cross-roads at the top of the town. Then hoping his former self would not be recognised, he went into the bar of the Belvoir Arms and sat on one of the stools. He ordered a pint of bitter beer, and drank it in two draughts, out of bravado; then he asked for another in the same tankard. The barmaid was the rather plump girl who rode on the flapper-bracket of the A.S.C. officer's Douglas.

When that person came in, dark eyes sunken, the blue-dark of his jowl combining with many craters of chicken-pox to give his face an uneven appearance, Phillip asked him to have a drink, hoping to talk about the comparative merits of single and twin-cylinder engines. He swallowed his pot of beer, and ordered two more.

"How does your Douglas behave up-hill with a pillion passenger?"

"Depends on the hill, and the passenger."

"Well, say the barmaid here. Would it go in top up to the Heath?"

The other eyed him. "Why do you ask?"

"I only wondered. Mine's a single-cylinder, of course. I say, if I asked the barmaid to come for a ride on it, d'you think she'd say yes?"

"I don't understand you!"

"Well, I saw her on your bus, and I wondered if she'd care to come for a ride on mine. D'you think she'd be offended if I asked her?"

"What exactly do you mean?"

Phillip saw that he was angry, but had no idea why. "I mean, she's game, isn't she?"

The A.S.C. officer turned his back. The barmaid, who was polishing a glass behind the counter, gave Phillip a cold stare. The A.S.C. officer said something, and she poured him a glass of gin, to which he added soda-water from the siphon on the counter.

The tankard of beer was still there when at nine o'clock the green-aproned cellarman came in, and the barmaid left. A minute or two later the A.S.C. man left; and going out, Phillip saw him taking his Douglas off the stand, and the barmaid getting on the cushion. Then the machine purred away in the direction of Six Mile Bottom.

Could the barmaid be the A.S.C. chap's bird? Had he thought he was trying to get her away from him? How funny, when he had a girl of his own—there it was, *Helena*, on the silver-grey tank of his own motor-bike!

Having nothing to do, Phillip returned to the bar and picked up *The Daily Trident*. There he read, under headlines of big dark type, "The Tragedy of the Shells. Lord Kitchener's Grave Error."

It was what he had always known, what everyone in France had known, there in print. Shrapnel, instead of high explosive, useless for cutting wire . . . "responsible for our Armies failing to gain their objectives, and the consequent appalling casualties."

"Dirty yellow rag that, sir. Been publicly burned in the Stock Exchange today, according to the evening paper. Several trade unions have condemned it, too, sir. Attacking Kitchener like that!"

"I think Kitchener deserved it."

"Really, sir?"

"I don't think that anyone at home has the slightest idea of what has been happening out there."

At this moment the senior subaltern came in, a half-smoked cigar between his teeth, followed by the adjutant, the second-in-command, and a strange lieutenant, wearing the same badges, whom Phillip had not seen before. All were smoking cigars.

"Good evening, gentlemen," said Phillip genially, as they made for the far end of the room. They did not appear to hear. He swallowed his beer quickly, thinking that he ought to switch to whiskey, since the adjutant at the other end of the bar had ordered four large White Horses for his party.

When he returned to the others sitting on the settle, upholstered in woven horsehair, which ran round three sides of the room, Phillip ordered a large White Horse.

The next to enter the bar was an old-faced man with a coarse voice, obviously a bookmaker. Phillip, perched on his stool, heard him say to the cellar-man, while pointing at *The Daily Trident*, "Castleton, who owns that yellow rag, is an ally of the Huns."

"Oh, no," said Phillip, swinging round on the stool. "Castleton's quite right. He's a decent chap. I met him when I was a boy."

Thereupon he declaimed his opinion of what was wrong in France, how Kitchener's mind, having been formed on problems of the East, was incapable of grasping the problem of the present war in France.

"The Germans have eight or ten howitzers to our one, all firing high explosive. Their shrapnel is a farce. So is ours. The people in this country do not know the truth. Do you know, f'instance, that the Germans believe absolutely in the righteousness of their cause? I've talked to many, so I know. They all said the same thing on the truce of Christmas Day. They can't lose the war, since it is a righteous war, and God is with them. No, no, don't go away—just listen a moment——"

"What are you, a Hun?" asked the bookie.

"My grandmother was German, but I'm English. No, really, honestly—what I'm saying is the gospel truth. What the Germans say is that they are an increasing nation with practically no colonies——"

"And those won't be theirs much longer!"

"Just a moment. They are a growing nation——"

"Were, you mean!"

"All right." Phillip gulped down his whisky. "Anyway, they have to depend on increasing trade, selling all sorts of things abroad, even toys, to keep going. They're shut in, you see. So they built battleships to protect their shipping, just as we have done, only we started earlier." Having rid himself of all his ideas on the subject, Phillip asked the other to have a drink. His offer was refused; and unperturbed, he ordered another for himself.

The cellar-man, his cropped hair ending in a water-flattened curl pressed low on his forehead, said, immediately the large beef-faced man had left the bar, "Lord Kitchener is very highly regarded in this town by the racing fraternity, sir."

"I like him, too; but he has let us down over shells. Our chaps, before an attack, are forced to try and cut enemy wire with machine-gun bullets. What a hope! There's no hope! Everyone anywhere near the front line knows it." The cellar-man polished a glass. "Including those who have found out by personal experience," muttered Phillip, to himself.

Then he began to whistle the tune of a song which Cranmer had sung during one of the peaceful bacon-frying mornings behind the Brown Wood Line, which ought to have been called the Bill Brown Line since the bunkers and rifle-pits in it had been dug by the Grenadiers. He sang to himself the words of the last verse.

> *If you want to find the old battalion*
> *I know where they are, I seen 'em I seen 'em,*
> *I know where they are.*
> *They're hanging on the old barbed wire.*
> *I seen 'em, I seen 'em,*
> *Hanging on the old barbed wire!*

Raising his glass, Phillip, now in a state of semi-exaltation with his own thoughts, drank to Cranmer, to Baldwin and to Elliot, to Peter and David and Nimmo Wallace, to the Earl of Findhorn and the Iron Colonel, to the wounded and the dying in No Man's Land, to faces seen in the pallor of flares and the glow of charcoal braziers, ration parties making a crude xylophone sound on the frozen corduroy path with their boots, fearful of the tearing scream and crack of shrapnel, to Tommy Atkins whose ghost must have come to help him out of the T-trench, to the *prächtige Kerls*, in field-grey on Christmas Day, and to that which, by God, cried inside him, Come back to us, come back—and with this feeling he hurled the empty glass upon the floor.

The cellar-man was used to that sort of thing; but only when toasts were drunk, on special occasions, such as banquets, in the private dining-room. However, he said nothing; but lifting the flap in the counter, came through with brush and pan, and quietly swept up the fragments of what had been a large wine-glass, and returned to his original place.

"That will be another sixpence, sir," he said, across the counter.

Phillip gave him half-a-crown, telling him to keep the change.

"Thank you very much, sir. You have been in France, I take it?"

"Yes, I was with the London Highlanders, as a ranker, and fought through the first battle of Ypres."

"Yes, sir?" He leaned over the counter. "But there are

others, sir, if you will pardon my saying so, who have not had the same experiences as yourself, sir."

"Quite! Quite!" and Phillip offered his hand to be shaken by the cellar-man.

Baldersby appeared, shoving past a circular three-legged table to the bar. He was going to order more drinks.

"I say, Baldersby," said Phillip, feeling extremely genial towards the entire world, "would you care to have a drink with me. Two large whiskies, please," to the cellar-man.

"I won't drink with you," replied Baldersby, almost violently.

"I don't really *mean* to chuck my weight about, Baldersby."

"Weight!" retorted Baldersby. "What weight have *you* got?"

"Ten stone four pounds, actually. But seriously——"

Baldersby turned his back on Phillip. His eye caught the heading of *The Daily Trident*. He picked it up, cried out "Pah!" and ripped it in pieces. This had also recently happened in the Pigskin Club, where Baldersby and the others had dined. The *Trident* had been carried by one of the members there to the fire-place, between polished steel tongs, and put in the fire.

The cellar-man put two goblets of pale yellow whisky on the counter. Phillip paid him, and was about to reach for the siphon when Baldersby seized it first, filled one goblet to the brim, raised it over Phillip's head, and tipped it. The liquid was still foaming down past his nose and ears, and fizzing on the back of his neck, when a fairly hard jet of soda-water struck him on the face, as Baldersby stood back, taking aim.

This was tremendous fun to Phillip: this really was like Fred Karno's Mumming Birds at the Hippo. He grabbed the glass jug of water on the counter, and sluiced it all over Baldersby. Then he gave Baldersby a push, which sent him clattering backwards into the three-legged table, which went over, Baldersby with it. Still laughing, Phillip put on his cap, which had been hanging on a hook, and walked out of the bar, over the cobbles, under the arch, and so down the moonlit street, with its echoes of a distant nightingale, to Godolphin House and his attic room; to undress and lie down, happily knowing, by the absence of saliva in his mouth, that he was not going to be sick.

The camp bed still smelt of carbolic fluid, and suddenly recalling the remark of the salesman at the Stores where he had bought it—*You'll find it redolent of the rigours of the campaign*—he imagined Desmond with him, and started to shake with laughter.

Chapter 15

SPREE—*continued*

LYING on his canvas bed, Phillip was listening to the far voice
of the nightingale, when up the stone steps beyond the open
door came the blast of an ill-blown hunting horn. This familiar
noise of Baldersby's made him get out of bed, and listen at the
top of the stairs. The horn notes came again, from the ante-
room, judging by their muffled effect: two shut wooden doors
between. He knew what was happening below, and went to
lock himself in the lavatory opposite Baldersby's room at the
end of the landing.

Then he decided not to hide but to face whatever was coming,
so went back to bed in his wide attic room, first having removed
the locket with the miniature from around his neck. Rising
footfalls on stone steps, horn notes down below; door pushed
open, flash-light dazzling.

"Come on, just as you are. You are wanted in the court."

"What court? Anyway, let me put on my British warm."

"Come as you are."

Held by both arms, he was taken down the steps in pyjamas,
through the mess and into the ante-room. There the chairs
and sofas, filled with subalterns, were arranged in a rough
square. Baldersby stood by a table in the centre, copper horn
shoved between brass buttons of his tunic showing water stains.
He was flushed, cigar-stub between teeth.

Phillip caught a glimpse of Major Fridkin, the second-in-
command, in an open doorway: the broad, easy, Chinaman-type
face of Hairy Harry, as he was known behind his back by some
of the subalterns. It disappeared. Baldersby removed the cigar
stub and rapped on the table with his heavy gold signet ring.

"Prisoner over there," he pointed. "Now, gentlemen, we
have a duty to perform, and as senior subaltern of the regiment
I have called this court martial to decide what shall be done
in the matter of Temporary Second-lieutenant Maddison. We
are all aware that he is not a member of the regiment, but only
attached for duty: even so, he comes under the jurisdiction of
this court. I would like to add, at this point, that the fact that

he is not a member of the regiment has nothing to do with the matter in hand, but only his conduct. There are other subalterns attached to us, and we regard each one as one of ourselves, as by their behaviour they do not let the regiment down. In fact, they are dam' good fellers."

Cheers greeted this remark. Baldersby took several puffs of his dead cigar, examined it, pinched it, puffed again in vain, then went on:

"Well, that's all. I have called this court to assemble, in accordance with time-honoured unwritten law, as senior subaltern, and not as Bertram Baldersby——"

"——of Baldersby Towers, Baldersby, Berkshire!" roared half a dozen voices in chorus.

"Quite, quite," blinked Baldersby. "But all joking aside, you fellers, Dimmock, just returned from the first battalion, is next in seniority to myself, and since I am standing down to be a witness in the case, not as senior subaltern, as I said, but as——"

"——Baldersby of Baldersby Towers, Baldersby, Berkshire!" roared the solid square of junior subalterns.

"Order," said Baldersby; and sitting down, he extracted a cigar from a heavy leather case, and lit it, puffing blue clouds of smoke.

Phillip recognised Dimmock as the fourth man in the Belvoir Arms, with Major Fridkin, Jonah the Whale, and Baldersby.

Dimmock, lean, fair, blue-eyed, sat on the table edge and said, "I accept the presidency of this court, which is composed of a junior subaltern of the regiment, another junior subaltern of the prisoner's regiment, and myself. Let the case be stated against the prisoner. Who is the prosecutor?"

"Here," said Baldersby, holding up a hand.

"Who is defending counsel for the prisoner?"

O'Connor stood up. He was a spare, dark man, with lean, clean-shaven brown face, and *pince-nez* glasses. "If the defendant wishes——" He went to Phillip. "The defendant is agreeable, sir."

"Very well, I call upon Baldersby——"

"——of Baldersby Towers, Baldersby, Berkshire!" roared the onlookers.

"Not so much noise, you chaps," said Dimmock, in a quiet voice, as he swung a knee from his perch on the table. "Carry on, the prosecution."

"Very well," said Baldersby, expelling smoke as he got up. He looked round for an ash-tray, upon which to lay his cigar. After a little fussing, he put it on the marble mantelpiece, and standing there, said, "General bad behaviour, lack of respect to senior officers, speaking when not spoken to first—often with a cigarette in mouth—all examples of bad form. It lets down the regiment."

"Can you give any particular instances?"

"Well, there is the incident of setting fire to the colonel's newspaper on guest night."

O'Connor rose; and being motioned to speak, said,

"I suggest to the court that the defendant has already purged his contempt for that gaucherie committed in extenuating circumstances. In addition, he has apologised to the colonel."

"What does the prosecution say?"

"Damned bad form," growled Baldersby. "No idea of good form."

"Do you agree that the gaucherie has been purged?"

"He's a little tick, all the same He cut guest night last week."

Dimmock turned to Phillip. "What do you say to that?"

"Sir, I forgot all about it."

Baldersby went on, "He lets down the regiment! Look at that bounder from the garage he goes about with! That feller who has the infernal impudence to wear Parthenopian colours on his boater and on his tie—a chap in a shop!"

O'Connor said, "I submit that my client is not responsible for an acquaintance who adds the feather of a paycock to the plumage of a crow."

There were ironical cheers from the chairs and sofas.

"Who is the man who wears Parthenopian colours? Is he a friend of yours?"

"Yes, sir."

"Is he teaching you to drive a motorcar?" asked O'Connor.

"Yes."

"Do you pay for the hire of the motorcars you use?"

"Yes, I do."

"How much?" interjected Baldersby.

"Ten shillings an afternoon."

Dimmock said, "Any further complaints? We have established one thing so far—cutting guest night. What other charges does the prosecution prefer?"

"I don't prefer any of 'em, I dislike everything about the feller," maintained Baldersby, stoutly. "Then there's another thing. He goes into the R.N.A.S. chief petty officers' mess-room in the Belvoir Arms without being invited, and ignores all hints to keep out. He isn't fit to hold the King's commission, and gives the regiment a dam' bad name by his presence anywhere."

"Do you agree about the R.N.A.S. mess accusation?"

"I didn't know, sir!"

"Haven't you heard that ignorance is no excuse?"

"How was I to know?" said Phillip, desperately. He thought that he was being court-martialled seriously. "I thought it was all part of the hotel!"

"One doesn't sound the 'h' in that word," growled Baldersby. "I saw and heard Maddison soliciting in the bar, having the dam' bad manners to ask an A.S.C. officer, who is friendly with one of the barmaids there, if the girl was 'all right'. The feller turned his back on him, I saw him, I was with three brother officers of the regiment in the smoke room at the time. So I cooled him down."

O'Connor said, "How did you do that?"

"In the usual way of dealing with a cad. I emptied my glass in his face."

"In the bar of the Belvoir Arms?"

"Yes. And I'd do it again."

"What happened then?"

"He poured the water-jug over me, gave me a shove which caught me off balance, and caused a table belonging to the hotel to be broken."

The whole room broke into laughter, except the faces of Phillip, Dimmock, Baldersby, and O'Connor.

"Order," said Dimmock.

"I would like to ask a question," said O'Connor in a mild voice, as he looked steadily at the ceiling. "Was the defendant in angry mood when he retaliated in kind? Was there a scowl on his face? Did he show his teeth? Did he reveal any desire for revenge? Or did he have upon his visage a familiar un-sophisticated inane grin, partly, perhaps, of embarrassment, partly, perhaps, of bewilderment? Did he, a newcomer to the life of an officer's mess in England, did he regard it all as a spree, similar to the fun we have in the ante-room during some nights, when natural high spirits and gaiety prevail over the sombre prospects of war? If it be claimed that it was an error in the most gross taste to confuse private behaviour in a regimental ante-room with lack of decorum—and I am not going to suggest that it be an error in the most gross taste, for that might involve a question beyond the scope of this, shall we say, unofficial court-martial, then——" The speaker paused, studiously avoiding the senior subaltern's face.

"Mr. President," went on O'Connor, in his clear voice, enhanced by his Irish accent, "speaking only as the counsel for the defendant, and not for a moment as a guest of the regiment, I suggest that my client, in giving tit-for-tat, in responding in the classic manner of Tit versus Tat, in returning a measure of water within a jug for a measure of Scots whisky and an additional measure of soda-water within a siphon, was only conforming to a precedent set by a distinguished member of His Majesty's Forces!"

Cheers greeted this speech, followed by the roared chorus of "Baldersby of Baldersby Towers, Baldersby, Berkshire!"

Baldersby retrieved his cigar, and striking one of the monster Bryant and May's matches in a giant box upon the marble mantelpiece tried to set fire to the charred end. Then puffing furiously he took it from beneath his teeth and waved it in the air.

"That's all very well, but what has it got to do with the fact that by his very presence here in the mess of the Cantuvellaunians he is an eyesore and we don't want him here! Let 'm get back to where he came from! That disgusting motorbicycle he rides about on, with a coffee pot stuck on the end of the rusty pipe! That isn't funny, it's utter bloody awful bad form! It makes the townee cads laugh. No doubt, it might be funny in a circus, dammit, but not when done among officers and gentlemen!"

Baldersby pressed the bell violently: almost instantly the mess-sergeant glided in, a deferential, enquiring expression upon his smooth face as he went to Baldersby, who said, "Six large 'Old Scotties'," and with a slight bow the mess-sergeant glided away.

"I'll tell you what!" roared Baldersby, waving cigar with one hand and tugging left section of tow-like moustache with the other. "I would like to see the outsider in the middle of twenty couple o' dog hounds now, here, at this very moment!"

and pulling the horn from between his buttons he drew a deep breath, pressed the mouthpiece to one corner of his mouth, hardened every muscle of head (including eyes), neck, and abdomen, and produced the series of piercing high notes known in the hunting field as the rattle or mort-blast.

"*Whoo Whoop! Whoo Whoop! Whoo Whoop!*"

Then from the side of his mouth came equally piercing yells, as the imagined lemon, black, white and tan foxhounds tore the hated figment of Maddison's face to bloody gobs of flesh and cracked bone.

Phillip ran for the door in his pyjamas, as "Hercules" launched himself in a flying tackle across the table—and missed his grab. Phillip opened the door and was gone before anyone could stop him. The effect of the whisky was still upon him; his mood was of wild self-annihilation. He would apply in the morning to go back to France. Near to hysteria, he ran out of Godolphin House and up the hill towards Freshwell's Garage, meaning to get his motor-cycle and ride as far towards London as he could on what petrol remained in the tank.

The mood did not last more than a few moments in the fresh air. He stopped, and looked back. In the moonlit street he saw figures. He waited until they had gone back into the mess, then crossed the road swiftly on bare feet and went along in the shadow-fringe of house-roofs on the opposite pavement, thus passing unseen the house on the corner.

Near the theatre he crossed over again, and waited by a shop window displaying saddles, boots, curry combs, bits, saddle soap, and spurs. He was going on tip-toe past the Pigskin Club, when two figures came out and walked slowly together, with clinking swan-neck spurs, the same way as himself. He kept behind them, distant about ten yards. They stopped when the notes of the horn came again. So did he.

The notes were muffled, seeming to come from the upper rooms of Godolphin House. Then they came clearly, with the noise of a window being opened up above. It was his bedroom. Immediately afterwards a glint appeared by the attic window, a dim object sailed downwards, and crashed upon the roadway below. Other major crashes followed at intervals, then a minor one. That's my soap-dish, thought Phillip.

"Damme, Willie," he heard the rusty voice of "Crasher", the Crimean veteran, say, "I thought for a moment that the

Russkies were carronadin' 'Old Strawballs' little lot, don't y'know."

At that moment a succession of wooden drawers, their contents flying, descended from the window above.

"An original way to move furniture, I must say, General."

"Damme, Willie, d'you suppose any more's to follow? They're not celebratin' me, d'you suppose, Willie?"

"Probably raggin' some unfortunate young cub, General."

"Do 'im world o' good, Willie."

A camp bed hissed through the air, and clattered upon the iron railings.

"Damme Willie, that looks like one of those new-fangled campaign beds we saw at the Stores t'other day! Damme Willie, I'm in half a mind to get me trumpet and sound the alarm, and rout 'em out again, Willie. What d'ye say?"

"Rather soon after last week, don't you think, General?"

"Mebbe you're right, Willie. Well, so long as they clear up this mess before the 'osses walk by in the mornin', Willie." The general paused. "Raggin', Willie, did ye say? That reminds me of the letter in *The Times* yesterday, d'ye recall it, Willie? That foreigner fellow the Prince o' Wales dubbed—what's's name, one of those Kimberley mushroom knights."

"Otto Beit, General?"

"'Ats'r feller, Willie! Son was a cornet, shot himself in the Cavalry Barracks at York, didn't know the form, so the others bully-ragged 'im. Chivalrous letter, I thought, Willie, well put together. Pleaded for consideration towards new types of officers in the Militia. I'm in favour of reasonable kindness, Willie—I served under that blackguard Raglan at Crimea, and b'God, Willie, when the 'Thunderer' got the news by electric telegraph, and m'lady mother thought I'd been snuffed out, she had the pair o' greys dyed black—did I ever tell 'ee that, Willie?"

"Yes, indeed, General."

"Well, the carronadin' seems over, so Bedfordshire, Willie, Bedfordshire!"

Followed the sound of a prodigious yawn, after which the two figures went jingling slowly up the hill towards brigade head-quarters.

Phillip had heard only snatches of what was said; he recog-nised the brigadier and his brigade major, and kept well back in shadow until they had gone. By now he thought it was all rather funny; and thinking to add to the fun, he turned to the left before Godolphin House, which was on the corner across the road, and going some way up the street, crossed over and so came to the back entrance in moon shadow all the way.

The interior doors were open. Listening, he heard laughter and the clink of glasses; and distantly, the nightingale singing. In a few moments he was up the stone steps, two and three at a time, silent on naked feet; and listening outside Baldersby's door. No sound within. He turned the handle, entered. It was a quick matter to open the window, and then to place white ewer, basin, soap-dish and chamber pot under the window, ready for a salvo. Then he went to the iron rail outside, listening. Reassured, he crept back, and stripped Baldersby's camp bed of rugs and sleeping sack.

These, with the pillows, went out of the window when he had dropped the drawers full of shirts, socks, breeches, trousers, and other things, and heard them spike themselves on the railings below. Then, one after another, hurled sideways to burst into the middle of the road, went the china bedroom-ware, each splaying out with a satisfactory ringing crash upon the void.

Soon there were voices below. Faces looked up. There were shouts. Phillip's heart began to thump. Should he await them, or dash down to the next floor, and through O'Connor's bed-room to the main staircase?

While he hesitated, he heard footfalls clambering up the stone steps. Could he get out of the window and so on to the roof, and hide among the chimney pots? He dared not; he would fall. So he awaited his pursuers in his attic room.

He was grabbed, lugged downstairs for what Baldersby called the kill. The sentence was in two parts: to run the gauntlet of wet-knotted towels, between two rows of junior officers across the ante-room floor, who lambasted him on head, shoulders, and back while cries of high delight came from them, while Baldersby sounded the mort-blast, and Jonah the Whale beside Hairy Harry Fridkin stood by the open door, much amused. It was Hairy Harry, Phillip learned later, who had, on both occasions, suggested to Baldersby the idea of the subalterns' court-martial. Phillip was glad that the towels were very wet, for they hid the marks of tears: tears not of pain, for the towels did not really hurt, but of loneliness.

The second part of the sentence was the more humiliating. He was ordered to stand naked upon the ante-room table, china pot in hand, and dance a jig. This he refused to do, so he was lifted up, while hands tore at the flannelette pyjama suit his mother had made for him, as he strained and pushed against them. Baldersby tried to crown him with the pot. Somebody—it was O'Connor, a spectator, holding towel in hand since, considering himself a guest of the battalion, he must make a token conformation with the ruling—shouted out "Steady!" Too late: the mind of the phrensied youth, as though torn across in response to the tear in the jacket his mother had sewn for him, momentarily passed into a lower stratum, where fear or death-thought ruled, akin to that which had screamed as a child under the cane of the father, to that which screamed out of men physically dislocated, mortally stricken upon the battle-field.

This fear, of one who had not learned to submit, charged nerves with power and muscles with strength, so that he writhed from the clutches of the laughing-weak, who received violent heel-blows upon chests and chins, catapult-like thrusts of legs straightening abruptly from bends, skull-butts in midriffs; and thus escaping from the worry, Phillip whizzed the pot sideways into the marble mantelpiece, where it shattered to many pieces.

He was lugged and tugged to the floor; so were many laughing subalterns, while Baldersby advanced, cigar between teeth, to add his weight to the *mêlée*. Phillip saw his light yellow shoes and managed to thump first one then the other on the toes with his clenched fist, making the senior subaltern howl and hop away, to the great amusement of Jonah the Whale and Hairy Harry Fridkin standing in the doorway. Major Fridkin saw Baldersby's discomfiture with a certain satisfaction: for if Phillip was an outsider, cause of anger and exasperation to Major Fridkin, he considered St. George Baldersby to be the fool of the regiment, and an over-bred nonentity: an attitude of interior scorn which may have had its origin in envy that Baldersby was the only member of the regiment, except Major the Hon. Arthur Wayland, whose particulars of family tree and pedigree, covering several centuries, appeared in Burke's *Peerage*, a copy of which, living on the colonel's desk, was frequently consulted by Major Fridkin, who longed to be armigerous.

He chuckled, cigar in mouth. "That will teach him not to chuck his weight about."

The adjutant agreed; while thinking that the outsider was putting up a dam' good fight.

Gasping and twisting, thrusting and sobbing, the culprit broke from the worry, and with one hand holding pyjama trousers, fled up the stone steps to the attic room. He would put in an application, in the morning, to return to the front: and this time he would take it to the orderly room. O'Connor followed him to the attic, and telling him not to take the ragging to heart, for it was all over, advised him to wash in cold water at the bathroom tap, put on his uniform, and come down to the ante-room.

"You acquitted yourself well, my boy. And we all have to go through a tempering at some time or other in our lives, to break the cast of our own conceit."

"Well, thank you, O'Connor, for what you did for me."

"Oh, 'tis very little, I'm thinking. But if you will take a tip, my boy, don't talk about the war, or the enemy. I know there is some truth in what you have been saying—after all, it is in *The Times* today, which hints that Sir John French himself has broken the news about the shell-shortage—but *timing* is important, indeed it is everything in life. A joke at a funeral will be in bad taste; the same joke at a coming-of-age party may cause a man to be considered the very soul of wit. Now to the bathroom, and don't forget a clean shirt, and hair brushed— it's wonderful how a change of linen can effect a change of mind."

Phillip, holding to the idea of going back to the front, felt strangely other than himself sitting next to Dimmock, who wore the magical two cloth pips sewn on his shoulder straps, and sipping a whiskey-soda that Dimmock had invited him to have. Most of the others had gone; unknown to Phillip, they were cleaning up the litter in the High Street outside.

Lieutenant Dimmock, who had come back sick from the B.E.F., after five weeks with the first battalion in a quiet sector around Arméntières, did his best to make the ranker officer see what was wrong with himself, as they sat somewhat uneasily side by side.

"Well, I don't want to preach, but when I heard that you had not been to school, I mean the kind of school most of us go to, with fags and prefects and particular codes—at Harrow if you turn up your trouser-ends in Lower School you get beaten, elsewhere if you don't turn them up you do, sort of thing—what was I saying?—Good luck!—Well, the best thing is always, when one is new in a job or school or 'varsity or regiment, to lie low, to conform like blazes, and certainly not to utter the first thought that comes into one's head, don't you know."

"I see."

"Where were you in France, by the way?"

"We went to Messines first, and then to Ypres."

"We were south of you, in the more industrial area, coal mines and all that sort of thing."

"Oh, I see. I say—er—well—I hope you won't mind my asking, but will you have a drink with me?"

"That's awful nice of you. There's just time before the hatch goes down. Just a small one this time, please."

The mess-sergeant was his usual gravely deferential, unsmiling self.

Phillip racked his brains what to talk about.

"Are you interested in motorcars—er—may I call you Dimmock?"

"Of course. No, not particularly. Why d'you ask?"

"I wondered, that's all. Well, cheer ho!"

"Here's luck!"

"Have you been in the Pigskin Club yet?"

"The Pigskin Club, I think, it is a place to avoid, really, unless one is really interested in bloodstock, and all that sort of thing, don't you know."

"Are you—er—Dimmock?"

"Oh yes, rather. It's in our midst all our lives, so to speak, friends, cousins, relations, you know, the horse is part of the life of the land."

After ten more minutes of this bleak conversation—Dimmock was not interested in birds, fishing, electricity, or chemistry—Phillip said he thought he would go to bed. Yet Dimmock seemed to want his company.

"Oh, must you, so early?"

Phillip wondered what was coming next. He found out the reason for Dimmock keeping him when he went into his bedroom. Somehow or other somebody had obtained another set of bedroom china-ware and chest-of-drawers; while his camp bed, although a bit twisted, stood with sleeping-sack laid upon it as before. What happened to Baldersby's things he did not think;

the idea did not occur to him until after the war that he should have made a gesture, at least, towards replacing them, and by that time Baldersby was dead, having been killed on the morning of his first day in action.

Dimmock's kindness gave Phillip hope again, he did not put in the application to be sent to the front. He was, of course, unaware that his other application had already gone through.

Now, in the late spring of 1915, the ivory hawthorn buds were dropping, blushet pink in death; nightingales sung out; nearly all the talk in the town bars was of the coming July Races. The marching companies with their yellow Japanese rifles passed strings of bloodstock, and saw the flying thin-legged centaurs on the turf. Songs rose above the dusty hedgerows—*It's a long, long trail a-winding, Into the land of my dreams*——

> Happy the soldier home, with not a notion
> How somewhere, every dawn, some men attack,
> And many sighs are drained.
> Happy the lad whose mind was never trained;
> His days are worth forgetting more than not.
> He sings along the march
> Which we march taciturn, because of dusk,
> The long, forlorn, relentless trend
> From larger day to huger night.

During the May Week inter-college boat races, held as usual for a fortnight in June, ladies appeared in Godolphin House for luncheon and tea, at the top table with the senior officers and their own particular friends in the regiment. The colonel had, before their appearance, addressed the junior officers on the matter of decorum. Among the visitors was a beautiful girl wearing a big picture hat, who was said to be going to marry Lieutenant Baldersby of Baldersby Towers, etc. She arrived with Mamma and Papa in a Rolls-Royce and they stayed at the Belvoir Arms Hôtel. How had Baldersby got such a peach of a girl, it was asked. The junior subalterns, warned to take no notice of the visitors, beyond the usual courtesies shown to guests of the regiment, took surreptitious glances and wondered among themselves in the ante-room afterwards.

The summery peace-time aspect of their lives received a jolt one day—when the names of four were posted on the ante-room board for Overseas. Rumour said Gallipoli, a place where all was not well. One of them was an attached officer, who was in Phillip's regiment.

By this time Phillip had learned more or less how to get from place to place on a horse, but it was still an embarrassment for him when it trotted, despite that he had learned to rise and fall in time, if not in harmony, with the rising of the various feet of the quadruped. He went over once or twice on horseback to the Green House, where he was now an old friend. A patch of oil was ever-fresh where *Helena* stood, against an out-house.

For some reason or other, he thought, Fairy fancied she was passionately in love with him. When he went over, as often as not her sisters left them alone, with the piano. Apparently she wanted to kiss him passionately sometimes on the lips, a procedure which embarrassed him. Hadn't he ever kissed a girl? she asked. No, he said. Had he ever *wanted* to kiss a girl? Not really, he replied. Had he ever kissed anyone? Only his mother; but it was so long ago he could not remember.

"Well, aren't you the strangest man! A heart of stone! I believe you hate me!"

"I like you. I say, do play that Chopin piece again, Fairy."

After playing, she looked at him as he knelt by her side to turn over the sheet music, and said, "You are the strangest person. You don't even seem to love your own self, let alone anyone else!"

"I hate myself."

Her hand moved to touch his head; but anticipating the move, he had already cried, "Good lord, I forgot to turn off my tap, and can smell the petrol dripping!" and hurried outside.

The July Races—during which the junior officers were warned by the colonel to keep clear of the Pigskin Club—arrived, and the town was filled with Rolls-Royces, Daimlers, and other majestic black landaus and landaulettes, many driven by chauffeurs in khaki; and one yellow Rolls, cheered by the stable lads when it passed down the High Street, the bewhiskered and genial figure of the Earl of Lonsdale sitting with his countess in the back.

After the races, Baldersby went away to be married. In the evening, redolent of ripening corn on the breeze, the captains

and the subalterns saw him off from the station. Bertram St[.]
George Baldersby, Esquire, in new barathea cross-woven uniform, sword and pistol attached to Sam Brown belt (he had been
persuaded by Jonah the Whale that these were indispensable
for any military wedding) and new flat hat which sat down low
and square on his forehead—making his eyes look almost fierce
under the peak—and new mustard-coloured puttees, was borne
to the station in the T-model Ford of Captain Wyman, said to
be the proprietor of two Electric Palaces, who wore the ends
of his moustaches waxed to rolled points. Where this captain
had come from Phillip did not know; he had appeared one day,
his kit in the Ford standing outside Godolphin House.

It was after mess-dinner: the sun yet glistened in the sky,
looking as though the day would never end, so timeless the
feeling, so far away the war. Captain Wyman's Ford held
fourteen men on its way to the station; eleven more followed in
a two-seater Singer belonging to someone else. Phillip rode on
the iron running-board of the Ford, holding on to Baldersby's
shoulder, while someone held to his belt strap, and someone
else to his collar.

"Oh, it's you again!" cried Baldersby, petulantly. Everyone
had been drinking champagne, toasting the lucky man. "Let
go, damn you!"

"I can't, I'll fall off if I do."

"Then fall off!" Baldersby puffed violently. Someone was
standing on his lap. The swaying load bumped on its flattened
springs.

"I can't! Someone's holding me, too!"

"Bah!" cried Baldersby, struggling in vain.

By this time Baldersby was the major joke of the mess; Phillip
the minor. The feeling of the send-off was part affectionate, part
scoffing. Baldersby looked to be a man who had lived much in
armour, with his strutting movements; his body, when seen in the
private swimming bath of Tonge Park, where subalterns had a
standing invitation to tea from the châtelaine, had appeared to
be the same width from top of chest almost to his knees. Yet
he was not fat; he was neither round nor rectangular; he was
Baldersby the man of ancestral armour, slightly scowling as
through a visor, long yellow moustaches turning down, long
hair of the same colour; his eyes, teeth, and big-toe nails, as he
stood for a dive on the edge of the bath—a belly-flop in the end—

all were noticeably yellow. The absence of all hair on the insides of his thighs showed where it had been worn away by friction against the ribs of horses.

Baldersby in the swimming bath of Tonge Park had swum slowly, on a breast stroke, puffing after Phillip to duck him in the traditional manner, in a horse pond. He succeeded, holding down the loathéd neck by a hand; but swallowing too much water himself, he was forced to let go. Phillip, all gasping over, bore Baldersby not the slightest ill-will. It was but another inexplicable act in the spree that was life.

The train came in. Baldersby stood there, flat hat, yellow boots, yellow puttees, sword scabbard scrubbed yellow and polished, not with saddle-soap (remarkable for a hunting man) but with light tan boot polish. There was no-one else in the train. Baldersby had it to himself.

The engine-driver waited, so did the guard. Watches, each as large as half a cricket ball, were consulted. Minutes sped by. At last the engine driver gave a little toot on his whistle.

"All right, all right," cried Baldersby, fluttering a hand. "Well so long, you fellers."

At this he was lifted up bodily to an open first-class carriage door, and flung in. Cheers as he got up, closed the door, leaned out, puffing his cigar.

"So long, you fellers."

"So long!" cried Phillip, with the others, cheering. Abruptly Baldersby left the window. Nor did he look out again. He was reading the newspaper he had brought with him for the journey —*The Pink 'Un*.

Phillip never saw him again. After his month's marriage leave, Baldersby went to the third battalion, then being formed under the command of Major Fridkin, soon to be promoted lieutenant-colonel. There Baldersby got his company, his longed-for third pip, and his own charger. On it he led his two hundred odd men on route marches; then another two hundred men; then another, and another; for it was a training battalion, feeding the two battalions at the front. At last, after the great battles of Somme, and the opening and middle stages of third Ypres, in the time of what was called the man-power shortage, Baldersby was sent out himself, and was killed almost immediately at the battle for Poelcapelle, one of scores of local battles, involving the British in 600,000 casualties, for the Passchendaele ridge overlooking the plain of the Scheldt, between the end of July and the beginning of December 1917. This was a little more than two years after Baldersby's marriage at the age of twenty-six; to Phillip in the summer of 1915, Baldersby seemed quite old.

Lieutenant-colonel Fridkin, five years older than Baldersby, saw out the war in England. For his services in training troops at home during the four years of the war he was awarded the Order of the British Empire, together with a foreign decoration: the Chinese Excellent Crop, 2nd Class, with Grand Cordon.

Chapter 16

ENDLESS POSSIBILITIES

MEANWHILE it was August 1915. Phillip was still haunted by the thought of having to return to the front. Cousin Willie, now commissioned, was in Gallipoli, of which many stories were told, of failure and disaster. Turkish snipers, their faces dyed green and their heads covered with grasses and twigs, were said to have been roasted after capture by the Australians; a division of second-line Lancashire territorials had broken at the recent Suvla landing, and stabbed the water-pipe from the off-shore barge, to fill their water-bottles: and the water had run into the sand. There was some talk, too, of a big push in France; two more subalterns in the mess had orders to proceed overseas, to join the first battalion. Soon the second battalion, it was said, was to fire its courses at the range near Southend, and then, with luck, go out as a unit.

He avoided the thought of far-off terrors by gadding about—never sitting still—always on the move lest something be missed in life that had no other horizon than death. He had no idea that he was escaping from his secret self, living in one dimension, from one moment to another moment, avoiding the thought of the length of his days.

Like a star, the thought of Desmond, his great friend, was fixed in his actual living, as the thought of Helena was fixed in his secret living, above his fears and uncertainties.

The gaiety of his friendship with Monty had gone after a

Saturday night and Sunday morning spent together at Southend-on-Sea, where they went, Monty on a Douglas motor-cycle, Phillip on his. They stayed in a cheap little house marked *Bed & Breakfast*, and on Sunday morning, as they packed their haversacks, Monty suggested that they creep out and leave without paying. At first Phillip thought this might be fun: then, thinking of the landlady's grey hair and thin face, rather like his mother's, he demurred. So the bill was asked for, and paid. Monty insisted that there would have been no risk; second loots like Phillip were two-a-penny, and who was to know where they had come from? Phillip felt rather inferior in Monty's eyes after that, coupled with the way Monty had sworn at him outside Ely; and the gay expeditions together seemed to be over.

Then there was a little trouble with the police, after a motor-cycle accident on the straight road across the Heath. The hell-for-leather Harley-Davidson owner, with whom Phillip had struck up a roadside acquaintance, was a subaltern in the Bucks, named Waterpark. He knew some people who lived in the red brick house among trees and stables lying off the Cambridge road. Waterpark, whose elder brother owned the racing Métallurgique, asked Phillip early one evening, when they stopped on the Heath for a chat astride their machines, if he would care to come to dinner with him at the House.

"The cove I was taking has just had his orders for overseas, and Mrs. Sweeting asked me to bring another cove. It's a pleasant little place, two jolly girls, still in the schoolroom of course, and they give you a good dinner. Old Sweeting trains the Royal String."

Greatly daring, for he suspected a trap, on the lines of *Downfall among Bad Companions* in the tableaux in Madame Tussaud's, Phillip said, "Thanks". What was a Royal String? Was it anything to do with a Royal Flush, like poker? A gambling house? What an experience to tell Mrs. Neville!

"I'll go back to the mess, and have a wash and brush up."

"Right. We'll meet here at seven."

As usual, Waterpark raced away on his twin Harley-Davidson, head down, eating up the road, as Monty said. Phillip dare not open his throttle wide, as the engine always began to vibrate, and cause a speed-wobble, at about forty-five. The Harley, with its high-compression pistons, could do over seventy.

He signed out for mess dinner, then went upstairs to change.

He left his money, except two shillings (possibly needed for a tip) in a drawer, just in case poker was the idea. He must be wary not to sign an IOU, which was legal tender, the new fellow in his room, drinking gin and water out of tooth-mug as he lay on his bed reading, told him in his dull voice.

This new fellow, called Flynn, was a curious fellow, Phillip thought. He was an undergraduate in his second year, and had recently been commissioned. Whenever Flynn could get a lift back to the university town, he went into the Blue Boar, and drank beer steadily. Flynn had a putty-coloured face, and long hair parted in the middle which often flopped over his eyes, which were dull grey. His hands were cold and damp. On his first night in the attic-room he had turned in his camp bed, while resting on an elbow, and muttered to Phillip in his thick voice that Phillip could do something to him if he liked, and then he'd do it to Phillip. Phillip pretended to have heard the word as "beggar", and replied with assumed innocence, "No thanks, I don't play cards for money."

"Who the hell's asking you to?" Flynn had growled, and Phillip saw that his putty face was sweating.

"Beggar my neighbour is a card game, isn't it?" said Phillip; whereupon Flynn repeated his offer, to which Phillip replied unconcernedly, "No thanks," and thought no more of it. Nor had Flynn mentioned it since. What Phillip did notice, however, was that Flynn was always wetting his bed.

Phillip told him that he was going out to dinner with strangers. Flynn grunted. "This town's full of four-flushers and three-card coves, so don't go getting into any fix-up. You really need me to look after you, you know."

"Oh, I'm only taking two bob. Well, cheer-ho."

He met Waterpark as arranged, and they went down the gravel drive to the house covered with Virginia creeper. The people inside seemed very quiet and nice. There were coloured pictures and engravings of race-horses, and many signed photographs in silver frames. He recognised Edward the Seventh, the Kaiser, George the Fifth, Queen Mary and others.

There was duck for dinner, and green peas that looked so very green that he wondered if they were doped. But more pressing was the problem, *Which way up ought the fork to be held?* Supposing he made a mistake? The thought was so painful that he decided not to take any peas.

"Oh, but they are just at their prime, the tomtits are beginning to peck the shucks! Won't you change your mind?"

"No thanks, really."

"Don't you like peas? And with duckling, Mr. Maddison?"

"Well, you see, the last lot I ate made me sick."

"Oh dear!"

The two girls, in white, long-haired with bows, were jolly sorts, he thought. By this time he realised that his fears about being lured to a gaming house were foolish, for these people obviously moved in very high society. Trying to make up for his awkwardness at table, sitting on his hands and hunching up his shoulders, he volunteered to sing songs at the piano in the drawing-room. Alas, he made a bigger fool of himself, choosing the *Indian Love Lyrics*, which he had heard sung only, but never sung himself; the result was rather like riding the white horse for the first time. To make it worse, he changed from tenor to bass, and blared out notes muffled in throat,

> *Less than the dust, beneath thy chariot wheels !*
> *Less than the rust which never stained thy sword ! !*
> *Less than the trust thou hast in me, my Lord ! ! !*
> *Even less am I, even less am I ! ! ! !*

They all clapped together, with smiling faces: perhaps it had not sounded too bad: so with elation he decided to give an encore of a different kind, his favourite poem *To a Skylark* by James Hogg, first heard when Uncle Hugh had recited it by his cot when he was nearly three, when the feeling in Uncle's voice had made his tears run in sympathy.

The words moved him now, with a feeling of all such things gone from his life, never to return: the lark singing high over the heather of Ashdown Forest, heard by Baldwin and his girl and himself on that Sunday before they had struck camp and gone to France. Were larks now singing over the graves of Baldwin and all the others upon the crest of Messines? And Uncle Hugh dead long ago, shrinking to skin and bone with cries of pain——

> *Then when the gloaming comes*
> *Low in the heather blooms*
> *Sweet will thy welcome and bed of love be.*
> *Emblem of happiness, blest be thy dwelling-place,*
> *O, to abide in the desert with thee !*

"You were a great success," said Waterpark, when they were outside after the goodbyes. "I think perhaps your métier is electrocution, or whatever the beastly word is, rather than singing. We must make our dinner call together in two days' time. Most hospitable people. Well, au revoir, many thanks for helping me out!" and leaping on his heavy brown machine, Waterpark rushed the dust away.

What happened afterwards was that he was blinding over the Heath, head down as usual, and did not see a motor coming towards him and went slap into it and the forks of the Harley were found somewhere near the flywheel of the motor car. Phillip heard the noise of impact half a mile away; and had to give evidence at the inquest. Afterwards he was served with a summons for not having the £1 annual licence required for a mechanically-propelled vehicle; and once again his name appeared in the local paper as a Young Blood in the Army Rushing About.

In mid-August the battalion entrained for a village near Southend-on-Sea to dig trenches and fire a musketry course. Several other regiments were in the district north of the Thames estuary. In one of the village pubs at night, in the saloon bar where some of the older junior officers, including Brendon, the Boer War gentleman-ranker, went after mess dinner, Phillip saw a most extraordinary officer. When first seen, as the Cantuvellaunians entered, he was seated on a chair in the little square room with the barmaid on his lap, one hand round her waist, the other holding a glass of stout. He made no attempt to alter his position as the half-dozen newcomers came in, but called out, "Cheero, cocks!"

The barmaid got up, a little flustered, to return behind the counter, thus enabling the row of variegated colours of medal ribands to be seen on the lieutenant's breast. There were yellows, reds, browns, blacks, and blues, an exotic section of butterfly-wings. He had a sort of butterfly-face, or a large caterpillar's, with his large black eyes, thin black moustache, little irregular teeth when he smiled, and parchment-rough texture of skin. Brendon, who wore the two ribands of the South African War, stared a lot at the fellow's ribands, Phillip noticed.

He was, it turned out, the adjutant of the Navvies Battalion of the Middlesex Regiment, recently formed by a Labour Member of Parliament, who had been made a lieutenant-colonel. Some of the navvies were to be seen in the district by day: many with grey hair, some very old and almost tottery, with campaign ribands going back to the Crimea, Ashanti, and long-forgotten Indian Frontier fights.

About the adjutant, Brendon was definite. He was, said Brendon, a sprucer.

"He's got both the Queen's and King's South African ribands up, *and* the Boxer Rebellion riband. Now to qualify for the King's medal you had to have two years' service in South Africa; and as the war lasted two years and four months, including the periods of transportation of troops from England, it isn't physically possible to have served two years there and to have got to China in time to get the Boxer medal. And there he is, with adjutant's pay and a captaincy in the offing, probably never having left the Liverpool docks, judging by his accent—and here am I, at the age of thirty-six, having to support myself, wife, and child on a second lieutenant's pay of seven-and-six a day, unable to afford even a second whiskey and soda."

After a while Phillip said, "Will you have a drink with me, Brendon?"

Brendon went on immediately. "Someone ought to tackle that fellow—Navvies battalion!—Fred Karno's Army!—You!" turning to Phillip. "Now there's the battalion for our prize young stumer, Maddison—he would fit in well there. As a soldier, Maddison is in that state known as *non est.*"

One more snub made little difference to Phillip: it was part of ordinary existence as he had known it from early consciousness: but it gave him an idea, that grew as he thought that the old navvies would spend the war digging trenches in England, or miles behind the front if ever they got so far as France. If only he could get into the battalion, he would be able to spend the rest of the war behind the lines!

He went to see the navvies' adjutant, who was billeted at the pub. He greeted Phillip as "Old Cock", accepted a double gin and tonic, and then said, "Well, what's your trouble?"

Phillip explained.

The adjutant said that he was expecting to be given the second-in-command of the reserve navvies' battalion about to be formed, and at the moment was officer in command of the detachment preparing a defensive line under the sappers; so at the moment he could do nothing.

"I'll tell you what, old cock. I'll give you the colonel's name and address in a moment, it's Alexandra Palace, near the race-course, you know, north of London, but we're leaving there any moment. When you write and ask for an interview, lay on the soft soap, but be regimental at the same time—if you follow my meaning—it can be done, cock, both ways, like most things in life, though some "—he bumped Phillip with his elbow, and leered—"can be done in a variety of positions, eh? Don't you agree?—to resume, cock—write the letter, say you were with the Londoners in France, no, don't say that, he'll think you're a skrimshanker, which you probably bloody well are, like the rest of us, but eyewash, cock, eyewash every time! Well, write your letter, see; and I'll put a word in for you, I'm going to Alexandra Palace in two days' time—and when I get to be second-in-command of the reserve battalion, I'll see you get a company, promoted to captain, how's that, cock?"

Phillip was delighted. He could hardly believe it. He didn't really believe it. There was the Boxer riband in the row, after the King's South African. He was a bit of a sprucer. He knew it when the other went on:

"I have some expenses to meet, in connection with forming the new battalion—comforts for the old boys' families you know—bless 'em, the old cocks booze every penny of their pay, and regularly forget to send a bit home—anyhow, an adjutant is out of pocket as often as not, with this and that, guests in the mess, et cetera. So how about fifty quid, worth it, isn't it, for a captaincy? Not now, cock—don't get me wrong—I'm not one of the fly boys!—later, when your transfer's through, not before, and you actually see your name—I'll tell you what I'll do— listen—— You give me five pun' now, to get the colonel's recommendation for the transfer. I suppose your C.O. will let you go?"

"Oh yes, I am sure he would, sir."

"Righto, cock. Five bradburys, and you're in, Meredith, you're in! Then when you're in, another twenty and you'll be in the second battalion soon to be split off from the first. Right, cock. Then when you see your promotion in the orderly room, going up to Eastern Command with the colonel's signature, the rest of the dough. And if you ever split, I'll deny every bloody word of it, and it'll be your word against mine. I'm no pushin' plaster saint, nor are you, so it's fifty-fifty, cock, are you on?"

"Can I get my transfer first, sir, and then think about it?"

"'Course you can! Tell you what, gimme coupla brads now, and I'll let you off the rest of the five pun'!"

Phillip gave him two one-pound notes, and took the name and address of the commanding officer. "And don't forget to put Em Pee after his name—he will be reminded of his constituents, and that will help your application, cock."

The next morning he went to see Captain Whale in the temporary orderly room. The adjutant said smoothly he did not think that the colonel would raise any objection: so Phillip sent off his letter to the address given him, and awaited results.

A week later, when they had returned to Godolphin House, a reply came. He was informed that a personal interview would be granted between the hours of 2 p.m. and 4 p.m. on the Saturday. Captain Whale gave him leave until Sunday midnight, and off he went, prepared for another weekend with Desmond, and possibly Eugene as well. Eugene was now in the Public Schools' battalion of the Royal Fusiliers, according to a letter from Desmond.

On his motor-cycle he drummed happily south, rubber belt smoothing away engine vibration, and in sunny weather came to Alexandra Palace. Everyone was still at lunch, apparently. Learning from one of the navvies, who clumsily saluted him, lifting up his whole shoulder and tunic with his arm, showing thickened, dispread fingers, that the "blokes" were billeted under "yon tall grandstand" of the adjoining race-course, Phillip thought he would take a squint at the rest of the blokes of whom he fondly hoped before very long to be a company-commander. What luck he had! Twelve shillings and sixpence a day, captain's pay, plus three shillings command pay, plus half-a-crown field allowance while under canvas or unfurnished billet—eighteen bob. He worked out that it would cost him fifty-five and a half days' pay to work off the bribe to Lieutenant Merrit. Well, it would be worth it. There might be a chance, too, of buying and selling motor-cycles, as he had the O.K. Junior. It was a good little bus, worth £22 10s. he had charged Chick, who had resold it to Flynn for twenty pounds, just before

Flynn, who had moved into Chick's room, had mysteriously resigned his commission.

He walked across the turf and peeped in a door in the boarded wall of the cutting under the grandstand. A smell reminiscent of Mr. L. Dicks coming into the office in Wine Vaults Lane smote him, of shag and thick-twist, beer and ammonia, sweat and feet. While he stood there several ancient shaggy-haired men, all wearing old-style forage-caps, came out of the opposite door and saluted him with varying goggle-eyed rather pathetic uncomfortable awkwardness. Then without further ado they faced the wooden wall in a row and urinated with the simplicity of horses.

"What are you chaps working on just now?" asked Phillip, when they had finished.

"Nought," replied one.

"It's pay day s'arternoon," explained another.

"Do you carry rifles?"

"Nah! On'y belts."

"I see. Do you have any leave?"

"Yus, when we feels like it."

"Don't you have to have a pass?"

"No, we pays our own fares, allus 'as."

"I mean, surely you only go home when given leave?"

"Not 'ere. Nobody don't stop us."

"Then you're absent without leave, aren't you?"

"Aye, an' th' ganger stops our pay."

"Who's the ganger?"

"The boss."

"Colonel Broad?"

"That's right!"

Phillip hung about until half-past three, when the colonel arrived in an open two-seater Vauxhall, driven by a small dark second-lieutenant. He was a big, heavy man with a large red face, wearing a service cap that looked as though it had been sat upon. He got out without a word, slammed the door behind him, gave the briefest hand-lift in return for Phillip's salute, and disappeared, loose chains of spurs jingling, into one of the Palace doors.

"That's a nice 'bus," remarked Phillip, eyeing the Vauxhall.

The small officer said with modest pride, "She's a Prince Henry."

"Is it Colonel Broad's?"

With some diffidence (he had a slight lisp), the other replied, "As a matter of fact, she belongs to me. I'm a sort of A.D.C. to the colonel. You're joining us, aren't you?"

"I hope so. I met your adjutant, Lieutenant Merrit, near Southend."

The small officer's face went blank; then looking on the ground he said, "Is he a great friend of yours?"

"Not exactly."

"Well, if you'll not mind me saying it, don't mention his name to the colonel."

"Isn't he very popular?"

"Well, hardly."

"Where is he, here?"

"Oh no, he's left."

"Left? How d'you mean?"

"Scotland Yard arrested him."

"Good lord! What for?"

"Bigamy, dud cheques, selling Army stores to civilians—all that sort of thing."

The little officer was leaning an arm on the bonnet of his motor car as he spoke in a matter-of-fact voice, without a smile, as though what he was saying was quite normal and ordinary. Phillip was about to ask for more particulars, when a sergeant with spectacles and two rows of ill-fitting yellow false teeth, came out of a door and said, "Is your name Maddison? The colonel will see you now!"

"Good luck," said the owner of the Vauxhall.

Colonel Broad sat at a desk, his great knees spread wide because it was too small for him. His flat hat lay on the desk with his gloves inside it. He had been a navvy on the yellow clay of London, with generations of endurance in his bones, and power in the strength of his back: centuries spent in skill of digging clay, in all weathers: none more hardy in the United Kingdom. By virtue of fist and gab he had become leader of his gang, from which he had developed to position of agitator for better pay, otherwise better conditions; thence to Trade Unionism, and a seat in Parliament (where he was known, among certain Tory Members, as the Buck Navvy) representing a working-class constituency on the flat clay lands of East London, once West Essex. A civilian one day, he was a lieutenant-colonel the next.

Pale blue eyes above moustaches waxed and rolled to considerable horizontal extensions looked intently at Phillip.

"Why do you want to transfer to us?"

"I fought with many ex-navvies at Ypres, sir, and miss them
in the battalion where I am now."

"If you like the company of ex-navvies so much why don't you
apply to go back to them in France?"

Phillip returned the gaze of the eyes regarding him steadily.
He did not know what to say.

"I'll tell you, shall I? You've got the wind up, and don't
want any more. All your chums gone west, and though you
miss 'em, you don't miss 'em enough to want to follow 'em to
where they've gone, eh? Am I right?"

Phillip thought it wise to agree.

"Get your present C.O. to forward your application to me
and I'll sign it and send it on."

"Thank you, sir!"

Outside the little officer said, "I knew you'd get your transfer.
The colonel showed me your letter. He said it showed sense. He's
quite a decent old boy. Did Merrit borrow money from you?"

"Yes."

"He did from me, too. And one or two others."

"Promising a company?"

"Yes."

"A pal of mine spotted that he was a sprucer, since he wore
the Boxer riband *and* the King's South African. You couldn't
get both, at the same time."

"He wasn't entitled to any of those medals. But he is to a long
police record."

"How did he get into your lot?"

"Bluff. He appeared in the mess one day—been formed a
week or two, three officers then—and said he was an expert on
catering. He took charge, and the colonel gave him a commission.
But he sold back to the grocer half the food he bought for us."

"Good lord, what a nerve!"

"Well, I must go now. I've got to take Miss Broad shopping
in Regent Street. See you again, I hope! Cheerio."

"Rather! Cheer-ho!"

Reaching the City, Phillip thought he would go down to
Old Ford and see his Aunt Dora. She was not there. Sylvia

gave him a cup of tea. She said Dora and she had come to the parting of the ways.

"The use of gas at Ypres shook her, then the *Lusitania* sinking apparently decided her. She sees the war as justified. She believes it is being fought on our side solely to eradicate Prussian militarism. She believes in the current cant of a new world *after* the war. What do you think of that, Phillip?"

"I really haven't thought much about it, to tell the truth."

"No, you're young yet, Phillip. Well, I shall keep on, providing a platform for our people, should they wish to end this murderous slaughter of the innocents. I suppose you're not sent here to incriminate me, are you? No, I'm sorry. The Home Office *does* send agents round now and again, you know. Well, dear boy, give my love to Dora if you see her. Oh no, we haven't quarrelled. I think, actually, Dora feels she has let me down. Still, even steel crystallises in the end, you know. Goodbye, and do look in again, won't you?"

Partridges flew in coveys over the big fields of stubble, the clover leys and pastures of a countryside whose life was very much the same as before the war. *Business as usual* was the national motto: sport as usual, too. Major Fridkin seemed to be shooting almost every day, and bringing back to Godolphin House rows and rows of partridges strung by their necks on split carrying-frames, which were sold to the mess. Captain Baldersby and his tweed-clad wife stayed at the Belvoir Arms, and went shooting too, with dogs, and two khaki loaders. In the mess there was cold partridge, both English and French, for breakfast; and various forms of partridge, broiled and roast, for dinner. "Awful good little feller, perdix perdix," remarked "Strawballs". "A cold bird makes the best breakfast in the world. Awful good eating."

Phillip wanted to agree but thought it better not to speak. He did not want any hitch to occur in his transfer to the navvies' battalion. "Strawballs" had signed the recommendation, and it had gone up to Eastern Command.

After parade one afternoon in the second week of September he decided to go over to the Green House, and tell Fairy. He had said nothing so far, as he did not want to upset her. The strange thing was that her sister still seemed to think that they were in love. "What a pity you two did not meet earlier, Phil."

He had not said or done anything to lead anyone to assume that he loved her, so why that remark? He had thought before that, as she was married, she could not possibly fall in love with anyone else.

Phillip's ideas of love had come almost entirely from stories in magazines published by the commercial houses of Pearson, Newnes, Harmsworth and Castleton, mainly for the urban masses of the industrial revolution educated to read and write in board schools. A sense of respectability and unreality permeated such stories, in which there was no kiss until the end, when several usually called smothering or devouring were "planted" on feminine hair, brow, hands and even feet; seldom on the lips, and never on the mouth. No editor of lower middle-class morality or respectability would have printed the word *mouth* in the context of romance except when a heroic fist crashed upon that of cad and villain.

It was all a little awkward: to avoid her cloying love, to sidestep her accusations that he was playing with her, that he was heartless and yet such a dear boy, to reassure her that she was pretty, sweet, and neither bold nor brazen. She asked what was *really* the matter, had he any secret he wanted to tell her, frankly, what was it about her that made him so shy?

"Nothing, Fairy, really."

"Do you think it is wrong to kiss anyone if they are married?"

"I don't know, I've never thought about it."

He pretended innocence, not to hurt her feelings.

"There you are again! I simply don't understand you."

"I don't understand myself."

"You are laughing at me all the time, I think. Ah, I heard you sigh."

"It wasn't me, it was the ghost of a hare shot by old 'Hairy Harry' Fridkin. I had it for lunch."

"Oh, do be serious. You are not thinking of Basil, are you?"

Phillip was not; but it was a way out. "Well, sort of, you know——" Supposing her husband came home on unexpected leave, and suddenly looked in at the window?

"You think it is dishonourable to kiss a married woman?"

"Oh no. I have often done so."

"Who was she?"

"My Father's wife."

"Idiot! Is it that girl you told me about?"

"Good lord, no! I seldom see her. She doesn't care a damn for me."

"Nor does Basil for me! So we are in the same boat, Phil, aren't we?"

Oh no, we are not, he thought; but said, "Judging by those letters you showed me—pages and pages of them—Basil loves you desperately!"

"So that is what is in your mind! Look at me, Phil! No, don't turn away! Do you think me a vamp?"

"How could I, when vamps are dark. Theda Bara, you know, and Nazimova."

"Well, that's one thing in my favour, since I am freckled and have carroty hair."

"It's not carroty, it's tawny, it has the gloss of the fox."

"Phil, don't mock me. I'm utterly serious. I told you I made a terrible mistake in marrying Basil. Oh, you think me shameless, don't you?"

"Not at all. But I think you are a flirt!"

She stared at him with face seeming thinner, the high cheekbones more prominent, as she grasped his elbow at arm's length. He thought she was putting it on. Then his feelings of dismay and satisfaction and faint scorn changed to dismay when he saw the tears in her eyes. She sprang up, biting her lips, and ran from the room. What an account he would be able to give Mrs. Neville and Desmond when he saw them! He was seeing life!

The thought of sharing this life with his friends in the flat lasted only a moment before he felt sorry for her. When her younger sister came in and sat on the sofa, he felt ashamed; and unhappy when she said, "Phil, be honest with me. You don't really care for my sister, do you?"

"Yes, I do," he said, sitting on his hands. "But I can't feel what I can't feel, can I?"

"You like her as a friend only?"

"I suppose so. I wish she were my sister, and you, too, Estelle. You're both so gay, and good fun to be with."

"Well, Phil, perhaps then it would be for the best if you didn't come here any more. Please don't look so hurt. I am thinking of Fairy, you see. She was always a highly-strung girl, and Father being what he is, always irritable, made her worse. That's why she married, really, to get away."

"I know, she told me."

"And marrying someone older than herself——"

"Out of the frying-pan into the fire."

"Well, in a way, yes; for now she is in the fire. She's desperate about you, Phil. Don't treat her as a plaything, will you?"

All he could think of saying was, "Why, when I am so ugly and thin and stupid?"

"That's your modesty. You're really terribly attractive."

He tried to stop his mouth from being loose and sloppy; and sat with a straight face beside her on the sofa. They both laughed. She was fuller-bosomed than Fairy, who was slim; he boggled at the word *flat*. Yet Fairy was very pretty, so alive and intelligent. Estelle was rather sly, he thought. Had Monty and she——? Monty was away at the moment, on holiday with his actress *fiancée*, who was rather like a Barribal girl, tall and fresh, dark, round reddish cheeks, a fringe, small round hat, many billowy blue diaphanous scarves floating around her neck.

He felt a flow between Estelle, with her white face and warm brown eyes and hair and bosomy white silk blouse, and himself. Awful! He was a Don Juan really. Mrs. Neville's remark, *Every woman at heart is a rake, Phillip. Could* they be like men?

"Yes, you're right, I'd better go."

"No, you mustn't do that," as she put a warm hand on his wrist. Again the trickle of fire.

"Have a whiskey? Help yourself."

Fortified by the slightly nauseating liquid, he told her that at any moment he would be leaving to join his new crowd.

"But -you won't be far away? You'll have leave? You'll come and see us, won't you?"

How awful of him, he wanted to embrace her! He was restraining himself when Fairy came suddenly into the room. She wore another frock, dark green, with a pale necklace of coral around her slender neck. She had brushed her hair. He noticed silk stockings, also dark green, very daring.

"Titania, how sweet you look," he said, feeling an ass's head over his own. "Haw, haw, Fairy. Your health!" He waved the glass.

She became serious and still when he told her about his transfer. At last she said, when Estelle had gone to prepare the supper in the kitchen, "And you never told me! Oh, Phil! You didn't trust me."

The postman knocked a double rap on the knocker. She ran out, returned with two thick wadded envelopes, said tragically, "You see? Every post almost, they come like this. What can I do?"

After another large whiskey and soda, he said, "Don't cry, Fairy. I do understand, really. Look, I'll write to you when I go away, though it may not be for months yet. But I'm not what you think me, you know. I'm really a throw-back. They say you can tell a man's real nature by how he is at home, well, I am simply *awful* at home. I dislike my father, I contradict my mother, I don't really care about my sisters. They aren't my sort, or I theirs. You once said I love no-one, not even myself. Well, it's true. I used to love birds, and the spring; but that has gone. I don't know why, but it just has. That's the real me, and also I'm cowardly. I'm only going to the navvies' battalion to avoid going back into that hell out there. Now you know! May I help you to some whiskey? I wish you'd let me buy you a bottle, I drink all yours up, you know."

"Don't talk like that, dear. You are honest, that is all. That is why I like you so much. And you are really very brave."

He scoffed; and emptied his glass.

"Oh no! I wangled my way home from France, you know. I bribed an orderly ten bob to be marked 'Bunk'. The real chaps, the really honest ones, like Cranmer, my old pal I told you about, and Baldwin, and Elliott, and the Wallace brothers, they're still out there. They had guts. I've got no guts. Now you know."

He poured himself another whiskey.

She went to the piano and played Chopin. She saw his glistening eyes when she had finished and sat beside him, holding his hand.

"Phil, dear, I am so glad you told me."

She sat at the piano, and began singing in a light, sweet voice the popular song of the moment, *They'd Never Believe Me*. Phillip knelt by the piano to turn over the music; but though she tried to make him sing, he was too shy of his voice. Besides, there was Helena . . .

He arrived back, without lights, just after midnight, ready with an excuse: he would say he thought he heard Zeppelins.

He had an acetylene lamp but no fresh carbide. No trouble; a wide and forsaken High Street. He stood his machine against the side-wall and went into Godolphin House. It was silent. A parallelogram of gas-light on the floor of the mess-room came from the open ante-room door. He went in, and saw the adjutant, Jonah the Whale, asleep in an armchair, snoring slightly, head back, long legs in tight Indian-cavalry breeches, and Tom Hill canvas leggings tightly buttoned to above thin ankles of long pointed brown boots.

Phillip stood there a moment, wondering if he should creep away to bed. He was filled with fear. Why had he done it? What would happen to him now? Supposing it happened to him what had happened to Uncle Hugh, and Uncle George Lemon? He might be done for.

Jonah the Wale opened an eye. He sat up, stifled a yawn.

"Hullo, I've been waiting up for you. Your orders have come through."

Before he could think, Phillip gasped out his fears. Jonah the Whale stared at him.

"But how do you know? You *are* a young ass! See the doctor in the morning, and for heaven's sake don't go blurting it out to others as you have to me. You're a case, you know, you really are! Well, you won't have much time. You have to report on Tuesday at ten pip emma to the senior draft officer at Victoria Station, and "—he looked at his watch—"it is already midnight. So you'll have to get a move on, young feller."

"Victoria Station, sir? Aren't I going to the—I mean to say, isn't it my transfer——?"

"I forwarded your application some time ago to return to the front, and assume that this has had priority over your later application for transfer. I have waited up specially to tell you in case you want to leave early in the morning. The first train to London leaves at six-thirty ack emma. I've warned your batman to come here at five, to pack up your things. The Maltese cart will be outside at six, to take your valise to the station. And take my advice, leave married women alone in future! Especially when they have husbands serving away from home, doing their duty by their country." The adjutant turned away.

Phillip did not know what to say.

Captain Whale went out of the mess, after a curt "Good

night". Phillip said "Good night, sir"; whereupon Captain Whale returned to say, tersely, "You might at least have the courtesy to say 'thank you' when a fellow stays up on your behalf! After all, it's only good form!"

"Sir!" said Phillip, coming to attention. "Thank you very much indeed for waiting up on my behalf."

"Don't mention it," said Jonah the Whale, adding without tension, yet still with a terse tone, "On second thoughts, you'd better, in view of what you've just told me, catch the later train, after seeing the M.O., who will fix you up."

"Very good, sir."

"Now don't be an ass in future! And when you get to your new unit, keep your thoughts to yourself! Be modest and quiet in manner!"

"Yes, sir."

"And do what you're told without questioning higher authority. Remember the saying, 'Speech is given us to conceal our thoughts'," concluded the county auctioneer.

"Yes, sir."

"Stand easy, for heaven's sake! This isn't the orderly room."

Jonah the Whale looked at the ingenuous face before him and said, not unkindly, "We all have to learn, you know, and there is no easy way to knowledge. Come and see me after you've seen Old Sawbones, and I'll give you your travelling warrant."

Phillip left on his motor-cycle, his valise having been sent by train labelled *Victoria Station*, after luncheon the following day. He was surprised at his send-off. Everyone was really quite decent, some even wanted to shake him by the hand. "Strawballs" was quite genial, in a massive sort of way, and both his and the handclasp of Major Howes were really meant, he felt. The face of "Hairy Harry" Fridkin, now with lieutenant-colonel's badges up, cigar as usual in suction, was inscrutable as ever. He had not spoken a word to Phillip in all the time he had been with the battalion; and he said nothing now, as he sat at table while the subalterns came out on the pavement or crowded the windows, eager to see the last of the cause of much amusement. O'Connor said, "Take care of yourself, my boy"; there were cries of "Good luck!" as he pushed off for the run and vault into the saddle.

Phillip, feeling himself almost to be liked, opened the throttle wide; there was an explosion in the coffee-pot, which blew off; and to laughter and cheers, part derisory, part affectionate, he sped away up the hill, retarding the spark to produce the loudest reports in the open exhaust, while sitting athwart the saddle in order to glance back and wave until the faces were out of sight.

Part Three

THE BATTLE OF LOOS
"A real British Victory at Last!"
(Headline in *The Daily Trident*, 27 September 1915)

Chapter 17

THE COCKEREL

DURING the past month of August many aspects of the coming campaign on the Western Front had been discussed among the privileged in London. It was known that, after the corn harvest was in, a major attack in the Champagne Pouilleuse was to be launched by the French, simultaneously with a minor thrust on their northern flank, in the sector of Artois recently taken over by the British. This northern thrust was to draw the German reserves away from the main attack by the French.

By the end of July the doubts of the British commander-in-chief, Field-Marshal Sir John French, concerning the ability of the troops under him to carry out such an attack, were generally known. Also known was the matter of dissension between the "Soldiers" and the "Frocks"—between the Imperial General Staff and the Prime Minister's Cabinet. The field-marshal had declared that the British Army in the field was exhausted after the wasting spring battles of Neuve Chapelle, Second Ypres, Aubers Ridge, and Festubert: that the recently-formed Territorial divisions, and the divisions of the New Army required further training—particularly the men of the New Army, who were without experience even of static trench warfare: that the heavy artillery, and reserve of shells (due to diversion to Gallipoli), were insufficient to reduce the German defences in the heavily-fortified coal-mining area of Artois, with its pit-heads and dominating spoil-heaps held by the enemy between La Bassée Canal on the north and the ridge of Nôtre Dame de Lorette on the south.

The field-marshal's protest had been over-ruled by the Cabinet.

The field-marshal had made further protest. In this he was joined by General Sir Douglas Haig, commanding the 1st Army. Both commanders were opposed to committing untrained troops to battle before the spring of 1916. Again the protests were over-ruled by Downing Street. The German successes in Russia demanded a relieving attack in France.

Among the "Frocks"—the term for politicians in use among some generals at the "War House" held a suggestion of derision—there was dissension, too: Mr. George, as the new Minister for Munitions was contemptuously known in the Tory houses and clubs, "the intriguing little Welsh lawyer", was trying to unseat the P.M., Herbert Asquith, who, though a new-comer, *and* a Liberal, at least had the manners and appearance of a gentleman. Mr. George characteristically was running with the hare of the commander-in-chief, and the hounds of the Cabinet. At the dinner-table and in the *salon* the facts were discussed and passed on, until the facts became rumours in the politer suburbs; to die out in those areas where the L.C.C. electric trams began their runs, where the war to most people was a simple matter of right and wrong, as they had been told by their betters, *via* newspapers.

Heading for the south-eastern suburbs, Phillip on battleship-grey *Helena*, O.H.M.S. in white letters boldly displayed across front forks, thudded around Trafalgar Square for the joy of hearing his open exhaust and taking various salutes; but none from a bunch of Australians, who were lounging against the pedestal of one of the bronze lions. Seeing one grinning at him, Phillip stopped, leaned the machine on a pedal against the kerbstone, and approached them. They were in slouch hats and long overcoats—tall, thin men, very wiry, with sun-burned faces. They watched unmoving as he came up to them, and said, "Good morning! May I enquire why you fellows never salute an officer?"

After an impassive regard of him, one of the Australians tapped him on his collar-bone: "Are *you* an officer, sonny?"

"Yes, can't you see I am?"

The tall soldier turned to his mates. "Can you see an officer, cobbers? Look around, can you see one anywhere?"

They shook their heads, and the spokesman said, "We don't see no officer, sonny."

"It's the uniform you salute, not the person, let me tell you fellows."

"Is that so? Now tell me, ain't you still in diapers?"

As he stood his ground, another Australian spoke. "Aw, git yourself an eyeglass, Archibald! We've come from where there's bin fightin'. Salute you? 'Archibald, certainly not!'"

Phillip, although slightly flattered by this reference to himself as a music-hall toff, felt he had had the worst of it; and continuing around Trafalgar Square, an idea made him laugh, so stopping at an optician's in the Strand, he bought a gold-rimmed monocle. Screwing it into his right eye, he returned to the area of the lions, dismounted, and walked to the Australians. Before the group he came to attention, and saluted them.

"That's because you've been in Gallipoli, cobbers!" Leaving them both unmoving and unspeaking, he vaulted on his machine and continued slowly, with soft-pumping engine, down Whitehall and so to Westminster Bridge, the flag on its post showing that the House of Commons was sitting. A newsbill *Artillery Duel in Champagne* quickened his sense of personal drama, and opening the throttle, with resounding reports from the open exhaust pipe he flew between the tramlines, feeling that the spectators might be thinking what he was fancying for himself: a thrilling rôle of carrying down the Dover Road urgent dispatches to be rushed by destroyer across the Channel, and so to G.H.Q.— "Ah, Maddison, how weary and travel-stained you are! But you have saved the day, as the London Highlanders did at Messines!" He had to slow up, to rescrew the monocle into his eye-socket, owing to the uneven cobble stones of Peckham Rye.

The sense of the dramatic began to leave him as he continued along the Old Kent Road, and turned up to Nunhead, to avoid the tramlines. Passing Wakenham Station, with its dreary, dead appearance, he removed the monocle and put it in his pocket, after a small boy had called out, "Swank on Old Iron!" Soon he was home; and trying not to feel overcome by dullness.

This time he would not go and say goodbye to the Rolls. He would let Helena learn the news of his return to France when he was gone: it would, then, perhaps, startle her into realising that she might lose him.

"Thank God that Desmond and Eugene will be home this evening, Mother."

"You won't be late dear, will you, as it's your last night? And Father will want to see you, I am sure."

That night in Freddy's it seemed natural that he should again and again pay for drinks for all three. Were they not all great friends? Eugene was in the Public Schools battalion of the Royal Fusiliers, and, like Desmond, a private soldier. "You coves are my guests—when you get your pips, you can treat me." Tom Ching came in, and then there were four of them. The more the merrier!

Tom Ching, still in the Admiralty, told them that all postal and telegraphic communication abroad was suspended, for— Tom rolled his eyes around the bar, before gathering their faces close to his own—there was to be a big landing on the Belgian coast, after a terrific bombardment by battleships and monitors of the Fleet. It seemed to be the Big Push at last; and visualising the German lines broken, with cavalry in pursuit, and hundreds of thousands of prisoners taken—the war over by Christmas— Phillip, monocle screwed into eye, convinced himself, with the aid of Haig's whiskey, that he was jolly glad to be going out again.

A few minutes before closing time "Sailor" Jenkins suddenly appeared, yachting cap on head, special-constable arm-band sticking out of greatcoat pocket.

"Hullo, Phillip! Your father told me you were home, and returning to the front tomorrow. Well, at least you'll be away from the dull routine of business life today. Which isn't being made any more cheerful, between ourselves, Phillip, by our sergeant's behaviour. I can fully understand now why you, as a boy, were a caution! It's 'not the thing' to pop in and have a quick one on a cold night, or to smoke a cigarette on duty, alone at midnight on a clear night, in case Zeppelins spot it! I ask you! Then if we talk about the war while inside the station—*inside*, mark you—he points to the poster hanging there, 'The ears of the enemy may be listening', and says it is our duty to give a good example to others. No, your father is not at all popular, I can tell you, Phillip. What's the eye-glass for, effect?"

"King's Regulations," replied Phillip, casually. "Have to see the enemy, you know."

"Go on with you!" replied Mr. Jenkins, as he upped his hot sugared Irish whiskey, and dabbing lips with silk handkerchief, he pulled the arm-band out of his pocket and slipped almost furtively out of the bar.

"Damn bad form," said Phillip, imitating Baldersby, as the door closed. "No idea of good form."

The next morning at breakfast he told his father what Tom Ching had said about the coming bombardment of the Belgian coast.

"Well," said Richard, as he laced up his boots, "all I can say is that I do not think that Master Ching has any right to disclose official secrets, especially in the place where apparently you met him last night."

"But the Germans surely knew as soon as the first shell dropped, Father? The *communiqués* have mentioned the Belgian coast bombardment for days, now."

"That is as it may be, my boy; but I am still of the opinion that official matters should not be disclosed. Well, Phillip," he said with sudden geniality, rising and holding out his hand, "I wish you all good fortune, and a safe return. Look after yourself, old man, won't you?"

Then taking his yellow straw hat—cleaned most carefully with an old toothbrush and salts of lemon every May Day for the past twenty years, the black band having been renewed twice in that period—and with umbrella on arm, Richard left the house. He thought of many things as, half an hour later, he crossed London Bridge for the nine thousand two hundred and eightieth time (he kept count annually in his diary)—this lonely, honourable, and stilted member of Outer London's middle-classes—believing all he read in his newspaper, impelled by what to him were the Victorian precepts of right living, punctilious in everything concerning the letter of his duty, at home and in the office; meticulous often to the point of pain—guarding ever, within his scope, the idea of his family's, and his country's, well-being.

Phillip was given an extra twenty-four hours' leave when, reporting at the R.T.O.'s office at Victoria Station, he agreed to take a draft to France the following day. Leaving his valise in the cloak-room, he hurried home. Although Desmond would be on searchlight duty that night and Eugene had gone back to camp, yet there would be friendly faces in Freddy's.

He was passing the gate of Turret House when he saw Mrs. Rolls, and had saluted her when, in the friendliest tones, she said, "You used to be a great one for birds, Phillip, I wonder if you could tell me how to pluck a cockerel?" Where did one begin, she asked, explaining that her cook had gone home to her mother the day before, after hearing that her only brother had been killed in Gallipoli.

"Gerard will be home at six, and I must give him a good dinner, dear boy, after his hard day's work, now that so many of the younger men have gone. Then there is the question of drawing it—I've never had to do such a thing in my life before, Phillip, and how fortunate that you came along when you did."

"Mrs. Rolls," said Phillip, going hot with the thought of his boldness, "I mean—if you like, that is, if it would help in any way—I'd be glad to do it for you."

"Would you? How very kind of you!"

"I'd like to, really."

He was invited into the house: it was the first time he had been inside, and everything seemed unreal. What would he be able to say when he came face to face with Helena? The sight of her hat and coat hanging on the coat-rack, with her tennis racquet, string bag of balls, and white plimsolls, made him quiver.

"Come through, Phillip, to the kitchen—d'you mind?"

Passing an open door, he saw within a piano and the music of *They'd Never Believe Me*. With racing heart he imagined Helena singing the song, thinking of him. In a dream he followed Mrs. Rolls into the kitchen.

"We can put some newspapers on the table. Or would you like to sit in the garden—of course you would! It's such a lovely day, isn't it? So you are on leave, are you? What has happened to your motor-cycle—what a noise it makes, to be sure."

"I've stored it at a place in the Lee High Road, where I bought it, Mrs. Rolls."

Mrs. Rolls did not appear to hear. She took a large basket, and put some paper in the bottom. "There now, do you think that will do for the feathers. We ought to collect them, don't you think? For the hospitals."

"For pillows?"

"Yes. Helena's Red Cross Party has asked for feathers, among other things. Poor boys, we must do all we can to make them comfortable, mustn't we? Now then, you would like a rug to sit on, wouldn't you?"

"Oh, please don't bother. I can sit on the grass, really."

"It is damp, Phillip. I wouldn't hear of such a thing! You always were a wild boy, weren't you? It would not do to mark your smart uniform, would it? Here, let me put Helena's nursing apron on you."

He stood still, thrilling with joy as she tied the tapes in a bow behind him. "Now you do look workman-like! Here's the basket. Have you everything you want? It is *so* kind of you— what a good Samaritan you are, to be sure!"

Happiness spread through him as he plucked, feather by feather, to prolong the exquisite feeling of being allowed to serve the beautiful people. The garden seemed to float in a golden stillness of peace and everlastingness, the summer of his boyhood had come again. It was a calm, mellow day, not yet heavy with the colours and dews of autumn. Then, lest she should think he was trying to prolong his presence there, he began to pluck faster. He must finish soon, and make his departure. Where was Helena? Hardly daring to lift his eyes from the task, for he must not appear curious, or betray Mrs. Rolls' trust in him in any way, he pulled fingerfuls of dark-red feathers; and coming to the back of the neck, wondered if he dare ask for some of the hackles which made the Red Spinner flies, according to the cobbler who tied flies at Lynmouth. Fishing: and he was going to the front tomorrow. How long ago, far back in the past, was his holiday in Devon—in another world.

When he had finished plucking, and then drawing; when the limp body, strangely thin and naked, was hanging from a branch of the lilac tree, he had to summon his courage before venturing to the open kitchen door, and, after further hesitation, to call out softly, "Mrs. Rolls!"

There was no reply. He waited in a mild distress of indecision, before calling again. Still no answer. What ought he to do? Where was she? Dare he go inside, and call into the hall? And waiting there, he heard the front gate bang behind its coiled spring, the crunch of gravel, and the plop of letters on the mat, followed by two short rings on the bell. The postman had come. Then footfalls downstairs.

"Mrs. Rolls, I've finished now."

"How very kind of you, Phillip! Come in, dear boy." She had three envelopes in her hand. He could not stop himself giving a glance their way. As though in response to his curiosity, she held one up.

"I expect you know that writing, don't you, Phillip?"

It was an *On Active Service* envelope, written in indelible pencil, a red rubber *Passed Censor* stamp, a signature in one corner, addressed to *Miss Helena Rolls*.

"From your cousin Bertie Cakebread. Such a fine young man. Gerard and I have always admired him, so upright, and such a good boy to his mother——"

Phillip did not know what to say. Why was Bertie writing to Helena? He did not know that the Rolls were friendly with Bertie. It was staggering news! Perhaps that was why he had been invited into the house! Bertie had given him a good name! *If ever there was a peach, it's that girl*. Bertie was helping his cause!

"His father was such a splendid man, wasn't he?" said Mrs. Rolls. "And it is nice to know, too, who was the grandfather of one's children's friends, don't you think?"

Phillip replied "Yes", not realising that she was referring to the Cakebread family connexion with the Coldstream. He thought she must mean Gran'pa Turney, until she said, "Three generations in one regiment! Not many people today can boast of a thing like that, Phillip. Well, thank you very much, dear boy," she was saying, when Helena came into the garden. She was smiling, she was radiant, she clung to her mother's arm, she looked into his eyes with frank delight; and Phillip's joy was complete.

"Isn't it awfully kind of this dear boy, Helena, to help us out like this? I think we ought to ask him to come in and eat it tonight, don't you? Or have you already made plans for this evening, Phillip?"

It was then that he saw that Helena was holding Bertie's letter to her bosom.

"Oh, yes," he heard his voice saying. Eyes on the ground: get away, quick, quick! "I'm afraid I have to see someone tonight, I'm going to France tomorrow morning. Well, I must go now. Goodbye."

"Going back so soon, Phillip? Surely you've done your bit?"

"I'm taking a draft of London Highlanders to the front, Mrs. Rolls. That's why I got an extra twenty-four hours. I was supposed to go this morning."

"Ah, I wondered why you had stored your noisy motorcycle! Well, I think you are a brick, the way you tackled that cockerel."

"Hear, hear!" said Helena.

"Well, goodbye," and hurrying away, almost he ran through the gate, and to the asphalt pavement of Hillside Road.

It seemed strange that men should be painting the spiked iron railing round the Hill the same bright green as in peace-time; that the milk-cart should be standing outside the flats, seen so clearly in the quiet sunshine. He could hear the footfalls of the milkman, with his white apron and straw hat, as he moved to put the milkcans at the doors, with his yodelling cry of *Milk-oo*. It was all as he had always known it; but now there was a sheet of plate glass between him and life.

"What shall I do, Mother, what shall I do? Did you know about Bertie all the time? Then *why* didn't you tell me? O, what a fool I have made of myself! Mrs. Rolls once said I was morbid. You all think this really, I know. All the lot of you! Aunt Victoria, Uncle Hilary—no-one seems to understand what it is to feel time passing, while life is also standing still. I'll tell you now why I never got on with Mavis and Doris! They laughed at me when I couldn't help them seeing the tears in my eyes years ago, when I spoke of the swallows soon to be flying away over the sea! It was in the kitchen during breakfast, Father had gone to the station. It was early October, and a high wind was rattling the kitchen window. I can see it as though it were yesterday. Doris pointing at my face, and Mavis jeering, 'Cry baby!' No-one understood in those days! No-one understands now! Sometimes I don't want to live any longer—I hope I shall be killed!"

When he was calmer, Hetty suggested a picnic on Reynard's Common. They could go by train from Randiswell, and be back in time for Mavis' tea. Doris could get her own; she would leave the key next door with Aunt Marian. It would be like old times, she said; and strangely quiet and still, his unhappy feelings settled or renounced for the time being, he said he would like to go with her to the Common.

Hetty was quiet, too; her bright nervous manner was shed. They were companions, as in the days after his scarlet fever, when they had gone together for a little holiday to Brighton. He was her little boy again, on that very same table they had played together with his bricks, or written letters to one another across the table—his handwriting a pencil squiggle; the early days when he had needed and confided in her his little secrets, and how he loved Da-da! Now he trusted her again.

They had the carriage to themselves; few people were going into the country at that time of day; and at the end of the line was the dear, familiar wooden turn-table for the engine, worked by cranked handle and cogs; then came the tree-shaded lane leading up to the Common, with its yellow-brick cottages and coppices and white dusty lanes through the woods. "O, to live here always, in a dear little cottage!" exclaimed Hetty.

Beyond the woods was open ground, where the gorse bore the last of its massive yellow nugget-blooms of summer. While they walked they heard little cracks, as the gorse pods split screw-wise and cast black beans upon the peaty earth. He collected some, to sow in the Backfield. Perhaps some other boy——

They sat down upon the sun-hot earth, in a space of sward where as of old the linnets were a-wing, their breasts faint-branded by the fire of summer suns. The corn-bunting still sang on the telegraph wires, the lizard clung warm upon the faded posts torn by the spiked climbing irons of the repairing men.

"Mother, I think I will give you my locket, and if I do not come back, will you give it to Bertie? And say I hope he will be very happy."

With piercing insight he thought of the human desperation, despair, and misery under the same sky which was so calm above this very Common, where all was peace, where the only movements were of cloud and bird and seed. Curled and bleached, the thin pods of the rose-bay willow-herb were loosing away their parachute seeds; they glistened and trembled in the webs of spiders hanging everywhere between gorse and thorn. Yet all life there had suffered; upon the pebbly spaces charred stumps showed where fires in past summers had burned the common black; but life had returned, for hundreds of sapling silver birches were now rising there. It was the land of linnet and stonechat, of bunting and goldfinch; of adders among the pans of pebbles anciently rolled by floods across the chalk of north-west Kent. Now upon this land the last heats of summer were dispread on fading heather-bell and carline thistle; only the yellow nuggets of the furze defied the sun's declension, while autumn's pale tickets showed upon distant elm and beech and oak.

This was perhaps the last time he would see the Common. How still and quiet everything was; even the twitter of linnets was finished. Time here was standing still; out there, Time was rushing fast, rushing upon life after life. Time rushed backwards for him, bringing winter scenes like transfers upon his mind; bearded faces, knife-shortened greatcoats, woollen bala-clavas, fire-pails, flares, mud-tracks through broken trees. Death was an instant away, the other side of the glass fixed between life and the soul.

His mother saw his face when he returned to where she was sitting, the sandwiches spread on a table napkin upon the ground, and said, "You won't forget your crucifix, will you, dear? It came from the convent, and was given me by Mère Ambrosine at Thildonck."

"I know."

"And don't forget your prayers, Phillip. They will help you in your duty towards others."

"Prayer never yet stopped a bullet."

"That is not quite what I mean, dear. Do you remember the poor boy you used to give bread and dripping to, because he was so hungry?"

"Cranmer. Yes, why?"

"Well, Phillip, when you thought of Cranmer being so hungry, you did not stop to think about any consequences to yourself, did you?"

"You mean Father forbidding me to go about with him?"

"Yes, dear, that is what I meant."

"What's all this leading up to?"

"Well, dear, you are now in a position to help others, the men under you, and if you always bear it in mind when you say your prayers, it will give you strength to continue through bad times."

"The Germans pray to God, too."

"Even so, God's help is always forthcoming when everything else seems to be lost." She turned away her face, to hide the tears.

Seeing them, he felt like scoffing; struggled against saying something unkind; strove to be kind; nearly gave way to black despair, but managed to say, "Cheer up, Hetty! I'm not dead yet. In fact, I'm rather glad to be going out again."

It seemed to her that her prayer was answered. "Of course,

dear! You came through last time, and you will come through again! You always did scrape through, somehow!" she laughed. Memory bloomed in her. "What fun we had during our picnics here, when you were all children! Oh, the sun, the sun! How time flies—it seems only yesterday when you were my 'little mouse', and Father was so good and unselfish, nursing you night after night, so that I should get some sleep, and be able to feed you——" She sighed; a tear started; to be lost in a sudden smile. "And then, in answer to my prayers, one morning, very early, there stood the old man who lived opposite, with a little jug of special milk; and oh, the relief when at last you stopped crying, and fell into a peaceful slumber in my arms! And Father could sleep too—do you know, never in all that time when he was awake with you, night after night, did he once complain. He was splendid!"

"Was—was Father *really* like that, Mum?"

"Yes, dear, of course, naturally. He loved his little son, very very dearly."

He got up and wandered away, and stood again by the massive gorse bush, its spines radiating the sun's heat with a strong sweet scent, and tried to feel clear, as he had when a child. Then Cranmer's face came into his mind, while it seemed that the air about him was warm and kind, and he was no longer afraid. Cranmer, he thought, Cranmer, are you near me, and it seemed that Cranmer was with him in spirit.

When he went back to his mother, and they spoke again, he felt that she was quite different, her way of talking was so assured, and there was now a sort of friendship between them, no longer that of mother and son, but of two friends who knew one another.

This feeling lasted all the afternoon and evening, which he spent at home, playing cards with Mavis and Doris and Mother, while Father seemed happy as he read the paper in his chair. When the morning came, Phillip was surprised to feel that he was looking forward to being at the front again, in a strange sort of way. And if he should be killed—well, he would go where Cranmer had gone, and Baldwin, and all the others who were now fixed faces in his mind.

Chapter 18

A CUSHY JOB

VICTORIA STATION. Thousands of soldiers, hundreds of officers returning from leave; a whole coach reserved for the staff, red tabs and gold-oakleaf hats; wives and mothers and sweethearts—some older women in black, with mourning veils, and crêpe upon their hats—kit-bags, valises, porters with hand luggage-trucks—tears, red-eyes, white-faces; serious old men in bowler hats and cavalry-cut of suits, and grey moustaches, standing by near-cheerful, pink-faced soldier sons in tall mahogany-polished riding boots and spurs—cavalry subalterns obviously going out for the first time.

Phillip had gone up alone, after a hurried firm farewell in the hall. At the last moment he was persuaded to take his father's mackintosh, despite his protest that he could get anything he wanted in France, at the base. He had not troubled about a revolver, or map-case; as for field-glasses, he would pick up a pair somewhere. Prismatic compass? Such gadgets were for the Fireside Lancers or "Strawballs" Staybacks. All he needed was a British warm, a haversack, and a walking-stick.

There had been one moment of panic after breakfast, before he had removed braid and cloth stars from his tunic cuffs, and, from his mother's work-basket, taken needle and thread with which to sew the pips on his shoulder straps.

"Let me do it for you, dear, won't you?"

"Leave me alone! I must hurry! Please leave me alone!"

The cuff badges would be obvious to snipers.

Reporting to the R.T.O. at Victoria he was taken to his draft of sixty London Highlanders, and signed copies of the nominal-rolls handed over to him by one of their officers who had marched them from headquarters. They were to be conducted to an Infantry Base Depôt at Boulogne, where further orders would await him. Among the sixty was a familiar face, clean-shaven and faintly brown, with *pince-nez* spectacles—little Kirk, of the original battalion, whom he had last seen at Bleak Hill, when he had motored there with Desmond in the early spring.

"How strange that we meet again, Kirky, old boy. By rights I should have been crossing yesterday, but got an extra twenty-four hours to take you blokes."

The uniform of the London Highlanders had been changed. The men wore a khaki tam-o'-shanter, with blue toorie and flash, instead of the old glengarry bonnet. They carried short rifles, wooded to the muzzle, and had boots and puttees half-way up their hose; but the old kilt of hodden grey was the same. He wished, in a way, that he was still with the regiment; but reflected that, as nearly all the old faces were gone, it was best as it was. What would his new crowd, the Gaultshires, be like?

The crossing was without qualms, the sea being level and blue as the sky. Rolling thuds of gunfire came upon the ship, from the unseen Belgian coast. Having left the draft on a lower deck in charge of the sergeant, Phillip climbed to an upper deck among the officers, seeing, in a reserved place with cabins beyond railings, the group of brass-hats, immaculate in appearance, entirely remote from the swarm of subalterns and captains for'ard. There was also a reserved space for field officers, the ordinary majors and colonels. Phillip thought that these looked, somehow, much more approachable than the staff officers, whose tunics all bore ribbons.

During the march up to the Base Camp on high ground above the town the draft sang *Tipperary* and other songs. It seemed rather flat; but he had made friends on the boat with two subalterns, one of whom had been out before, wounded at Neuve Chapelle, who told him of a good place where to get lunch in Boulogne. There was also an Officers' Club, he said, where it was possible to wangle an extra night there if you were on your own; but with a draft you were tied like a nursemaid to a perambulator. There were other possibilities of a night in Boulogne, too. This officer confirmed the stories about the un-cut wire, and lack of high-explosive shells.

It was strange to see German prisoners working in the Base Camp, white-washing rows of stones leading to the big brown huts, painting doors, and even digging in garden plots. They had big round blue patches let into their grey tunics and trousers. Phillip spoke to one: immediately the prisoner leapt to attention, snatched off his pork-pie hat, and stood rigid before him.

"Stand easy," said Phillip. "*Sprechen sie Englisch?*"

"A little, sir."

"I hope you are all right here. I had many talks with you chaps—*prächtig kerls*—last Christmas Day. Do you understand?"

"Yes, sir."

"*Prächtig kerls*—I liked them. This war is no good."

"I understand, sir."

"We are all homesick, you know. Well, keep smiling!"

"Many grateful thanks, sir."

"Cheer-ho!"

That night the draft had to be marched down the hill again, to the station. The destination was Béthune. Phillip thought, we are all for it: the talk in the officers' mess had nearly all been of the coming push, in the mining country north of Arras. Béthune was the rail-head. Practice assaults, he learned, had been going on in the country round about since the middle of August. The attack was to take place south of the La Bassée canal, the objective being Lille, through which all the railways ran behind the German lines. With Lille threatened, and cavalry pouring through the gap, the old Hun would have to go back to the Scheldt. Just as Gran'pa had said! It was all rather exciting.

"And," said someone, "the attack is to be preceded by a new kind of stupefying smoke which will conceal our advance right up to the German parapets, and lay out the Germans for a couple of hours, after one whiff. It'll be a walk-over for our chaps."

"Like bloody hell," said the chap who had been wounded at Neuve Chapelle. He seemed quite angry. "Latrine rumours!" he snorted.

Béthune. Enormous naval guns on multiple bogies standing in railway sidings, sixty-foot rifled snouts lifted eastwards, towards the German lines. Enormous stacks of shells in fields; rows and rows of Ford ambulance cars with khaki covers painted with red-crosses; thousands of mules and horses tethered to endless picket lines. Soldiers crowding square and market place; dingy buildings, tall water-tower, a few cracked roofs; shops with chocolate and bread and meat for sale; military police wearing revolvers and red caps at every street-crossing; rattle of wheels and hoofs, trail of white puffs in the high blue overhead following a white speck moving east, above the sullen booming of big guns. No beards, no fire-pails, no short overcoats, no boots worn to the uppers, with toes showing. All this looked like a new business!

A peasant in peaked cap was being led away by red-caps, a handcart following loaded with brown army blankets. Officers on horses, long columns of wagons and limbers, scarlet-banded hats in motor cars. Rattle of wheels on cobbles, filthy grey drain-water in gutters half-dried in the sun, white chloride of lime sprinklings. Oh, for a base job, to be able to watch the war, all so tremendously interesting, without the dread of having to go over the top: the odds in the infantry were three to one against being killed.

Beyond the town, in evening light, shocks of yellow-brown corn stood in fields, looking strange with vast dark mounds and pyramids rising above them, with tall chimneys and the tracery of iron-work above the coal pits.

A fellow subaltern in the camp of khaki canvas huts told him that this was Artois. Coal seams ran everywhere under the skin of chalk. The whole depressing landscape was crowded with khaki, and hazy with smoke. Even so, he felt a sense of freedom to be in the midst of such varied movement, glad to be one of the hundreds of thousands of troops. Life was everywhere interesting, on such a vast new scale. He told himself that he would not have missed it for anything; and there was satisfaction in thinking that his army pay was accumulating, together with his salary from the office. This was the real thing, not life with that "Cantuvellaunian" lot! "Strawballs" ought to be covered with woad. Well, he had seen the last of them, thank God! What matter if the water tasted of chloride of lime, when whiskey was three francs fifty a bottle from the Expeditionary Forces Canteen? Grub was good, too.

What luck, they seemed to have forgotten all about him. There were many decent restaurants in Béthune; and nobody bothered what time they got back to their Nissen huts. This was the life, lived against the flickering rumble of gunfire. Most of it was British; the Germans seldom replied. Roll on, the Great Push. Berlin this time!

On the fifth morning after his arrival, looking at the notice-board in the mess, he read that officers with experience in

chemistry were requested to give their names to the office of the
D.A.Q.M.G. What was that when it was at home?

"Deputy Adjutant and Quartermaster General, old boy.
Some sanitary job," the Sussex officer beside him said.

A cushy job, perhaps! He went to give in his name at once.
After all, he had had some experience in the laboratory at school,
and there was his shilling magician's set years ago. There was a
policy he had made out in Wine Vaults Lane, for a chemical
factory at Silvertown in the East End somewhere, and Mr.
Hollis saying one morning that he had inspected it. *So I considered my experience entitled me, Mrs. Neville*—— He imagined her
shaking with laughter when he told her. *Oh, there are no flies
on you, Phillip!*

That evening he was called to the orderly room and ordered
to proceed the next day to Helfaut, together with two other
officers. Thither, wondering what they were in for, they went
by Crossley tender—a wonderful journey, with a stop for lunch
at a restaurant in Hazebrouck of many memories. The old
Rossignol estaminet was still there, but the cabbage-painted
Long Toms gone from the Grand' Place. After the meal, which
was taken with two bottles of champagne, the Crossley roared
down the narrow cobbled road to St. Omer, past wide fields
where corn was being carried in blue-painted tumbrils looking
like wooden boats on high wheels. He enjoyed the thought of
the last time he had come along that way in the darkness, nearly
a year previously, riding beside Baldwin on the top of a London
bus, and so into the battle for Ypres. All that was over!

The course. A lecture given by a junior subaltern of the
Royal Engineers, on the method of using liquid chlorine gas
in trench warfare, illustrated by a sergeant unscrewing the
rounded top of a cylinder and fitting the connecting or discharge
pipes. Then a field demonstration in trenches dug for the
purpose. Gas was turned on, damp grey P.H. goggled helmets
worn over the head, the ends tucked under the collars of tunics.
Phillip got hold of a spare one—what fun to ride up Hillside
Road like that, on his bike!

Squads, all of N.C.O.s, were formed, each to an officer.
Phillip had three sergeants and thirty corporals, half of whom
had been under fire in the infantry, the remainder specially
enlisted as chemists. On the last afternoon of the course there
was a lecture by a staff officer from G.H.Q. on the tactics of the

use of gas, and its application in trenches before an infantry assault. The prevailing wind, said the staff officer, on the western front was from the Atlantic, from the south-west; and as the enemy lines were, generally speaking, to the E.N.E. of the Allied lines, the prevailing wind was in favour of the Allies. The idea was to drench the Hun positions with smoke and gas of such density as to render the infantry and machine-gunners *hors de combat* before the infantry assault; while the gunners, particularly during X and Y days and nights, already would have destroyed the Hun wire, emplacements, and dugouts.

"The bayonet and the bomb, gentlemen, will eventually decide the issue. It is our job to saturate the enemy positions before the assault. In doing so, we shall only be paying the Hun back in his own coin, and with interest! It is known," went on the staff officer, after a pause, "that the Hun infantry is supplied with respirators that will last for about a quarter of an hour only. After that, they require to be redipped. On the other hand, their machine-gunners have oxygen helmets which will protect them for about thirty minutes. There will, therefore, be two periods of discharge. The first period will continue for a period sufficient to ensure that, in the surprise caused by the use of gas, the Hun will neutralise his helmets during the pre-liminary dosage. The second period of discharge, the disabling one, will then follow. It will be accompanied by smoke from candles, to screen the infantry assault. I need hardly add that secrecy in every particular must be observed by every officer and non-commissioned officer here in this room. Upon your absolute discretion will depend the element of surprise, as much as upon the employment of the asphyxiating gases themselves."

The cylinders were of steel, about thirty inches high, weighing over a hundredweight when filled with sixty pounds of liquid gas. The armoured parapet pipe was ten feet long; this was to be connected to a further pipe, flexible and about seven feet long, the other end of which was secured by a nut holding down the union joint to the cylinder head. This head was protected by a steel dome held over one end of the cylinder by a large hexagonal nut.

When the course was ended, Phillip left with his squad in two motor lorries, and was "decanted" at Verquin, two miles south of Béthune. On the way there they passed the bivouacs and lines of many cavalry regiments, and also an aerodrome, on which biplanes were standing; and nearby, an observation balloon tethered by steel cable to a winch. Nearer the front were the great dumps: rolls of wire, piled boxes of S.A.A. under tarpaulins, boxes of bombs and hand-grenades, limbers and wagons, shells, picks and shovels, angle iron and screw-pickets—acre upon acre of materials, all giving a feeling of power.

When the time was come to go into the trenches again, he felt curious, excited, and pleased; for it was to be a visit only, to observe the lie of the land, and to see, in particular, the emplacements in the new forward assault trenches that had been built for the cylinders.

What surprised him was the length and order of the communication trenches, the only danger being from shelling so occasional that it was said the old Hun had pulled out most of his heavy artillery to face the major attack that was coming down south by the French, in Champagne.

All across the gently sloping downland burdened with huge sombre pyramids and dumps of slag and stones, arising above the fringe of tall yellow grasses and weeds beyond parapet and parados, line upon line of chalk could be seen—the assault trenches. He was told by an infantry captain who invited him into a shelter dug under the parapet that the attack had been planned for two days previously, the 15th September, but it had been postponed. The day before, said the captain, who was in the first battalion of the Gaultshires, the old Hun hoisted a board before the wire in front of his trench just below the Lone Tree ridge—he had carried it and fixed it during the night, so that it could be read through field-glasses—

WHY HAS YOUR ATTACK BEEN PUT OFF?

The infantry captain, mug of whiskey in hand, looked at Phillip across the dugout table in his company headquarters, and spoke in a voice of deadly fury under his restraint.

"They've removed all ranging marks for our artillery, and their rifle fire is conspicuous by its absence. Why, do you ask? Because they are saving ammunition. And why, you wonder? Because for weeks past bumff has been going around with full details of the push. Our staff has done everything except send a complete copy of the plan of attack to the Hun opposite, who has watched us digging jumping-off ditches, putting up wooden bridges over the trenches for the eighteen-pounders, and scaling-ladders for the infantry, from his comfortable quarters in the Tower Bridge; and so interested is he in it all, that he has not sent over so much as a whizz-bang. Why?"

"Perhaps they're waiting for the actual moment of attack, to break it, sir. Once I saw——"

"Allow me to speak," said the captain, his eyes fixed upon Phillip's. "I will do the talking here! Why, you ask, is the Hun waiting until he has got us jam-packed before him, every trench and assembly point bung-full, and then, when he can't miss, CRASH——!"

The pale captain smashed his fist upon the table, starting up a score of flies, some to settle upon his sweating brow.

Alarmed, and a little shaken by the outburst, Phillip replied, "Exactly, sir! That's what our Guards did at Klein Zillebeke, during First Ypres. They let the Alleyman cut their wire, in order to catch all of them coming through the gap."

"Were you there?"

"Yes, sir."

"Who were you with?"

"The London Highlanders."

"Then shake hands!" The other leaned over to give him a hurtful clasp. "Help yourself to a spot of old man whiskey!"

"Thank you, sir. By the way, I'm also in the Gaultshires. I removed my badges in case the sniping was hot. My name's Maddison. I haven't served with the regiment yet, sir."

"Mine's West. I hope you're posted to us, one day. I'd like you in my company. I take off my hat to any man who went through First Ypres!"

Phillip felt important with the new brassard on his right sleeve, of red, white, and green vertical stripes. In a way, he was a staff officer, he considered. The R.E. colonel at the gas school had said that the duty of a squad officer was to stay with his cylinders until they were emptied, lest their presence endanger his own men: therefore no officer, wearing the brassard, could be ordered to join in the assault. What, Phillip had said to an imagined Desmond, could be more cushy? He would see all that happened, and be under cover when the machine-guns started. He had his spare P.H. helmet, in case of accidents, such as a shell breaking a cylinder.

There were fourteen emplacements in his sector, each having been made by digging away the fire-step, and replacing it by a wooden platform resting on stakes driven into the chalk. Under each platform fifteen cylinders were to be laid. Turned on full bore, the gas from each would escape in under three minutes.

The captain showed him a trench map. The German lines lay just over the crest of the slope rising imperceptibly across the wide and grassy wilderness of No Man's Land. "The Hun can see us against the skyline, when we go out on patrol, particularly when the moon is going down. We can't see him, because the ground rises again out of the Loos valley behind his front line." To the south, the British lines lay up another slope, with No Man's Land an imperceptible hollow in front. Behind the enemy front line was Hill 69, rising to the skyline, and the much-wired Loos Road Redoubt. Farther on, to the south, and in the direction of Loos with its upstanding colliery gear, the German lines lay on and behind more rising ground.

Phillip looked cautiously over the chalk-bagged parapet. Dark-brown docks in seed were visible in the thin yellow grasses; thistle floss floated into the haze of the eastern horizon from which arose the chimneys and machinery of pitheads, and dark sullen heaps of stony slag faintly green with grass. Out of the hazy, almost level scene arose the bursts of shells, like waves breaking upon an invisible reef.

Dominating the view was a tall structure in lace-work iron, of twin pylons surmounted by a flat top, called by the men the Tower Bridge. It arose high above a red-brick village with a church. That was Loos, one of the main objectives of the attack, which had to be captured, said Captain West, in the first rush. Beyond it was the large town of Lens, which was never shelled, since the civilian population was still there, working for the old Hun.

"Yes, they're still mining coal to make the shells which will be blowing us all to hell next week. And we not only pay rent for our trenches in this blasted country, but have to pay for the blankets we're buried in. Still, what the hell? A soldier's life is short and merry. Come into my shelter and have a spot of old man whiskey."

Enamel mugs jinked; down went a generous slop of whiskey and chlorinated water.

"Thank God we're being relieved tonight," said Captain West. "But we'll be back in time for the alleged Big Push. When are you going to bring up your beastly gas bottles? God's teeth, if the old Hun gets a direct hit on one of your emplacements——"

Phillip saw that Captain West's hand was shaky. He had a very white face, with a high forehead that seemed to think for itself above the clouded blue-grey eyes when he was silent; but when he spoke, it was usually through his teeth, and he had a grim look when he clenched his bony jaws. He was a strong-looking man, he thought; though his strength was more in his will than in his physique. Phillip had learned that his nickname among the other officers was "Spectre". It suited him, he thought.

"What provision have you made for leaking gas?"

"Two extra Vermorel sprayers will remain in the sector, with two of my corporals, when we bring the cylinders up, sir, to neutralise any gas."

"We had to piss on our handkerchiefs during Second Ypres. I've got the blasted gas in me still." Captain West thumped his chest, and cleared his throat. Phillip noticed how dirty his nails were. He was not like any regular officer he had met before.

On the 18th of September the cylinders arrived in the special tram, which was shunted into a siding. Each cylinder was in a wooden box. Phillip was ordered to remove them by unscrewing the tops of the boxes, then to loosen all the dome covers of the cylinders before replacing them in the boxes and refixing the wooden lid with one screw only.

Remembering that chlorine was corrosive, and that his father had always put screws into wood with Vaseline, against rust, he got hold of a tin, and returned with his squad to the siding.

While they were unscrewing the boxes, and were about to loosen the dome-cover of the first cylinder, a general arrived on the scene and asked what they were doing. Phillip called his men to attention; then repeated his instructions.

"Put all the boxes back in the train at once," ordered the general. "Those safety domes are not to be touched."

"Sir!" replied Phillip at attention. He saw, with some alarm, from the gold crossed-swords and crown on the officer's shoulder-

straps that he was a major-general. So the screws only were
removed from the box lids; and one screw replaced in each,
after being smeared with Vaseline.

Violent blows were splitting the sky, singly and in multiples
of four; rarely was there silence; but in a rare interval when no
guns were firing, he was aware of a quivering of the air, of a
ground-bass seeming to shake the very earth and all upon it.
At night the tremulous flickers of the French bombardment
were to be seen in the sky, far away down south, where the chalk
escarpments of the Champagne Pouilleuse were set sparsely
with fir-plantations, now a wreckage of poles. When would the
Big Push start? No-one knew; rumours were almost as numerous
as the flies. His servant, an old soldier nicknamed "Twinkle",
told him all the rumours, obviously to get him to talk; Phillip
listened, but made no reply; he knew that the gas cylinders
were not all in place.

On the night of 19th of September, while a slight breeze was
blowing from the German lines, the boxes of cylinders were
loaded on to G.S. wagons, and taken to the forward dump.
The feet of the horses had been enwound with sacking, and then
put inside treble sand-bags, and tied; the wheels were muffled,
too. Extra care for silence was taken lest enemy shelling destroy
the loads. The British shelling had slowed down, as though in
sudden anxiety about retaliation.

Without incident the wagons unloaded, and went back quicker
than they came, the horses needing no encouragement to
return to the picket line, where a string-bag of hay and fifteen
pounds of oats was their daily ration. The box-lids were unscrewed, the cylinders removed, and slung on poles, each to be
carried up to the front line, via communication trenches, by
two fatigue men from the infantry. As they were heavy, and
movement would be slow, there was a relief of two extra men for
each load.

Progress was tedious up the communication trenches, as many
other fatigue parties were passing up and down upon the duck-
boards. At last the front assembly trench was reached, and the
sergeants in command of the various carrying-parties led their
men to the emplacements. The cylinders were laid on the chalk,
and sandbag revetments built around them. It was nearly
dawn when, having visited his emplacements and seen that all

was in order, including the two men left with Vermorel sprayers, with rations, and water in a petrol can, Phillip led his squad back to the cross-roads at Philosophe, where the disused railway passed through the Lens–Béthune road. About half a mile down the road they turned left at the next cross-roads and about a mile farther on arrived at their billets in the village of Mazingarbe, which they entered as the flares were shrinking in the first pallor of dawn.

The billet was in a terrace of brick-built and tiled cottages, or *corons*, leading off from the square. He had a bed in an up-stairs room, chosen for its airiness, while the widow and her children slept in the cellar, on top of half a dozen layers of bully beef in tins.

It was a bare room, with one small cracked window facing east, and a floor of broad poplar boards. The bed was a rusty frame on which was some straw under an army blanket. Thereon his valise was spread open, the flap turned back, for the tooth-less old soldier acting as his batman fancied himself as a valet.

Phillip supposed that "Twinkle", as the batman had said he was called by everyone, was a sapper, although he wore no shoulder letters. He had appeared one evening in the billet, and offered himself as Phillip's batman, telling him that he was the only man in the British Army to have earned two Rooti, or bread-eating, medals. He explained this curious position by declaring that he had first joined the Army in India as a cook; and when after twenty years he had got the Good Conduct Medal, and his regiment was on the point of returning home, he was left behind accidentally, and had carried on, maintaining the cookhouse on his own, "up-'olding of the British Raj, sir, wiv various punkah and other wallahs, sir", until the next regiment arrived, when he re-enlisted and after another twenty years had qualified for another Rooti medal. That, said "Twin-kle", brought him up to the little old Boer War.

To substantiate his various experiences, across the old soldier's left breast there stretched a band of ribands from which the colours had faded and been replaced by grease and smoke. When Phillip asked what they were, the old soldier replied with an uninterrupted flow of sounds and spittle-sprays from tooth-less gums in which the originals of Good Conduct, Coronation, Durbar, Chitral, Egypt, North West Frontier, Afghanistan,

Omdurman, Fuzzy Wuzzies, Boer War Queen's and King's, might, with a little knowledge of British military history, be made out.

After his second time-expired discharge, according to a "Twinkle" garrulous with rum or whatever it was he got hold of at night, he had worked in the kitchen of a sandwich shop in Covent Garden, where after boiling the haunches of old boars, sows, and horses, he sliced them cold to make "thicks" or sandwiches for the porters and carters in the vegetable market. If he was to be believed, most of the great names in opera and ballet had dropped in at his "Ham and Beef" at one time or another, including Caruso, Melba, Scotti, Chaliapin, Destinn, Pavlova, and Nijinsky. Phillip was never tired of hearing the old man's stories, which usually were told while he waited at table during his solitary dinner in the cottage kitchen at night.

The experience in the Ham and Beef shop in London now seemed to serve the old fellow well, for in the Demi Lune in Mazingarbe, "Twinkle" did a roaring trade in beef sandwiches, which he cut up in vast quantities in the billet, after boiling great chunks of meat in saucepans over a fire in an outhouse. Where the meat came from, Phillip did not know. "Twinkle" probably scrounged it, he thought.

During four more nights cylinders were taken up in the same muffled wagons, and emplaced. On the 23rd of September a big fire broke out in Cité St. Pierre, within the German lines; vast drifting smoke filled half of the forward sky seen from the trenches, and at night the low clouds, (for the weather had broken) glowed a dull red. The work was completed that night, when all the discharging pipes had been carried to the emplacements, and laid on pegs driven into the parapet. It was hard, sweaty work, and slow, too, owing to the ten-foot lengths being most awkward to manipulate round the traverses, amidst oaths and curses among the numerous soldiers in both communication and front trenches.

The R.E. major came to Phillip, and taking him aside, said, "This is X night. Keep it to yourself, my boy."

"Certainly, sir."

A violent thunderstorm that night broke with lashing rain upon waterproof capes and chalk-bags, bringing great clogs of white slather upon boots; but the fire in Cité St. Pierre burned as brightly as before, when the storm had gone away over the plain of the Scheldt.

By now he was fairly familiar with many of the officers and men of the infantry holding that section of the line farthest from the Germans, a little more than half a mile from a solitary tree visible just in front of the enemy wire, known as Lone Tree. As Phillip left one of the reserve infantry company's dugout, happy with whiskey inside him, he felt he was enjoying the adventure, despite the falling rain. Thank God he would be able to sleep in a billet that night; and he was comparatively dry, in his Father's mackintosh, which gave him an extra feeling of security.

"Twinkle" was to have hot soup and sandwiches ready at 3 a.m., when he got back. Before going to his billet, he saw that the N.C.O.s of his squad had their hot tea and rum, and canteens of skilly.

"Well, good night you chaps, have a good sleep, while you can."

"Very good, sir," replied the senior sergeant. "Beg pardon, sir, but have you any idea when the big push will start?"

"The wind is blowing from the west, sergeant, that is one thing; and listen to the guns, that is another. We shall know very soon, I think. Cheer-ho!"

The night was electric with white flash and orange-red bulging flame. Walls and roofs and shattered rafters along the meagre wet street were revealed in flash upon flash of field-gun batteries massed in the fields and lanes all around. To the south, above the wooded hills of Nôtre Dame de Lorette, the sky was fluttering and quivering as though filled with a thousand butterflies. He stood a while near the broken church, letting his sensations possess him entirely—the awfulness, the strangeness, the majesty, the terrible beauty of it all—to which was added a feeling of secret relief that he would not be going over the top.

Morning came with drizzle and mist, the wind being from the south at noon. Hourly reports, during the past few days, had been sent in to Brigade H.Q., and transmitted back to Division, Corps, Army, and G.H.Q.

At ten o'clock in the morning of the 24th of September a motor-cycle despatch rider on a Triumph gave Phillip an envelope marked *Secret*, for which he signed. Inside were orders for the

Special Companies, R.E. All ranks of the specially employed sections were to be in position by 7 p.m. on Y/Z night.

All officers i/c sections were to report at their respective Brigade H.Q. for instructions regarding zero hour. All anti-gas helmets were to be dipped in hyposulphite solution before leaving billets.

"At the moment," said Phillip, to his senior sergeant, as he wetted his finger and held it up, "there is no wind at all. If we let off in present conditions, our own chaps will be gassed, and not the Germans. We are supposed to discharge for thirty-eight minutes, before a final two minutes of smoke. D'you know how long the German helmets last?"

"Fifteen minutes, sir."

"How long will the hypo last on ours?"

The sergeant, an old soldier of Mons and Ypres, laughed shortly. "They don't tell us that, sir."

"Well, I've got to go to Noeux-les-Mines now, Sergeant Butler. I am leaving you in charge. If anyone asks for me, say I've gone to get some equipment from Dados. I'll be back about two pip emma."

"Very good, sir."

Dados, he had recently learned, was short for Deputy Assistant Director of Ordnance Supplies. From listening to Captain West he had come to believe that the extraordinary silence of both the German guns and machine-guns might be due to a plan they had to attack, should the wind change, and the British be gassed by their cylinders. The jam-packed troops would be caught, unprepared for the defensive. From what he had seen and heard of the plan of attack, every infantryman had been given instruction, in training, to the smallest detail; and if the old Hun attacked, the whole thing would be a muck-up.

In his unsophisticated mind, his unawareness of the thoughts of others (except of the rank and file) Phillip wondered if he ought to tell the R.E. major of this possibility. Supposing the fire of the German artillery was being held back for a terrific bombardment in the event of the British gas blowing the wrong way? The gas would paralyse everyone in the deep and narrow chalk ditches: the German infantry would be able to come through the gaps which had been cut in the British wire. It would then be Second Ypres again, but this time not with the "devilish

German gas". However, his experiences in his recent battalion at home had partly subdued him; so he suppressed his fears; and thinking of his own safety, decided to get himself a revolver from the ordnance stores. He could sign a chit for it, his pay would be debited.

D.A.D.O.S. was at Noeux-les-Mines, a couple of miles behind Mazingarbe. He got a lift on a lorry, and was soon there. To a remark by the quarter-master-sergeant at the store, as to whether or not he had lost his revolver in the line, he replied, "Yes. During some shelling", which led to the information that by filling-in a claim form and signing it, he might get a refund. He left with a new Smith and Wesson .45, and fifty rounds of ammunition; and after a meal of steak and chips and red wine in an estaminet, got a lift back to Mazingarbe. No one had asked for him during his absence.

The wind was now from the south, and very slight. What if it were south on Z morning?

He went into an overgrown trench, part of an old system where mouldy pieces of French uniform and equipment, an occasional bone or red fez could be found, and set up a mark in the side of the trench directly opposite him, about eight yards away. He took aim and fired; and to his surprise the bullet returned by his head, almost hitting him. It must have bounced back almost exactly along the line of flight. What an escape! That was the fourth time he had been lucky, including the Spandau bullet in 1914 that had cut across his greatcoat. He decided to practice no more, and never again to fire directly at a solid object.

The R.E. major paid the section a visit in their billets at Mazingarbe. Afterwards, as the Major was about to climb into his car, Phillip asked him how long the detachment job was likely to last.

"Ah, I expect you are keen to get back to your regiment," remarked the old soldier, genially. "Well, I can tell you that you will be required only for the morning of the assault, as far as I can foresee at present. Then you will, I suppose, be returned to your regiment."

Ominous words. Saluting the major, Phillip fought the feelings twisting within himself.

At twilight the wind was moving, almost imperceptibly, from

S.E., and E.S.E. It was moving, where it moved at all, up the lines of trenches, and, in places, aslant from the German lines.

The strange silence of the German batteries was still being maintained on the afternoon before the attack. No rifle fire from the unseen trenches came across the dry yellow grasses, with their occasional patches of wildered cabbage plants. At twilight Phillip left with his section, carrying the two kinds of spanners, one to tighten the nuts of the jet tube, the other to turn on the gas. There was a time-table for each infantry unit taking part in the assault: when to leave billets, when to enter a named UP communication trench, when to be in a further named assembly- or jumping-off trench. Nearby a quarter of a million British and French infantrymen of twenty-six divisions were on the move under the dull rainy sky of Artois, moving along narrow roads and lanes, and tracks of chalky mud gleaming with the dilating pallor of the sky: British infantrymen, in khaki, French in the new *bleu invisible*, replacing the red trousers worn in earlier battles to serve as aiming-marks of their own field-gunners; while south of this minor battlefield, in the Champagne Pouilleuse, a further three hundred thousand men of thirty-six French divisions were moving into their positions for the major attack.

Chapter 19

Y/Z NIGHT

PHILLIP and his section struggled through the new and unrevetted UP communication trench, in places up to their knees in white pug, and eventually reached their positions; and then, trying to loosen the domes of the cylinders, which was to have been done at the railway-siding until the general stopped it, found that neither of the two kinds of spanners "dished out" to them would shift the nuts. What should he do? He was in a state of fear and acute anxiety, afraid to telephone to brigade lest he be reprimanded; afraid to go back to the R.E. dump, lest he be reported absent from his post.

Shortly afterwards, to his relief, Captain West's company filed into the forward trench, covered with wet chalk from the UP communication trench.

"I'm awfully sorry to bother you, Captain West, but have you a large screw-wrench, by any chance?"

"What the hell d'you think I am, a damned ironmonger?" shouted Captain West in sudden rage. "Are you so bloody inefficient that you, with damn-all to do for the last few days, have to depend on the poor bloody infantry to provide you with the tools of your poisonous trade?"

Phillip saw in the light of the candle stuck on the table of piled ration boxes in the shelter that Captain West's pale, high forehead had beads of sweat on it, while the line of his jaw was ferociously set.

"I can't help it, the spanners dished out to me——"

"If you don't bloody well shut up, I'll put a bullet through you!" retorted the other, now whispering tense. "How dare you, one of the original nineteen fourteen army, and more-over a soldier of the Gaultshires, how in hell dare you stand there and talk to me as though you had not already sized up the whole bloody war, the real war, the *only* war, which is between the infantry and the staff, who sit on their bottoms and collect all the gongs with their hampers from Fortnum and Mason's before issuing reams and reams of bumff—orders and counter-orders—modifications and alterations—thus making a complete balls-up of every battle since you fellows' marvellous defence of Ypres against the flower of the German Army! *Then* Sir John French left the work of fighting, which is *their* job, to local commanders —God's teeth, don't you look at me like that, young Phillip, or I'll have you reduced to the ranks! I would probably make a worse balls-up of things if I were on the staff! Help yourself to a spot of old man whiskey, for Christ's sake—and stop talking!"

Captain West grabbed a pile of paper memoranda and threw it up into the air, then took an enamel mug off its hook—a bayonet thrust into the chalk wall—and pushed it, with the bottle, across to Phillip. "Help yourself. Knock it back! Then pass me the mug."

Phillip swallowed, making a wry face; he returned the mug. Captain West poured a stiff peg, and tipped it down his throat; then to Phillip's amazement, he helped himself to more.

"It isn't my fault, Captain West——" began Phillip.

"Call me Westy," said the other, staring intently across the table. "And most certainly it *is* your fault, Phillip. What if the general did tell you to leave well alone, it was still up to you to see that you had the right spanners! *You* were in command, *not* the general! Anyway, 'Never explain, never apologise'—that's the only attitude. You've heard of Jacky Fisher? You haven't? Where were you educated?" Phillip lowered his eyes; and Captain West, seeing this, said immediately, "Well, the Services' world is a narrow one, of course. Jacky Fisher practically made the navy what it is today, and all the way he was up *against* people like that general who said Nay to a better man's Yea at rail-head. Have you read Nietzsche? The most misunderstood and misquoted philosopher of our time? Anyway, I hope I have now made myself clear, you blue-eyed wonder, in the matter of personal responsibility?"

"I think I see what you mean, Westy."

"You think you do, do you? Well, that is something. The next step from thinking is doing. Now, I'll answer *your* question. No, we haven't got a screw-wrench, as you call a monkey-spanner. But if you don't want a court-martial, I'd advise you to get hold of the right spanners. Don't ask me how. It's your job to find out. I'm not your blasted bear-leader, even if you were at First Ypres!"

While Captain West was speaking, Phillip had thought at first that he was joking; then, seeing the sweat on his forehead, as though forced through the skin by the violence of thought, he had felt over-awed. This was followed by the fearful thought that, if the cylinders in his fourteen emplacements could not be unscrewed, causing untold losses, he would be court-martialled . . . and perhaps suffer the death-penalty.

There was no time to be lost. He hurried through the damp gas-blanket of the shelter, and sent his runner, waiting outside, to bring the senior sergeant, a regular of the Royal Engineers, to him. The old soldier was reassuring.

"I've already sent a corporal to borrow some from the next sector, sir. 'E's gone over the bags, it's 'opeless to try and get along the communication trenches now. 'E knows where to go, and said 'e can find Mr. White's dugout with 'is eyes shut. Lieutenant White had the same trouble, sir, but 'e won some adjustable spanners from the A.S.C. as soon as 'e saw as 'ow the ones dished out wouldn't fit."

"But they were only issued yesterday, sergeant."

"True enough, sir, but Mr. White come up 'isself and made sure, 'aving observed as 'ow the spanner they give us in the railway siding was different to both the issue spanners. The ones they give us yesterday are for to connect the stiff jet pipes and the armoured copper flexibles, sir."

"What shall we do if the corporal can't find Mr. White in all this muck-up?"

Phillip had to shout, for sudden flights of shells were now racing overhead, following almost continuous double-cracks of sixty-pounder batteries behind the ruined *corons* of Le Rutoire. "It's that general's fault—I wonder who he was?"

"Someone from corps—black-and-red brassard, sir."

Phillip felt panic, remembering that he had orders to report at brigade headquarters, a little over half a mile behind the front line, at ten o'clock; and it was now 8 p.m.

"Well, carry on, Sergeant."

"Very good, sir."

He hurried back to Captain West's shelter, and peering round the blanket, asked if he might come in, to be greeted by the inevitable, "Just in time for a spot of old man whiskey."

He was too agitated to think of drinking. Captain West reassured him.

"The wind is so slight that in all probability you won't have to let off your beastly gas. We, the infantry, have a double set of orders—one for use with gas, the other without gas—if one excepts, I need hardly add, the inevitable hot air, itself a kind of poison gas, from the staff. Anyway, you can't help by worrying. Your corporal has gone to get long spanners. Help yourself." He pushed over the bottle. "Wait here until my subalterns, who are seeing that the men have their hot soup, come here in"—he looked at his watch—"half an hour's time, at eight-thirty pip emma. What about your men's rations? Have you thought of that, blast your eyes? God damn it, am I your bear-leader?"

"They've got haversack rations, for tonight and tomorrow, in addition to their iron rations, Captain West."

"I told you to call me Westy! God's teeth, don't you ever obey an order?"

"Now and then," said Phillip, feeling sudden elation.

"To you, as a 1914 soldier, I am 'Westy'. Go steady with old man whiskey, for you've got to see the brigadier tonight.

Everything will come all right, which means that nothing ever goes according to plan. God's teeth, what's that blasted row on top? The bloody rats are getting as big as elephants! They're fat as cats, after feeding all the summer on the French stiffies lying out in front since last May."

The bumping about on the chalk-bags above the corrugated iron roof ended with the thud of someone jumping; then a face looked in past the blanket, and a broad Scottish voice asked if anyone knew where the adjutant of the 7th King's Own Scottish Borderers was. The face was invited in, and became the captain of a company which had been lost on the way up. The visitor explained that the marching column had been split, two files on either side of the road, to allow wheeled transport to pass in the middle; and when the Hun had started strafing, they had left the road. The big, dark-haired Scotsman was too anxious to accept a drink. He belonged to the fifteenth division, to the New Kitchener's Army. The guide had hopelessly lost direction; they had come across many communication and assembly trenches. His men were waiting.

"You're on the right of us," said Captain West. He opened a map, and spread it. "There's your divisional boundary, two hundred yards from the crossing of the tracks to Lone Tree and this one into Loos. There's a gap in the line here"—he pointed—"and the left flank of your division rests on this other track, also to Loos, approximately five hundred yards due south. It's less than three hundred yards from the Old Hun, so don't let your hearties start singing Roamin' in the Gloamin', or you'll start the whole Brock's Benefit prematurely, and our blue-eyed boy here hasn't got his little spanner yet. Now for a wee Doch an' Dorris!" He got up, handed the newcomer his mug, said "Knock that back," went to the blanket, called out, "Runner!", returned, and said, "I can give you a guide—he comes from Dunstable, and knows this kind of chalk country; besides, I get my liquor at night the way I am going to send you, so you should have no difficulty in following the winding tracks of myself and porters. Here's your guide. Au revoir, and the very best to you and your bonny lads. Good night!" and rising, with grave courtesy, the pale captain opened the curtain for the other to leave. The K.O.S.B. captain, new of uniform and equipment, his eyes constantly returning to the ribbon on the other's tunic, was equally formal in his thanks.

"Where would we be," said Captain West, when the kilted figure had gone, "if we hadn't got a navy?" He helped himself to half a mugful of whiskey.

Phillip saw another aspect of what he thought of as the most extraordinary men he had ever met during the candle-lit dinner in the shelter. Captain West had told him that he was a schoolmaster at a preparatory school before the war, what he called an usher. "It was there that I earned the loathed appellation of 'Spectre'." He had been up at Oxford with the Prince of Wales, whom he spoke of as the "Pragger Wagger". Captain West at mess-dinner was quiet and friendly; he ranted no more about the staff; the coming attack was not mentioned. He talked of cricket, in the Duke's Deer Park, in the early months of the war; of partridge drives over the Duke's property, with more than a hundred beaters, and all the game going to the county hospital, for wounded soldiers: and how the Duke made it his business to visit every man of the Gaultshires back from the front, in that hospital; how he had provided money for the wives and dependents of men called up at the outbreak of war, entirely out of his own purse. How in those early days he himself had been sent, senior subaltern of the third or militia battalion at the depöt, to command a company of one of the new service battalions encamped in the Duke's park; how the Duke provided most of the food for the entire battalion—grouse, beef, mutton, venison —and made it his business to know the name of every officer and man under him, and details of his family, too. One day there was what the Duke called a grand charge of the entire battalion of companies in line, led by the Duke on his famous Arab stallion (which before the war was sent to serve one approved mare for every officer of the Gaultshire Yeomanry) —the Duke, sword flashing aloft, crying in a loud voice, "Men of the Gaultshires! Let loose the dogs of war!" and, said Captain West, sitting back with a mock grin look, "Every one of the camp dogs gave tongue exactly a moment afterwards, and led the charge! They knew his Grace's ways as well as anyone!"

Before they left for France, he went on to say, every officer was presented with a pair of field-glasses. The Duchess, too, made it her job to go round and visit the wives of the rank and file, in their cottages, to see that they lacked nothing.

"And that!" said Captain West, holding his mug of whiskey

at arm's length, and regarding the solitary candle through half-closed lids, "is Good Eggery. That is the minimum that one expects from an Englishman with responsibilities going with high station. Gentlemen," he said, half-standing up, "I give you the King, coupled with the Pragger Wagger!"

They drank; then Captain West said, after a glance at his wristlet watch, "The Duke, coupled with the name of his lady wife, the Duchess."

Phillip saw the sweat on the pale domed brow glinting once more; noticed the clenched muscles of the jaw locked tight. The servant cleared the enamel plates; then put upon the table a cubic foot of black cloth, which, on being opened, revealed the nickel-plated enclosed horn of a Decca trench gramophone. "Not now, Boon," Phillip heard Westy mutter, his jaw muscles setting and unsetting. Immediately he changed his mind. "Put on the duet from Tonight's the Night." Then in the momentary silence in the shelter before the needle was put on the disc he said, "My word, the French are going it down south! Listen!"

The air was shaking; Phillip could feel a trembling under his feet, and through the chalk walls of the shelter. Gunfire beat in muffled waves upon the hanging door-blanket; the two candle-flames were quivering nervously. Upon this undertone of the earth's rumbling the sweet and tinny voices of the gay London night came from the open lid, heard by the heads held towards it.

> *And when I tell them, and I'm certainly going to tell them*
> *That you're the girl whose boy one day I'll be,*
> *They'll never believe me, they'll never believe me*
> *That from this great big world you've chosen me!*

Smoke came from pipe and cigarette, hot tinned *café-au-lait* from the primus stove next door was poured steaming into mugs by the attentive Boon. The record ended; was put on again.

"I've got the corks done, sir," Phillip heard him say to his master.

Captain West was looking at his wristlet watch when the blanket parted, and a sentry said, "Corporal asking for Mr. Maddison, sir." Phillip went out into the night. "Sergeant Butler says he's got the right spanners, sir, and the domes are being removed according to plan."

"Oh, good! Tell Sergeant Butler I'll come and see him, and

inspect all emplacements with him in half an hour. And give him my thanks. Have a bit of chocolate. Have you had your grub?"

"Not yet, sir."

"Have some of mine. Half a mo', I'll get it."

"That's all right, sir. I've got my haversack ration intact, sir."

Feeling quivery as the multiple play of light upon the sky beyond Nôtre Dame de Lorette, Phillip went back into the shelter. It was now empty except for "Spectre" West putting on his webbing equipment. A transformation had come over the tall figure: his face, recently so pale, was now black. Burnt corks lay on the table. A sergeant of the Gaultshires, similarly darkened, stood beside him.

"Stop that blasted record!" cried Captain West, as he took up a knobkerry and said tersely to Phillip, "I'm going out to look at the Hun wire. It is now nine pip emma. Since you seem to have about as much initiative as a chick just out of the egg, all wet, I will exceed my duties as a mere company commander of footsloggers to tell you that you will leave this trench at nine-thirty pip emma, to be in plenty of time to report to brigade at ten pip emma. You know where brigade is, don't you? In one of the cellars of Le Rutoire farm. Give 'Nosey' my compliments, and tell him that I look forward to dining with him in Lille tomorrow night."

"Are you serious, Westy?"

"God's teeth, am I ever anything else? Now pay attention. Each battalion going over tomorrow has orders to get as far as it can into the blue. The limit is the Haute Deule Canal, where we shall stand and await the cavalry going through the gap and on to the plain of Flanders and the Scheldt."

Phillip felt excited. Again he remembered that Gran'pa Turney had said the very same thing.

"'Nosey', is that his real name? I can't very well ask for 'Nosey'."

"What is good enough for the regiment," said Captain West, "is good enough for a brigade-major. Now sling your hook and go and look at your emplacements, and next time don't rely on bicycle spanners. Come and see me when you get back from brigade, you blue-eyed wonder! Boon!" to his servant, "why the hell have you stopped the gramophone? Put on They'd Never Believe Me."

Taking the tall ash-plant he had cut from a thicket at Helfaut, Phillip followed the guide through long grass, around shell-holes, and over wooden bridges laid across trenches, to the ruins of Le Rutoire village. There was enough light from the gun-flashes to see ahead. A mild wind came from the west with occasional spots of rain. Troops were moving everywhere. From the two roads in front, leading from Vermelles, came the pro-longed grind of wheels. Buzzing salvoes of howitzer shells passed overhead, to burst with red-black splashes upon the German lines. There were no German shells coming over. He passed waiting men in groups—individuals revealed suddenly by the little glow of cigarette held in hand-palm, so that a stealthy draw glowed upon cheek and chin. He bumped into an aiming post, painted white, by a hidden lamp: with a start realising that he was in front of a battery of field-guns.

"Who are yer?"

"Officer in charge of special emplacements, R.E."

"Pass, sir."

Broken, lonely walls were discernible along a narrow cobbled road forlorn with watery craters. The guide said they were at Le Rutoire farm. Here were many figures, the phut of motor-cycles, the rattle of bits, the roll of wheels. Stretcher-bearers passed, breathing heavily; there was an aid post, lit by a hurri-cane lamp, in what looked like a cellar, the door covered by a gas-blanket, and within, walls covered by white sheets. Perhaps it was an operating theatre. "This way, sir," said the guide, leading him down some sandbagged steps behind the ruin-heaps facing away from the lines. He went down a dozen steps, saw many telephone wires, and tables. At one sat hatless clerks and two officers with red tabs, also bare-headed. He saluted the grey-moustached officer with gold on his tabs, and a blue brassard, who looked up a moment and went on writing at another table. He had crossed swords on his shoulder straps: the brigadier. The third table had a large map pinned on it.

"What is it?" said a captain with a thickly mended bridge to his nose, and a D.S.O. riband, sitting at the other end of the table, beside a telephone. Obviously this was 'Nosey'. Having confirmed from a clerk that he was the brigade major, Phillip gave in his written report, that all his emplacements were in order. It was quiet in his sector. They had had no casualties.

"You are to wait here until you are given the time of zero

hour, which will come later from division, and then you will be responsible for taking it to the adjutant of the battalion on the left section of your front, the Gaultshires. Do you know where the commanding officer's battle headquarters are?"

"No, sir."

A frown came from the brigade major. These temporary officers of the New Army! He said evenly, "Don't you know your sector?"

"Yes, sir, as far as my fourteen emplacements are concerned." He remembered what Westy had said about never explaining. "I'll find it, sir. My guide belongs to the battalion."

"Good," sighed the brigade major. He looked very tired. He sat back in his chair, and stretched his elbows behind the blades of his shoulders. He belched slightly, as though he had eaten bully beef. "Is it raining?"

"Slight drizzle now and again, sir."

"What effect has rain on your gas?"

"It dissolves it, sir, partly in relation to the volume of rainfall."

"What will it do in fog or mist—apart from the smoke of the candles? Hang about?"

"Yes, sir. Chlorine is heavier than air, and so tends to flow to the lowest level."

"I see." The brigade major looked thoughtful. "You will, of course, remain in close touch with the adjutant of the Gaultshires. Here's the weather report. Look at it later. You know, there is an alternative plan for the assault at zero plus forty minutes for the infantry, should it be impracticable to employ the gas discharge. Unless you hear from me, or from someone else here at brigade, that no discharge is to be made, you will carry on according to the time-table you will receive later. Is that clear? Then repeat your instructions."

"Yes, sir. Unless I hear from brigade to the contrary, my cylinders will be turned on according to time-table."

The brigade major took a hand-made Goldflake cigarette from the yellow tin on the table, and pushed the tin to Phillip. "Help yourself. You were with the London Highlanders at First Ypres, 'Spectre' West tells me. Stout fellows, all of 'em. They're on your left, along the road outside. How did you leave 'Spectre'? Fulminating against all with gorget patches?"

"He was just going out on patrol, sir, with blackened face, to look at the Hun wire, opposite the Lone Tree."

"He should have sent one of his subalterns. But 'Spectre's' a chap who won't ask subordinates to do anything he isn't prepared to do himself. He'll have plenty of chance to get moving to-morrow, when we get over the La Bassée–Lens road, into their un-wired and unoccupied second position, and so into open country."

"By the way, sir, he asked me to say: 'Give my compliments—there was a nickname, sir, but I'm not sure what it was—and will you dine with him in Lille tomorrow night'."

"The deuce he did. He said the same thing before Neuve Chapelle, and again at Aubers Ridge—— Well, you'll have to hang about until I can give you zero hour."

"Very good, sir."

He was dismissed, but with a feeling of exhilaration that he had been spoken to as an equal. He was proud of being in the Gaultshire Regiment. This pride awoke a keener interest in what was taking place. He leaned against a wall by the telephone exchange board, listening to the cryptic replies of the operator. The operator seemed to be taking calls and plugging lines all the time. Likewise orderlies were coming and going, handing envelopes for signature to the clerks, while two sergeants were also writing out messages, taking them either to the staff captain or brigade major for signature, and then, tearing out the top-copies, taking them to a compartment separated by a hanging blanket where two signallers at morse-buzzers were sitting on the floor, each with a diaphragm fixed to one ear. It reminded him of the cigar-box telephone he had once made and fixed between his bedroom and mother's; and he began to see what a lot of work there was behind the lines. Those telephone wires by the road-sides on blue and white R.E. poles, scores of them, must link up battalions, batteries, and other units with each other, through the little spider-webs of brigades, and farther back, through divisions and corps headquarters, to Sir John French himself in his château somewhere.

It was hot in the cellar. He went outside, after telling a sergeant that he was going to relieve himself, should he be wanted. He wore the mackintosh under his webbing, with haversack, P.H. helmet, revolver in holster, and ammunition outside. It was not cold in the night air, but fresh. Followed by his guide, he tapped his way along the road which, said the guide, led to the Chapel of the Consolation, on the Vermelles to Hulluch road.

"Who are you?" It sounded like an officer's voice.

"Special Section, R.E."

"Advance, and prove yourself."

Phillip went up to a dim group of figures, with strange head-gear, he could just see.

"I'm the officer in charge of a special section of the R.E."

"What is your rank? And your name?" the authoritative voice demanded.

"Second-lieutenant Maddison."

"What is your Christian name, and where were you born?"

Phillip gave the particulars, and was about to ask why, when the voice said, "Does the name Bleak Hill mean anything to you?"

"Yes, I was there in August 1914 with the London High-landers."

"Do you remember me? My name is Douglas."

"Good lord, Sergeant Douglas! I heard you were gazetted to the Highlanders. But what is the idea—you scared me at first."

"We were warned that spies were about, masquerading in British staff officers' uniform," replied Douglas. "One was reported this afternoon on a bicycle near Verquin, asking various troops who they were. So we were warned to keep a look-out."

Douglas shone a torch on Phillip for a moment, and then asked what the brassard was for. Phillip told him, after which he and Douglas enquired about mutual acquaintances, and how they had fared. Mr. Thorverton, the old platoon officer, had gone home sick, and was now a district recruiting officer in the West Country. "Fiery" Forbes commanded the battalion, which was in an assembly trench as far as the cross-roads, to advance, after the first waves had gone over, to the front lines, and fill the gap between the division's right flank and the left flank of the Scottish division. With another battalion, it was known as the Detached Force. Then Phillip mentioned the draft he had brought over, including Kirk of their old tent party.

"He's in my company," said Douglas. "In fact, he's my run-ner. Kirk, are you there?"

"Here, sir. Hullo, Phillip."

They shook hands. Phillip asked what were they wearing on their heads, and learned that the turban-like effect was due to the rolled gas-helmets sitting upon the tam-o'-shanters, ready to be pulled down.

He told them about the gas and smoke, and feeling optimistic, said that no German in the trenches opposite would survive the double effect of shell and gas bombardment. "Well, we'll all be dining in Lille tomorrow night! Au revoir, you chaps—I've got to see the general in the basement of Le Rutoire farm—so long, and the best of luck!"

When he returned to Brigade H.Q., he saw that the brigade major was reading a message held in one hand, while he picked his teeth with a gold pick concealed in the other. Then he got up and spoke to the general. Together they looked at the map on the third table. Phillip could see the crenellations of the German trenches marked in red, line behind line along the contour marks opposite the blue trenches of the British, for the table was only a yard away from him.

The brigade major was saying, "From this point, General, two hundred yards north of Lone Tree, to a further three hundred yards south of the track——" The brigadier said wearily, "Why can't the gunners observe their own shoots effectively? Ring up division, and ask if they can arrange for the corps heavies—better still, get on to the B.G.R.A. corps himself—I'll speak to him. No, wait a moment." The brigade major waited. Phillip pretended to be examining his field service message book, while he listened. "I'll speak to division myself." He turned to the telephone operator, a pale-faced lance-corporal with oil-smoothed hair and spectacles, and said, "G.S.O. One, division."

The night dragged on. The three other gas-officers waiting for the information of zero hour had long exhausted all topics of talk. They wanted to sleep; they were new to the war; they kept on their feet, hoping that the next moment would be the moment of call to the cellar.

The fourth gas-officer, Phillip, had found a brazier inside a shelter, from where the headquarter guard was mounted; he dozed beside it, while his runner waited, with orders to exchange with him every hour. On one of his "rests" he walked to the front of the farm, seeing the battlefield in fancy as a skeleton ribbed with phosphoric lights: a skeleton which would sink to invisibility at daybreak, issue its poisonous breath upon the day, dart forth its eyes in hundreds of thousands of bullets every minute, its body of nothingness break into thousands of burning sores. The dogs of war would lick this Lazarus turned Sisyphus, rolling backwards and forwards, in attack and counter-attack; and all in vain, for the German *mutter* was the British *mother*, the German *Gott* was the British *God*, German *Freiheit* the British *Freedom*. He yawned wearily, his tongue sharp with nicotine.

He returned to the cellar, and peered in. It was nearly 2 a.m. He heard the brigadier say, "Well, 'Nosey', you'd better turn in for a couple of hours, it will probably be your last chance for several days."

The night was quiet, with the least movement of damp air. Going to the front of the ruinous buildings he stood and let the wise-like feeling between his legs possess him, and so to a sense of detachment from life, the feeling of loneliness that was, deep within, strangely satisfying. He waited, detached, sunk in stillness, while an occasional shell passed with chromatic whine into the vaporous hollow before him, to burst redly, seeming sullen by distance; while away in the south the sky was filled with a multitudinous play of light under distant clouds. What did it all mean, what was it all for, why had it come about? Both sides, along the vast front from the North Sea to the Alps, were waiting, with the same hopes and fears. And yet there was something wonderful about it all, despite the truth that people at home could never know.

An hour seeped away. Exhaustion thinned him. There was no wonder left; the war was really one great horror, a nothingness, everything that had ever been becoming nothing, in pain and fear. Well, he had nothing now to live for: the dream of Helena Rolls was ended, and Nature was gone from his life. What could he *do*, in the broken nothingness all around? The old black depression had fixed itself upon Phillip.

Chapter 20

Y/Z NIGHT—*continued*

Every hour during Y/Z night meteorological reports had been coming in to First Army Headquarters from observers in the army area. At midnight, the speed of the wind, from between south-west and west, five feet above ground, was variable from two to four miles an hour; by midnight it had fallen to a calm.

In the early hours of the morning reports from London gave details of wind-speeds at different places in the British Isles. When at 3 a.m. the meteorological expert saw General Haig and his chief general staff officer, he said that conditions were still favourable for a south-west wind in the morning, but a change back to south might occur.

"At what time is the wind likely to be most favourable?" the general asked.

"The wind usually begins to increase after sunrise, sir, and goes on increasing in the forenoon; and in the case of wind from the south-west, the increase of speed is accompanied by a change of direction towards west."

"*Towards* the west, Captain Gold, did you say?" asked the C.G.S.O., as General Haig stiffened.

"The term applies to the direction whence the wind is blowing, sir. The south-west wind tends to veer, to come from the west. I must add, sir, that owing to the general changes I have mentioned, it would be unsafe to rely on the wind increasing at all."

"When, in your opinion, will be the most favourable time?" the general asked again.

"As soon as possible, sir."

Sir Douglas Haig considered this for some moments, then he asked again if the possibility existed that the wind might increase with the rising of the sun; and on being told yes, turned to his C.G.S.O. and said that zero hour would be at sunrise, 5.50 a.m., for the releasing of the gas, the infantry assault to follow forty minutes afterwards at 6.30 a.m.

Phillip was watching the staff captain as he listened on the telephone. The staff captain was glancing at the chronometer on the table with its black and almost-heart-beating second hand moving round the large face, and checking with his wristlet watch laid beside it. The large chronometer and minute gold watch reminded Phillip of the picture on Father's bedroom wall of a very large and a very small dog in the same kennel, called *Dignity and Impudence*. He heard the staff captain say, *Thank you, colonel, I'll give the brigadier your message*, before the receiver was replaced. Then he wrote something upon a message pad; and beckoned the four subalterns who had been waiting for the past six hours.

"Gentlemen, zero hour is at five-fifty ack emma. I repeat the time of zero. It is at ten minutes to six this morning. You will take this information immediately to your commanding officers, by word of mouth. Here is the time-table of gas and smoke discharge. There is a copy for each emplacement, with extra copies for yourselves. Will you now synchronise your watches." When this was done, he repeated once more that zero hour was at 5.50 a.m. They all saluted, and went up the steps, and after "Cheerios" and "All the best" went their ways in the darkness.

A guide led Phillip to the battle headquarters of the first battalion, the Gaultshire Regiment, nicknamed "The Mediators".

The commanding officer of "The Mediators" came of a family of professional soldiers. He was a temporary lieutenant-colonel with the substantive rank of captain in the first battalion. Lieutenant-Colonel Mowbray wore the D.S.O., and silver rosette of a bar to that decoration, awarded for leadership and selfless devotion to duty as a company commander in the retreat from Mons in August 1914, and again during the battle of Ypres. He was a heavily-built man, with a manner of great courtesy that went with his simplicity. Now a widower, he had been happily married, with the peace of mind that a matched marriage had given him, even as a happy childhood had given him peace in his soul. It was said by some of his brother officers in the regiment that Colonel Mowbray had suffered a great tragedy in his life when, a junior captain, serving in India, he had returned to his house after a week's absence on manœuvres and watched from the bottom of the stairs his wife, running to greet him, trip and lose balance and fall; and when he picked her up her neck was broken so that she died. The grief of Captain Mowbray had been deep; but his faith was deeper. He maintained his faith with prayer as regular as his other habits in both his private and professional life. Thus he kept his spirit free; thus the habit of courtesy, which, beginning as an imitation of his father's manner towards subordinates, had since youth been part of his personality. The stress of war had not shaken his integrity, for Colonel Mowbray within was as Colonel Mowbray without. For him there was only one tragedy in life: to fail in duty towards others.

It was the message from Colonel Mowbray which had disturbed the brigadier and his brigade major, the effect of which Phillip had observed, when they had looked at the trench map on the table. Colonel Mowbray had reported that the enemy wire north and south of Lone Tree was still intact after the bombardment.

The guide stopped before a dugout, which went down ten feet under the surface. It had a roof of timber baulks and bags, with an air-space to act as cushion in the central layers. Sods on the top hid the bags of chalk.

Colonel Mowbray was sitting at a table reading Malory's *Mort d'Arthur*. He put down the book when Phillip entered.

"I have to report that zero hour is at five-fifty ack emma, sir," said Phillip, saluting. "And may I show you a copy of the gas time-table?"

"Thank you," replied the colonel, quietly. "Sit down, won't you." He examined the time-table; looked up and said, "How is the wind?"

"Almost nil, sir, but what there is, is moving north-east by east."

"Can you tell me what the effect of our final bombardment will have, particularly as regards the low-trajectory eighteen-pounders, on a slowly moving gas cloud?"

"They will tend to disturb, it, sir, and so break it up," replied Phillip hurriedly.

"Will they carry forward, or impede, the cloud?"

"They will tend to carry it forward, sir," he said, trying to appear as though he had not made up the reply.

"I see. Now when the cloud reaches the enemy's wire and front trenches, will the bombardment disperse the gas, owing to the heat of the explosions?"

"Yes, sir. But the gas, being heavier than air, will settle again."

"Thank you." The colonel looked at his watch. "The time is now twenty minutes past four. In one hour and thirty minutes you will be discharging your gas?"

"Yes, sir."

"Are your cylinders intact?"

"They were when I saw them last, sir."

"When was that?"

"Between eight and nine o'clock, I mean pip emma, sir."

"Where have you been meanwhile?"

"Waiting at brigade headquarters, sir, to be told the hour of zero, and for the revised time-table. I was ordered to be there at ten pip emma."

"You have had to wait a long time. Well, I must not keep you. You are going to your emplacements now, are you? Goodbye, and good luck!"

The wet night was turning, with a rise of temperature, to-wards the dawn, soon to reveal a morning of mist and drizzle in places, to cast the first wan light of day upon innumerable watery boot-marks left by those who, having said goodbye to life, were now become spectral to themselves and to one another, grey with fear, barren with the thoughts of men whose lives might soon be taken from them.

It was eerie to be passing men trying to sleep in all attitudes in the reserve trench; and coming to the communication trench marked UP, Phillip went on to the front line. Here it was like-wise crowded with men in sagging attitudes, heads bowed over knees and resting on elbows, faces hidden away from dreadful thoughts of aloneness and obliteration. He passed by the half-sleeping, the thought of Captain West guiding him. When he reached the shelter, all within was quiet and dark. The orderly sitting on a box just inside the blanket whispered that the captain was asleep.

"He told me to wake 'im when you come back, sir. He's only bin down to it an hour. He was out acrost to the Jerry wire, and then with the colonel until nearly two, sir. Shall I wake him, sir?"

"No, let him sleep. I'll go and see my chaps, and come back later."

He was about to go out when Captain West's voice said, "Don't you ever obey orders, Phillip? Where have you been? Come and tell me. When does the balloon go up? How's the wind?"

"Zero is 5.50. I've told your C.O. Wind is fairly faint. There's also a revised time-table for the gas discharge. I haven't read it yet. I've got to give a copy to each sergeant in charge of my emplacements."

"Let me see."

Captain West rose on an elbow, switched on his electric torch.

"God's teeth, my eyes are seeing double. Read it out."

"Zero to 0.12 minutes, six cylinders gas

    0.12 to 0.20 minutes, four smoke candles

    0.20 to 0.32 minutes, six cylinders gas

    0.38 to 40 minutes, two triple smoke candles

    0.40 minutes—Assault!"

"So we go over at half past six," said West. "Boon! Bring tea, hot, thick, and *no* sugar this time. I've got a mouth like the bottom of a parrot's cage. So they've changed the plans again."

"Yes. The original idea was thirty-eight minutes of gas right off, to use up the German helmets, including a second dip in the hypo. They last for fifteen minutes only, without a re-dip. Thirty-eight minutes of gas, then the smoke cloud for the final two minutes, to give the infantry complete cover from view. This new arrangement isn't so good, in my opinion."

"It's to get the main body of Hun troops out of their deep dugouts, when they see the smoke, to meet our assault, then to catch them in our final bombardment," replied Captain West. "But if the Hun doesn't come out until the guns lift, and if furthermore, my lad, your gas doesn't put him down, we'll be for the high jump again. For, I will tell in strict confidence, the gunners haven't cut the wire along our front."

"Good God!"

"Not a word, mind," said Captain West, through clenched teeth.

Phillip was startled to realise that the great "Spectre" West was afraid. The revelation gave him, in the same moment, the thought that what Westy could do, he could also do. In this extraordinary feeling of having shed his old feeble self, he said, "It says here that local commanders may give orders to run the gas concurrently with the smoke, if necessary, so if you like I can easily let it all off in the thirty-eight minutes. That will saturate their masks. I think it must have been your report I heard the brigadier discussing. Is the German wire intact two hundred yards north of Lone Tree, to three hundred south of it?"

"Yes. What did he say?"

"That he'd ring 'B.G.R.A.' at corps, whoever that was."

"Brigadier-general of gunners. What happened?"

"He changed his mind, and rang 'G.S.O. One, Division'."

"Well? Hurry up! You're too damned slow!"

"I didn't hear any more."

Captain West said sharply, "Not a word about this outside, or to any of my subalterns, mind!" in such a tone of command that Phillip automatically said, "No, sir!"

Then, after a pause, he said, "Well, I think I'll get along to my emplacements, and warn the N.C.O.s in charge of the change of time-table."

"Come back here when you have done so. I may have something to say about how you release your gas, and blast every staff wallah! Boon! Hold that tea back until Mr. Maddison returns. I'm now going to sleep for half an hour. Shut up, you bloody thing!" he shouted at the alarm clock, ticking loudly on the table as it lay on its face in disgrace. Captain West covered it with his balaclava helmet, before rolling upon the bed again and pulling the blanket over his head. But not to sleep. He lay in the darkness fighting to overcome a picture of men bunching in front of thick rusty wire until cut down by the screeching blast of machine-guns firing at point-blank range. He clenched his hands, drew up his knees, made himself rigid as he tried to dissolve the picture; but always it reformed itself before his closed eyes, to the loud ticking of idiot Time.

Phillip moved along the assembly trench, passing company after company of men in all attitudes of unquiet sleep and quiet despair, huddled on duckboards or leaning against chalk-bagged walls of each traverse. Sentries stood in the fire-bays, patient and thoughtful as they took moments of privacy with shut eyes, with subdued sighs. Through the damp and stagnant air, in the hour before dawn when the thoughts of waking men, in peace or war, are often catastrophic, the body vacant of soul, Phillip moved among herded men, his slow progress revealed by the wan light from a torch whose glass lens he held between his fingers. Strange thoughts of his new self passed in his mind; *he* was commanding men; *he* was one of those superior beings to whom men looked, as having power over their lives. It was a surprising thought that he, Phillip Maddison, could stand up to real officers like Captain West, M.C.; could speak to staff officers as an equal. How remote seemed his old self, that used to feel small in the presence of such people as Captain Whale, Major Fridkin, and Lieutenant Brendon, who had remarked, with slight contempt, "As a soldier, Maddison is in that state known as *non est*."

He was sweating when he reached the first emplacement, to hear the sergeant say, "I thought perhaps you'd copped it, sir," to which the reply, "Oh, no, I'm too wicked to die just yet," while Cranmer's face seemed to be upon his own, strangely. He left a time-table sheet, and pushed his way on to the next emplacement, while telling himself there was no need for hurry, there was a full hour before the balloon went up. The strain ended only when he had come to the last emplacement; then a further anxiety developed when the sergeant, asking to speak in private with him, said, "I don't like the look of this quiet air, sir. The men are saying that the gas will hang about, and they'd rather go over the bags without it. If you'll excuse my saying it, sir."

"Of course, naturally. I'm going back to my Number One emplacement now, and shall be in telephonic communication with brigade, and will send word if the plans are changed. Meanwhile, unless you hear from me, you will carry on with the time-table I've given you."

"Very good, sir."

"I'll be round to see you again, in any case, before the boys go over." He turned to go back.

"Sir!"

"Yes?"

"The infantry's talking of the wire not being cut, I mean the jerry wire, sir, along by the Lone Tree. I thought I'd tell you, sir, just in case——"

"That's been taken care of, Sergeant. I was at brigade when the report came through, an hour or two back, and the gunners will attend to it."

"Very good, sir. Is there any harm in telling the boys?"

Phillip hesitated. Then, remembering what Westy had said to him, "Rather not. See you later, Sergeant."

By 5 a.m. it was growing light. General Sir Douglas Haig walked outside his château, into what was almost a calm. With him was his senior A.D.C.

"Light a cigarette, will you, Fletcher."

The smoke drifted in little puffs towards the north-east. The two men stood still. The commander of the first Army did not speak; his aide kept the cigarette down, while holding himself in pliant immobility, emptying himself of thought, lest he disturb the general.

At 9.20 p.m. on the previous evening Sir Douglas Haig had ordered the general offensive with gas confidently; but owing to possible variance of the wind, staff officers of corps had been ordered to wait by their telephones to receive instructions. Without gas, owing to the insufficiency of heavy artillery, the attack would suffer heavy losses, and had small hope of success; furthermore, the enemy, from his superior observation posts in pit-head tower and spoil-heap, would be able to direct devastating gun-fire on troops massed in the front trenches, and in crowded communication trenches, if an attempt was made to withdraw the infantry of the four divisions not required for the limited alternative attack.

A few minutes after 5 a.m. the wind began to move slightly. At 5.15 a.m. General Haig gave the order to carry on, and then climbed to the top of his wooden look-out tower, to think alone. While time passed slowly as the wind he began to fear that the gas would hang about the British trenches. He bore himself up under the grave responsibility with the aid of prayer for guidance, a man seeking clarity within his own soul.

While he stood there one of his staff telephoned to the commander of the First Corps. When Lieutenant-General Gough replied, he asked, "Is it possible to stop the arrangements for the attack, General?"

"The gas is due to be turned on within half an hour," said General Gough. "I do not consider it practicable to get word in time to the front trenches and to all the batteries concerned. Therefore, I am of the opinion that it is now too late to cancel the arrangements for the attack."

By 5.40 a.m. the First Army commander felt a less heavy weight upon his spirit, when a slight breeze sprang up and rustled the poplar leaves in the green country behind the coal-fields. But a weight remained on his mind; for he had no immediate reserves to exploit a break-through should this happen in the morning. He had asked for the reserve divisions to be put in his immediate rear as soon as the assault took place; but to all his requests Field-marshal Sir John French had replied that he would keep the general reserve for the battle under his personal command, and await events before ordering them to move forward.

With the exception of the Guards Division, and the Cavalry Corps, the divisions of the general reserve were all untried troops, who had only recently arrived in France from England. The field-marshal had several reasons for keeping them back; Sir Douglas Haig knew only one reason why they should be well-up at the moment of assault.

Behind the trenches, artillery observers sitting in their sand-bagged posts were waiting, in calm excitement, headphones to ears. The battery commanders had received orders to be prepared to move out of their pits at the shortest possible notice.

Along the British line all was quiet; but from the south, from behind the ridge of Nôtre Dame de Lorette came the subdued deep roar with flickers as of distant lightning where the French had been fighting round Souchez and the strong German redoubt of the Labyrinthe continuously for the past week.

The gunners were now standing-to, in the gun-pits of batteries pointing into the whitening east: the great howitzers with blunt barrels rising steeply up; the long and comparatively slender high-velocity guns; the eighteen-pounder field-guns with their horses picketed a couple of hundred yards in the rear, waiting to hook-in and go forward over the prepared wooden bridges. Thousands of gunner-officers were imagining, again and again, the thrilling order of *Hook your lanyards!*, then *Fire!* as slowly the hands of watches passed the half-hour mark, and crept to the three-quarter-hour mark, and the small ticking behind luminous dials became heart-beats thumping in ears.

Captain West's company headquarters was alive when Phillip returned. Equipped for battle, bombs hung on webbing braces, revolvers oiled, gas-masks rolled on heads under shapeless trench-caps from which badges were removed, platoon commanders were taking last looks at their maps. Their runners stood outside, holding yellow flags on sticks, to mark the boundaries of the advance for the artillery observers hidden up chimneys, in house lofts, and on haystacks behind the series of chalk seams cut in the level-seeming pan between the groups of *fosses* or *puits* held by the British and those on higher ground occupied by the Germans.

Ladders were in position, to scale parapets; the new Lewis gun-teams held fast to their hollow black weapons.

Boon the servant brought hot mugs of tea. Shakily the captain poured whiskey into each. Then he sat down suddenly, as though hit, on the edge of his wire-net bed. From there he lit a second candle, putting it in front of the alarm clock now upright on the table. As the flame rose up, Time became his enemy. He put the clock between him and the stump, complaining, "God's teeth, that blasted light stabs my eyeballs." He gulped the contents of his mug. "This tea is cold, dammit." Then, "What's the time?"

"Four minutes to go, skipper."

Captain West sprang off the bed, and touching Phillip on the shoulder said quietly, "Come with me."

Phillip followed him through the blanket, damp with liquid from the Vermorel sprayer, and out past men standing up in a sickly light, ominous with rain that hung everywhere in threat above the dead-white parapet. Some were smoking; a few talking; but all were silent as they watched the two officers climbing two scaling ladders, placed side by side, to look out over the dreaded top.

"No wind," said Captain West. "Do you agree?"

"Yes, I do."

They got down the ladders.

"Ring up Brigade. Ask for the general. Tell him I have ordered you not to turn on the gas."

They returned past the silent faces, and entered the shelter. There in the same silence filled with a quaking sense of doom Phillip took the telephone and spoke to the general, saying, as he tried to keep his voice firm, "I am unable to carry on with the time-table, sir. I don't trust the wind, sir."

A remote, impersonal voice replied, "I've already spoken to Division about the wind being unsuitable, and received a direct order to carry on. Therefore you will release your gas according to your orders. Is that understood?"

"Yes, sir."

Faces were looking at him. He was about to speak when the candle flames fluttered and went out, as in fright before a concentration of heavy buffets that shook pieces of chalk out of the walls and caused all the men within to flinch. When the blanket was drawn back Phillip saw the forms and faces of men holding

rifles, the scaling ladders, the wrinkled parapet line of chalk-
bags in the rain as a scene in one of the scratchy flickering early
bioscope films at the Electric Palace.

It was the intensive bombardment before the assault. It was
5.50 a.m. on the 25th of September 1915. The battle of Loos
had begun.

Chapter 21

LONE TREE

THE gas was already rising into the air and forming into a
rolling grey cloud. Showers of small chalk fell among the waiting
men. The top layer of hessian bags on the parapet was breaking,
lifting ragged ears to the dull sky. Through the rolling thunder
of the bombardment could be heard a shearing-of-glass noise,
as the air above the trench was torn across by machine-gun
bullets. Distant rockets soared and broke into colours; down
fell the German shells. The waiting men crouched.

Away to the north a big mushroom of dark smoke hung in
the sky, above a blown mine. In places along the German lines
fires were being lit, to dissipate the gas which was moving slowly
towards them. It seemed to be hanging about in No Man's
Land, eddying.

Followed by four runners, Phillip pushed his way down the
trench, to visit his emplacements. Shrapnel was cracking above;
men were being hit. In all the first four emplacements some
connecting pipes were broken, and gas had come into the trench.
The sergeants in charge had turned off the flow. Smoke candles
were billowing away. He felt he could get no farther: he told
the runners to tell their respective sergeants to use smoke only,
rather than let their own men be gassed. When they had gone
he put on his smoke helmet, and soon felt an almost insufferable
heat. The eye-pieces misted over with sweat; he could hardly
breathe; he stood as nearly upright as he dared, remembering
that chlorine was heavier than air.

Some of the infantry lifted the bottom edge of their helmets
to get a breath of fresh air. He saw, as from undersea, several
figures doubling up, staggering about retching, wrenching

off helmets and clutching at the air. They made movement in the trench almost impossible.

Phillip looked at his watch, but it was invisible. He must wipe the eye-piece of his good eye. Holding his breath, he felt up from the end of the grey cloth tucked under his tunic. It was a desperate movement, made with the right hand while with his left he clutched the damp cloth round his neck to stop any gas coming in. It felt as though his right hand were trying to fight his left, the guardian hand. If it did let in gas, there would be no escape out of the trench. The top bags of the parapet were now in rags as machine-gun bullets struck them.

Smoke from the candles poured into the trench. This was not deadly, like chlorine, but it made breathing most heavy.

He tried to get back to Captain West's shelter. He would be able to see the face of the alarm clock. While he was shoving his way forward, there was a change in the muddle of the trench; men were forming into some sort of line about the scaling ladders. The smoke having drifted a little, he could see through the eye-pieces that bayonets were already fixed. He got back in time to see the first wave of the Gaultshires climbing up the ladders. It was zero plus forty minutes. One of them appeared to slip. He fell back into the trench. Others pushed past him. All were wearing pulled-down smoke helmets. The helmet of the man who had slipped was torn. He lay in the trench, in an attitude of relaxation, while the helmet trickled blood.

More waves of attackers were coming from behind, up the communication trenches. Near the entrance to the fire-trench they began to cough and choke. Those who could do so, climbed out, and hurried along behind the parados, trying to find the crossing bridges. There was some confusion, as the trench was under fire; but somehow they got across, extended, advanced; and one by one dropped out of the advance.

From where he was standing behind the parados of the trench, under a continuous screaming of eighteen-pounder shells passing, it seemed, just over his short-hairs, Phillip could see pale-yellow grasses stretching away in front of him to the crest behind which lay the concealed German lines; but now all between sky and grass was hidden in smoke and gas. Into the hanging fog, in twos and threes and fours, shells were bursting. The waves of advancing men were disappearing in the smoky drag of the

horizon. He thought that to call them waves was the opposite
of what they were; the waves were against them, throwing up
black spray, surging over little figures like specks of jetsam.

A continuous flight of bullets was passing, most of them
whipping the air, but a few striking the ground and whining
away as they spun over and over. As he watched a voice shouted
in his ear, "Your blasted gas has done enough damage already,
and I don't want you on my conscience as well, so get down,
damn your eyes."

Phillip got down; but Captain West, now marble-calm, stood
as before and focused his field glasses upon the advance.

The German first line, curtained by their own protective fire,
was not in view from where Captain West was observing; it lay
just behind the turn-over of the imperceptible slope, marked
by a stark and solitary tree near the wire-belt concealed by the
grass. This front line, on the reverse slope, was connected later-
ally with the Loos Road Redoubt on Hill 69. The Redoubt
was a massive work, the centre one of three dominating the
British positions, with the Hohenzollern to the north and Hill 70
to the south. There were many steel cupolas, with splayed slits
for machine-gun fire, a few inches above ground level, each so
placed that it could enfilade attacking troops at a distance;
and the German machine-gunners were equipped with oxygen
masks. The German defensive system of cross-fire was designed
to strike attacking waves sideways on; and as Captain West
watched, he saw men falling like stalks in the sweep of a scythe.

The Loos Road Redoubt was the objective of the brigade of
which the Gaultshires was the leading battalion. Its garrison
had been safe from heavy shell-fire in dugouts twelve metres
underground; now it was protected in fire-trenches revetted with
stakes and faggots, made with firing-steps well above a deeper
trench which provided a passing place as well as shelter from
shrapnel. The deepness of such shelter was its security from
shells and bullets; but that very deepness, filled by asphyxiating
gas heavier than air, would be as the deepness of a grave.

The Loos Road Redoubt, from where Captain West stood,
was visible only as a skyline above the slightest of rises in the
down-like landscape. It was sixty-nine metres above sea-level;
the British front line, where the gas was still eddying in places,
was between forty and forty-five metres.

The wounded and gassed began to totter, crawl, and drag themselves back through the sere grasses, some helped by others, but this was rare; most of them struggled alone, desperate for safety, for water, for rest. Nothing could be done for them; there were too many; the first-aid post had been blown in, the doctor and his corporals killed. Some got over the trench bridges; others fell in, and writhed about, gurgling and retching in chlorine which lay there stagnant. The Vermorel sprayers had used all their liquid.

The crackle of rifle-fire came undiminished from over the grassy battlefield pocked by white craters of chalk, and strewn with figures in khaki, their heads defaced by grey masks set with circular goggles, with little rubber beaks or mouths giving them an appearance of miming in death to the hammering of machine-guns, the rending of shells, and the crackle of rifle-fire that told its own tale of what had happened to the Gaultshires and their sister battalions in the brigade.

To Captain West, ordered to remain behind during the first assault, it was happening to himself. He longed to rush upon the wire. Indifferent to the whip and hiss of bullets passing over, he continued to stand on the parados, and, looking up, Phillip saw his face working with curses.

Phillip stood up. Unknown to him, the effect of his presence upon "Spectre" West was calming. Phillip felt no fear. He was a mere spectator; he had no part in what was happening. He was free.

"We should be getting a message back soon," said Captain West, sitting down. "When are you taking your section away? Here, get behind the parados. I told you before, I do not want to have you on my hands——"

"They've gone. I sent them back under the senior sergeant."

"What were your orders?"

"I ordered myself. I said I'd follow on later. I want to see what happens."

Captain West focused his glasses to search the ground to the south, towards Loos and the Double Crassier just perceptible in the mist and smoke. "If I apply for you, will you join my company?"

So far Phillip had put away the thought of rejoining the infantry; the direct question came as a shock. Before he could think what to reply, the company sergeant major came up to

Captain West and said, "Runner coming, sir. Looks like Croot, sir."

The runner came limping towards them. His boots were clogged with loam and grasses, his puttees balled with mud, his trousers ragged. He carried his smoke-helmet in one hand. His face was red, his hair matted with sweat. He picked his way over a wooden bridge, took a crumpled sheet of message paper from his pocket, and gave it to Captain West. While Captain West was reading it, the orderly spoke to the C.S.M. in a high, hoarse, wheezing voice. The boys were lying before the wire. Many had fallen down on the way, owing to gas. They were in the grass. The shell-holes were full of gas. Stretcher-bearers were wanted. He showed a small hole in the back of one trouser leg, where a shrapnel ball had gone into his thigh.

"Well, you've got the blighty one you wanted, Croot."

"Yes, Major, but the boys——"

"We'll take care of them. Now, my lad, you look after Number One now. That's your way!" The C.S.M. pointed to a communication trench marked *Walking Wounded Only*.

Captain West spoke on the telephone to Colonel Mowbray. After giving his report, he seemed to be listening for a long while. Phillip was transfixed with fear at the thought of being ordered immediately to join the battalion. At last he heard Captain West say, "They should soon be in a position to pinch off the Hun opposite, Colonel." Then, "Yes, Colonel. I'll come now. Yes, I'll bring Maddison with me."

Putting down the instrument, Captain West said to Phillip, "Those damned fornicating idiots on the staff! They do not even listen to one of the finest surviving regular soldiers of the original British Expeditionary Force, Edward Mowbray! Their minds are paper, paper, paper! They stare at maps, they stick in their little pins with flags on them, and that is all a battalion means to them! They've never been stopped by barbed-wire, unless it was the wire outside a prisoners' cage! They can think only frontally, from staring at reams and reams of their own bumff! They have now ordered us to make another frontal attack on uncut wire! Do you realise what I am saying? Then what in Christ's name are you grinning at?" yelled Captain West, his face contorted, a thin white lather working in the corners of his mouth. "Take that grin off your face, and listen to me, you horrible gas-merchant! The London Division is over there." He stabbed the air towards the Double Crassier. "They are on the extreme right. They have got into the Hun front line with little opposition, but have had to stop to make a defensive flank, because the French next to them haven't started yet. Don't ask me why! They have not yet started! That is a fact! So the Londoners' advance is stopped; while the Scottish Division next to us are going strong towards Loos. Their left flank is exposed, because we are held up. On *our* left flank"—Captain West's voice was now less strident—"on *our* left flank the First Brigade has got through both fire and support trenches of the Hun first position, and the leading troops when last seen were crossing the Loos–Haisnes road. So their right flank is exposed, because our fellows, or what is left of them, are lying down before belts of uncut wire. That is the situation. The Hun position behind Lone Tree is threatened on both flanks. So what does the staff order? Shall I tell you?" screamed Captain West, above the screaming of eighteen-pounder shells. "The staff has ordered a second frontal attack against uncut wire! Does that, or does that not, strike you as the quintessence of criminal stupidity? Well? Well? Say something!"

Phillip did not know what to say.

"God's teeth, I thought you had brains!" went on Captain West, contemptuously, the froth working in the corners of his mouth. "Look at this!" He flung open his map, knelt down to spread it on the ground, and pressed it with a finger as he cried, "Here is Lone Tree. And here"—the finger shook on the linen-backed, squared paper—"is where the First Brigade is now, just about to outflank Lone Tree to the north. And here"—another prod—"is where the Jocks on our right have got to. Yet here"—driving his finger through the map into the loamy clay underneath—"is where we are ordered to attack the same uncut wire frontally! And this in modern war—not in the Crimea!"

The C.S.M., lying a few yards away, grinned at Phillip, as much as to say that he knew the captain of old, and there was nothing to be done about anything anyway. Phillip said, "Surely the reserves should follow the First Brigade and get round behind Lone Tree? Why, as a Boy Scout I learned that!"

"The staff," said Captain West, "have never been Boy

Scouts. They know everything except nothing. Now come with me." To his batman he said, "Fill my water-bottle with the remains of the Johnny Walker, Boon—and *no* chlorinated water this time." Then to Phillip, "Come with me to the colonel."

Outside a dugout among the lines of chalk-white trenches stood Colonel Mowbray with his adjutant and R.S.M. The colonel wore a trench-coat concealing his rank. With his walking-stick and air of authority the massive deliberate figure looked like a country gentleman with his steward come to inspect part of his estate. Phillip saluted, and the feeling of awe before the colonel's massiveness vanished when the big red face became kindly with a smile, and "Good morning!" said the colonel. The words, spoken with the charm of an open face, made Phillip feel happier, yet with a certain nervousness that he did not deserve to be treated as a proper officer. He moved away a few paces, in case the colonel wanted to speak to Captain West alone, but hurried forward when the voice called to him, and the colonel held out his hand. When they had shaken hands, the colonel said, "How much gas have you left in your cylinders, Maddison?"

Pleased and surprised that so important a figure already knew his name, he replied with a slight stutter, "N-none now, sir, it was all l-let off before the assault."

"Then your duties on detachment are ended?"

"I have to send in my report, sir."

Colonel Mowbray began to talk to Captain West, so Phillip once more went a few yards away, and looked towards the smoke of battle. Bullets passed; he was pleased that he did not flinch. He hastened forward when the R.S.M. said the colonel wanted him. "You had better hear what I have to say, Maddison." Colonel Mowbray went on to say that the attack was generally going well on both flanks: that the temporary check on the brigade front was to be dealt with by the Divisional Detached Force, consisting of mixed troops. They were about to advance from their assembly trenches of the Fosse Way, and occupy the front line, with a view to carrying on the attack towards Lone Tree.

Phillip wondered if he would be ordered to go with the attack. If he said that his gas brassard prevented him going, would they know he was afraid? How could he get away? The colonel was explaining that the rôle of the Detached Force, as originally intended, was to fill the gap between the two brigades when the first enemy position had been carried, and maintain touch with them.

"The First Brigade, as you know, is advancing due east to Hulluch, while our brigade has still to strike east-south-east over the Loos Road Redoubt to the slag-heaps of Puits Fourteen. Now the Detached Force, the liaison force, is, unless the brigadier can prevail upon division to prevent it, to be thrown in to repeat our attack, with Lone Tree as their centre. We are concerned in that the reserve company of the Gaultshires is to support the attack."

Captain West replied with distinctness, "Surely division knows, Colonel, that the Hun position behind Lone Tree is now a salient, and that it should be pinched off? If the reserve company were to debouch to the left, by the Bois Carré, which has been overrun by the First Brigade, we could outflank the entire position."

"I know, Harold, I know. But those are my orders."

Colonel Mowbray then said very quietly, "The reserve company has only two junior subaltern officers left, as Hopkins was killed and Whitfield wounded by the same shell this morning, so I am putting you in charge of the attack. I'm afraid you will have to go straight for Lone Tree again, Harold. I asked to be allowed to go myself, but the brigadier has ordered me to remain with the cadre. Ah, here's Bimbo—he may have some news——" The staff-captain was coming towards the dugout. The colonel went to meet him.

Phillip, feeling icy cold, watched Captain West staring into the sky. He strove against a feeling of being fixed to the ground; he wanted to go away, while the chance was there; but he could not move. Westy would know why he went, if he went. Then Westy went towards the dugout, and suddenly he felt free; and with trepidation, and sickness of his fear, he set off to Le Rutoire farm, with the excuse to get the correct time. His wristlet watch had stopped, due either to grit or gas, probably both. He lit a cigarette, to show his nonchalance; but the smoke tasted of rotten eggs. The Germans must be sending over lachrymatory shells, called pear-drops by the men, after the farthing-an-ounce fruit-drops in the sweetstuff shops at home.

It was shortly before eight o'clock, he learned at brigade headquarters. He thought it best not to be seen hanging about, so he made for the white line of trenches beside the track leading to the Chapel of Consolation, where he had talked with the London Highlanders the previous night. Would it have been wiser to have gone back to the billet in Mazingarbe with his section? But if he had gone back, by now he might have been ordered to join an infantry battalion, his detachment duty being over. And while he remained where he was, no-one would be able to find him, even if anyone thought of him, which was unlikely in the continual movement of all kinds of troops, once he was clear of the Gaultshires.

He walked in the direction of the chalk thrown up beside the Fosse Way; and was almost at the beginning of them when shells began to drone down, as salvo upon salvo dropped upon and around Le Rutoire farm. The air, too, was again being scorched with swift hissings like water spilled on red-hot iron. The smoke and gas had cleared across the dim, dull plain; and the old front line was under fire again from machine-guns and rifles.

He started to build for himself a rough bunker by piling chalk-bags on to a length of sheet-iron crossing the trench, obviously someone's shelter during the past night. That would make it shrapnel-proof. While he worked he saw what had caused the German fire. Away on his left, up the track, several columns of infantry were advancing. It must be the Detached Force. German shrapnel now started to burst in the air in places over the old front line. It was the high-explosive variety known as woolly bears, which had yellow smoke.

Now the columns of troops were running sideways, extending to open order, advancing on Lone Tree, while the scorching hisses of machine-gun bullets were increasing. He kept down his head; he sat back and tried to sleep; but all the time his mind was working. If discovered there by the Battle Police he would say that his heart was bad, owing to the gas, and that he had not gone back to Mazingarbe because he had been asked to join his regiment; he had wanted to take part in the attack, but had dizzy spells, due to gas. That anxiety being allayed, he decided to remain where he was for the time being, and watch what was happening.

He peeped over the chalk parapet, and saw that some of the kilted infantry—they must be London Highlanders—were stumbling, their rifles dropping out of their hands first. Now the smoke had cleared off, they were easy targets across No Man's Land, since the German front line was still in the same place as the day before. Bullets were cracking sharply overhead, so he crept under his narrow shelter and, suddenly weary, lay down with face on one arm, to get some rest. His throat felt sore. Could he be slightly gassed?

Sometime later he was aware of noises of slipping feet and heavy breathing, and, looking up, saw men leaping and sliding into the trench. They were the Gaultshires. Intense fire was now cracking and hissing over the trench. From a sergeant he learned that they were in support. Thank God, he thought, for his gas brassard; he could not be ordered to take part. How strange it was that this was part of the Big Push, that he was actually in it. To be hit at such a distance from the enemy was not so bad as being aimed at: it would be rather like being in a street accident. When he asked a sergeant what the time was (for his watch had stopped again) he was surprised to learn that only an hour had gone by since he had been at Le Rutoire farm.

Sitting in the trench was rather like being behind the corn-stack on Messines ridge nearly a year before, in the same slow meaningless drag of time that was dead; hour after hour, while half a mile in front the London Highlanders, part of the Detached Force, were lying behind the shallow parados of the original front line, exposed in the weak sunshine to prolonged enemy fire as they waited for orders: from nine o'clock to ten o'clock: to eleven o'clock: to twelve o'clock: to one o'clock.

"Are you Lieutenant Maddison, sir? Captain West would like to speak to you, sir."

With thudding heart he followed the runner along the trench. Captain West was sitting beside his telephone signaller, eating bully beef and biscuits. He offered his water-bottle, which was empty. He was now apparently in better humour.

"Have a spot of old man whiskey. Boon is making tea. Where the hell did you get to? Our attack has been washed out. We are standing by. Only when those coves, who help themselves to all the gongs, have had their luncheon of potted Morecambe Bay shrimps, chicken in aspic, truffles, Camembert cheese and Romary biscuits, coffee and brandy, will the order to infiltrate through the gap on our left come through; for, by the teeth of God, what else but staff luncheon is preventing us from filing to the north along the trenches and debouching by the Bois Carré?"

"I don't know."

That was the only reply he could think of. Why was Westy staring at him so intently? His face was changed; it was slightly unpleasant, with its paler blue eyes and little pin-pointed irises. The sweat on the white forehead was rather nasty. He was now indeed his nickname of "Spectre". Staring at him intently, "Spectre" West said, "I weep tears of blood for you, Phillip! Look at me, my poor young friend!" He flung away his lump of bully beef. "Look at me! Now listen carefully! On our right the Fifteenth Scottish Division has gone out of sight over Hill 70! Got that? They've broken through on a narrow front. A narrow break-through is dangerous. It is vulnerable! Got that? But Hill 70 is the key to the battle. It gives observation over everything else. Do you know what Hill 70 in Hun hands is?" He paused. "Death peering with folded wings."

"I understand that, of course, for they can shell anything moving——"

"Listen to me! Don't turn away your head! I have told you that the Scottish Division, or the Fifteenth, if you prefer staff-like precision, has got into the suburbs of Lens, beyond Hill 70. The Seventh on our left has got almost to Hulluch. So I asked permission to lead all available reserves through the Bois Carré, and so get behind the Lone Tree position, and pinch it off. And what was the result? Pass me the bottle. Hell! Who's drunk it? Boon! Boon! Where the devil is Boon? Send for Boon, s'ar major!"

"Here, sir!"

"Good. Another bottle, Boon."

"Napoo, sir. You've had the last bottle," replied Boon, pumping the Primus.

"No excuse! Get one! Help yourself, Phillip."

"Spectre" West passed the empty bottle.

"No thanks, I think I've had a whiff of gas, it makes my taste seem rather funny."

He wanted to get back to his shelter, but he must not make it too obvious. Was Westy blotto? Or even mad? Boon the batman continued to sit by the canteen of water on the Primus stove. When Westy spoke again, he was suddenly his old self once more.

"I'll give you a mug of *café-au-lait* in a minute, Phillip. Sergeant Jones! Has the company s'ar-major come back yet?"

"Not yet, sir."

"I sent him to the colonel with a message, asking permission to move to the flank," remarked Captain West, to Phillip, as though he had forgotten his former outburst, "and so give fire-support to the frontal attack of the Detached Force. Hullo, it looks as though it has started." He looked at his watch. "Two pip emma! The staff have finished luncheon," he announced, almost cheerfully.

A whipping fury of bullets passed over the trench, followed by a distant crackling. It was now impossible to hear what Westy was saying, for almost simultaneously the field-guns behind Le Rutoire had opened up. They sat there, unspeaking, until the rugged face of the regimental sergeant major was seen, bending low, pushing its way to them. Kneeling by Captain West, he bawled through cupped hands:

"The colonel has been hit, with the adjutant, sir."

Phillip saw Westy's jaw tighten. Then his nostrils opened wide.

"What happened, Mr. Adams?"

"The C.O. was leaving battalion headquarters to go to brigade, sir. A coal-box burst right beside them, sir. You are now in command of the battalion, sir."

Phillip watched Westy open his message book. While he was writing, it was a good moment to slip away. He went back to his shelter, and put on the red-white-green gas brassard that he had taken off on the way to the farm, to be inconspicuous.

After five minutes the storm of rifle-fire died away. It became intermittent, with a traversing machine-gun now and again, telling plainly that the attack of the Detached Force was stopped before the wire. Then shrapnel, black German smoke, began to burst over the trench. He got as far as he could under the parapet, while the smoke drifted sideways overhead. The rising wind would shift the pockets of gas. Some of the infantry were looking at him curiously; they had been in reserve, and evidently had not seen a gas brassard before. Soon the shelling ceased, both ways, and he heard the rumbling of guns to the south. It was wearisome waiting; it was cold; but there was nothing else to do, but wait for twilight, and then get back to his billet. He closed his eyes, to sleep; and was aware that someone had touched him on the shoulder. He saw Boon, the batman.

"Captain West's compliments, sir, would you please come to him. He's been hit, sir."

"Captain West?"

"Yes, sir. Whizz-bang, sir."

Phillip resisted an impulse to say that he was not really anything to do with the attack. He followed the servant. Westy lay on the floor of muddy chalk, working his jaws as though chewing. There were tiny white specks in the froth on his lips. A stretcher-bearer with red-cross armlet was kneeling by him, holding a field-dressing pad to the wounded man's cheek. When the pad was lifted, Phillip saw that the eye beneath was a broken pulp in a bloody star-fish of flesh stripped away from the cheek-bone. Then he saw the left arm lying askew to the body, with two fingers gone from the hand and purple sinews at the wrist broken and shredded. The shell had brought down some of the trench wall; chalk partly covered the wounded man's left leg. The exposed end of the puttee had little tears in it, the boot had slight cuts in the leather.

Phillip knelt beside him, saying, "So you've got a Blighty one, Westy."

Captain West turned his head, with its one staring eye, minute of pupil. "Morphine—give me my box—get round the flank," he muttered. Blood was now staining the froth on his lips. "Morphine—give me my box—get round the flank——" the voice kept repeating, while the right hand fumbled at the breast pocket below the stained riband of the Military Cross.

"He keeps 'is little box there, sir," said Boon, bending down to speak against Phillip's face. "His syringe's smashed with 'is haversack, sir. He 'as had to keep 'isself goin' since he got that little lot at Neuve Chapelle, sir. He 'ad 'eadaches something awful, sir."

Rolling his head Captain West repeated, "Morphine—Phillip, come nearer——"

Phillip knelt to hear the voice, feeble and whispering, "The Grapes, Lime Street. My mother—tell her——" His hand sought Phillip's. Phillip held the cold hand between his own. "See my mother—The Grapes, Lime Street—the City—tell her—all my love."

"I understand, Westy. But you'll be all right."

Boon meanwhile had taken a small silver wax-vesta box from the breast pocket, opened it, and let two tablets roll into his palm. "That'll settle you, sir," as he put them into his master's mouth.

"More—more——" complained the voice, as the chin stretched back. "Put six under my tongue."

"And don't forget to put the requisite number o' crosses on his for'ed at the aid post, my lads," said the R.S.M. to the stretcher-bearers. "All right, I'll see to it," and with the indelible pencil from the message book and spit from his mouth he drew two thick crosses on Captain West's forehead. "Now then, gently does it—mind that leg—lift 'im careful——"

Blood running from bitten lower lip, eye closed, the man on the stretcher lay feebly with pain; then through clenched teeth came the murmur, "Get round the flank——" and then a strangled screaming broke from his bloody lips. "Morphia——"

The bearers waited while the paroxysm passed, then Boon opened the mouth and put two more tablets under the tongue.

The jaws worked; the slow, partial swallow; the struggle to articulate. The batman said, "All right, sir, don't you worry yourself no more. Mr. Maddison 'eard you, sir. 'Get round the flank.' Didn't you, sir?"

"Yes, Westy, I heard. I'll carry on. Leave it to me. We'll get round the flank."

The uninjured hand again made to find Phillip's; but the wounded man was sinking into a coma.

"The bearers will get him back to the dressing-station as soon as we've moved off, sir," said the R.S.M. "I think you are senior to Mr. Allport, sir? The captain told me you was out in 'fourteen, sir. Will you take command of the battalion, sir? The orders come just before the captain was hit, to carry on the attack acrost to Lone Tree."

With forced jocularity Phillip heard himself saying, "Mr. Adams, I have not heard any order, beyond that given by Captain West!"

"Very good, sir."

"Have the men got their rations, water, ammunition, Mr. Adams? What about bombs?"

"Each man carries two bombs, in addition to what the bombers have, sir. It's bombs we need in this sort of work. The Jerry trenches are eight feet deep, you've got to hand it to Jerry, sir, he knows how to protect his infantry in trench warfare, all right. Shall I send a runner for Mr. Allport, sir?"

"Yes, please, Mr. Adams."

When the slight, fair-haired Sandhurst youth came, Phillip, feeling Colonel Mowbray on his face, said in the colonel's manner, "'Spectre' West's orders are to get round the flank. Who is the senior of us?"

"I was gazetted last July."

"I was March. Righty ho. I'll tell you what we'll do. I'll go to the end of the trench, and lead the company through as far as I can get. Then we'll go over the top and string out and make for the Bois Carré then swing round by platoons, in an arc. No covering fire, remember—it will only advertise that we're going to attack. Will you, company sergeant major, tell the platoon sergeants? Mr. Allport, will you bring up the rear-half company?"

"Shall I report back to the farm, sir?" asked the R.S.M. Then, "You'll send a runner back with any information, of course, sir? I'll take them. A negative report is as valuable as a positive report, sir. I'll see that all reports get to brigade, sir. The battalion ammunition dump is behind the H.Q. dugout, sir. I shall be there, sir."

The R.S.M. saluted, and Phillip said, "We'll be dining in Lille tomorrow night, with any luck, Mr. Adams!" And with a swiftly thought prayer, he turned away with a wave of his walking-stick.

Chapter 22

"A BIT OF FAT"

His exhilaration soon settled to determination, now that he was moving. Men cumbering the trench were in his way; he climbed out and walked along the parapet, swinging his walking-stick, indifferent to occasional bullets, mere strays and spents, as he thought of them. Looking down into the trench he said, as he passed, "We're going round the flank, you chaps, wait there till you get word to move from your sergeant." Then looking to the east, he saw the stumps of the Bois Carré about a quarter of a mile away on his right front, beyond the white lines of trenches lying parallel and numerous in the yellow grass spreading to the smoke-laden horizon of the Hohenzollern Redoubt and the great spoil-heap known as the Dump.

The Fosse Way trench extended to the Vermelles–Hulluch road, along which in the distance wheeled transport was moving, under shell-fire in places. He waited by the road, while the men came up, to halt by him. He did not know what to do, so he said, "Keep at intervals of five paces, and follow me up the road."

The stumps of the plantation were now slightly forward on the right. He walked on, followed by his string of soldiers. The mackintosh was hot, so he took it off, and slung it over his shoulder. Odd walking wounded could be seen coming down the road in front; bullets hissed by overhead; figures in khaki were everywhere lying and crawling in the grass. Some called out, with cries for help, for water. The less badly hurt were grateful when he said, "Help is coming soon, boys." Others stared with drawn faces the hue of clay. Forcing himself not to heed the cries, he walked on, while arms rose waving and from some came despairing wails and weeping. What a game it all was, what a game. From the Bloodhound Patrol to the First Gaultshires!

The company was now strung out along the road. He halted, and said to the nearest men "Right turn". They turned all along the road, and walked forward in line across the old No Man's Land, towards the plantation. The ground was pitted with shell-holes, many of them occupied by wounded men. Dead figures lay about in all attitudes of complete repose, however stricken: joined to the ground in its stillness. He had a curious sensation, from part of himself in detachment, that invisible parts of their once-bodies were still about in the spaces of the air, looking down at the poor little bodies rather curiously as they became smaller and more remote. He thought of Cranmer; it was almost as though Cranmer's face were beside him, very near him, knowing all that he was thinking. It was strange how the feeling was bearing him up, almost leading him on, the other side of the glass. It was wonderful not to be afraid.

The stumps of Bois Carré were in front. It was a tumbled

wreckage of chalk and posts and wire, splintered boles and branches, roots in air upheaved by shells, through which the bag-lumpy parapets of trenches straggled, with their broken faggot-like revetments, and everywhere the first *feld-grau* dead he had seen since 1914—flung upon the ground with English dead—passive among the crawling and crying wounded.

There were no direct shots coming over now; only tired bullets flopping down, some making their last eccentric spins as they fell with their deadly little music. From over the slight rise to the left, in the direction of the brown roofs and chimneys of Hulluch, a heavy racket of rifle and machine-gun was mingling with gruff thuds of bombs; but nearer in front the comparative silence was strange. Were the Germans waiting to open up, when they got nearer? He was not bothered: if they did, they did.

Even so, having left the plantation behind, and with the stark little ruin of the Lone Tree less than a quarter of a mile away, Phillip began to feel alarmed. It must be a trap. He walked closer to the tumbled wire of the captured German front line wondering if he dare try and cross it and take shelter in the shell-holes which had churned up the level wilderness into a frozen sea of chalk stuck with splintered balks of wood and crumpled sheet-iron—a petrified foreshore horribly untidy with a jetsam of broken rifles, stakes, machine-gun tripods, *pickelhauben*, torn grey tunics—and the sprawled dead. So he gave the order to cross the front trench in lines of platoons as that was as good as anything he could think of.

"We'll advance in four waves, Mr. Allport."

"Very good, Sir!"

"*Sir!*" He thought of Mrs. Neville, and what a tale he would be able to tell her, to match that of Mavis' bogus staff officer, Wilkins, who ordered the recruiting parade on Blackheath. How long would his luck hold? Anyway, he was only obeying a superior officer's order. He *was* getting round the flank!

He walked in front of and away from the leading platoon as the men were moving round the cratered chalk, extending to the new formation. He was about a hundred yards ahead when he saw a German standing up so near that the band of his pork-pie hat was a bright red. The German waved. Phillip beckoned, his heart beating fast. Other Germans were clambering up beside the first. One carried a white flag. With a calm feeling Phillip waited until his runner, clambering to reach him, was near enough for him to speak to in a low shout, saying, "Tell Mr. Allport to remain in charge until I come back, and not to advance until I give the word."

"Very good, sir."

Taking long, but slow strides, and using the walking-stick, Phillip approached a group of five German officers in long over-coats. One had a fur collar. He felt that he was being drawn along, as on the afternoon of Christmas Day when he rode on the Belgian bicycle towards the Hôspice. When he got within talking distance, he shouted out, "Prächtige kerl, ja?" and then, before he could think, "Ist Mittagessen fertig?" which was about all the German he knew. With relief he heard them laugh. He straightened his brassard, and walked towards them.

Other Germans were now appearing out of the frozen sea, while a line of British troops advanced from the rear of the German position. Very soon scores of Germans were standing up, hands raised above their heads. Then right away down to Lone Tree and beyond he saw that the garrison in the salient had surrendered. Poor old Westy, he had missed it all.

His lack of German was made up by the fur-collared haupt-mann with the numerals 51 in red on his grey shoulder straps. He spoke English almost like an Englishman, and wore the silver-black riband of the Iron Cross. He clicked his heels and said, "Ritter!"

Remembering from what his father had once told him about Germans introducing themselves by their surnames, Phillip succeeded only in stumping muddy loamy heels, as he replied, "Maddison". Hauptmann Ritter bowed again, as he stood by the framed entrance to a shelter on a level with the trench fire-step.

"You are a little late for Mittagessen. We expected you some time ago, awaiting the inevitable, since our ammunition was used up. Please to enter."

Inside the shelter was a carpet, a bedstead with coverlet and white sheets, pictures on the matchboarded walls, an enamelled stove, a chair, a table. The German officer spoke sharply to an orderly, who sprang up stiff and went outside.

"I have ordered coffee, Herr Leutnant." He put a box of cigars beside Phillip.

"Not at the moment, thank you, sir. This beastly gas——"

"Where did you learn our slang expression, 'Prächtige kerl', may I ask? Ah, Christmas Day! We, too, had hopes, after Tannenberg, of the war being over by Silvester—the New Year. Do not let us talk of war. Ah, here is the coffee. Sugar? It is beet sugar, we cannot just now supply Jamaica cane sugar!"

Phillip wondered if the coffee was poisoned; the German captain seemed to feel his thought for, having poured two cups, he made no attempt to pass one, but, "Do help yourself, won't you?"

There was a vase of cornflowers on the table. The hauptmann explained that they had been grown in a garden in the support line. They were a favourite flower in Germany, he said, as he took one out of the vase and gave it to Phillip.

"Now, if you will excuse me, or rather, since I am your prisoner, sir——"

"Well, thank you very much, sir," replied Phillip. He heard shouts outside, English shouts, with Welsh accents, and going out of the dugout, saw that some of the kilted troops with bayonets outheld were on the parapets. Among them an officer, revolver in hand, was violently beckoning with the other, and crying "Keep them covered! Keep them covered!" It was Douglas of the London Highlanders.

"Don't shoot, don't shoot!" Phillip cried out. "They've surrendered!"

At first Captain Douglas did not recognise him, but when he did, he said sharply, revolver in hand, "What are you doing here?"

"Looking round the place."

"How long have you been here?"

"About five minutes."

"How did you get here?"

"Through the Bois Carré—we advanced after a flank movement."

He felt amused that Douglas was suspicious of him. Douglas knew that he had German cousins. There were stories of German officers in British uniforms. Even Westy had believed that one had given false orders behind the British lines to cause confusion. Like the Mayor of Arméntières being shot, for telephoning through to the Germans, in 1914!

While Captain Douglas was waving the prisoners to climb the parapets, under escorts with fixed bayonets, a whizz-bang arrived with a scream and crack and shower of chalk and

Douglas afterwards was lying on his face, kilt in ribbons, and his backside a mass of blood. Seeing that he was cared for, Phillip walked back to the Gaultshires, which under Allport had advanced, seeing that the German resistance had collapsed. The Gaultshires looked delighted, not unnaturally: for they had expected to be killed. Phillip was wondering what to do; he felt light-headed with relief; and was saying to Allport, "I think we had better lead on, to the Lens–La Bassée road, and attach ourselves to the nearest battalion. Then I'll report where you are——" when he saw Allport looking with delight at a short, sturdy figure with an ugly face, approaching through a gap in the wire, followed by a string of soldiers. "'Pluggy' Marsden!" said Allport. The figure recognised him: a full lieutenant of the Gaultshires. He had been in the first wave, and had been lying before the wire since early morning.

"Well," said "Pluggy" Marsden, "this is what I call a bit of fat, boys!" After some more enthusiastic talk, Phillip said that he ought now to hand-over his command.

"I am due to report back at Mazingarbe." After further explanations, it was agreed that a runner should go back to Le Rutoire, to report the position to brigade.

"Stout fellow," said Marsden. "By the way, aren't these *your* prisoners?"

"Well, the Welsh and the London Highlanders seem to have collared them. I'll say goodbye now. For all I know, my C.O. will put me under arrest for not having gone back with my blokes this morning!"

Lieutenant Marsden looked up from his field message book. "Au revoir!"

"We'll meet again, I hope, sir," said the C.S.M., saluting.

"Yes, I hope so," added Allport.

"So do I," said Phillip, as he turned away, swinging his stick. He added to himself, "'Archibald, certainly not!'"

He wanted to see his emplacements, not from a sense of duty (which he did not as yet possess) but out of curiosity. His mind, formed in ancient terrors, brooded romantically on the war: not the war of waves breaking, and so dying, upon the foreshore of terror: not the war of each actual laborious moment, but War, an extended dream, the jetsam of combat become quiescent under ceased movement and lost hope. He wanted to walk about and stand and stare and let his feelings possess him, so that he could lose himself in a dream that was beyond nightmare—the romance of war, the visual echoes of tragic action. Gas brassard on arm, he was free; no-one would question him if he appeared to be going about his job. He must visit the Lone Tree, imagine the barbed-wire as it was when holding up the assault.

The Lone Tree had a smooth brownish bark, or what was left of bark after hundreds of bullets had scored it. The bark was speckled with yellow. It smelled like a sixpenny cherry-wood pipe he had bought once. A few brown-edged leaves still remained on three unhappy stumps of branches.

All around the cherry tree the pitted chalky ground was strewn with dead and the movements of wounded. The white bottoms of London Highlanders were conspicuous among the grasses, as kilts of hodden grey lay torn and flung over still bodies. Hands lifted among the yet-alive crawling and dragging themselves, smeared with grey loam, around shell-holes, ghastly of face, torn of tunic; others were lying palely quiet beside patches of coagulated blood, where blow-flies stood, drinking. Others, less hurt, talked reasonably, asking when stretcher-bearers were coming. He spoke to many, as appeal after appeal arose to his face. He recognised little Kirk, still wearing his *pince-nez* as he lay back, bare-headed, a thick dark stain down one side of his tunic. Where was he hit? In the chest, came the whispered reply. Were the stretcher-bearers coming? Phillip told him that they would be coming soon. Anyway, the Germans were now a mile back, and the Fifteenth Division was in Lens.

He made little Kirk as comfortable as he could, then saying he had to go on, he left him, after promising—as he promised others again and again as he walked on—that he would report the need for stretcher-bearers.

He became weary, almost irritable with so many promises, all along the line, all through the thin grasses extending up to the gradual rise of Hill 69. How strange that there should still be skylarks among these thin yellow grasses clustering upright a dozen inches above the loamy soil pocked and gashed white with shell-crater and trench: chalk-white the kiltless rumps of the bulleted dead, those cleanly killed, not savaged and destroyed by high explosive, which had cast a litter of severed legs and arms and fractured shin-bones sticking out of laced boots. He began to feel hollow as though his life were ebbing away; he felt helpless, for himself and others; his throat was sore; and only when his breathing suddenly was sickly trapped, and a petrifaction came upon him, that he was in chloride of lime hopelessly trapped, did he realise that he had come into an area where chlorine still hung about. So he hurried away east out of the hollow until he came close to the German front line beyond the tumbled wire along the slight ascent of the terrain which was the foot of the Loos Road Redoubt.

Here he met a Scottish major, who was examining the ground of his battalion's attack. He said that the Fifteenth Division had started eight minutes late, as the men had crowded together, trying to find the gaps in the British wire, which had been cut only the night before. There had been some casualties from shell-fire, but practically no opposition from the Hun infantry. In twenty minutes his battalion had got through the fourth enemy line, and "were into the blue". The major was optimistic; the German front was broken; the R.F.C.—Phillip had not seen an aeroplane so far—had reported a concentration of horse transport outside Lille, which looked as though the old Hun was in a panic, and shifting his headquarters further back. Did he know where were our reserves? Had he seen any? Why hadn't they come up? Had he seen anything of the cavalry? What?

"No, sir."

The dead in *feld grau* lay everywhere in their old front line; they had got the gas. He crossed over, and walked beside a communication trench leading up to the redoubt. It was choked with German dead piled upon one another, three and four deep. Obviously they had been caught in the *Allee*, or communication trench, trying to get away; bomb after bomb, to judge by shattered heads and faces, must have been lobbed on top of the struggling masses. Many had hands blown off, as though they had been crying *Kamerad*. It looked like a massacre of prisoners, which was understandable, so soon after zero hour, because attacking men were nearly insane with fear, and the exhilaration succeeding intense fear. It was awful; he had seen enough; and when he got to the top of the down-like rise, and suddenly saw troops moving along the skyline, and saw very close to him the twin pylons of Loos and the brown cluster of broken roofs down below on his right, and heard the gruff coughs of bombs, with the hiss and cracking of bullets passing him, he turned back, determined to make his way to his billet in Mazingarbe, and report sick with gas. With luck, he would get down to the base.

This idea became an obsession. He must get away from all the horror, which really had no purpose, since both sides thought they were fighting for the same thing. He began to stride along fast, but the going was heavy; boots were clogged with grey clay, puttees thick with plaster. He went down the slope to what looked like a track, along which, in the distance, wheeled transport, strung out, was visible. At last he got to the road beyond, after floundering through more trenches blown in, their withy-and-stake revettments in a horrible mess, *feld grau* and khaki dead lying outside the tilted beams of dugout and shelter, and came to the top of the rise where the old front line had been. He walked down the road for the best part of a mile, and saw no fresh troops moving up. Shells from field gun batteries in the open were flashing and barking under the leaden sky, into which reared the dark pyramids and heaps of the fosses, the strange iron towers of the winding-gear of coal-pits. He thought how it all looked like the scenery of the nightmares he had had as a child.

It began to rain. The churned-up road, pitted with shell-holes, gleamed hopeless like the sky. The flashes of guns were indistinguishable from large and nervous blinks of the eyes. He passed hundreds, thousands of wounded limping, or lying on stretchers in the mud above ditches, and no-one to take them away. He hastened on, desperate to get to his billet.

The elderly major of sappers said, "Ah, so you are back again. We feared something might have happened to you."

"I was with my regiment, sir. They had lost most of their officers."

The old man looked at him benevolently. "Well, you look to be in need of a good night's rest, my boy. Perhaps you had better see the doctor. That hoarse voice sounds like a whiff of gas."

"I think I'm all right, sir."

"Well, better to be on the safe side. Chlorine is not so easily got rid of. I think we'll have the doctor run over you. How were things going on your sector?"

"The Lone Tree position was surrendered by the Germans, sir."

"Yes, we heard that. Things are going as reasonably well as can be expected, though Horne's Second Division is still checked. The gas blew back, I am afraid. Thesiger's Ninth has over-run the Hohenzollern Redoubt, and both Big and Little Willie trenches, and has taken Fosse Eight and the Dump. Capper's Seventh has captured the Quarries, and is over the Lens–Béthune road, and reached the second German line about Hulluch." He looked at a message on his blanket-covered table. "Yes, things are going well. The First Division, as you know, is now astride the Lens–Béthune road after initial checks at Lone Tree, and has captured six hundred prisoners." He put down the Corps battle report. "Well, let me have your written report first thing in the morning, will you? Now I think we'll get the doctor to vet. you."

Phillip saw the M.O., an elderly Scotsman with a rugged face and drooping grey moustache yellow with nicotine. A cigarette smouldered on his lip. He had a scurfy scalp, Phillip noticed, as he put the stethoscope over his chest.

"Do ye play bridge? We need a fourth in the mess." He folded up his red rubber tubes, and pulled down his patient's lower lids. "A bit of inflammation, you're lucky to have got no more than a whiff of that gas."

"No, I don't play, Doctor, I'm afraid."

"Ye'll soon learn. A few days' light duty won't hurt you. Your heart's intermittent, and a wee bit on the rapid side. We play for sixpence a hundred. Did ye see anything of the new Kitchener divisions as you came down the Harrow Road?"

"No, I didn't, Doctor. But the wounded were still lying out in No Man's Land. I think it ought to be reported to someone."

"Oh, things are bound to be in a muddle at this stage. Don't worry yourself about what canna' be helped. The Hun front is broken, but our reserves are on the way. Two Kitchener divisions from home have been marching up during the past three nights, to avoid being seen from the air. Then some dam-fool military policemen held up the leading Brigade for an hour, on a standing order, for trench warfare only, that platoons going into the line must have a hundred yards' interval. You were with the London Highlanders at Messines, were ye not?"

"Yes, sir."

"I had a nephew of mine killed at Ypres—Elliott, did you know him?"

"Yes, Doctor. He was in my company."

"Well, you've done your bit. Take things easy. I'm giving you four days' light duty. Now go and sleep. Have you got four francs on you? I can let you have a bottle of Johnny Walker, only don't drink too much. It's the best sleeping draught." Phillip handed over a five-franc note, and took the bottle.

"Right, you're a franc in credit. And don't forget to come to the mess for bridge after dinner tomorrow. We only play for sixpence a hundred."

Phillip hurried away, thinking jubilantly that it was indeed a bit of fat. His jubilant mood soon went. He was cold, his throat was metallic; depression returned as he crossed the wretched little square filled with limbers and wagons, files of led mules with pack saddles, and echoing to the tramp of a weary-looking column of soldiers passing through towards the line, and went on to his billet, one of a row of drab little back-to-back cottages, the *corons* of the French miners. The village had been shelled during his absence; more rafters gaped, new shell-holes in the road had been filled in with bricks, the blackish mud was streaked with red by the passing of files of pack-mules taking up eighteen-pounder shells, and wagons.

He found his batman sitting by the fire with the widow and her children; they got up when he entered, and all except "Twinkle" disappeared into the scullery. Thinking to celebrate the break-through, Phillip invited the old fellow to have some whiskey with him.

"Twinkle" handled lovingly the bottle of Johnny Walker, and insisted on pouring for Phillip what he called a chota peg, which meant that a cup with a broken handle was filled nearly three-quarters full. Then "Twinkle" helped himself, as invited, and proposed his officer's health, which Phillip took appropriately seated, while the batman swallowed his cupful in two swigs, champing his bare gums afterwards, and uttering deep sighs of satisfaction.

"Twinkle's" bare gums were in the nature of a permanent insurance; he had told Phillip that he had hidden his dentures against the possibility of being ordered into the trenches; for, toothless, he would be unable to eat iron rations.

"I could do with some breakfast, Twinkle."

"Breakfast, sir? But I got your lunch all ready! No matter, sir, no matter! Breakfast you shall have, forthwith," and going to the stove, the servant took up a canteen and returned to tip the contents into a plate. It was an oily mess of lumps of yellow fat and meat surrounded by cabbage leaves, dumplings made of flour and lumps of biscuit, onions, and watery potatoes.

"Breakfast up, sir! Just a moment, sir, I've got a French flavour for you."

Phillip sat back, wonderfully warmed by whiskey, with loose lips and stretched legs, and watched while his servant covered the plateful with cheese shavings. "You're not only a chef, you're a conjurer," he said, feeling he was falling to pieces. "Dinner into breakfast without even the wave of a napkin." He raised his glass. "I drink your health, Chef!"

"Thank you, sir, I don't mind if I do," promptly replied the Chef, helping himself to another quartern from the bottle. That, too, was as rapidly disposed of as the first, with appreciative suckings, and clappings of gums and lips.

"Come on, sir, aren't you 'ungry? My word, sir, you oughter've sin them rookies of the new Kitchener's mob what come up this arternoon! They'd 'ad no food all day, and was wet through and proper flogged out by forced rowt marching. Thank Gawd we've got the Guards a-comin' up, that's what I said to misself when I see'd'm."

Like all old soldiers of the file who had seen much military endeavour come to nothing, the Chef went on to prophesy doom. The young soldier agreed.

"I don't like the look of the whole business, sir. It gives me the shakes, all them rookies goin' in for the first time, arter three nights' forced foot-sloggin' on the *pavé*, and no grub under their belts, and none seen a shot fired in anger. It ain't Sir Garnett." He took the bottle, and helped himself. "Here's your very good health, sir. Aren't you 'ungry, sir? What would you fancy like, for afters? I got prunes, and tinned milk, and a cupper kawfy. If I'd've knowed you was comin' I'd've got the old gal to frizzle you hup han rhum souffle like the bellarenas and the ballet boys used to take afore the shows at the old Crawl fer Pardon, that's rhymin' slang for Covent Garden, sir, wanting something light, to settle their nerves. They was the days, or rather nights! Twinkle me boy, they used to say, Twinkle, they'd say, in their foreigner's lingo, they was all furriners you see, sir, cor strike a light, what 'abits some'v'm 'ad, proper Oscar boys they was, talk about nancies, some on'm was jealous've me, sir, would you believe it, jealous o' Twinkle! Old enuff to be all their farvers! The chorus boys all come, fur coats over tights, 'ungry as 'unters, into my 'Am an' Beef, and wolfed thicks in the interval, that's 'ow I got to know 'em, you see, sir, they give me their confidences, like a lot of kids they was. What you lookin' at, sir, suthin' in me mutton 'ot-pot?"

"Only a hair. Your sheep must have tails like horses', Chef."

"Can't 'elp a little fing like that in war-time, sir, it must've come off'r butcher's daughter, Marie, she's called, sir. Eat up, sir, stoke up. What about those rookies comin' up, arter nights o' forced marchin', on empty bellies, sir?"

"That's one way of looking at it, certainly. By the way, surely this *is* a horse hair? Perhaps Marie's father was a horse?"

"It must've got in somehow," remarked the Chef, thrusting his greasy hand before Phillip's face and taking the hair away, to hold it up to the light of three candles before dropping it on the floor and remarking, "Nature's a wonderful thing, sir, to my way o' thinkin'. Didn't you never 'ear as 'ow eels growed out'r 'ossairs, sir? I sin 'm wriggling in the Wandle near Wandsworth when I were a boy. Many a time I've taken of'm home in a jemjar, a proper mystery, it was, them 'ossairs a-wrigglin' away accordin' to nature's law. Makes yer fink, don't it? Yes, eels come aht'r 'ossairs."

"So you think the father of an eel is a horse, Chef? Well, I think I'll have the prunes now, I'm not very hungry."

"What? You ain't goin' to eat yer plateful, sir? Wiv all them fresh dried veg I wangled aht'v A.S.C., sir? Go on, 'ave a try, sir! Must keep yer strength up, you know." The old fellow stifled a yawn. "Manners, Twinkle!" he reproved himself. "Kripes, I could do wiv some kip, sir. I ain't slepp a wink for nights, what wiv them Long Toms a-crackin' off double each time just be'ind me an' liftin' the tiles over me 'ead. Go on, sir, stoke up! It's me special mutton stoo!"

"No thanks, I really can't eat any more. It's too fat!" He laughed to an imagined Desmond. "I'd like the prunes. I'll put the milk on myself, thanks all the same, Chef!"

"Very good, sir," exclaimed the Chef. "Just as you say, sir. Prunes, sir, now comin' up. Very good for the bowels, sir. Cawfee to follow, sir, tout suite."

"I'll put the milk in, Chef!" Phillip didn't want the blowing-act to be repeated, the old man's breath upon the milk, as on a previous occasion with prunes. To divert his mind off the blowing he offered him another drink.

"Come on, Chef, help yourself to a spot of old man whiskey."

"Very good, sir," said the Chef, promptly putting down the tin of milk. "Here's hopin', sir!" Down went the raw spirit in the skinny neck. "Now, sir, polish off them prunes. Very 'ealth-giving, sir. Now for some cream———" He seized the tin before Phillip could get it, and put his lips to one of the two holes punched in the otherwise unopened end. This was the servant's idea, to keep away flies, which swarmed in the billet.

"Can't let you do my work, sir, I know my duty, sir. Many's the time I waited in the officers' mess in India, sir, and served the young gentlemen just out from Belaite, sir—what the ignorant calls Blighty today, with no knowledge of Hindustani."

No cream coming from the yellow-crusted hole, the Chef shook the tin, muttered, "Them flies bin an' bunged it up agen," listened at one hole, for some reason; then, putting the other hole to his lips, he drew a deep breath and blew with bulbed cheeks so that a jet of cream was directed expertly upon the prunes. They were watery prunes; why didn't he soak them, as suggested, for twenty-four hours, as Mother did, to get the rich, dark brown sweet juice? Now they would be tasteless, the juice mere cold coloured water.

"There you are, sir," and putting the plate before Phillip, he stood back, shaking the empty tin. "Not a drop missed the target, sir! Go on, sir, stoke up, it's very health-giving, is cream."

Phillip began to laugh to himself, as he thought of a shag sitting on its favourite rocks. If only Desmond were there with him, to share the fun!

"What, don't you want no prunes neither, sir?"

"I don't feel like any food just now. By the way, you old rogue, about those sandwiches you have been giving me—where do you get the beef from? Pinch it from the ration dump?"

"Me, sir? Me half-inch and get the wrong side of the red-caps, sir? Not Twinkle! Nearly fifty years of good conduct, sir, why, I wouldn't be so daft as to spoil me record, sir."

"But don't you supply that estaminet, what's it called, the Demi Lune, with beef sandwiches? Come on, where does it all come from, you sprucer?"

"Promise you won't let on, sir, if I tell you? Well, me and a business partner oo is a butcher in civvie street do a little tradin' with a Frenchie what buys up 'osses, sir, a nice clean beast the 'oss, a clean feeder like a bullock, sir, flesh comin' from good oats an' 'ay, sir, what more could you want?"

"Where does the French knacker get 'em from, Chef?"

"That ain't my business, sir. I arst no questions, and get told no lies, in a manner of speakin'."

"Killed by shell-fire, you mean, Chef?"

"What cleaner end to an 'oss, sir, than a sudden shell? It's as clean as the sled on its skull in a knacker's yard, in my opinion. Why waste good meat? Corn-fed beef, or corn-fed 'oss, where's the difference? An Irishman'll eat a donkey, a Hitalian a pussy cat, diddekais eat 'edge'ogs—everyone to 'is own taste, sir. I'll tell you what, sir, only a little while ago, just before you come in, all the lot I'd cut up for tonight in the Demi Lune went like 'ot cakes, bought by an officer for 'is men, sir. My Gor, they're sending out the gran-fers now. When I went to Nooless Mines this mornin', to get them veg you refoosed, I seed the column 'alted by a redcap, and an old gineral on a 'oss come up from the rear, a-roarin' and a-bawlin', because the redcap wouldn't let the head of the column carry on without a pass. 'E got a move-on, 'e put everyone in sight under arrest. I recognised 'is face, 'e were a proper hot-tempered bloke in India, a proper broth of a boy. Often I see 'im in Quetta when I were a boy just 'listed, sir, a real ole pig-sticker 'e were. 'E were in the charge of the Light Brigade at Balaclava, we all called 'im 'Crasher'."

"Crasher, did you say? Brigadier-General Joliffe-Howard?"

"That's 'im, sir! 'Crasher' by name an' crasher by nature! When I see'd 'im gallopin' up this morning, I says to myself, 'That's caused it, Twinkle, me boy,' I says. 'It's all up wi' the old Alleyman now,' I says to myself. Nobody can't kill Crasher. 'E'll never die—'e'll only fade away—but if 'e 'as 'is way, that little lot under 'im 'll soon be with the Underground 'Oozars."

"He was commanding the territorial brigade I left little more than a fortnight ago in England! They had no idea, then, I'm sure, of leaving for the front! Well, I'm damned!" exclaimed Phillip. "Look here, I must go and have a look at them. Fancy Crasher and old Strawballs, and all those others, out here! What good can they possibly be, at their age?"

In the excitement the Chef helped himself to more whiskey. He poured it down his throat; then squaring his shoulders, while a wide grin split his face, he began to hold forth with his real personality, hitherto partly suppressed in the presence of an officer: the old soldier freed by drink from the old soldier cowed by discipline.

"There's cunnin' in an old dog, what takes the place o' life, sir. Though I must admit that the other orficers looked a proper lot of twots, all waitin' there, wiv the big push goin' on, and them the reserves what were needed, and all allowin' of theirselves to be 'alted by a pushin' redcap because the leading C.O. bin a naughty boy and gone and lost 'is late-night pass. They talk about man-power, why not the women to do the clurkin' down at the base, then they can send that little lot o' skrimshankin' fireside lancers and Royal Staybacks up 'ere wiv' a rifle and baynit——"

But Phillip was not listening. He sat still, while within him various feelings were in conflict—curiosity, desire to show off his staff brassard, warm friendliness, caution based on self-interest—but they could not touch him, he was still on gas; besides, he had been placed on light duty. Even so——

"Twinkle, get me a good packet of sandwiches! I'm going back for an hour or two, just to have a look at Crasher and Co.! I'm on light duty for four days, so tell the senior sergeant to carry on. I'd like to have a last look at that lot. My God, they've got a nasty surprise coming to them. Fill my water-bottle three-quarters full of chlorinated water, then fetch me a dry pair of socks. Quick!"

When he was ready to go he topped up his water-bottle with whiskey, and slinging it with haversack and map-case outside his mackintosh, went out of the billet, walking-stick in right hand, brassard on arm; and coming to the square, walked beside the tramping column of weary infantrymen with long strides that overtook the files continually stopping and breaking to allow down-moving transport and ammunition limbers to pass them; and coming eventually to the cross-roads over the main road to Lens he arrived level with the halted "poor old 'Cantuvellaunians'," recognising the weary, bedraggled faces of many of his old acquaintances, including Chick, O'Connor, Captain Rhodes, Infant Hercules, and others. He avoided looking at them directly and walked on, until he came to the head of the column, and saw Jonah the Whale, and Strawballs talking together. "It's bloody rot," he heard the colonel say querulously, "taking away our cookers!" Not wanting to be recognised, Phillip walked on.

Chapter 23

HISTORICAL PERSPECTIVE

THE reserves which had come upon the edge of the battlefield (as Phillip was returning to his billet) were tired, hungry, and bewildered. For the past five days two divisions of untried troops fresh from England had been marching from the area of the Channel coast. They had paraded each evening at 6 p.m. and continued along the roads bordered by poplars until shortly before sunrise each morning. Many of the battalion transport sections were without experience of horses and driving; battalion, brigade, and even divisional staffs were likewise without experience of moving masses of men in the field. Some brigades had less than half a dozen officers and N.C.O.s who had seen service in the present war; in the brigade commanded by "Crasher" Joliffe-Howard not one man or officer had been in France since the war.

The night marches had been ordered lest the columns—each division took fifteen miles of road when on the march—be seen by German reconnaissance aircraft. Troops had remained in billets during each day.

On the night of the 24th the divisions were lying about twenty miles from the battlefield. At 7 p.m., the time when Phillip was in the front assembly trench with his section being placed at the gas emplacements, the leading brigades started their fifth night march, a short one of from between seven and eleven miles, a distance taking, normally, from three to four hours. The march took double that time. All along the narrow roads to Noeux-les-Mines and Béthune there were prolonged halts. Horses drawing wagons were unable to get up slight hills. The infantry columns were marching in fours; there was a yard to spare on one side of the road only, then came the deep ditches. The roads used had been marked *Down Traffic Only*; convoys of lorries and motor ambulances, with lines of horse wagons, were continually passing the upgoing troops, who were forced to walk in files beside the road, often scrambling in and out of ditches. At every cross-roads were blocks, causing the broken columns to lose touch, and some even to turn off at right angles in error. There were level crossings with long white painted poles across the road, while trains shunted, whistled, stopped, rolled on slowly. At one crossing there was a delay of one and a half hours due to an accident on the line.

Corps headquarters had made arrangements for the free passage of marching troops with the French railway authorities, but the French could not carry out the time-table. Those portions of broken columns which had lost their way and taken wrong turnings came back and found themselves in the great congestion of heavy supply transport behind an imminent battle. Thus very tired infantry, many with no hot meal at the end of the march, since the travelling steel cookers had been lost, lay down just before dawn under hedges and beside ditches and tried to sleep; but hardly were their eyes shut against the light of a drizzling dawn revealing distant pyramids and dumps when the guns opened up, forty minutes before the battle was joined.

The reserves, which the First Army commander fighting the battle had requested, again and again, to be two thousand yards behind the British front line, were then six miles back, and in no fit condition to march on until they had rested.

They had been kept back deliberately by Field-Marshal Sir John French.

The field-marshal was sixty-three years of age. His body was heavy on its frame, with abdominal muscles sagging from desk-work, not from indulgence in food. He had reached the time of life when a man reflects rather than acts; and for over a year of war he had been continually frustrated. He had lived with grief: the flower of his army had been destroyed. Anxiety gnawed him, a fox under his cloak.

During early September the field-marshal had passed on to his First Army commander, the spare and active Sir Douglas Haig, Lord Kitchener's direction for the battle—". . . to act with all energy . . . even though by so doing we may suffer very heavy losses"—while in the field-marshal's mind were grave doubts of the success of an attack which he had been ordered to undertake against his judgment, and with too few guns and gun ammunition, and too few men. The field-marshal had been under great and continual strain for over a year; and now constant dread of committing the men under him too deeply—together with a wish to keep raw troops out of battle if the attack was shattered on the strong German defences as previous attacks in the first half of 1915 had been shattered—at Neuve Chapelle, Aubers Ridge, Festubert and Givenchy—possessed him.

Against these sombre thoughts a bright, contrary idea persisted with the field-marshal. If all went well in the opening stages of the battle, he, by keeping the reserves under his own direct orders, would be able to give the *coup de grâce* to the enemy. Put in at the right time, used with the Cavalry Corps held within his own command to pursue the enemy's disorganised forces across the plain of Flanders, he could take the Germans in flank before they could reorganise behind the Scheldt.

Reflection can, with an ageing man who has suffered many strains, become rumination; and rumination, a vice. The field-marshal, for various reasons within himself, had decided to keep the general reserve for the battle behind the area of battle. Thus, on Y/Z night, the two divisions, tired from England, had lain up to twenty miles behind the British front line.

General Haig, who was to fight the battle, had more than once suggested that they be moved nearer. He was supported by General Foch, commanding the 10th French Army on his right, who had proposed to the field-marshal that they be brought to within two thousand yards of the corps reserves (which, in fact, did not exist: for the six divisions of the two corps comprising Haig's First Army were all to be used in the assault; and he had no reserves whatsoever).

General Haig once more urged that the two divisions be held ready, by daybreak of zero day, to move forward directly into the battle of pursuit. To this the field-marshal had replied merely that he did not agree: he, as commander-in-chief, would keep the whole of the general reserve in the Lillers area, sixteen miles back, until the course of the battle was known. The field-marshal's two-mindedness in the matter revealed itself in the words of his formal order to Sir Douglas Haig—"Once the enemy's defences have been pierced . . . the offensive must be continued with the utmost determination directly to the front . . ." while at the same time the field-marshal kept the reserves back.

General Haig persisted. He wrote yet again, repeating his request for the general reserve to be well up behind the assault—"on the line Noeux-les-Mines–Beuvy by daylight on 25 September": to this the field-marshal, committed in the first place by politicians to a battle he had no belief in—fearing to send untried troops into a forlorn hope, yet wishing to support his First Army commander with the loyalty of a good soldier—replied "Two divisions . . . will be in the area referred to in your letter by daybreak on the 25th September".

They were indeed there, shortly after daybreak; but in no condition to move forward.

The assault that morning, of which Phillip with his gas containers and "Spectre" West with his company of Gaultshires were but two small items in the wave of European life destroying itself, had been made by eighteen British brigades of infantry, against a comparatively small force of three German regiments—equivalent in numbers to three British brigades—with one Jäger battalion in support. At a quarter to eight that morning the German front was breached in two places; and at that hour the British reserves were still lying under the hedges and beside the ditches, six and seven miles away. When eventually they did march forward, a military policeman on duty at a railway crossing told the brigadier of the leading brigade that the troops could not enter the battle area, because he did not have in his possession a pass. The military policeman, a lance-corporal, was obeying orders; the leading brigade was halted for nearly an hour.

The field-marshal, with only his personal aides, had left his headquarters at St. Omer unexpectedly to visit the Château Philomel three miles south of Lillers on the evening before the battle. From the château there was no communication by wire with his armies; and only the civilian French telephone system to St. Omer. Sir Douglas Haig sent, at 7 a.m. the next morning, a staff-officer by motor car to inform the field-marshal of the success of the assault by the 47th London and 15th Scottish divisions towards Loos and Hill 70, and to ask that the two reserve divisions be put in immediately.

Again at 8.45 a.m. General Haig sent another messenger, to report that all the brigades of the 1st and 4th Corps were either in the German trenches or on the move there; and to request that the reserve divisions be pushed in at once. Two valuable hours had already been lost.

At 9.30 a.m. (when Phillip was dozing in the Fosse Way trench) the field-marshal replied by telegraph, that the divisions would "move forward to First Army trenches as soon as the situation requires and admits".

At 11.30 a.m. the field-marshal visited Sir Douglas Haig and told him, at last, that he would arrange to put the reserve divisions under his orders.

From First Army at Hinges he motored to Noeux-les-Mines, where he arrived about noon. There he saw the corps general under whose command the divisions had been placed. Having discussed the general situation with him, the field-marshal, at 12.30 p.m., gave the corps general the order to move his divisions forward. Five and three-quarter most valuable hours had wasted away.

Fifty minutes later, at 1.20 p.m., the corps general informed Sir Douglas Haig that the reserve divisions "were under him and marching to the areas ordered, but were delayed on the road". Sir Douglas Haig, a devout man, had meanwhile spent some minutes in the privacy of his room, praying on his knees. He was a Scots Calvinist; his mind and conscience were settled in beliefs about righteous living in this world as well as in the next; so to his staff he was invariably courteous and restrained in manner, concealing his anxiety about the field-marshal's procrastination like the Spartan boy with the fox under his cloak.

Meanwhile (as "Spectre" West was sinking into a coma), from various parts of the front, according to many regimental officers, the Germans were on the run. Some had thrown away arms and equipment: field-gun batteries had been abandoned. It was only when they saw that the British had paused after their efforts, and were not being reinforced, that they halted, and came back to their vacant trenches, and took up the fight once more.

Messages sent back took a long time to deliver, owing to clogging mud, and the mêlée of movement upon degraded soil;

thus Sir Douglas Haig believed for some hours that his First Army was "on the crest of the wave of victory, that it had broken through the second and last line of defence in two central and vital places, Cité St. Elie and Hulluch; and that a break-through at Haisnes and Cité St. Auguste was imminent".

The truth was the First Army had spent itself, like a wave with none behind to gather its waters and follow on.

And the jetsam of that wave was two men out of every three men in the battalions of the original assault fallen, broken or dead, to the ground.

Chapter 24

"CRASHER" & Co.

THE sun was going down behind the battlefield like a septic wound upon a dying world of great loneliness. It was, by Phillip's watch, a quarter-past seven. Father would now be walking down the gulley from the Hill, swinging along, strawyard in hand, to feel the wind on his forehead. Desmond, unless he were on searchlight duty, would by now have finished his supper, and perhaps be thinking of going down to Freddy's. Would there still be tennis on the Hill, and rooks flying home to the elms, above whistles and warblings of boys in the twilight? A light in the turret bedroom of the top house of Hillside Road—would she have his photograph beside Bertie's, or only Bertie's, on her dressing-table? No, not his; that was gone now, for ever. Everything was gone. Perhaps if he were killed Desmond would soon forget him, happy with Eugene—with such melancholy sunset thoughts he walked on, aimlessly.

While Phillip, going towards the battle, was overtaking weary files of laden men in greatcoats trying to move along the margins of a narrow road congested with down-traffic, pocked with shell-craters, and lined with irregular rows of wounded recumbent and sitting amidst clustering blow-flies, a tattoo of gunfire arose from in front, from beyond the old front line crossing the Lens road upon a swell of the ground. Shells from the unseen German guns were dropping into the dip beyond. He could see red spots of bursting shrapnel in dirty drifting smoke. Some poor devils were copping it there, he said to himself.

Soon he found out what had happened. Two Yorkshire battalions of the advance reserve brigade, in full marching order, in fours with a hundred yards' interval between platoons, and horse transport following, had reached the crest of the slope leading down to the Loos valley, crossed the wooden bridges over the old front line, turned left-handed towards the Tower Bridge, and so come into full view of the German batteries hidden among the *corons* of Cité St. Pierre on the further slope of the valley. The transport was destroyed, and its wreckage blocked the road; the Yorkshiremen, followed by a battalion of Green Howards, having no idea of where they were, with no guides and only maps of the 1/100,000 scale, reformed and marched on towards Lens, and, as "Twinkle" said afterwards, "straight into the open jaws of 'ell".

Meanwhile Phillip had returned, and was hanging about, not wanting to reveal himself to the battalion about which he had so many mixed feelings; but, reassured by the thought that, being on light duty, he could go back at any moment he wanted to, continuing to find interest in all around him.

The sun was dead and its last light draining away as the reserve divisions began to form up two thousand yards behind the old front line, on the grass north of the Lens road. The rotund and steaming cookers, and the water-carts of the twenty-four new and untried infantry battalions, as well as their transport wagons, had been left behind by the unwritten order of some unknown officer, probably a deputy-assistant-adjutant-and-quartermaster-general in the rear areas. In lines of companies on a two-battalion frontage, with companies in columns of fours at ten paces' intervals—each brigade upon a frontage of one hundred and twenty yards —the divisions rested in mass, a thousand yards apart.

In front of the leading brigade Phillip saw red hat-bands, among them the red gorget patches of "Crasher" and "Little Willie"—evidently a conference was being held. He moved away to find the Cantuvellaunians. They were on the left, the men squatting or lying on the chalky grass in their great-coats, uneasily, with packs on backs. Their rifles were piled in lines beside them. The company officers were standing, their floppy service caps without wires, he noticed.

He heard a slight cheer. Surprised, he saw men of his old company looking at him, their faces expectant. The cheer came again, more strongly. He looked behind him, expecting to see someone else. Could it be for himself? He went forward to them. Bellamy's tired, but still grinning, face, said, "Hullo, sir! It's lovely to see you, sir, honest!" Bellamy he remembered as the company comic.

O'Connor, now with three pips, saw him and came towards him. Others crowded round.

"I thought, with regret, that probably I had seen the last of you, my boy! Never was a face more welcome!" O'Connor glanced at the brassard.

"Hullo, O'Connor, congrats. on your captaincy. I heard you fellows were here, and came along to see you."

"Very decent of you, Maddison!"

"What's happening?"

"Have you seen our transport?"

"Have the Germans gone?"

"They told us we were in for a long march——"

"They said the front was broken——"

"What's the arm-band for?"

"Are there any billets in front? The men are dead beat."

"Where can we get water for the men?"

"Has the cavalry gone through——"

"We were held up on the road by squadron after squadron of lancers——"

"Why haven't they taken the wounded by the roadside away? It's bad for the morale of our chaps——"

Jonah the Whale, on long thin legs in tight breeches and canvas leggings, stalked up smiling grimly from his taller height, unshaven, tie awry, legs bowed a little, breeches-strapping rubbed dark by the horse-sweat of much riding. "Good evening, Maddison! Do you know this line of country? You do? Splendid! You're the very man we want. Come and see the colonel."

"Strawballs" looked thinner and more stern, until he shook hands, when Phillip saw the white stubble on his chin and the lines between his eyes as the result of sleeplessness, the same strain on the faces of staff officers in the cellar of Le Rutoire farm. Captain Rhodes, now with crowns on his shoulders as second-in-command, spread a map and opened a compass. "We'll be moving up about midnight, Rhodes," said "Strawballs". "On a compass bearing of one hundred and twelve degrees."

So these were the people who had tried to crush him, and his ideas—these amateurs! Marching on a compass bearing, like Boy Scouts who could only light wood fires with paraffin! He could keep silent no longer.

"Sir," he said to the colonel, "why not get right up straightaway past Lone Tree and the Loos Road Redoubt, and send patrols forward until you find the Germans? It will be easy to go up now, before they come back, with their reserves. The front is open, sir. The Germans must be some distance off, judging by the fact that only a few field-gun shells with black smoke are visible. Then again, sir, the only small-arms crackle we can hear is on the right beyond the Tower Bridge on Hill 70, and on the left away out over by the Hohenzollern Redoubt and the Dump behind it."

"Come with me to the brigadier," said the colonel. "And repeat to him what you have just told me."

"Crasher" looked very old and bloody irritable, thought Phillip. His brigade-major, tall crown of cap, long nose, long face with wispy moustache, looked more than ever like a caricature of the Crown Prince.

"What happened?" asked O'Connor, when Phillip returned.

"I told Crasher he ought to get up as soon as possible, while the men could see, and not wait for useless orders. Obviously we ought to go on and fill the gap. We ought to push on, the quicker the better. It's common sense! Get up while it's still light! I said that they'd find it hard to make out the crossing places in the dark. Also, to get up while the Germans were not there."

"You told Crasher that, did you, my boy?"

"Yes."

"What did he say, then, my boy?"

"Nothing. I was up there this morning, as far as the other slope of the valley, and there were no Germans anywhere near when I turned back."

"Why did you turn back?" asked the eighteen-year-old captain nicknamed "Infant Hercules", who now commanded Phillip's old company.

"I was only sight-seeing. I happened to be with the Gault-shires when a great friend of mine, Captain West, was badly hit, and asked me to take over his company for a bit. The colonel had been knocked out, too, and also the second-in-command, so I carried on. There was nothing in it. We walked round the flanks, and as the Welsh and the London Highlanders had already got behind the Lone Tree position, and others were attacking from the rear, the Germans surrendered. If I'd have obeyed staff orders, we'd all have been shot down in the third useless attack on the uncut wire in front of Lone Tree."

"So you took your own line, my boy?"

"Of course. Everyone knows that the staff are no good."

"Did you tell Crasher that?"

"No. He told me. By the way, are you chaps hungry? I've got some sandwiches if you care to have them."

"Thanks, but we've got our iron rations, also extra cheese and bread, and an issue of pea soup. We were told we were in for a long march, and would be on lines of communication."

"Yes, they always tell you that."

"Do you think the Germans *are* on the run?"

"Not now. They were this morning. I met a major of the fifteenth division, which had gone right over Hill 70, which is the pivot of the advance, beyond the Tower Bridge over there. He asked me where you chaps were."

"We were told we wouldn't be put into the attack until a gap was made."

"Those staff idiots again! Why didn't they put you with regulars, as we were when we first went into the line? What can an entirely new division know, all on its own? You want to be sandwiched in with the old sweats. My God, if we'd have had the old first brigade here, which we were with at First Ypres! The Grenadiers and the Coldstream! And the Jocks! We'd have been through to the Haute Deule Canal now! Still, it will be good to get back to real soldiering, when this is all over, won't it? Where's old Brendon, by the way?"

"He's Home Service. Non est," murmured O'Connor.

More subalterns had come up, and were listening intently to this talk.

"Can't you persuade 'Strawballs', Maddison? If the German reserves aren't here yet——"

"It's nothing to do with me, anyway. I saw regular officers

before the attack weeping tears of blood about the inefficiency of the staff."

"Certainly what we have seen so far confirms what you say, my boy."

"We had it cushy at First Ypres, compared with this. We weren't mucked about, you see."

O'Connor, the Dublin barrister, was convinced that what had been said was true. He went to the adjutant. He returned for Phillip. After some more talk, a brass-hat wearing the black-red brassard of corps ordered Phillip to stand by to act as guide to the brigade when the orders to move off should be given. Hell, I'm for it, thought Phillip. Oh, what an idiot I am, as the clouds in the sky broke, and a harsh rain shut down the last of the dimming battlefield. He could hear his mother's voice saying, *Why can you never leave well alone, my son?* as when he had taken his first watch to pieces to see if it could be made to work faster.

Faintly, like sad thoughts searching, the first calcium flares of night began to rise in the distance.

The General Officer commanding the First Army still knew nothing of the heavy losses of the battalions in the line by the time night had fallen. Sir Douglas Haig believed, with many others in the back area, that the Germans had been driven entirely from their first line; that their second and final line of defence, behind the Lens–La Bassée road (until it turned at right angles, west of and around Lens) was but weakly held, and most of it without barbed-wire. If this last position were taken by an advance through its centre, the German position around Lens would be turned.

But a division, occupying many miles of road when on the march, was not as easily manoeuvrable as a battalion, or better still, a Detached Force under its local commander.

Sir Douglas Haig's original plan of action was dependent on the French on his right. Lord Kitchener had ordered "a continuous and vigorous attack"; but an attack has flanks which are always vulnerable. They are like blows upon a man from the side. While he fights forward, he must be guarded. Enemy thrusts to get in at the flanks and so through to the undefended rear-areas, must be countered in advance by strong defensive flanks, so that frontal attack may be made with confidence. Not only had the French behind the Lorette Ridge failed to start until five hours after the First Army assault, but they had failed when they did start, about noon. The Vimy Ridge, which overlooks the wide plain stretching away to the Scheldt as the Hog's Back in Surrey overlooks intervening English country to the Thames, remained in German hands. The French advance line still lay three miles away.

So a break-through by the British north of the Vimy Ridge had its dangers from the southern flank. Two British divisions, the 47th London and the 15th Scottish (which, as Captain West had told Phillip, had gone through the first German position in the early morning) would have to dig in and wire their positions east of Loos and on Hill 70 to stop any heavy thrusts into the southern side of the First Army's further attacks.

General Haig decided to press on with the attack, to take away German strength against the French. The orders went out at 11.30 p.m. that night from his headquarters at Hinges. The two reserve divisions were to attack at 11 a.m. the next morning, get through the weak German second position, and line the Haute Deule Canal in the plain beyond. The cavalry would pass through the gap to the plain of Flanders.

The field-marshal, loyal to the Cabinet's directive, and to the French Allies, did not restrain General Haig, although he felt "the futility of pushing reserves through a narrow gap in the enemy's defences". He informed his First Army commander that the last reserves, the Guards division, was on its way "to be at his orders", to relieve the 15th division, which would be withdrawn into general reserve.

While this order from the First Army was being transmuted into detailed orders at the headquarters of First, Fourth and Eleventh Corps, comprising the eight divisions now upon the battlefield, the Germans, unknown to the staff, had brought up their reserves, many of whom were by this time in their second position, putting out stakes and barbed-wire in the long grass, without interference from the British; while others were advancing to the long straight road between Lens and La Bassée, for the counter-attack.

"Forward!" cried "Crasher", in a croaking voice, just before midnight, as he laid the right-hand reins of snaffle and curb on the neck of his charger, and turned to face the white stalks of light in the distance.

"Lead on, scouts!" said "Strawballs", gruffly, out of three mufflers round his neck and a balaclava elongating his egg-shaped head by quite six inches. It had been made hurriedly by his wife, with a generous allowance for shrinkage.

"Follow me, chaps," said Phillip, as he set off, ignoring the compass bearing of one hundred and twelve degrees; to cross, for the second time that day, the wide and open space of tall stalky grasses and glimmering lines of chalk towards the ruddy glow that was the village of Loos-en-Gohoelle on fire. How strange, he thought, that he was doing what he was doing; it was all like a dream; the yellow grasses were those in the Backfield of boyhood, the slag-heaps like the ballast heap he had played on, and rival bands had tried to drive him off the heap, and out of his "lands". It was worse than any dream; the great ruddy glare away in front was like the all-red nightmares he had had as a child, walking on Randiswell Bridge down into Randiswell, where everything was burning with a dull red glow, and he was powerless to find Mother, powerless even to walk, powerless to escape all the world on fire. Even after he had awakened, and Mother was holding him sitting up in bed, wet with perspiration, and the fire was only a candle on the chest-of-drawers, the awfulness of the nightmare, of never being able to find a way out, remained to haunt him throughout his childhood. He saw the Tower Bridge black against the burning village, rising up like something lit by a Crystal Palace firework display. What a set-piece for the destruction of the world!

They stopped to check the compass bearing. What piffle! A compass wouldn't get them past the wire!

While they halted, wails and groans came out of the grasses, from unseen wounded.

"Stretcher-bearers!"

"Give us a moment, chum!"

"Water, for Christ's sake, matey!"

"Hi! Help! Oh-h-h."

"Can't we do something, my boy?" asked O'Connor.

"Nothing. Apart from the fact that it will only bring false hopes if we stop, it's against orders. Damn orders, anyway. For God's sake let's get a move on!"

"Not so loud, my boy." O'Connor came nearer. "The men——"

Drifts of mist enclosed them. Then a glimpse of a full moon, apparently hastening through a gap in the clouds. They floundered into a schemozzle of wire and buried stakes. Here grey upsurged chalk was the old German trench.

"How do we get over, my boy?"

"Find a plank, or a bridge. If not, we'll have to scramble over."

"How can Crasher and Strawballs get over, on horseback?"

"Transfer into the Foreign Legion, and try with camels, I suggest."

"Not so much sarcasm, my boy. We are relying on you, you know."

"I was only joking. We'll have to halt here and look for the bridge. We had to scramble this morning."

"Pass the word back to halt, Sergeant," said O'Connor. The word chain-linked back into loamy darkness. "I'll blow two short blasts on my whistle if I find a bridge," said O'Connor. "Will you do the same?"

"I left mine with the Bloodhound Patrol."

"I've got a whistle, sir," said a sergeant.

"Then go with Mr. Maddison, will you."

Phillip took the sergeant and Bellamy as a runner and they floundered up the line, trying to avoid the dead. Phillip had no idea where he was. He knew only that, once through the trench lines, they would be in the valley with gentle sloping sides where he had walked that morning, leading up the rise to the Lens–La Bassée road. Once there, he would leave them. He began to feel tired, and took a swig at his bottle. He hesitated to offer the ̲ners a drink, remembering Lance-corporal Hack, a regular, who had been out since Mons, who had got five years' hard labour, to be served after the war, for pinching rum and getting tight all alone in a Belgian barn.

"I heard Captain O'Connor's whistle, sir." They listened. Two blasts came again. On the way back the sergeant said, "To my way of thinking, there's a lot of firing over yon, isn't there, sir, for the Germans to be in retreat?"

"Probably our chaps, firing at the whistle. The Germans sometimes blow them. Bloody dangerous things, whistles. For God's sake don't blow yours, Sergeant. It may start the wind-up, when both sides fire all night at nothing."

"I begin to see why Horatio Bottomley says the war is costing five million pounds a day, sir, when I see all this waste of men and material. Last week's *John Bull* said he was coming out to see for himself."

"A fat lot of good he'll do."

"Don't you think his trenchant articles have done some good, sir?"

"I don't know. But I do know that a prominent man in the City once told me that he was the biggest rogue out of gaol."

"Still, there's good in all of us, sir."

"There's some good in my water-bottle, Sergeant, if you swear you won't say I gave you any. Or Bellamy."

"We're not children, sir," replied the sergeant.

"Stuff to give the troops, sir," said Bellamy.

It took the brigade nearly an hour to get through the old German line, with its narrow gaps in the wire and few single planks. On the farther side the men, still in greatcoats with webbing equipment outside, and carrying extra bandoliers of rifle ammunition, were so exhausted that a rest was ordered. Rain was coming down in the pattern of the clouds, with intervals of veiled moonlight revealing haggard faces and uptilted empty water-bottles. Both Phillip and O'Connor thought of the same thing at once, from different sides, speaking together.

"Where shall we be able to fill——"

"You probably won't get any water—— Sorry, you were saying——?"

"Go on, my boy."

"Well, I was thinking that there won't be any water in shell-holes now, and probably the pumps and wells in the villages will be out of action."

"There's the battalion water-cart, Phil."

It was the first time O'Connor had called him by his Christian name; and the warmth of gratitude he felt for O'Connor, added to the warmth of the whiskey-water-bottle shared with O'Connor, caused Phillip to stay with the battalion when, having left their packs behind, they went on and, half an hour after midnight, reached the road in the valley leading to the ruddy glow of Loos on their right and Lone Tree and Bois Carré on the left.

While they sat there, the company asleep despite the cold and wet, a file of men from the brigade on their left, carrying empty petrol cans and seeking water, stopped to give the alarming news that Hulluch had been re-taken by Jerry, causing a retirement from the Lens–La Bassée road.

"The Prooshan Guards are on the way, chum, wi' bags'r other reinforcements! That's the way we're treated out here, chum; first they tell us we'll only be used to follow up the rout, and the next thing we know is that, not having had any proper grub or kip for forty-eight hours, we're expected to fight the Prooshan Guard, and all our Lewis and machine-guns back with the transport."

"Write to *John Bull* about it, chum," said Phillip, derisively, in a cockney voice, feeling Cranmer's face on his own.

"Who are you, old man?" asked the partly educated North-country voice.

"Old Man Whiskey, mate."

"I don't see ought to be foony about."

"It's the only way out here," said Phillip, getting up, and now talking in a rough throaty voice, as befitted the old soldier. "To hell with your pushing Prooshan Guards! They're all rows of little crosses around Ypres, where they came over at the jog-trot, carrying rifles at the porte. We met them with the bayonet, when they came through the Nun's Wood. They're all ghosts now, so no need to get the wind up."

"Well, that's something definite, at any rate. What are you, may I ask."

"I belonged to the First Guards Brigade at Ypres, but I am specially employed now," replied Phillip, in a precise voice, as he saw himself in the character of Colonel Mowbray.

"I say, you're a good mimic, you are, chum! You're not by any chance an officer are you—sir?"

"About your water. I don't think you'll find any this way. Loos is on fire, and fighting is still going on there, if you listen." The gruff thuds of German stick-bombs could be heard among the crackle of rifle-fire. "There are two pumps in Le Rutoire farm, and they are probably the nearest source of supply, until your water-cart comes up. It's about a mile and a half back from here. There is a lane back from Lone Tree——"

"We came up that way, sir——"

"The farm is the turning to the right, about a mile down past Lone Tree."

The sergeant thanked him, saluted, and the squad went back almost cheerfully.

"You're a dark horse, Phillip, my boy. You ought to be on the staff—or at the Coliseum!"

"Well, you see, Shaun, I happened to be at Le Rutoire farm last night, and saw the two pumps. All pumps this way are shelled to hell. Why didn't the staff give each of the new battalions a squad of guides? Or better, mix them up with the old sweats. As I told you, when we came out, I mean the London Highlanders, we were put in among regulars, old sweats from Mons, who looked after us like nurses. It was hell when we first went in before that, alone, at Messines. No-one knew anything. We were just like the chaps of these two divisions. I wonder how many officers in your division have been under fire before?"

"Probably only Crasher, I imagine. Certainly there are none among the Cantuvellaunians, with the exception of your explicit self, Phillip. What I like about you, Phil, is a total absence of either callousness or malice in your character. Do you mind me speaking so personally? Have a Gyppie cigarette?"

"Thanks. Have another spot of old man whiskey?"

"Not just now, thank you. I suppose it's safe to strike a match? I've got one of the new trench fusees, somewhere, but it's in my pack, which I doubt I shall see again."

"We must be careful, Shaun, me b'hoy, for look what happened when a fag-end was thrown down, careless like, in Loos!"

Captain Whale joined them, sitting down, accepting a Gyppie. He smoked it vigorously, then, "Shaun, I'm worried about the transport, particularly the Lewis-gun cart, the cookers, and the water-cart. Lambert is due to be at a place called Le Rutoire farm at eleven o'clock."

"Here's the very man for you, Jonah. Phil himself appears to know this line of country as well as he knew the staircases and bolt-holes of that equally watery place, Godolphin House. Le Rutoire farm is a mile and a half west of Lone Tree, where he was in action only this morning, in an unofficial capacity, let it be understood, and took the surrender of three hundred Germans."

"It was all luck, sir."

"It's certainly our luck that we came across you today," said Jonah. "We thought we were never to see you again!" He patted Phillip's knee: and the upshot was that Phillip, with the same sergeant and Bellamy and a dozen other men, led the way down the route to the crossroads and so past the shambles of Lone Tree to Le Rutoire farm, to find the transport and bring up the rations, water, Lewis guns, and ammunition.

"Oh my God!" said Phillip, after the slow walk down the road from Hulluch, where an attack was going on, judging by the rattling and roaring. "God's teeth," he said, in a different tone of voice, as the party stopped near the mass of the farm, with its barns, sheds, lofts and courtyard walls in brick-heap ruins; but alive with every kind of voice and movement of hoof and wheel. Here were voices of Glasgow and the Cairngorms, of Northumberland and Durham, Yorkshire, London, Kent, Bedfordshire, Devon, and others amidst the cries of the wounded, laid out upon stretchers, ground-sheets, and the wet sett-stones; while shells swooped and bassly growled down, to burst with flash and rattle in the air and red spouting rage upon the earth. There were so many horses that at first he thought the cavalry was there; but getting round motionless wagon after wagon, amidst a chorus of identical questions and answers— "Are you the——? No, have you seen the——?"—repeated all around, he realised that the jam of vehicles included field-guns, strings of pack-mules, ammunition limbers, Maltese carts and every kind of transport for almost every branch of divisional troops. Having arrived, nobody could move on or back or sideways; some wagons were already ditched; one field-gun team, with a dozen plunging animals, had gone over a row of wounded lying by what originally was the roadside. Oaths and yells and high-pitched nervous cursings filled the tawny darkness; and when the full moon raced out of the clouds, a feeling of nightmare unreality, of the pale hopelessness of it all, stopped Phillip's further movement. He had already shared his sandwiches and emptied his water-bottle—a mere sip each—and felt suddenly hopeless.

How to find Lambert in all that congestion? He thought to go to Brigade H.Q. in the cellars, and telling the sergeant to wait where he was, walked to what had been the door of the farm. Hurricane lamps inside revealed a change. Wounded men sat on cellar steps; from below came the warm, acrid smell of sweat, and then of an open latrine, causing him to return at once. God, what a muck-up; and the old doctor in Mazingarbe playing cut-throat bridge while this was going on!

"What shall we do, sir?"

"Do you all know Mr. Lambert? I think the men ought to go out, in pairs, and try and find him. Each pair must get back here, just where we are now, after about an hour. Obviously the roads will be jammed. Mr. Lambert may try and get here, on foot, to find the ration party. Understand? Well, you wait here, sergeant, in case he comes. When the moon is about there"—he pointed into the sky—"will show roughly the time to be back here, for the couples going out. Probably the wagons and carts are held up somewhere between here and Vermelles, which is the first turning to the right about a quarter of a mile down this road. So two couples go that way, and three couples straight on to the main Lens road we came up this afternoon. Just a minute, before you go."

He could not think any more; he went a few yards away, to try and think out what to do. The men were hanging on his words. As though he knew anything! Quick, what could he tell them, supposing the wagons were jammed immovable in the traffic? What would Cousin Bertie have done? For a few moments he felt like crying. Why hadn't he told Jonah that he had to be back at Mazingarbe, as ordered by the M.O.? Then he thought of Mother praying to St. Anthony when she had lost anything, and automatically he said the phrase he had often heard her speak aloud, *Please, St. Anthony, let me find the transport.*

"As soon as anyone finds where it is, come back here and tell the sergeant."

"Very good, sir."

His words gave hope in the ruinous moonlight.

"The efforts to get the first-line transport forward with the brigades," says the official history, "failed. That of two brigades struggled through the mud and shell holes of the Lens road on its way to Loos, but was held up by the original front trenches, the road here being blocked by derelict wagons broken up by the German artillery that had been shelling the road throughout the evening. In the same way, the transport of other brigades was held up by the Corons de Rutoire. Here, no authority having arranged for the co-ordination of the movements of the two corps troops in the same area, the bridges across a back line of British trenches were blocked for some hours by ammunition wagons of the First Division, returning to be filled, and by a stream of ambulances from Le Rutoire farm. The confusion in the darkness was considerable, and the transport was therefore parked off the road by the Corons.

"Every infantry brigade having apparently ordered its vehicles to be at Le Rutoire, as the only place that could be identified on the featureless plain, the mass of wagons on the way thither led to much confusion in the darkness, and interfered very considerably with the passage of the batteries.

"Not only for the artillery, but also for the infantry of the reserve divisions, the conditions under which the attack (the next morning) was to be launched were most unfavourable from the outset. In spite of tremendous efforts, it had been impossible to bring the ration wagons and cookers up to the battalions. The quarter-masters had made many attempts during the night to get in touch with their units, but, after wandering aimlessly in the dark through the mud and débris of the battlefield, abandoned the search."

"I'm awfully sorry, sir, but I could not find Mr. Lambert, or any of the transport. I tried to borrow some petrol tins, and was put under arrest by a gunner major, sir."

"O-oh," said a grim white-stubbled "Strawballs". "What did you do then, Mr. Maddison?"

"I put him under arrest for using language unbecoming an officer and a gentleman, sir—then I thought it best to clear off."

After a long pause, the colonel said, "Did you manage to pick up any information as to Mr. Lambert's whereabouts?"

"No, sir."

"O-oh," growled the colonel once more. "Jonah, why didn't you send——" The brigadier and his brigade major were standing beside "Strawballs".

"What's 'at I hear, damme?" said "Crasher".

"Did you make enquiries?" asked the brigade major.

"Yes, sir. The traffic blocks extended for miles. It was the artillery, sending back their limbers for shells, and the ambulances for the wounded going down, with the transport coming up at the same time, from the other direction, sir."

"Did you see the batteries in position, as you came up?"

"Yes, sir, everywhere in the mist the other side of the Lone Tree ridge. I thought they were in the wrong place, sir."

"You are being asked for facts, not for opinions, Mr. Maddison," said the colonel, very distinctly.

"I thought it might be useful to know, sir. I thought that negative information would be important at this juncture, sir. The batteries are all in the open, sir, and in full view of the German observers where they are now, almost wheel to wheel. I think they missed the way, sir, and also the place."

At that moment salvoes of German shells began to scream overhead, to burst in unseen ground below the Lone Tree ridge.

"You can go now," said Jonah to Phillip, quietly.

He saluted and left the long narrow chalk pit, fringed by trees, and went back in the pallid light of early morning to where O'Connor was sitting with his company beside little scrapings in the chalk hacked out by entrenching tools. This trench was perhaps fifteen inches deep, and wandered for a couple of hundred yards in the wet and flattened grasses beside the Lens–La Bassée road, whither the brigade had moved before dawn. A guide, left by the old position, had led the ration party there, three-quarters of a mile eastwards. This was now the front line. A yellow flag, stuck in the ground near others with broken shafts, showed where the advance had reached the previous day.

"What did they say, Phil?"

Seeing the bleak look on the other's face, O'Connor got up to stand beside him. "Look out, sir, there's a sniper active!" cried out a voice from the ground. "Better get down," said O'Connor. Lying beside Phillip, he said, "Don't let it worry you, Phil. You did your best, I am sure."

"It's all been such a frightful muck-up, from start to finish! Like my life, before and during this war. I begin to see why most people never liked me. I've often thought of that ragging I got. I thought it was because, as Baldersby said, I couldn't speak the King's English. Was it?"

"Well, pronunciation of words varies from place to place, and from age to age, my boy. For myself, I doubt if I can speak the King's English—I can only be reasonably sure that it approximates to the English spoken by m'forefathers who out of politeness—for I cannot think there can have been any other reason—began to imitate the immigrants from a foreign country in the reign of your Queen Elizabeth. But to answer your particular question, I consider that your voice is both soft and pleasant, generally speaking, so do not let the idle remark of a vain fellow put you out of harmony with yourself."

An orderly arrived, bent low at the double, with a message in a pale buff enyelope. Captain O'Connor read it.

"We are advancing to their second line at eleven o'clock this morning, Phillip. It should not be too difficult, for at the company commanders' conference we learned that it consists of a single trench, and no wire in front of it at all. It is also unoccupied. You will be going back now, I suppose? What about your gas job?"

Phillip looked away into the sky, and after an inner struggle he said, "Do you mind if I come with you? I don't like leaving you in the lurch, now." He stuttered as he went on, "I—I've done this sort of job before, y'know." Leave me alone, leave me alone, he cried within himself, to his mother's imagined face.

Unknown to the brigadier, the attack had been postponed by First Army until midday; but as no counter-order had arrived by 11 a.m., the advance went forward without artillery support.

Moving in various directions, some of the untried units, mistaking other advancing troops for Germans, lay down and fired at them. The fire was returned; but the main attack straggled eastward across a long and bare stretch of ground between the strongly-held flanks of a bastion, its objective being the second German position a thousand yards beyond the Lens–La Bassée road.

This second German position, empty and unwired the previous evening, was now protected by wire almost as thick as brambles, as high as the waist of a man and five to seven yards deep. The wire had been put up by newly-arrived German reserves, who had worked without interference in the moonlight.

A strip of copse, originally planted as covert for pheasants, and known as Bois Hugo, lay down the centre of the advance. Here German machine-guns had been placed early that morning.

Thus the advance, caught in a cross-fire of machine-gun and rifle fire from the flanks of the bastion, was also enfiladed by machine-gun fire at short range from the edge of the wood; while German field-guns fired shrapnel and tear-gas shells over open sights from Hulluch.

The straggling lines faltered, became thin, fell away.

Jonah the Whale was cut across by a dozen bullets, which spun him round twice as he fell.

The colonel, no man of straw, continued to go on at a crouch, swearing loudly, until he appeared to stumble, and was no more.

Major Rhodes ran forward to take his place and wave the battalion on. He and a score of men in line with him went down almost together in the screeching amazement of machine-gun death.

Phillip saw Captain O'Connor, his hand vaguely seeking his *pince-nez* spectacles which had been splintered into the space left vacant by his nose and eyes, blundering about; and then the line, thin and useless, faltered and lay down, Phillip with them, wondering why he had not felt any fear at all, why his own self seemed to be entirely detached from it all, away from what was happening.

Chapter 25

FRIENDLY FACES

HE seemed to have been lying in the grass, his nostrils near to clover leaves, his arms and legs swelled with heat, for a long time, when he realised that firing had stopped. There was only the sound of distant guns booming, the distant racket of small-arms fire; no immediate crackling and swishing of bullets. Cautiously, slowly raising his face, he saw with a clutch of sickness that Germans were very near, looking among the grasses. He lay down again, but when nothing happened, no shot or shout, he lifted his head once more. Two Germans came towards him, rifles slung on leather thongs on shoulders. He stared up at them, trying to speak, but his tongue was stuck in his mouth. He was trying to say *prächtig kerl*. Then with an incoherence of trembling he saw that several Germans behind the leading two had red cross brassards, carrying stretchers. He held up his hands, to show he was unarmed, and rose shakily to his feet.

"Are you wounded?"

He shook his head. How strange to be taken prisoner. He kept his hands up, until motioned to put them down.

"Gas?"

He thought they meant his brassard. "Yes, but it came back on our men," he said shakily.

"There are too many of your wounded for us to deal with," said one of the Germans. "So our Oberst has ordered us to tell you that you may take your wounded back the way you came."

Phillip stared, shaking uncontrollably. He tried to speak, impotently.

"Does it surprise you that a German colonel should give such an order?"

When he could speak he said, "I met some of your fellows, prächtig kerls, last Christmas Day, when we were all good friends."

This remark was ignored. "Are you an officer? Yes, then you may lead back your wounded who can walk, back to your own lines. You will not be fired on. The order has gone forth from our Oberst! We are not 'perfidious Germany!' Let me explain one moment, please! What did your Coldstream Guards do last month, in the trenches by the mine craters of Cambrin? I will tell you, Herr Offizier Engländer! Your Guards had their band in the trenches, and played *Die Wacht am Rhein*, then your *God Save the King*. Just before one o'clock Berlin time, when our soldiers were clapping hands and applauding in polite manner, what did your Guards then do? Even before the last note of *Rule Britannia* sounded, they responded with a drum-fire of bombs, grenades, and mortars, killing and wounded many of their musical guests. So what did your clever gentlemen do? The very next night they played the band again! But this time 'Fritz' was not fooled by Tommy! So do not ask me if you will be fired upon now! *Deutsche treu*, Herr Engländer!"

"It was a dirty trick, I agree," said Phillip. "My father is half-German, I am proud of it. You are very kind people, I think. Prächtig kerls, in fact!"

They exchanged salutes. Phillip was light-bodied, his spirit fluttered in his throat, he felt the darkness of the world to be overcome.

He walked to a quiet waiting group in khaki, with yellow, drained faces, some with bandages on heads, others with arms in slings under cut-away jackets, or standing with slit trousers revealing flesh-wounds that had been bound.

"Don't bunch, men, don't bunch," he told them as they hobbled away. "Single file is safest, and don't look about you.

We're in luck, my boys, but show no interest in anything, and for God's sake don't loiter! It's almost as though it's over, not a shot anywhere." He was speaking to himself, the only un-wounded man. He waited for them to pass him, seeing them as a mixed lot, some Jocks, all sorts of regiments. They moved on slowly, faces set, they had lost blood, they were unspeaking with thirst and the puffy feeling of mind and body stretched after tension.

They came to the main road, and he saw in the wide spaces before him hundreds, thousands of walking figures, extending as far as he could see, on all sides. Good God, what had happened, was the war suddenly over? The entire British Army seemed to be leaving the battlefield.

The centre of the British front had broken, beyond shame and the fear of death, in a mass movement of starved, dry-throated troops of the reserve divisions extending from the higher slopes of Hill 70 on the right to the Hulluch–Vermelles road on the left, a distance of nearly three miles. The brigades of the two reserve divisions, after every other man had become a casualty, had lost cohesion, and individual men, and groups of unspeaking men, were leaving the battle. The Germans stood up and watched them go.

But not all had gone. A few remained. Some of the stragglers, coming upon steady troops, hesitated, and joined them. Phillip, mind set on billet, walked at the head of the slow file of wounded. He led them down into the long dip of Loos valley, and hearing sporadic rifle and machine-gun fire from Hill 70 over his shoulder, guessed what had happened. And bloody sensible, too, he thought, to want to leave that ghastly and meaningless hell behind.

He led the way down the track to Le Rutoire, which he was beginning to know now. God's teeth, was it only yesterday that he was listening to "Spectre" West, eye hanging on cheek, as he whispered the order to get round the flanks? It was a life-time. Here was the Lone Tree rise. How was little Kirk, and Douglas with his bloody behind and kilt in rags? Wounded were still lying in the grasses, calling out, raising arms, crying for help. He saw them without emotion. There were too many. He was not being stopped this time. He was going to get out of it. If only he had had a bullet through an arm. They were all dragging feet now, his rag, tag and bobtail brigade—the man beside him, with head-bandage and skewed jaw set with smashed teeth, was gurgling with every breath; but shook his head when asked if he wanted to rest. Surely there would be ambulances at the farm?

The batteries he had seen in the first light, the *prima luce* of the dear old Magister (Phillip had had a pleasing letter from him, and ever since had thought he was a fine old boy, really), had copped it. Dead horses lay about in dozens, guns turned over, ripped and pocked and knocked skewwiff by the old Hun. What a tragedy it all was.

The file of hobbling wounded was now one of many little groups going back; but coming towards them were about a dozen officers and men whose appearance was in striking contrast to the battle stragglers, with their torn and chalk-mud uniforms, slacked-off puttees, and faces fixed in exhaustion. The soldiers coming towards them bore themselves upright, the officers walked with an easy stride, withal bearing themselves with a calmness that seemed to take in nothing about them, as though indifferent to the scene. The officers' moustaches were brushed towards the lobes of their ears, their caps set level on their heads, the peaks correctly aligned; while the stars on their shoulder-straps, though in miniature like their buttons, were more spread, efflorescent, than the miniature pips of ordinary officers. The men following in step bore their ruddy faces and necks upright, giving the impression that their rations were better in every way than those of ordinary soldiers; as was their bearing, which had a kind of brutal pride about it, the effect heightened by their cap-peaks drawn down to an even level with their eyes, so that their chins were drawn in, and the backs of their powerful necks pronounced.

When this group was about fifty yards distant from Phillip and his party, they stopped; and he saw the leading officer speak to a straggle of retreating men. A sergeant shouted at them to stand to attention before an officer. At this other stragglers stopped, and stared at the group. The officer, who was elderly, and a captain, said something; but the stragglers addressed began to move on as before, when a younger officer near the captain raised his hunting whip, and seemed to throw the plaited leather thong at one of the men, who held up an arm as the cotton lash cracked in his face. The officer, with similar stroke of lower arm and flick of wrist towards another man, caused a howl as the lash whipped a second cheek.

"About turn, you damned cowards!" shouted the officer, who was a full lieutenant, Phillip saw. Near him another officer, a second-lieutenant, had on his face a look of faint scorn; and staring at the face, Phillip, standing still with his party, some of whom had mouths open with fatigue, saw that the officer was his cousin Bertie.

At the same time Hubert Cakebread recognised Phillip. With a slight smile he said, "What are you doing here, young Phil? How long have you been out?"

"About a fortnight."

"Are you wounded?"

"No."

"Going the wrong way, aren't you, old man?" said Bertie, coming near to him. "Where's your battalion?"

"I haven't got one, really. I'm——" He could not say anything further.

"What is your division?"

"It was the First."

"*Was?*" said Bertie, sharply. Then, "Better come along with me, I think. These walking wounded can find the dressing-station by themselves. They don't need an officer to conduct them, you know. There are ambulances at Le Rutoire farm."

"Oh good. That's what I wanted to find out."

Phillip found himself walking beside the broad upright figure of his cousin towards Lone Tree for the third time in the past two days. "Mustn't let the side down, you know, old man," said Bertie, now his amiable self.

Phillip walked with the others in silence. No more wounded were coming back now; but on the ground arms were still being raised, voices were calling. The elderly Coldstream captain spoke to some, saying that help was on the way.

At the old German front line beyond the scarred cherry tree some sort of reorganisation seemed to be taking place. Two staff officers with red-tabs were moving about, urging slow and exhausted troops to organise the line for defence, though it was very deep and narrow, revetted by board and posts, and a boarded fire-step: much better-made than the British trenches. The party of Guards officers crossed by a plank. Here Phillip forced himself to say, "I am a gas officer, Bertie. I'm supposed to be at Mazingarbe."

"Then what are you doing here?"

"I was excused duty after we let the gas go, so I came up to have a look round."

"Been out all night?"

"Yes."

"When are you on duty again?"

"In two days' time."

Bertie laughed. "I've heard of some odd ways of spending leave, but yours takes the biscuit. But you were always a bit crazy. How did you leave them all in England?"

"Very well, thank you."

"I heard you'd been in to see the Rolls. Plucked a cockerel didn't you, and then weren't asked to help eat it? Old man Rolls likes his Friday night dinner strictly in the bosom of his family."

Hubert went on to say that his advance party was going up to look at part of the line they were taking over that night, relieving part of the Fifteenth Division.

"You look a bit tired, Phil, why not get back to Mazingarbe?"

"Yes, I think I will, now you mention it. Goodbye!" He gave his cousin a long look, in which resignation, sympathy, appeal were mingled; and holding out his hand to be shaken, turned away and walked back, his eyes ringed with tears.

Coming to the old German trench, he put on his brassard; if questioned again, he would say that he had come to inspect the effects of the gas—as, in a way, he had.

But no staff or other officer took any notice of him. Thinking of Kirk, he went along the uncut wire to see if he had been rescued. Voices, feeble and croaking, called out at his passing; hands were raised among the grasses. Two men, one behind the other, were laboriously going back on hands and knees; others dragged themselves on elbows, one with a twisted, shattered leg, alive with maggots. "The ambulances are up at Le Rutoire; it won't be long now, boys," he said, again and again. Haggard faces responded with such gratitude that he could hardly keep back hysteria.

He came to an area white with the unkilted bottoms of the sprawling dead. Among them, composed like a stone crusader on a tomb, lay little Kirk. He had made himself comfortable. His neck rested on his valise, arms folded on chest. Phillip knelt by him, and thought, as he stared at the pale, delicate face in repose that Kirk had arranged his own laying-out; for he was dead. Phillip sat beside him, to rest himself in the silence and immobility of the dead man; then, opening one of his breast pockets, to take letters and photographs, the first thing he felt was the pair of *pince-nez* spectacles which Kirk had been wearing when he had passed him the previous afternoon. Kirk must have given up hope when he put them there; for he could not see without his spectacles.

When he had taken letters, a small Y.M.C.A. khaki Bible, and other possessions from the pockets—soon the usual battlefield thieves would begin their night-searches—he lifted Kirk's cold hand, held it for a moment, whispered goodbye; and rising, walked back to the road marked on the sullen plain by a long line of slow movement, turning wheels and tramp of feet stretching away to the far horizon of mist and smoke and massive pyramid s.

He got a lift back beside an ambulance driver. At Mazingarbe he thought it advisable to see the doctor. "Yes, yes, yes! My dear fellow, of course there are still wounded lying out. And maggots act as scavengers, removing putrid flesh," said the doctor, cigarette smoke staining his ragged moustaches more yellow. "Don't you worry about what canna' be helped, laddie. Watch that heart of yours, and don't concer-rn yoursel' with what canna' be helped! The wor-rld has gone mad, quite mad, young fellow!" He held out a packet of yellow perils. "I've been working fifteen hours at a stretch. How about a game of bridge tonight? Well, come an' join us if ye feel like it. Sixpence a hundred, that's the limit," he wheezed, lighting another cigarette from the stub of the one held between brown finger-tips.

Chapter 26

"TWINKLE" PROPOSES

A NEW "Twinkle" greeted him in the billet, with spruced-up moustache cut to a stubble between rolled and horizontal waxed points, and an exaggerated mouthful of new false teeth. The top row was of gold, in contrast to the lower peg-like objects upon which, in the intervals of speaking, he appeared to be champing.

"Breakin' of 'm in, sir. I took this little ol' lot off'v a Frog, in lieu of services rendered." As he spoke, loose rivets in the gold teeth were jumping about. He gave two rapid champs, which caused a faint rattle. "The ol' girl's getting you some soup, sir; I expected you back last night, had a very nice 'ot-pot waiting, sir."

"I'm thirsty, give me some water." He drank nearly a quart.

"'Ere, have a swig o' this, sir, I kep' it for you." From his kitbag "Twinkle" pulled a bottle of whisky, labelled *White Horse*. Phillip drank from the bottle; and feeling better, said, "You look very smart tonight!"

"Yes, sir, I'm a noo man, sir, now I got me noo snappers."

"Have you seen anything of the special detachment?"

"The 'ole lot's gone back to Helfaut, sir. The major sent for you, sir, then 'e came 'isself, sir, and I told 'im you got the gas bad, and was out for a breath o' fresh air. Now drink your soup before the scum forms on it, sir."

"Don't you belong to them?"

"No, sir. I stayed to look after you, sir."

"But, my dear chap——"

"That's right, sir. I know what you're thinkin'. 'Ere today and gone tomorrow, that's 'Twinkle'. But you'd be wrong, sir. I'd be pleased if you could take me with you wherever you goes, sir. Put me on the strenghth, like. Now, sir, you look proper done-in, sir, if you'll pardon the remark. I don't suppose you 'ad no kip last night?"

"God's teeth, it's a muck up, this whole attack, 'Twinkle!' No water! No cookers! No rations! Nobody knows where anybody else is! And Christ Almighty, the casualties! Thousands and thousands of our chaps lying everywhere, at least ten killed for every one German. I went over with my old lot this morning, but God knows what happened, I was with them one moment, and then I was going on practically alone, so I lay down among some other lot, all mixed up, until a cease-fire."

He put the bottle to his mouth, and drank till he choked; then sat down, and after coughing and spluttering, with loose lips finished his account to the old man, ending with the Irish Guards officer lashing out with his whip; then sighed deeply, feeling sick.

"Them Micks always was a quarrelsome lot, a-roarin' and a-bawlin'," mused the servant. "Why, in the boosers of Aldershot and Caterham they was allus the first to up-end their beer-mugs soon as they see a Bill Brown or a Lilywhite come in for a wet. Then up goes the 'ole balloon, belts off, buckles whizzing, fists bashing, boots stampin' on faces. My word, sir, they was wild boys, them Micks. Them horse marines in Union Street Plymouth was never near 'em for a real rough 'ouse. The wild geese, they calls 'em, but they're more like wild wolves in my opinion. The Micks loves scrappin' for its own sake. I'll tell you what I seed once in Kingstown Docks, in Dublin, First, let me fill your plate with soup, sir—very 'ealth-giving."

Phillip was very sleepy; and regarding him, the old soldier said, "My best respects, sir," then carefully inserting the bottle of White Horse between his loose gold teeth, drank; and after lip-smackings accompanied by a rattling of miniature rivets, went on with his story about Kingstown Docks.

"I were on sentry go, and I seed a bloke on a tug-boat pickin' up with a boat-'ook a familiar object all the world over, sir, what floated by out of the sewer. This one 'ad a baby's 'and on the end, and when 'e fished it out, it was 'alf filled with water, so for devilment 'e slung it at a bloke rowing acrost the 'arbour 'oo was a little tich. This object, sir, if you'll pardon the mentioning of it——"

"Go on, go on, I wasn't born yesterday——"

"Thank you, sir," promptly replied the servant, taking the opportunity to take another swig at the bottle. "Yum-yum!" Again the little percussive noises, then—"Well, sir, this object, without a word of a lie, catches the little tich full in the face, and seeing what it was, 'e let out a lot o' wicked words and made for the tug, rowin' like billio. I were on dock sentry, so I seed it all. The big bloke run off when the boat come alongside, pretendin' it were a joke, but the little tich went arter 'im, but couldn't catch 'im before the big bloke what chucked the letter 'ad shut 'isself in 'is 'ouse. The little tich come back blindin', and said 'e'd get the big bloke one day. 'Alf a mo', sir, I'll get the 'otpot. Nah don't go to sleep yet, sir, I ain't finished the story."

"Very amusing. I was wondering why the baby's hand, as a matter o' fact."

"The women likes it, sir, fascinates 'em, sir. 'Tes nature, in a manner o' speaking, though it's agin' nature, if you understand my meaning——"

"Quite! Quite! What happened—did the two meet again?"

"Eat your 'otpot, no heel-taps now! You bet your life they did, sir. In Rufferty's it was, sir, a booser. The tug-boat bloke 'ad been boasting what 'e'd do to the little tich when he see'd 'im; and one night he was leaning on the bar, talking big about 'ow 'e'd turn 'is empty glass down when 'e saw 'im—that's a free-for-all challenge, sir—when in comes the little bloke. 'Good evening, all', he says pleasant like to the customers. 'Nice night for a wet—even for those 'oo are wet enough by themselves already, the big streaks o' piss in a gaspipe an' all.' At this the big bloke turned down 'is glass, bottom up on the counter. The little tich ignores 'im. 'Pint a porter, please, miss,' he sings out, putting down 'is tuppence. 'Ee were just about to pick up the wallop, when the big bloke taps 'im on the shoulder, then reaches out and grabs the wallop and knocks it back. Then, all in silence, 'e puts the empty glass down.

"The little bloke still takes no notice, but says cheerful as anyfink, 'Pint o' porter please, miss,' and puts down two more coppers. Then he turns to the big bloke and says, 'If you drink that one I won't say what's coming to you,' but the big bloke reaches over again and grabs the glass, throws back 'is 'ead an' drinks the wallop, and is just on the point of turning the glass to the verticle from the 'orizontal, sir, when the little bloke swings an upper-cut what catches the bottom o' the glass acrost· 'is knuckles."

The storyteller paused dramatically; the dental orchestra played a few bars. "It took sixteen stitches to sew up the tug-man's big marf! The little tich," he concluded, "was the ex-lightweight champion o' the Royal Navy!"

"Wonderful yarn, wonderful. I could see it as you told it. Now I think I'll have a bit of old-man shut-eye. Oh, hell, I suppose I'll have to go back to the infantry now."

"You go sick, sir. You got the gas. Affects the 'eart, sir. They can't rumble it, sir. And if you chews some cordite, they can't find it aht, neither. This war's a bad 'un, sir, mark my words. I sin 'em all."

"What about you?"

"You put me on the strength, sir, and you can take me wi' you into 'orspital, and we'll get back to Blighty pronto. You can put me on the streng14h, sir, or tell 'em I come out wi' you, private like, your valet, sir. I'm a time-expired man."

"*You* are? Since when?"

"Any day I like, sir. You see, I ain't on no strength14h."

"I don't understand."

"I managed it, sir, like."

"But what about your pay?"

"I managed that, too, sir."

"But if you aren't on the strength of any unit, how did you manage to come out here?"

"Cookhouse wallah, sir. Nothin' in it, sir. You've got to 'ave the experience, of course."

"What experience, my boy?" Phillip felt O'Connor on his face, and his voice took on a slight Irish brogue.

"Dry firewood, sir. You appears with a noo lot puttin' up tents, an' goes to the cookhouse with a harmful o' good dry firewood, sir, an' start makin' a fire. Then you carries on. 'We're in, Meredith, we're in!' No-one knows 'oo is 'oo in a noo unit, sir."

"How did you manage about pay, if you weren't officially on the strength?"

"I turns up, sir, on pay-parade, an' tells the orfficer the truth, that I ain't bin given no pay-book, so 'e gives me one for interim, until the Pay Corps records come, which they don't 'cause there ain't none, an' the dossier gets bigger an' bigger, then we gits to France, an' there the matter rests, as the Marine says to the Admiral's quarter-deck when 'e were took short on sentry-go."

"So you're not really in the army, then?"

"Twinkle" drew himself up and glanced down at his ribbons. "What, me, sir, arter fifty year and more wi'out a single crime? Not *this* army, I grant you, sir, possibly. Anyhow," he concluded inconsequentially, "an army marches on its belly, as little ol' Boney said. They can't touch me, sir, I ain't signed no papers since 'ninety-nine, when I went back for the South African war. I don't want to stay 'ere no more, sir. I want to pack up them thicks, an' the ol' major an' mud-'ook, an' see me old mother again, sir. I'm fed up, sir, that's the truth, with everything aht 'ere."

"So you've got a crown and anchor board have you? You must be worth thousands of francs, 'Twinkle'. Good luck to you, you deserve it!"

"Look 'ere, sir, I wants to arst you a favour, sir. Will you put me on the strenghth, sir, an' write a letter, sir, to me old mother, an' let me put in some frog money? I can trust you, sir, can't I? I want to 'elp the old woman, she's on 'er last legs, sir. Ninety-two next birfday, an 'ad seventeen kids, only me left now, sir. She can change frog money in Lunnon, can't she, sir?"

"How much do you want to send, 'Twinkle'?"

"Tharsand-franc note, sir."

"I'll tell you what. The exchange is about twenty-five francs to the pound, so if you like I'll send the money to my bank, and ask them to send her the equivalent in forty pound notes."

"Blime, she'll get boozed up when she gets forty jimmy o' goblins by post, sir."

"Why not arrange for half quarterly payments? A bank would send them, if you deposited the money and gave instructions to that effect."

"I don't trust no banks, sir, not since that there penny bank went bust."

"Well, I have a bank account, and trust it, any old how."

"Ah, you're a gentleman, sir, and no bank wouldn't put it acrost you, that's why I ast your advice, sir."

Phillip thought of his father. "If you give me your mother's name and address, 'Twinkle'——"

A look of hardness and cunning flitted over the old man's face; then with his former manner he said, "Blime, the shock'd kill her! The most she ever 'ad was nine bob one week from the factory when we was all kids. Me dad was killed in the Crimea War when we was all very young, you see, sir."

The talk seemed aimless to Phillip, so he said, "Well, I'm going to sleep now."

He wondered where he had seen that hard cunning look before, as he went upstairs to his bare room. There, too tired to remove boots and tunic, he got into his sleeping-sack, to be lulled by the familiar double cracks of the sixty-pounders flashing away beyond the village. Soon he was asleep. He awoke once in the night, to see through the dirty little window panes what he thought of as the pale lilies of the dead—the flares rising along the distant Lens–La Bassée road from Hill 70 to Hulluch. Thank God that he could sleep, he said to himself as he pulled the camel-hair cloth closer round his neck.

He lay in in the morning, aching all over, ruminating, depressed by the feeling that life had come to ruin, that all human hopes were vain. He thought of the men who had slept in the room before him, who had left their records upon the walls. Where were they now? Scrawled on the plaster walls were dates, initials, badges, all in purple pencil digging into the whitewash. There were sketches and inscriptions, including a cartoon of Bernard Shaw and Dr. Lyttleton, both of whom he knew vaguely from casual glances at *The Daily Trident* to be anti-British, and therefore rotters. They were hanging side-by-side from a gallows, with the text underneath *Love your Enemies*. Near them was a warning, *Abandon hope, all ye who enter here*, an idiot's face grinning with the explanation, *After six months in the R.W.F.* There were verses.

> *Gentlemen the Guards*
> *When the Brickfields they took*
> *The Germans slung their hook*
> *And left the Gentlemen in charge.*

Another hand was more poetical.

> *A thousand suns I've seen above*
> *A thousand moons watched quiver*
> *But by sweet Thames my feet shall roam*
> *Ah nevermore, ah never!*

To which a critic had replied, *Take more water with it, matey!* There was a new inscription on one wall, he noticed. Was this an addition by "Twinkle"? The words read,

> *The wages of sin and a soldier is death.*

Chapter 27

CLIMAX

AFTER a good breakfast of fried bacon and eggs, he decided to take sandwiches and full water-bottle, and watch the new attack from high ground. The Guards were going over sometime that day. Part of the battlefield could be overlooked from Maroc, a mining village just inside the old front line, "Twinkle" told him.

Immediately in front of Maroc the right flank of the attack rested on two long, grass-grown spoil-heaps, the best part of a mile in length and forty feet high, extending into the German lines like two slugs side by side. This was the Double Crassier.

"Now don't be late tonight, and fret an old man's heart, will you, sir? And pardon the liberty, sir, but you won't forget to git me taken on the strenghth of your lot, will you, sir?"

This unexpected tenderness delighted Phillip for a moment; then he felt that "Twinkle" was playing, with his pink and tooth-less gums (the gold riveted teeth had vanished) the part of a harmless old granddad: and as he looked at him again he thought that he detected hard cunning under the grinning.

Maroc was no good, too near the front line. There was the hole-in-the-wall "Twinkle" had spoken of, at the end of the village, but streams of machine-gun bullets and balls of black smoke dotting the roof-lines showed that it was under observation. So he returned to the Harrow road, now white with chalky mud, and thought to cross below the crest of the spur on which the old front line continued north until it descended slowly into the fold of ground in which lay Le Rutoire farm.

He went on up the straight road, leaving it when whizz-bangs spirted a hundred yards in front, and threaded a way around shell-holes and over communication trenches, full of German dead, thinking that a solitary figure would not be fired at when there was so much fighting going on in front, on the rising ground beyond Loos and the tall Tower Bridge.

He peered into a steel telephone-box in the German trench that had a bomb-buckled door, and a sniper lying dead inside it—he must have been a sniper, because his rifle was fitted with a telescopic sight. Phillip thought to take it as a souvenir; but the butt, on which half-a-dozen notches had been cut neatly, was split, so he left it, and went on his way—whither?—striding fast, clasping his thumb-stick, walking from nowhere to nowhere, urgently, his face strained, his blue eyes with their characteristic speculative look intensified: a man beginning to think for him-self, maybe on the wrong lines—for what so far in his life, and the war that was an intensification of that life, could he have recognised as the right lines? Phillip was thinking of "Spectre" West: thought took the form of imitation. He could be as Westy!

Bullets whistling overhead and falling with tired little buzzes in the grass all around were spent bullets, coming from all directions. A passing despatch-rider told him that the Germans were back in the Hohenzollern Redoubt, their old front line a mile or two north of Lone Tree. No wonder, the reserves being so late! The blasted, inefficient staff!

The day was misty, with low clouds and scatters of rain. When he reached the outskirts of the village, walking round shell-holes half-filled with yellow lyddite water, his boots and puttees were clotted with grey-white mud. He plodded on past a ceme-tery with trenches around and through broken crosses and bits of artificial marble-chip flowers, and making for the church, found the empty square, or *place*. This looked to be sinister, open to a thousand unseen eyes, so he kept to the protecting houses, picking his way over splintered rafters and heaps of bricks below gaping roofs and standing walls. He went carefully, lying down when shells swooped to throw up red brick dust amidst dark fragments. He wanted to get to the Tower Bridge, which now seemed, with its criss-cross iron-work, and flat roof, as high as the water-towers that flanked the Crystal Palace seen from the entrance gates at the top of Sydenham Hill, when he had marched there six years before with a thousand other Boy Scouts, for the Grand Review. Even then, in the mock battle, Mr. Purley-Prout had tried to get round the flanks of the defenders, instead of being like the other scoutmasters, content to charge direct, and cross broomsticks with their rivals. God's teeth, he heard Westy's voice saying, the Germans knew how to protect their flanks. He could hear their stick-bombs going off, gruff noises like old men clearing their throats in the shelters on the Hill, as the Germans worked down the chalk trenches on Hill 70; while their machine-guns were chattering, rigid as German discipline.

He sat down, and let his thoughts rest, when he came to the troops in the cellars beyond the church. Smoke of wood fires arose, with a smell of frying bacon. So some rations had been got up. After ten minutes he went on, around fallen walls and window-frames towards the Tower Bridge. Where was the front line? he asked a soldier, obviously cavalry, in breeches, puttees reversed, and leather bandolier. He turned out to be the North Somerset Yeomanry, and told Phillip that the Germans were half a mile away, in trenches from Chalk Pit Copse to Hill 70, up behind the Tower Bridge.

"Plaize to kape your 'ade down, zurr, there be znipers auver thurr"—pointing to Cité St. Pierre—"over thurr"—the grey-green mass of the Double Crassier—"and in they brick 'ousen of yon mine-shaft. It ban't exactly a 'ealthy place, midear."

"Any up the Tower Bridge, do you know, by any chance?"

"Not now, zurr, but they cleared out one on'm yesterday, 'twas a telephone chap, so I did hear. 'Twas a Jerry all right."

"Can one get up the pylons?"

"Aye, aye! There be a round ladder, like up a church tower. But 'tis risky, zurr, what wi' they znipers about!"

That was enough for Phillip. He crept round shallow places in the rubble, bending low until his neck ached; he went on upright—until a bullet spat on a brick wall, and pinged away like a metal wasp. Cautiously he reached the base of one pylon, around which the usual rubble of brick and wood was piled, with a scattering of glass, amidst rifles, water-bottles, tins of beef, biscuits, and half-buried dead.

What was unusual was the sight of two light-draught horses, their harness hanging awry, waiting side by side near an up-turned G.S. wagon, the lower part of the driver's body lying beside it. Obviously the old cushy days of the transport were over, he was thinking, when with howls ending in clanging cracks four woolly bears broke to hang yellow above the Tower, and their splinters swooshed down upon tile and brick. The shells had obviously come east, from Lens.

He ran to cover, through a tangle of ironwork and brick which must have been the engine house; a huge fly-wheel lay in pieces near a riveted and rusty boiler full of holes and tears, and girders split and wrenched about; while above, seen through a tattered iron roof, the steel platform where the trucks had been loaded to be run off on rails along the crassier or dump were visible. He thought that the twelve-inch naval gun on the railway at Béthune must have hit it, to have caused such upheaval. And yet, despite the destruction below, the steelwork of the towers seemed to be untouched, except for gashes in the metal. They looked immensely strong.

Had the search party which had found the German telephoning

climbed up the framework? It looked impossible. His thought was broken by the fat buzz of howitzer shells, coming from the opposite direction, from the north, probably in Hulluch. So guns were placed for cross-fire, the same as machine-guns! He wondered if the staff knew this: it might be a discovery.

Yes, it was definitely a cross-fire! Four more yellow bears appeared in the sky, coming direct from behind Hill 70, from Lens. The gunners had shifted range and direction, to burst over the square. He stood up, and saw an open iron door half hidden by scrap metal in between the feet of the towers. Insinuating himself there, he saw an iron stairway leading upwards, spiral and very narrow, enclosed by sheet iron. It was like the iron staircase up to the mezzanine room between the Town Department at Head Office and the directors' floor. Up the old Bloodhounds!

It was with thoughts of past days with Cranmer as corporal of the patrol that Phillip started to climb the iron stairs. Round and round he went, his feet sometimes fumbling at a tread, not daring to look down, or to think of what would happen if a shell made a direct hit on it. Shrapnel had struck it many times; hundreds of jagged holes were in the boiler-plate walls. He paused for breath, to ease the ache in his legs, while the dim tube whispered hugely of the noises of battle, then *whang*! the blow went right through him, as a splinter of woolly bear opened an eyelid-shaped space six feet above his eyes.

After hesitation, he decided that the law of averages—no shell ever fell exactly in the same shell-hole as another—would protect him; so he climbed on, to rest again a dozen yards higher up, and to see large gaps in the boiler plate above him. Would that bare space be watched by a sniper? Why were there no British observers up the tower? Perhaps because they could see all they needed for the moment from their old O.P.s in Maroc, and the huge crassier near Vermelles, with telescopes?

He came to the top of the staircase, and found himself on an iron floor strewn with shell-splinters and broken glass. He was in a circular room, like a turret, with breast-high windows all round it. Cold wind moved past him from the empty spaces, with their serrated glass edges.

He began to tiptoe around the platform, under the steel roof. At the far end was a table, with one leg fractured, leaning sideways. Below it was a small pile of newspapers, apparently slidden off, with an empty wine bottle and a piece of dry black bread; and in one corner, a single grey Zeiss glass. He picked it up, screwed the adjustment, and saw that it was unbroken. What luck! He put it on the table, and took up a newspaper, making out the thickly carved German letters, *Berliner Tageblatt*. Then there was a little book of cartoons, with a picture of Big Bertha, a fat smiling woman bending down, face turned back to look at her posterior, which was a gun pooping off a shell with the motto *Gott Strafe England!* He examined other pictures of smiling, moustached soldiers, wearing the round nob of gunners on their *pickelhauben*, in scenes of snow. There was a Russian bear, with the Czar's face under its peaked cap, ambling big and stupid right into the muzzles of a German battery. On another page was a long lean lanky Highlander, with bony knees and a narrow face and brow with glengarry slipping off, and buck teeth holding a huge curved pipe, and a marmalade pot in one hand, running away from a laughing German soldier labelled *Michael* with rifle and bayonet.

Phillip sat down and studied the book, while he ate his lunch. He was keeping the best things of his adventure for after his meal—the view over the battlefield from the window. "Twinkle's" sandwiches had never tasted so good, with their French mustard. They were horse all right, browner and more tender than beef, with a wider grain that made the slices easier to bite with the bread, and softer to chew. Then, having folded his sandwich paper, and put it back in his haversack, he opened his map, and going to the window with the grey Zeiss monocular, looked out.

The morning mist had cleared up, and the country lay spread out below him, with its faintly blue pyramids, tall brick chimneys, —some of them white—and thickly congested pithead villages or *corons* of brick, lying as though pressed upon the wide spaces of rolled-out downland. The downland itself looked flattened, as though it had sunk down with all the stone and coal lifted out from under the coverlet of chalk. On the map-like scene little men in groups and files were moving, all one way, amidst the booming of cannon and the burst of shell. He focussed the glass on one group, but they were without interest: mere slow-moving figures. It was better to look with his eyes only, at black spouts of shell-bursts amidst the thin and wandering lines of white in the brown-green grassy flattened downland. He saw

the flashes of guns, tiny winks of light, and imagined the air
torn in strip upon strip above the tiny men moving so slowly,
so far away—always so slowly, so far away.

He went to the dangerous side of the tower, towards the
Germans, after covering his face with his khaki handkerchief,
to blend with the rusty iron. North lay the shallow valley
between Lone Tree ridge and the crest of the Lens–Béthune road,
with its lengths of coppice concealing the machine-guns which
had cut up the Cantuvellaunian attack of the day before; and
farther down the valley, into which the straight road dipped,
lay the brown cluster of Hulluch, and beyond it a stream in
a green valley, with trees in full foliage just beginning to turn
to the colours of autumn. Farther away and beyond, five miles
or so, lay La Bassée and the canal. West of La Bassée lay smaller
Auchy, and this side of it miners' cottages, *corons*, near the big
sullen Dump, and a tall chimney by the pit-head; and in front
of it, semi-circular in a dressing of sulky chalk, wreathed in the
smoke of many shells, lay the Hohenzollern Redoubt, which
had been taken and lost, and was now being attacked again,
judging by the white British shrapnel smoke over it.

He saw Vermelles, comparatively untouched by shell-fire; and
the big grey pyramid that was the crassier at Philosophe, tun-
nelled along its peak for shrapnel-proof observation posts. Back
behind the British lines lay the tall slag-heaps of Noeux-les-Mines,
the square tower of Béthune, and the dark mass of a wood.
How small and remote everything seemed!

He saw the trenches of the lost and dying soldiers' world like
lines of waves white-crested: low waves frozen white on the
green and dun underswell of a frozen sea—frozen with pain and
despair—waves of burst chalk-bags strewn with punctured men.
Through the glass he could make out the criss-cross of larch
poles, the knife-rest obstacles with their coils of wire; and the
dead men caught in the tangles.

Turning to the south, he saw the high, tree-billowing crest of
Nôtre Dame de Lorette, running into another wooded height,
which must be Vimy Ridge, which the French had failed to
take. The Germans were too strong. Their dugouts, forty
feet down in the chalk, made them safe from bombardment.
How could men so brave and clever be beaten? Would they
not hold out for ever, since they believed that God and Right
was with them in their struggle for their Fatherland?

A terrific clang shook the turret; an equal fear possessed him. Supposing the stairway was blown away, and he would not be able to get down? The air was acrid; a yellow bear had hit the steel frame somewhere. Well, if it happened, it happened. He peered out tremulously from his high place. Yellow bears were coming over almost as regularly as clockwork from Lens, and Black Johnsons from Hulluch, or from Auchy—two horns of a bull goring the attackers. He could just discern the flashes of guns.

The noise was greater now, the attack of the Foot Guards must be starting. He could see a row of dots, in perfect alignment, coming down from Lone Tree ridge into the shallow valley beyond the brown fracas of the village. Soon black spots of shrapnel found them; and woolly bears were breaking above them. Through the Zeiss glass he saw a tiny figure fall; then another threw up its arms, and fell, and another, and another, while the line went on steadily. The air was solid with metal hammering. Was Bertie down there?

He felt fascination and excitement. The Foot Guards! He recalled the charge through the Nonne Bosschen before Ypres in November 1914. Oh, why wasn't he with them, and Cranmer, and Tommy Atkins? But this wasn't like that faraway charge, this was like a field day before the general, all correct in line and spacing. He began to swear as more and more figures in those straight lines dropped out. If the Guards failed, all was lost. Ought he to get down the tower? Would the Prussian Guard division counter-attack down the slopes, if the Foot Guards' attack was broken by the terrible hammering?

Then he saw thick black smoke rolling along from the direction of Hulluch, two miles away in the shallow openness of the valley. The wind was very slight, it brought it billowing forward so very slowly. Would it get up the slight slope in time, to hide the advancing lines? Even if it did, the fixed machine-guns would sweep through it, as before. Oh hell, hell, hell!

Looking farther back, towards Vermelles, where the lower sky was grey with drifting smoke of another kind, obviously shrapnel, he saw that the supports were coming forward in diamond formation; and in between was a column of slowly moving transport. Black dots began to spatter the sky above it, as he watched.

Turning north again, he saw the black smoke screen moving towards the Lens–La Bassée road, but so slowly. Quick, quick, quick! Get to the coppice around the Chalk Pit this side of the road, and Bois Hugo the other side of the road! That was where the hammering came from! Then above the rolling smoke all the woolly bears began to gather, in sixes and sevens, while howitzer shells spouted up from the ground. Obviously the Germans were taking no chances, for there were no troops under the smoke screen. Go on, waste all your ammunition on the smoke! Poop it all off before the line of Guards came up the slope! He felt great excitement and anguish.

The shells were coming from behind the Hohenzollern Redoubt, three miles away, and the dark mass of the Dump, from Auchy; where the infantry was back again in the original British front line. He could see little nicks of flashes in the village, from the German batteries.

Trembling and taut, he turned away to the south again, and saw troops leaving the shelter of the houses immediately below, and making for the little plantation beside the road into Lens. From Hill 70 redoubt, less than a mile away east, came the hammering noise, while a few British shells burst upon the chalky flatness. As he moved his glass from figure to figure, taking the boiling feeling of each one upon himself, he gave a start: for in the retina of his right eye he saw a dark-blue movement, and with a rush of fear turned round prepared to see a German covering him with blued barrel of automatic.

To his relief he saw that it was a swallow, flying round and round inside the turret, crying with beak open above the tawny stain on its throat, crying inaudibly. Looking up, he saw a nest upon one of the roof girders, in a space where it was crossed by a lighter length of iron. There was the lip of grey mud, dry grasses showing, and shrunken marks of droppings on the floor.

He climbed on the table, and felt in the nest. It had young, a late brood, probably, he thought, coming from rich feeding on the flies which infested the battlefield. The swallows would be migrating soon; the little ones would be left behind. He thought of the tragedy of the parents, torn between love and the urge to migrate when the inner call came to leave. Would it be kinder to kill the nestlings, and so decide for the parents? Perhaps they might be able to feed their young in time for the flight down to the Mediterranean and across to Africa? After all, they had built there, and had been able to rear them so far during the war.

The hen bird slipped through the open window, and he saw her flying in the air, catching flies. He thought it wonderful, that in all the noise, she had carried on; but if a woolly bear were to burst near her——

The attack of the Guards had become a feeling of mourning. They moved so slowly, they were but figures walking on, with wider and wider gaps between each little fore-shortened figure. Only a ragged suggestion of a line reached the Chalk Pit and its trees; and when, after an interval, a few scattered figures appeared beyond the trees, in the terrible exposure of flat open country beside the narrow road, they withered away almost immediately: and looking through the glass, he saw that they were lying on the ground. About a dozen figures got up to run across the road, but they too, in ones and twos and threes, went down under the hammering.

He felt empty and weary. The afternoon light was going. He must try not to think as he went down the spiral stairs. He must go slowly, lest be become giddy. One last look at the nest on the rusty iron girder, *bon chance mes hirondelles!*; and slinging haversack and water-bottle, he left the turret.

It was dark when he got back to his billet, after passing troops winding up along the road, amidst the usual roll of wheels on mudded *pavé*, through all the desolation and the raging of guns. It was dark, the moon not up; but far away, around the Hohenzollern and beyond, the flares were rising, like curious lilies of the dead.

"Ou est M. 'Twinkle', madame?"

"Parti, m'sieu!" The tragic face of the woman, her children staring behind her thicknesses of black skirts, looked into his.

"Gone?"

"Oui, m'sieu! Les 'redcaps'."

"Comment, madame?"

"Pardon, m'sieu?"

"Pourquoi les 'redcaps' avent prendre prisonnier 'Twinkle', madame?"

"Mud Jeck, m'sieu!"

"Comment, madame?"

She spelt it out, he was the more puzzled: she wrote it down in pencil: *Mad Jack*.

Mad Jack! The name seemed familiar, but only when he learned that "Twinkle" was a deserter, and had been one since *'quatorze*, did he connect Mad Jack with the old deserter he had once seen at Villeneuve railway junction outside Paris, in September of the first year of the war. Mad Jack used to sleep behind hay-bales, he had a sack of bully beef as his capital, and swopped tins of it for red wine. When last seen, in those lines-of-communication days, Mad Jack had been humping his sack across the tracks, having seen redcaps on one of the platforms.

The news of his batman's arrest depressed Phillip, and he went to bed after an omelette and lay in his sleeping sack un-sleeping, a prey to thoughts that he too was a sort of deserter: the R.E. detachment had gone away, and to whom should he report? And how explain his absence? Even if the doctor had verbally put him on light duty, he had never reported anywhere for light duty.

Chapter 28

ANTI-CLIMAX

In the morning his fears seemed to come true. At first, when the military police appeared to search the premises for stolen army property, including blankets, the talk was of Mad Jack, who had been caught with nearly twenty thousand francs, which, said the redcap sergeant, came from flogging army property to civilians.

Apparently "Twinkle" had been given away by a woman in Noeux-les-Mines, after he had "taken on the mam'selle in the Demi Lune, sir, if you understand my meaning", said the sergeant. It seemed rather sordid to Phillip, and he wondered how much of "Twinkle's" tales were true. He mentioned that he was, anyway, a good batman; whereupon the sergeant asked him casually how he had come to get him for a batman, when he wasn't on the strength of any unit? Phillip explained about the gas detachment.

"Aren't they back at G.H.Q., sir?"

"I heard they were, I suppose my job is ended now they've gone."

"Yes, sir," said the sergeant non-committally. "I suppose you come up with the reserve divisions, sir?"

"Oh, no. I was First division."

"Oh yes sir."

A few minutes after they had gone, wheeling away over four hundred tins of bully beef, ham, tinned butter, with a dozen blankets and other articles on a barrow, there was a knock on the door. Madame opened it. An officer stood there, a captain with a red brassard on which were letters in black *A.P.M.* The sergeant stood behind him. Phillip felt as though shot.

The assistant provost marshal was curt. He wanted to know who he was. Why he was not with his unit? Why he had not reported back for light duty? How long he had known his so-called batman? The A.P.M. ended up by saying that he was under close arrest. His belt and revolver were taken away.

"Your kit will be packed up and be brought to you. You will come with me."

Round the corner was a motorcar. Through lines of curious troops Phillip was driven to corps headquarters, feeling what Father would call white about the gills as he thought of court-martial. He recalled what Cranmer had told him about men being shot for leaving their units only for an hour or two, and felt even whiter about the gills. "Pluggy" Marsden, Allport, the R.S.M., Mr. Adams, of the Gaultshire—probably dead. He would have no witnesses.

After interrogation at corps he was taken away in the motor-car; and to his immense relief he saw "Nosey", the brigade major, who vouched for him. He was set free, belt and pistol returned, and told he could join the Gaultshire mess. "Nosey" now wore a crown and star; Gaultshire badges replaced the red gorget-patches.

"Meanwhile, write out a report, will you, Maddison, about those batteries you saw in Auchy, and let me have it immediately."

"Very good, sir."

He wrote with the speed of jubilation, and took it to the orderly room.

In the mess, he learned that "Nosey's" nickname had been given at a pre-war inter-battalion heavyweight boxing contest.

He heard that the Gaultshire casualties had been very heavy, nearly seven hundred in the battalion. All attacking officers had either been killed, wounded, or taken prisoner. Both "Pluggy" Marsden and Allport had been wounded. It was the same with most other units. Three divisional generals out of the eight divisions engaged had been killed. Over forty battalions had lost their commanding officers. Beyond that, no-one in the mess spoke about the battalion attacks. They seemed very quiet. Among the rumours was one that the field-marshal had been recalled to London. The reason, it was said, was that the new-formed Guards division had been almost annihilated, owing to Sir John French having put them into a hopeless attack, when it was too late. An Irish Guards major came to visit "Nosey" Orlebar and Phillip learned that they were out at rest at Verquineul quite near. He wondered if he could go there, and find out if Bertie got through all right. Perhaps he could borrow a horse from the transport officer? He heard that "Spectre" West was down at Le Touquet, at the Duchess of Westminster's hospital; he had lost an eye and a hand, but had dictated a letter to one of the nurses: a brief letter, wishing the battalion good luck, and apologising to the commanding officer that he was "not able to return to duty at the moment". To Phillip it was rather a frightening letter. It was pinned on the ante-room board, showing a ducal coronet embossed in black.

On this ante-room board battalion orders were put up every evening. Phillip learned that he was posted to No. 1 company. With a shock he read that he was acting company commander. During a route march he felt pride and a new determination as he rode in front of his thirty-seven men, and wondered, in intervals of doubt about his ability to remain mounted, if he would be given his second pip. Or even a captaincy. But no, it must be only temporarily.

The battle was still going on, never pausing night or day. As soon as drafts arrived from England, it was understood that the brigade would be going back into the line. The odd thing was that when some officers did join, with a draft, he remained in command of No. 1 company. "Nosey" was always very friendly when he saw him. But he was friendly to all the new officers.

In battalion orders one evening was a paragraph that officers i/c companies were to read out on three successive parades the names and regiments of five deserters who had been condemned to death by sentence of general courts-martial, each sentence duly having been carried out.

"Hell to that," said Phillip to his acting company sergeant major, "I'm not going to put the fear of God into these new chaps by reading them this bumff."

He threw down the orders, thinking that Westy would approve.

In the same issue of orders all officers not on duty the next afternoon were informed that they were free to attend a lecture on *The Opening Phases of the Battle of Loos*. It was said at luncheon that it was to be given by a war correspondent of a London newspaper, in a marquee outside Béthune. Phillip went, with two other subalterns.

The lecturer stood on a daïs by a blackboard, with a pointer. He drew diagrams in chalk, and spoke in a soft voice, so that, with the canvas walls of the marquee flapping with gun-fire, no-one could hear him properly at the back. Soon voices were calling out, "Speak up". The lecturer cleared his throat, and spoke louder, but still his voice did not carry, so that after ten minutes or so even the young officers of the new drafts, spick and span and eager to learn everything in a quiet way, became restless. Phillip had a seat half way down, to one side, from where he could see backs of heads in rows of red-tabbed and senior officers in front. One head, constantly moving as though with impatience, was familiar—the white curly hair, the mulberry cheeks and scowling brow of—could it be?—yes, it was—"Crasher"! Phillip looked for the white head of "Strawballs", but could not see it.

The audience became more and more restless as the voice continued in its sympathetic monotone. At last the lecturer laid down his pointer, came forward to the centre of the daïs, and said:

"Gentlemen, I feel I must ask your indulgence for what must appear, to many of you who had to do the fighting, a most imperfect account of it. I do assure you all that I, as a mere distant spectator, feel most humble when I think of what you were called upon to do—and what you did was magnificent. Our great national poet Shakespeare said that all the world was a stage. This remark has never been more truly illustrated in all our island story than in the past two weeks. You, gentlemen, are the actors; we who stand and wait are but the audience, or to be more exact in the metaphor, not even the audience; for we can see little or nothing of what is happening, we are *behind* the scenes, or backstage to use the jargon of theatre-land. But while you are acting your valiant—I will not say tragic parts, for that would imply a condition that I am sure you would not yourselves ever consider, or wish to be admitted on your behalf—as I was saying, we who are in the rear do not share your particular experiences, varying with every trench and rise and fall of ground—but this I can say, that just as the landscape painter's perspective is always remote from actuality, so is the remoteness from the battlefield, for mere scribblers like myself in the rear, a clearing-place of often contrary messages and reports. Only gradually can the whole picture of what is happening be built up. Thus in one sector all may seem, for the time-being, to be lost; while that aspect, by its very pessimism, may enable troops a mile away to overcome the enemy position and so effect a break in his defences."

The lecturer paused. There was dead silence among the audience.

"Well, gentlemen, I have done my best to give an outline of the general position on the first, second and third days of the battle; I am always open to correction; and if any of you would like to ask any questions, or to amplify what I have said, in any particular, I shall do my humble best to reply."

The lecturer bowed, as though awaiting applause. Phillip felt a slight distress when none came. The silence remained. Perhaps people did not clap at military lectures, even when given by civilians? He felt a little sorry for the speaker; he was obviously nervous, and must have known that what he had said was only a sort of newspaper account.

"Well, gentlemen, have you any questions?"

There was a stir in the front row. Phillip saw "Crasher" slowly getting on his feet. Then he heard the curt, growling voice, "I want to ask only one question." "Crasher" paused, and glared at the lecturer.

"The other day I took part in the battle of Loos. Now, having listened to the lecturer, he has proved to me that I was never there. I would like to ask 'im to explain that."

The marquee was filled with cheering, clapping, and laughter. The meeting broke up. On impulse Phillip went to the brigadier, came to attention, bowed and said, "Excuse me, sir, but I am the guide who took you up past Lone Tree on the evening of the twenty-fifth. I have been wondering, sir, what happened to the colonel of the Cantuvellaunians?"

"Caught a ball," growled "Crasher". "Every other man jack of 'm caught a ball. As I told 'em at First Army, it was the charge of horse against the Russkies guns at Balaclava all over agen. They put me on ha' pay after that one for telling 'em what I thought, and b'God they put me on ha' pay after this one! No dam' progress in the human race! That feller Darwin was right. Who the devil are you? I've seen your face somewhere before, dammit."

"I am the guide who took you up past Lone Tree——"

"That don't account for your name, dammit."

"Maddison, sir. I met you in the Cantuvellaunian mess in England."

"Did you b'God. More people know Tom Fool than Tom Fool knows."

Misunderstanding this remark, Phillip said, "Yes, sir, I was a bit of a fool, I admit."

As the old general did not reply, but continued to fix him with his pale blue eyes, Phillip went on, feeling more and more awkward, "I mean, sir, in setting fire to the colonel's newspaper."

"Why, bless my soul, you must be the young feller o' spirit they bully-ragged for speaking out o' turn, but b'God, if no-one spoke out o' turn——! I have, b'God, and blotted me copybook! Yes, 'Strawballs' told me about you the other night in that damned cold quarry, said it was a pity you have never been to school. Well, don't let it worry you, I never learned a dam' thing at Eton, except how to hunt the hare with those dam' jelly-dorgs they call beagles."

The anciently-dressed brigadier lifted his hand in dismissal, and Phillip went away, thinking what a wonderful old boy he was.

The next afternoon he started to ride with a groom to visit cousin Bertie at Verquineul, about three miles distant, behind Noeux-les-Mines; but the chronic congestion of the roads, and the fact that he was still not able to "sit down to it", in the groom's phrase, made him turn back. It was now into the first week of October, and the battalion was nearly up to strength. The further attacks had got nowhere, all the attackers who survived had gone back to their jumping-off trenches. Training with smoke-helmets pointed to a new attack with the French, who had now come into the sector north of Loos. And the following afternoon, when he walked to Verquineul, hoping to see Bertie (and yet hoping not to meet him, now that his face had partly eclipsed that of Helena) he learned that he had missed him by one day. Bertie's battalion was in the line up by the Hohenzollern, which, except for the forward trench, was once more in German hands.

A day later, in Béthune, whither he had gone to draw the battalion pay in francs, he saw the Coldstream G.S. wagons being loaded with gas-cylinders, and heard that another assault upon the Hohenzollern Redoubt was being prepared. It was part of the renewed attack all along the line.

He took the company the following day to the bombing range beyond the town, a hot and suffocating business with gas-helmets; and on return, when he went into the ante-room, to see what post had come in he saw a khaki envelope in the M pigeon-hole of the letter rack—*2/lt. P. S. T. Maddison to report immediately to the orderly room*. With trepidation he went there, to hear the worst.

The adjutant and the colonel were working late, before dinner. Cold water in stomach, with drying throat, Phillip stood to attention.

"Good evening," said the adjutant, amiably. "Your exchange into the Diehards has come through. There's a train leaving Béthune at nine ack emma tomorrow morning." He pushed over a yellow ticket for Victoria. "Your dossier has been following you about, from here to Helfaut, and back again. The colonel wants to see you."

Lieutenant-colonel Orlebar was genial as ever.

"So you're leaving us, Maddison. ' Spectre ' West will be sorry to hear it. You belong to the county, don't you?"

Phillip tried to smother his betraying hesitancy—yet he did have cousins at Beau Brickhill—Wakenham, black on the map of the County of London—Baldersby—"little Cockney"——

"Yes, sir!" he replied, eyes on ground.

Worse was to follow, for offering him the tin of hand-made *Goldflakes*, the colonel asked where he had been at school. Dreading a repetition of the pause, the non-committal "O-oh", when the same question had been asked in the orderly room of the Cantuvellaunians, and in panic lest his lie be detected, he pretended not to have heard the question and replied, eyes on floor, "I was at Fitzwilliam Hall, Cambridge, sir."

The colonel made a few pleasant remarks, then shook hands, and wished him luck in his new regiment. The colonel was sorry to see him go; there had been a chit from division about the excellence of the report sent in by a junior subaltern of the Gaultshires who had remained up with the attack on Lone Tree, taken command in an emergency and led a flank attack which was successful, and then, on light duty, had nevertheless remained up with the attack and sent in valuable information about the position of enemy batteries. Colonel Orlebar had only that afternoon decided to confirm Maddison in the command of No. 1 company, with the rank of temporary captain.

Early the next morning, the 13th October, the guns were booming upon the dull eastern horizon as Phillip set out for rail-head. The new attack had begun, from Hohenzollern Redoubt on the north, to Bois Hugo in the south, towards the higher ground held by the Germans along the La Bassée–Lens road. The deadly horizon was white with the drifting smoke of the bombardment, brittle with remote crackling and hammering. Waiting on the platform of Béthune station, Phillip saw transport men with brass letters C.G. on their shoulder-straps; and going up to the officer wearing the Star of the Garter badge on his cap, to ask what news of the attack, he learned that "Marie" Cakebread had been killed the night before, while on patrol by Big Willie trench, looking at the Hun wire. His body had been brought back for burial at Vermelles.

After the comic little toot upon the horn, the steam-dribbling black Nord engine drew away from the country of pyramids and broken *corons* while he could scarcely realise that he was leaving it all behind, for ever; and yet in a way he was sorry he would not see the Gaultshires again. What nice people they were, from Colonel Mowbray and "Nosey" down to the new second-loots from Sandhurst. There had been a genuinely free and easy feeling in the mess, and a foremost regard for the men, under the unspoken disciple of good form set by the colonel, by his very friendliness. Perhaps that was what Baldersby had been driving at; but somehow it had not been the same thing as in the Gaultshire mess. Every officer in the Gaultshires seemed to belong to the county, nearly all the officers knew about each other, or their families had known each other, and the senior officers at the top table were like elder brothers. "The Duke" was often spoken about, and always with respect, so different from Uncle Jim's angry Radical attitude against him for being a large landowner.

Oh, damn, damn, damn! Why was he leaving? Anyway, he had spoiled himself by pretending that he had been up at Cambridge. Still, he had left them for good, he would never see them again. The thought of another winter in the trenches was unthinkable, and he had to tell himself again and again of his wonderful luck. The papers said it would be a long war, as Kitchener had forecast; probably two more years before the Germans cracked. Two years like the past seventeen days! Ah, but he would be a non-combatant, in charge of those white-headed old navvies, digging trenches far back, building rest camps, laying railways——

He settled in his corner, looking out at the green country of poplars, willows, and dykes along the way to Calais, and thought of his arrival that night, unless there were submarines in the Channel, in Hillside Road. He fixed in his mind the surprised faces when he walked down into the sitting-room. He thought of warmth and light in Freddie's. He thought of Bertie, always so easy and smiling; he could not imagine Bertie dead. Nor could he imagine Helena Rolls' face when she heard the news; he could not think of her, something put her out of his mind, he could not see her face, but only a blank.

It was about that time that Helena Rolls was told of Hubert Cakebread's death by her mother.

Chapter 29

LONDON, S.E.

THERE were no submarines in the Channel, but there were waves. He spent the crossing hidden in the shame of sickness, lying upon the floor of one of the lavatories, only half-conscious that his life was torn away to the last froth. Wan-faced he walked off the ship at Dover, and settled to shivering sleep in the train.

At Ashford he had a small pot of tea, and a brandy to settle his stomach, as it had in childhood's train-sickness; and after being sick again, he lay in the locked lavatory until just before Victoria. He was surprised to see "Crasher" and "Little Willie" getting into a taxicab, followed in another by their two servants loaded up with about a dozen *pickelhauben*, several sandbags of nosecaps and saw-bayonets, and other souvenirs. He wanted to speak to them, but did not like to risk the "Tom Fool" remark again. So he watched them depart, as old friends; and feeling that all was strange and empty, went into the buffet where beef-tea gave him back the warm idea that all life was adventure.

He went by Underground to Charing Cross, wondering at the quietness of everything. Sight of the river from the Embankment cheered him. He was back again! All the same——

He walked up Villiers Street to the Strand, and found himself in a scene so poignantly different from what was really happening that he felt like screaming. How could women sell white and yellow chrysanthemums out of large wicker baskets, and talk cheerfully to an officer buying some for the girl with him when a paper-boy was running past with a bundle under his arm and crying out, "New attack on Western Front! Loos battle flares up!" He bought a *Star* and read the *communiqué* from G.H.Q. ending with the well-worn phrase: *The morale of our troops is excellent*, which belonged to the scene all around him, of the world beyond the pallor of the flares which he had forsaken. But it would have been too lonely without Westy, without "Twinkle", without Kirk, and all the others.

He crossed over to Trafalgar Square, drawn by longing to see again the faces of the Australians who had been in Gallipoli. Something was happening around the pedestal of Nelson's column where a large crowd was pressing forward. On the plinth above he saw that a woman was trying to speak. Other women were standing beside her, and a small girl and two old men. They were holding banners. The crowd, among them Australian soldiers, was heckling the speaker. A man stood at one corner of the plinth, with a camera. Below one of the lions a number of men were yelling in unison, to drown the speaker, who, he saw, was Sylvia. So it was a Suffragette show. He did not want to be seen by her, so kept on the outskirts of the crowd, coming to where some more men were putting red and yellow powdery stuff into paper bags. One looked at Phillip and said, with a grin:

"This'll dust the old cow all right!"

"What are they?" he asked, pretending ignorance.

"Who, them?" sneered the man, jerking his thumb upwards. "Why, it's all paid for by the Germans! Tryin' to stop the war! Stabbin' our boys aht there in the back, that's what it is!"

"Who are you? Where did you get that powder?"

His questions remained unanswered, as the group moved off to bombard the speaker. Bags were thrown. He saw the little girl on the plinth crying, her dress spoiled by red powder. Another bag hit her in the face.

"Stop it, you cads!" he shouted, "or I'll have you all arrested!" They flung what was in their hands, then made off. Moving nearer, he saw the face of his Aunt Theodora in the crowd. She was watching with a strained expression, her mouth slightly open, showing her projecting teeth. How old and worn she looked. She smiled when she saw him, and did not look so old.

"Where did you spring from, Boy? I thought from what your mother wrote to me, that you were in France, doing something rather secret."

"We were told not to write home any mention of the gas."

"Tell me, Boy, are you well?"

"Yes, thank you. But did you know that Bertie has been killed?"

"Bertie Cakebread? Oh dear——" Her eyes became remote. She was thinking of Sidney, his father, dead in the Boer War: Sidney, the only man she had ever loved, or would ever love. And now his son had followed him——

Phillip thought that Aunt Dora looked very thin and cold, with a faintly red tip to her nose.

"So little Bertie has been killed——"

"Apparently he was nicknamed 'Marie'. I wonder if it was after the Marie biscuit, a play on his surname, Aunt Dora."

He told her about meeting Bertie at Lone Tree; and what he had heard of the night patrol at the Hohenzollern Redoubt.

"What are you doing here, Aunt Dora? This 'Stop the War' movement hasn't a hope, you know. The soldiers are the only ones who could stop it, I think. But both sides think the same things, you know. Willie believes that is why it could be stopped, if only each side could realise what the other side thinks; but

I've been thinking, you know, and see that while both sides think as they do, it is bound to go on. It's a bit confused, I'm afraid, but—well, anyway, it is a deadlock, in my opinion. How is Willie? Still in Gallipoli?"

Aunt Dora said he was, when last she had heard of him; and she went on to say that she had left the Movement, as she could not agree to Sylvia's further opposition to the war. "It is a war of systems, Boy, our democratic way of life against an autocratic and military tyranny. But Sylvia and I remain good friends. It is the babies who matter!" she smiled, a light coming into her fragile face. "The Mothers' Arms!"

This reminded him of "Twinkle". "I don't know what her name is, the old chap kept it dark, but he said his mother was the oldest member of the Movement."

"How very strange that you should mention such a thing, Boy! For I have been to the War Office about such a matter this very afternoon! If it is the same person, then it must be a most extraordinary coincidence. But read for yourself."

He took the thin, cheap, clay-coloured sheet of paper from the O.H.M.S. envelope.

> Infantry Office
> Hounslow.
> 10.10.15
>
> Madam,
>
> I am directed to inform you that a report has been received from the War Office to the effect that No. 431 Pte. Nobbs J.S. 1st Battn. Essex Regt. was sentenced after trial by court martial to suffer death by being shot for desertion, and the sentence was duly executed on 8 October 1915.
>
> I am, Madam, Your obedient Servant,
>
> > P. G. Hendley,
> > 2nd-lt., for Lt.-Colonel Infantry Records.

"Grannie Nobbs is over ninety, Boy, so it seems most likely that she is this poor fellow's mother. She refuses to believe it, saying that he has already been reported killed in two previous wars, and that he will turn up again after it is all over. She is the very spirit of our people—undefeatable."

"I am afraid he won't come back from this one, Aunt Dora," said Phillip, feeling weak. Good lord, it must have been about "Twinkle" that the story was told in the Gaultshire mess, of how

one deserter had insulted the firing party, drawn from the
Guards, who had shot him.

He said goodbye, and made his way to the station, where he
took a first-class ticket to St. John's, thinking to walk over the
Hill. Blinds must be drawn; Zeppelins had been reported over
the Thames estuary. The dear old South Eastern and Chatham
Railway!

Seeing Tom Ching on the platform, he made for the nearest
carriage, a third-class with pale gas flame wobbling familiarly
within dirty enamel and glass dome in roof, mantle broken,
war-time gas turned low. Buck-navvy-smelling carriage, thick
boots, stale beer, shag, and coal. Hoarse voice of unseen porter
on platform of London Bridge station, calling familiar names of
stations . . . *Greenwich, Woolwich, Gravesend, Erith* . . . foggy
riverside names, muddy-water-ebbing-tide names, shivery melancholy names, hurrying working-class pale-faces names, truck-
shunting-in-darkness names, ammunition loading at the Arsenal
. . . and, from another platform, there was the mysterious *Paddock
Wood*, green leaves and woodpeckers, far beyond the black
county of London, with its shunting of trains, hiss of steam, bang-
ing doors, and *Hurry along, please*.

The door was opening, railway gangers with copper-peaked
caps getting in, empty tea-canteens in hand, too tired to speak
after a few words to one another, no glances at himself, lying
back close-lidded. Smells of glue, vinegar, hops . . . rattling
over points at New Cross. Plate-layers getting out, door slammed,
alone. Quietness, sadness: what sorrows and despairs had the
carriage known, weeping women, broken-hearted children, poor
old men . . . He got out at St. Johns, and felt lost in an un-
bearable silence of nothingness.

Walking over the cold and windy Hill he saw searchlights
leaning upon the clouds. The beams moved about; died out;
others sprang up and wavered hesitating; moved together to a
common apex, seemed to fumble; moved away again. Then
one swept half round the sky and came to rest pointing upwards;
and the others rushed to join it, and the dark greyness of the
Hill became lilac, as though slightly powdered, when a new
strong beam stared upwards from the roof of the old West Kent
Grammar School, now the L.C.C. Modern School. He heard
throbbing: a lorry in the sheep-fold showed dark, mounted with

running engine. Voices, a shout; the violet beam died reddish then black-staring in his eyes.

London lay in darkness once more. His footsteps crunched on the gravel, the wind rustled all the grey birch leaves at the corner of the gully. His feet resounded on the circular iron grating of the drain by the spiked iron gates; he saw a thin yellow line under the blinds of the Rolls' house. He hesitated; drew back; waited unseen by the railings. Then, assembling himself, he went in past the gate, hollow and thudding. It was too late to turn back now; he had rung the bell.

It was Wednesday, and Mr. Rolls would be away from home, he was always away from Monday to Friday. He waited. It was worse almost than going over the top, all the early fears possessed him. Then a deep baying came from beyond the door. It was too late to clear off now. Mrs. Rolls was opening the door.

"I am very sorry if it is inconvenient——"

"Phillip, dear boy! Do come in, you look so cold—I thought at first it was a ghost. Come by the fire—so good of you to come. Don't be alarmed by Rastus—down, sir, down! Noisy creature, Rastus! Sit down, Phillip. Helena is upstairs, lying down, she has a headache, poor child. Yes, we have heard the news about Hubert. Then a letter came from him, by the six o'clock post this evening. So sad, isn't it? You are shivering! Sit down on that chair, draw it up to the fire—turn Rastus out."

The dog, a gaunt animal with drooping ears, loose skin, skull-like brow and sunken eyes, had climbed into the armchair, the only one in the room, and lay there, head on paws, looking despondently at his mistress, but not moving. "Get down, Rastus! Get down this instant, sir!" Rastus, looking broken, crept off the chair with a groan of displeasure. Then, turning round, it nipped a square of carpet with its teeth, and carried it to beside the copper coal-scuttle, where it lay across it.

"Good boy, Rastus!" cried Mrs. Rolls. "Rastus is one of Colonel Anthony Rolls' bloodhounds, Phillip. Anthony sent Rastus to guard us, while Gerard is away. He is Gerard's cousin, you know."

"Oh, I see," as he perched on the edge of the chair. Could his patrol really have resembled Rastus? He had to suppress an idiotic desire to laugh at the idea of Rastus being Mr. Rolls' cousin.

"Have you just come back, Phillip?"

"Yes, Mrs. Rolls."

"All you poor boys——" she said, in a voice caressing and tender, while she sat on the other side of the fender, on a straight-backed chair, her khaki knitting on her lap.

He thought that her name, Flora, meant flower; she was a violet, the colour of her eyes. Her voice was rather like Aunt Beatrice's voice—he winced away from the thought of the too-soft skin of Aunt Bee's cheek, like a silken bag holding in the flesh of her face—but Aunt Beatrice's voice had a sort of metallic hardness behind it, when she laughed or spoke suddenly. Mrs. Rolls' voice was deep unexpectedly, with a sweet lovingness in it. It was strange that she was Helena's mother; in a way, she seemed younger, like a bunch of violets to a sunflower.

"You are shivering so, Phillip—break up that lump with the poker——"

Could it really be true that he was sitting in the red plush armchair glimpsed in rare moments through the window as he had hurried past outside? He was taut, unable to stop his shivering, unable to sit back, afraid to speak lest he stammer. He sipped coffee that was too hot, and burned his lips.

"Do smoke, Phillip—I think a fireside without a man with a pipe is not really home, don't you?"

"I-I-I've given up smoking, Mrs. Rolls, thanks all the same." Why had he said that, when he had pipe and pouch showing in his pocket. He must give up smoking now.

"Why is that?"

"The gas makes the taste rather awful." True then; but not afterwards. Hopeless.

"Oh, that awful gas! They used it, didn't they, in the battle. Thank goodness, I said to Gerard, when he read it aloud from *The Times*—thank goodness that we have not used the gas those fiends used, but a stupefying gas that lasts only for an hour or two. Rather like dentist's gas, I suppose, only not the laughing kind, Phillip?"

Jonah the Whale's voice saying, *Speech is given us to conceal our thoughts*. "I think that dentist's gas is nitrogen dioxide, Mrs. Rolls. Or was it—n-no, I think that was the brown, choking gas we made in the laboratory at school. I rather think that it is nitrous oxide and not nitrous di-oxide."

"What a lot you know, Phillip. Now do tell me, what has brought you home so soon?"

"I have transferred to the Middlesex Regiment, Mrs. Rolls."

She stared at nothing, her thoughts elsewhere, her hands paused in their knitting. Then in lowered voice, "Tell me about Hubert, Phillip. We were *all* so fond of him. Such a pity that all the fine ones are going, isn't it? I remember his father—*such* a gentleman. He wrote to Helena, you know—they were *such* chums. Poor girl, she is *most* upset. Yes, your cousin spoke of you in the letter we got today. You were wandering about, looking quite lost on the battlefield, he wrote."

Phillip told of the meeting, leaving out the whipping incident, and indeed, all that had really happened. He did not omit the truth deliberately, for he had not formulated any aspect of truth in his mind as yet; and the details of his own living had always, from those early years when punishment had entered and dominated his life, been something to conceal. He spoke in the idiom in which his letters home had been written.

"It was a bit trying for the reserves, without food and water. It's all rather strange at first, you know, and when someone thought the order to retire had been given, everyone began to go back. I was with some wounded fellows, going to the aid-post at Le Rutoire, when I met Bertie and some others of the Guards Division coming up, an advance party. It was all a bit of a muddle, one way and another, I suppose."

"I know, it must have been terrible for you poor boys," the voice almost crooned. "Then you don't know where he—where it happened, Phillip?"

He told her what he had heard that morning, adding, "Death was instantaneous. He is buried at Vermelles, Mrs. Rolls."

Violet eyes stared into the fire, the khaki sock drooped on her lap.

"I was making this pair for him, Phillip. You must have them now, dear boy."

The moment was dream-like, the coal-flames fluttering in the grate drying his eye-balls, while in drowsy warmth he rested, feeling that it was all happening to someone other than himself —as indeed it was, for the Phillip sitting there was not so much person, as *persona*: he was acting a part, unconsciously, all the time, while the real Phillip was hiding behind the past.

The moment was dream-like, beyond gratitude, beyond words, as in a dream when words are neither spoken nor heard by the remote point of life which is innocence, and the soul.

The real Phillip looked at Flora Rolls for a brief instant: a glance that seemed to her to be of dismay, of surprise, of fear; perhaps he had not heard her, she thought, he is so very very tired, he has been so near to death, the quietness of this room must be strange to him, after what he had gone through. Her thoughts were in the space of a glance, then she saw his head turn again, and yes, there was fear indeed in his eyes, as he turned his head to the door, and saw Helena coming into the room.

Flora Rolls went on knitting, composed within herself, at ease within her world, which was a world of love, of a loving father and mother, of a loved and loving husband: so she had always lived in a world ordered by a loving God; she knew no other world. There were evil things in the world, but they were not of God, they were of the devil—and evil things in the German nation had made the war. It was all foretold in the Bible. But the evil things were not oppressive upon her, for she was a loved woman.

She went on with her knitting, while her daughter walked across the room; and as Phillip got up from the chair, she said, without lifting her head, "How kind of Phillip to come, isn't it, Helena, when he has only just arrived from France."

"I came to tell you——"

He could not speak further. His throat had closed. She stood before him. He saw that her face was different. Always it had shone; smiled when he had met her. (It was this which had given him hope for his dream. Phillip had never thought, and did not now, that what was lacking in his own home he had sought in her face—the peace, the harmony, of beauty, which comes from the shining face of heaven.)

"Oh, he is so tired, poor boy," said Flora Rolls. "Let him sit down, Helena. Rastus! Where are your manners, sir?"— for the bloodhound, seeing the empty chair, had picked up its square of carpet and was advancing to lay it upon the comfortable and draught-free seat that it shared with its master. But Rastus had been born and bred in a military kennels;

without asking why, he turned round again, spread his bed diminutive, and curled again by the copper coal-scuttle.

Laughter at the sight brought ease. Helena laughed; but he saw her tears, so looked upon the carpet, while he spoke of the lighter things he had seen, in the spirit of the Bairnsfather cartoons in *Tatler* and *Bystander*. He made semi-nervous little jokes, which seemed to be appreciated, thus, "There is no glass in the windows of the *corons*; it has all been called up." "Twinkle" was a joke—"of course he managed to escape from the police; trust 'Twinkle'."

"Thank goodness there is a lighter side to this terrible war," said Mrs. Rolls. "Now, Helena, you must have a good hot bath and go to bed, then I will bring you up some hot milk. You must give your best to the hospital ward tomorrow. Phillip, too, is in need of a sound night's sleep."

He got up, accepting the hint; and so did the bloodhound, who was back in the chair almost before he had said goodbye.

"See Phillip to the door, Helena."

He carried away the vision of a white throat and a black gown, the Star of the Garter badge pinned above her heart, of frank eyes withdrawn in shadow behind the long lashes, of a tall brow with its wave of hair sweeping beautifully back, of curve of cheek and chin so sweet, of head held up in pride.

"Goodbye, Helena."

"Goodbye, Phillip."

Searchlights were puzzling star-spaces in the clouds, grass and pavement and roofs lay dim under the shining swords of light. He felt strangely exhilarated, almost heroic; he wanted to go back to the line, to meet his fate as bravely as Bertie had met his. Words sang through him, flowing from Helena, as he walked down the pavement. She is Night, her neck and brow are as the lilies rising, so gently o'er the disentangled dead. He hesitated to go into his own home. At length he rang the bell.

"It's Phillip, Mother, it's Phillip!"

"Oh, not so much noise, for God's sake!"

He stood there.

"What's the matter? Don't you want to come in?"

"In a moment."

"I say, I can't keep the door open, you know! There are Zeppelins about! I suppose you've heard about Bertie?"

"Yes."

"Isn't it awful? I say, what's the matter? Have you been drinking?" Mavis giggled from nervousness.

The giggle hardened him. He turned and walked away.

"Phillip! Phillip!" His mother hurried out under the porch. "Why, dear, this is a surprise," she said, with forced gaiety. "Is everything all right?"

"Quite." With an effort he said, "I thought I heard a Zeppelin engine, that faraway churning growl."

"Don't, whatever you do, tell Mavis, Phillip!" she said in a low voice. "She is terrified. Father has just been called out——"

"Mother, Mother, come in——!"

"Poof, what's a Zeppelin!"

"Do come in, dear, just to please me," pleaded Hetty. "Polly is staying with us."

"I don't care."

"You needn't see her now, dear, she and Doris are upstairs, having their baths together."

He nearly said that that was how he would like to see Polly, but suppressing the thought, he washed in the scullery, before going upstairs to change into mufti; and after boiled eggs, tea, and toast, said he must go out.

"Must you, so soon, dear? Anyway, take the key, and please don't be late——"

He called to see Mrs. Neville; then on down to the High Street, his mental gaze fixed steadily upon the face of Helena, looking down steadily on all grief. Oh, if he could give his own life to bring back Bertie to her. But the thought was not genuine, he knew. Thank God he was out of it! He fitted the monocle into his right eye, for the entry into Freddy's.

Chapter 30

ZEPPELIN

FREDDY's bar was almost empty. Only two strange men were there, and one gas-mantle alight. Acute disappointment: emptiness: he had been imagining, to replace Desmond on duty with searchlights, the faces of their last visit together—Cundall, Eugene, Mrs. Freddy, "Sailor" Jenkins, even Tom Ching. The two strange men looked at him. Both wore bowler hats, dark suits, big boots, and rolled umbrellas hung on their left elbows. One was tall with a wispy black moustache; his older companion had a full meaty face and ginger hair, and being clean-shaven his projecting rabbit's-teeth were the more noticeable.

The door leading into the unlighted billiard-room, set with pieces of coloured glass in leaden panes, opened to reveal Freddy wearing straw-hat, celluloid collar and bow-tie, striped shirt, elastic arm-bands, brown trousers and yellow shoes. At once the straw was tipped.

"Good evening, sir." He lifted the mahogany slab across the bar, and said to the two men, "All ready for you, gentlemen." He pushed on the stained-glass partition level with his head, and a little oblong peep-hole opened aslant. He bent over and whispered: "You'll take the usual? On the house, of course?"

The two bowler-hatted men went into the dark billiard-room. "I won't keep you a moment, sir," said Freddy to Phillip, as he poured out quarterns of Irish whiskey into two squat glasses, added hot water, sugar and lemon, put in glass rods; and opening the door behind the bar, took them to the strangers.

"What's yours, sir?"

Phillip decided to drink milk stout, to build up his strength. "Very quiet tonight, Freddy."

"I only hope it stays quiet," smiled Freddy. He kept his face still, but moved his eyes sideways towards the billiard-room. Then he said conversationally, "Your friend's on searchlight duty tonight, I suppose? A fireman from the station was in earlier, and said the warning was out."

"A lot of fuss over nothing, Freddy."

"I don't know. Those aerial torpedoes they carry can do a lot o' damage, I hear. I expect your father's on duty tonight?"

"Yes. What are you drinking?"

"Thank you, sir. I'll have a gin."

Freddy poured the usual fourpenny tot of water for himself, proposed and drank Phillip's health, and taking out his pocket-book, leaned over the bar and showed a snapshot of his wife and baby. Then coming close, "Two flatfoots from the station, they're hopin' for a pinch, nice little camera, isn't it, only a No. 1 Brownie."

"Jolly good!" said Phillip loudly; then, "Who are they after?"

"That sprucer Wilkins, who dresses up as a major on the staff —the Galloping Major people call him, since he ordered that parade review of the territorials. He's bin in here lately. Don't let on to those coppers I told you."

"I've never seen him."

"Very nice-spoken fellow. He told me his father was a parson in the country, but I have heard he comes from Leytonstone, the other side of the river. He usually comes in 'ere from the Roebuck, he's very hot at billiards. Your friend Desmond knows him, and that Brazilian fellow often with 'im. Took five bob off them last time!" Freddy tittered.

"What do they want to arrest him for? He has paid for his uniform, and helped recruiting, which is more than those plain-clothes flatfoots have done. They ought to be in uniform themselves."

Freddy winked slightly, then raising his voice, said: "Yes, she's a very nice young lady, sir, and I'll introduce you two to each other with pleasure."

Phillip began to feel a return of the black depression, sitting by himself on the horse-hair settee, while behind the stained-glass partition waited two pairs of cold, man-catching eyes. He thought of "Twinkle", and wondered again if the story of the defiance of a deserter shot outside Béthune belonged to him.

The shooting had taken place behind a high brick wall of the garden of the château used for corps headquarters. The deserter, an old sweat, had been tied to a post, his eyes bandaged, a piece of white paper pinned over the heart. The firing squad's rifles were loaded by the provost sergeant, some with blank, others with ball, so that no man would know who shot him. Before his eyes were bandaged, according to the story, the deserter had made a speech to the twelve marksmen, all from the Brigade of Guards, lined up before him. Sitting on the horse-hair settee, Phillip could imagine the rivets in his gold teeth working like miniature rifle-bolts as he spat out his insult. "I 'ave sojer'd all round the globe, I 'ave fought niggers, chinees, wogs, an' fuzziwuzzies, but I never thought till now that me, a reel sojer, would ever find 'isself anywhere near to such a row of tailor's dummies, what is all you little lot ever was, s'elp me Gawd." That insult delivered—so ran the story—the old sweat stood to attention. He made his last remark to the two chap-

lains standing near, prayer-books in hands. An extra chaplain,
a non-conformist with one of the two new K 3 divisions from
the north, had come along in case the prisoner was a Methodist.
The prisoner had refused to discuss his religion with either padre,
until he said, while being tied to the post, "No talkee talkee
about what religion a stiff belongs to, thank you, gentlemen."
By God, Mad Jack or Twinkle, the old boy had guts!

Sitting there, with his fourth milk stout, Phillip wondered what
had happened to the old chap's French money. No doubt it
had gone into the red-caps' pockets—or more likely into that of
the sergeant who had brought the A.P.M. to him. From
"Twinkle's" face he thought to "Spectre" West's—and of how
Westy had asked him to see his mother at The Grapes, near
Leadenhall Market. Could Westy's mother possibly keep a
public house? But he had been to Oxford University! All the
same, sometimes Westy's voice had had a different intonation.
And he had a pre-war commission in the third, the special reserve,
battalion. Of course, Westy must have come from the University
O.T.C.!

Then there was "Twinkle" and *his* mother. It was a strange
coincidence; the two of them, so different, yet both asking him
to see their mothers—but why a coincidence? Didn't everyone
have a mother? He heard in his mind the cries of German
boys, wounded and afraid—*mutter, mutter*. And of Helena,
with her lily-in-death look. He could not sit still. Pacing about,
he said suddenly, "Give me a spot of old man whiskey, Freddy.
Anyone—yes, that'll do." He did not want the whiskey; he
wanted the spirit of "Spectre" West, and "Twinkle".

He was in half a mind to walk down to the Roebuck and warn
the billiard sharper Wilkins; but he stayed in the bar, for its
warmth, safety, association. He sat down again, feeling sleepy;
but his mind would not rest, it descended into shadow and
melancholy, and so to the edge of frenzy that nothing in the
world was really right. And never could be. He had another
whiskey to avoid the great loneliness that was life, feeling that
death was the only true companionship of souls, and was drinking the last drop when the door opened and Desmond's Brazilian
friend, Eugene, came in.

Seeing his face, Phillip felt a surge of warmth and gladness, to
which the newcomer instantly responded. The wide mouth
in the sallow face smiled, revealing even teeth; the small natty

figure in bowler hat, light raglan coat, carrying wash-leather gloves and black silver-topped cane, came quickly forward on small highly-polished shoes below blue serge trousers.

"You do look a swell, Gene!"

"When did you come back? I'm frightfully glad to see you, Phillip."

They clasped hands, looking delightedly at each other. Freddy behind the bar simpered with reflected amity, prepared to tip his straw when his customer should turn to the bar.

Eugene had left the army; his feet would not stand the marching, he said. He had a job in the City, in the warehouse of a friend of his father's, Charley Mayer, of C.M. corsets. Eugene was learning the business, eventually to return to Brazil, and an import agency, he said.

Phillip felt a stab of regret. Gene leaving England? It was one more link with the past breaking. Eugene apparently felt the same, in the flush of sudden affection for Phillip. "It won't be yet awhile, Phil. Not during the war——"

"Oh good! Freddy, two hot rums, and have a drink yourself."

"Thank you, sir!"

Freddy added more of his especial water to his glass, while Phillip, his eyes on the other man's, told Eugene not to look, but behind the glass screen were waiting detectives. Gene's eyes fought against Phillip's in order to look; but Phillip's gaze won.

Phillip said to Eugene, as they walked down to the Roebuck, that he couldn't understand how the bogus major had managed to get away with it for so long. There he was, in khaki shirt-sleeves, showing his new leather jockey-braces, as he leaned over the green baize table, going in off the red again and again; while his tunic, and soft khaki trench cap, its neck-cover hiding the red band beneath, hung on a peg for all to see. How had he the nerve to appear like that, despite the well-known story of his disappearance after the Blackheath review last May?

Phillip thought that he had rather a nice face, with curly hair and pink cheeks. His hands were delicate, he wore a gold wristlet-watch. Obviously he was a very good billiard player. Everyone watched as he went in off the red again and again, bringing the red back every time to the same place near the spot at the top of the table. Sixty-four, sixty-seven, seventy, seventy-three, seventy-six—then he caught Phillip's monocled eye.

Phillip had put on mufti before leaving home, rather in the hope that he would attract attention to himself in the Castle, perhaps to be given one of those white feathers that some pretty girls were said to be presenting to slackers.

"A break of seventy-six, Major," called the marker; and there was desultory clapping in the room.

The man in jockey braces glanced quickly again at Phillip. Then he came over, and with a slight smile said, "Haven't we met somewhere? Surely you were at Sandhurst?" as he put on his tunic, which had only two stars on the shoulders, Phillip noticed.

"I say, may I have a word with you?" said Phillip.

Eugene, his coffee-coloured face slightly simian with curiosity, made to accompany them; but seeing Phillip's slight head-shake, he remained behind when they went into the private bar.

"I'll come straight to the point," said Phillip, when two drinks had been bought. "Purely as a friendly tip, the police are after you. I saw them in Freddy's, ten minutes ago."

"After me? My dear old thing, what *are* you talking about?"

"Aren't you Wilkins?"

"That is my name. Devereux-Wilkins. What police? Oh, I begin to see it! You are confusing me with my cousin, who got up that rag last May, on Blackheath, for a bet that he could stimulate recruiting! If you're after him, you'll have to apply to Secret Service. More I am unable to tell you. It's all sub rosa. You're from Horse Guards, I suppose, Provost Marshal's Office, and all that?"

"Good lord, no! I just came along to tell you about the coppers in Freddy's. I don't like policemen, civil or military."

The other looked at his gold wristlet watch. "I'll have to go, old thing. I'm an A.D.C. for my pains. Care to see?" He removed the wristlet watch, and showed Phillip the words engraved on the back. Phillip read *To Second-Lieutenant Charles Devereux-Wilkins, from the men in his platoon at Suvla Bay, May* 1915, *as a token of esteem*. The watch was strapped on again.

"You live in this salubrious neighbourhood? Nice place," isn't it?" said Devereux-Wilkins with such charm that Phillip felt he was not sarcastic. "Surely you were up at Oxford before the war? I seem to remember you in the common room at Keble?"

"I was up at Cambridge—at Fitzwilliam Hall," replied Phillip.

"Fitzwilliam Hall? Do I know it? Surely——? I don't

recall such a college, old thing," said Devereux-Wilkins blandly. "Where exactly is it?"

"Oh, at the corner of Jesus Lane," said Phillip, hurriedly guessing.

"Sounds very suspicious to me, old thing! Well, I must be going. See you some time," and taking up his leather-covered cane and gloves, the debonair Devereux-Wilkins left the Roebuck and sprang on a motor bus going towards London.

"He's a mystery," said Phillip to Eugene. "I believe that he *is* on the staff, all right—but I feel also that he gave that watch to himself. Even if his platoon could afford a gold watch, how could they all get together to put money in the hat to buy one out there? There aren't any shops in Gallipoli, as there are in France, anyway. He's a bit of a sprucer, all right! Told me he was up at Oxford before the war, so I told him I was up at Cambridge—so we're two sprucers together! Would you like my monocle as a souvenir? It doesn't really fit my eye."

Eugene took it eagerly, and screwed it into his own eye. "Well, cheer ho, Gene, my boy!"

Two years were to pass before Phillip saw Devereux-Wilkins again, in the company of "Spectre" West, when, as it happened, all three met in the reserve battalion of the Gaultshire Regiment at Felixstowe.

Freddy's was alive when Eugene and Phillip returned. With a surge of delight Phillip saw Tom Cundall standing by the bar, in what he called his new maternity jacket—the Royal Flying Corps tunic that wrapped across stomach and chest and fastened down one side. He wore his pilot's wings. Half a dozen people, including Ching, were listening to him on the subject of Zeppelins. After greeting Phillip, Cundall went on to tell, in his dry, ironic manner, how he had been training at the Norwich aerodrome, during the late summer, when Zeppelins were reported making for the city. Instructors, the only people who could fly, went up in the darkness with Véry light pistols.

"Talk about wind-up among the civilian population of our great big nation of hot-air merchants! We had to mark the corners of the 'drome with petrol flares for the homing birdmen, by cutting off with hacksaws the tops of petrol tins. The native population of spy-hunters, seeing the flares, rushed across the grass and put them out, just as two of our chaps were coming in to land. So they crashed their undercarts and got 'orribly mixed up with the office. To make more certain of their demise, the mob smashed the ambulance head-lamps, so the two blokes in aspic got to hospital a bit late. Talk about Julius Caesar and the stinking breath of the mob——"

"Talking about the staff at Loos——" and Phillip, standing just below the open spy-hole in the stained-glass partition of the billiard-room, went on to give them details of what he had seen during the past month, ending up with a declaration that the Germans were really quite decent fellows, that the stories about them in the papers were lies, and that no war correspondent would have had the guts to tell the truth, for example, of how the walking wounded were allowed to go back unmolested after the Sunday morning attack on the 26th September across the Lens–La Bassée road.

"And you should have seen the face of one of the war correspondents when 'Crasher' asked his question! I tell you, people at home have no idea at all of what really happens out there. Take the gas, for instance——" He repeated what Mrs. Rolls said she had read in *The Times*.

"Oh, it's Bonaparte eating babies for breakfast all over again," remarked Cundall. "Well, let me stand you a drink, my beamish boy, and let's drink to the national motto, a variation of the Nation of Shopkeepers' 'Business as Usual', which includes the Fabrication of News by the Press, all of which has now gone completely yellow."

It was some time later that Mr. Jenkins touched Phillip's arm. "Can I have a word with you, Phillip?" They moved to a vacant space away from the stained-glass partition. Then "Sailor" said with motionless lips, "Follow me into the private bar next door, in about a minute."

Phillip, having gone there, listened with amused impatience to what "Sailor" had to say. There were spies about; there were also the police, and nearer than Phillip imagined; and it was his duty, as well as theirs—"We're all in this war, Phillip, we must all pull together"—to report anything of a nature likely to impede the war effort. And from what he, Phillip, had been saying, he might find himself in queer street.

"To spread alarmist reports about what is happening over there, Phillip, is tantamount to acting for the other side, you know. It's all very well to scoff!"

"Look, Mr. Jenkins! What happens out there and what you and Father and other civilians read in the papers are two utterly different things! Besides, what did I say that could upset anyone in particular?"

"Well, Phillip, you praised the Germans as brave men, yet in the next breath you boast—and between ourselves, is it anything to boast about—how you dodged the fighting by pretending to be a chemist. Anyway, the last time I saw you, you said that you were only taking over reinforcements, and that you hoped you would take no part in the fighting. No, Phillip, you're not doing yourself any good by talking like that!"

"I said I took no part in the fighting, but I saw quite a lot of it, as a matter of fact."

"That sounds like a quibble. Anyway, I am only giving you a tip, as a friend, Phillip. Don't talk too loudly, for there are quite a number of people in the neighbourhood who have known all about you from early boyhood, you know! There's another reason, Phillip—is it entirely fair to your father to praise the Germans openly? I mean to say, some people have not forgotten what your house was once named, and why, you know! So take a friendly tip from one older than yourself, Phillip, and lie low."

"Thanks, Mr. Jenkins. That's what I intend to do henceforward. So low that I'll be beneath the dust!" He laughed at his own joke. *Less than the dust.* He *was* less than the dust, beneath her chariot wheels—— He felt tears coming into his eyes, and looked on the ground.

"No offence taken, Phil? I'm only trying to help you, you know."

"Thank you, Mr. Jenkins. Now I'd like to ask you something. *How* are you sure there are spies about, Mr. Jenkins?"

"How I know, or from whence my information, I am not at liberty to divulge, but you can take it from me it is as good as official, Phillip. There's one about disguised as a War Office staff man, with scarlet hat-band; and "—Mr. Jenkins whispered—"he is always seen when Zeppelins are coming over, Phillip! The warning's been given tonight, you know!"

"By Jove, Mr. Jenkins, supposing you were to catch the spy!" he exclaimed, trying not to laugh.

"Well, one never knows, does one, Phillip? Your friend was quoting the Bard just now, two can do that, you know! 'There's

more things in your philosophy, Horatius, than were ever
dreamt of in heaven and earth', as Shakespeare once said. Well,
keep smiling, and don't forget what I've told you, Phillip!"

"No, Mr. Jenkins, I won't."

Back in the saloon bar, Phillip told Cundall some of what
had been said, with the comment, "He's full of wind and Woggle-
dagger, and doesn't know the difference between Julius Caesar
and that bloke who kept the bridge."

"What bridge?" asked Cundall; and when Phillip told him,
"Oh, such shocking iggerance, and from an Old Heathian!
Horatius kept his bridge to himself—no inquests on why his
partner went to bed with his ace—while it was to Horatio that
Hamlet made that celebrated remark about heaven and
earth——" Cundall, the brainy bird, was saying, when "Sailor"
Jenkins pushed open the door and going to the bar said to Mrs.
Freddy, "I've just got time for one more very quick one!
It's going to be a hot night tonight, my dear," with several
quick nods of his head. Then turning to Phillip, he said behind
his hand, "I've just seen the sergeant, who has come from the
station. Five Zeppelins have crossed the coast! Better get home
while you can, Phillip."

"Oh, they don't worry me."

"But there's your mother and sisters to think about, Phillip.
Get them into the coal cellar! That's where my wife and children
will be tonight!"

Phillip thought this funny; and when "Sailor" had hurried
away, he told Cundall and the others.

"What's that you're saying?" asked Mrs. Freddy, paler and
more child-like than usual. Phillip told her, and to his surprise
a hard line came on her mouth and she took a kick at Freddy,
helping himself to four penn'oth of water.

"What's biting you now, my dear?" he tittered, sipping his
drink.

"*You*, you bleeder! I to'd you you ought to take me back
to Mother!" She turned to Phillip. "She works in the Dragon
at Farnborough, you see, while Dad's in the Army."

"Jolly good place to work in, Mrs. Freddy! Next best place
to a brewery!"

"I don' want none of your lip, see?" she cried. Phillip was
surprised at her anger. He had not connected it with her fear,
for her baby, Freddy, and home. "We can do without your

sort! And you!" whipping round on Ching, who was merely looking at her with his prominent eyeballs. "You ain't got your uniform yet, I see! And what'r you doing, you with angel's wings, why aren't you up arter them bleedin' gasbags?"

"No plane," said Cundall, simply. "No bus. No kite. Not even a sausage. So, not being a Knight of the Air, I did the next best thing, and decided on a Night with Wit and Beauty."

"Very well expressed, sir!" chimed Freddy, touching his straw. "Very neat. I'd take it to be an honour if you'd have one on the house, sir. All of you gentlemen join me, please."

They were drinking Freddy's health, and Freddy was drinking it too, when a deep grinding sensation was felt everywhere in the bar, coming through ground and air at the same time. It caused two wine glasses on a shelf to chime against one another. There was a colourless pause, in which every face seemed fixed; then female cries arose, one from Mrs. Freddy, another from a woman in the unseen public bar opening direct on to the High Street pavement, and further shouts from outside. From the billiard-room door the two bowler-hatted plain-clothes men, umbrellas in hand, strode out unspeaking.

Phillip, Cundall, Ching and Eugene went out into the street to see the fun. A tram came to an abrupt stop opposite. People hurried off. One woman was moaning. A man who looked like a coster, with a rag round his neck, shouted out, "Put them lights out!" in a hoarse voice. On plimsoled feet he ran to the tram-driver. They seemed to have an argument. The tram lights remained on. People stopped, or hurried to listen, then many voices demanded that the lights be put out. Someone shinned up a lamp-post, fumbled at the glass, put his fist through, smashing the mantle. Other people were now inside the tram, pulling out electric bulbs above the cane-woven seats along both sides. Screams were heard far off, then shouting; faces were looking up, lit by searchlight beams sweeping round in circles to come to a common apex in the height of the sky.

Running to the centre of the road, with Eugene, while Ching and Cundall stood on the pavement, Phillip was in time to see a long thin cigar-shaped object, yellow at the point of a dozen beams, lifting its nose almost lazily upward while faint smoke came from under it as it climbed, now with gathering speed, and moved out of the haze of light. Distant guns began to fire from all directions. Phillip looked at his watch. It was just after half past nine. He glanced around for sight of his father; then went back with the others to the warm bar, now with one mantle alight, and that turned down. But the life had gone from the place, and after one more drink, he thought to go on the Hill for a view over London.

How to shake off Ching? He wanted to be alone with Eugene. He was delighted that he and Gene had become friends. Before, he had been puzzled, slightly hurt, that Desmond could see anything in his Brazilian friend. Like many youths coming from small houses awed by Victorian fathers, to Phillip all the world was his feelings: he was only now learning to think apart from them. Now that he and Gene had warmed to one another, he felt more secure about his friendship with Desmond: it was doubled.

"I'll see you up to your house, Phillip. You might need a friendly arm, you don't look very well, you know."

Ching, too, wanted friendship—and the love of Mavis.

"I am perfectly all right, Ching. Anyway, Gene and I have to see Mrs. Neville, who may be worrying."

"I'll wait outside while you go in."

"We may be an hour or more, eh, Gene?"

"I don't mind how long I wait, when it's you, Phil."

"Well, I do."

They walked over the bridge in silence. Occasional beams of light pierced the sky. Randiswell was dark and seemed deserted, until a solitary figure approached, holding an open umbrella over a bowler hat, although the night was now fine and starry. The umbrella stopped; and a cultured voice said, "Middleton, I presume? Surely I am not mistaken? Middleton, I think—yes!" Having delivered this greeting, the squat figure staggered sideways; immediately to recover balance, using the umbrella like a tight-rope walker. Stability having been maintained, the stranger advanced for further sociability.

"How do you do?" A hand was held out. Phillip shook it.

"Middleton, my dear boy——! England owes a debt she can never repay to you, and to others like you. Will you gentlemen honour me by coming with me to the Conservative Club, the bar of which remains open until eleven o'clock, and drink to the victory in France?"

This seemed to promise high adventure, so they went back

beside the man with the umbrella, who said he was Dr. Dashwood. Phillip had heard of Dr. Dashwood from Mrs. Neville;
he was a popular man, with beautiful manners, the only trouble
being that, "under the influence", he was liable to stagger
about during confinements, or while testing eyes for glasses;
and, solely on that account, as a medical adviser he was not
altogether reliable, although he had not so far poked a finger
in anyone's eye or dropped a new-born baby. Apart from that,
Dr. Dashwood was a gentleman of the old school, said Mrs.
Neville.

The Conservative Club was next to the railway bridge. A
lonely figure standing under the shelter of the bridge turned
out to be "Sailor" Jenkins. "Ah, Middleton—my dear fellow!"
exclaimed the benevolent Dr. Dashwood, as he persuaded Mr.
Jenkins to come in out of the cold night, and share the umbrella.
Paying attention to each of his guests in turn, he walked beside
them up to the club entrance beside the pawnbrokers, remarking
"Very handy for members, don't you think."

Phillip saw a room full of polished leather armchairs and
sofas seeming to be of great age, for most of the leather was
cracked. There were prints and engravings of the borough in
past ages. Dr. Dashwood, his heavy jowls and cheeks revealed
in the gaslight to be of a shade between maroon and purple,
ordered double Haigs. Having drunk his, with concealed shudders, Phillip thanked him, and said he must be going; but the
doctor protested.

"The night is but young, my dear Middleton. Fill the glasses,
will you?" to the barman. "If you will excuse me, gentlemen, I
will leave you for a moment. Do you know the geography of
the place? Permit me——" he ushed them all towards the
lavatory, which was only large enough for two.

"Come on," whispered Phillip to Gene. "This is our chance."
Suppressing giggles, the two hurried out of the club, passing
the pawnbroker's three gilt balls at a run, and on the pavement
exploded in merriment. "What an extraordinary man! Fancy
calling us all by the same name! I wonder who Middleton really
is? Anyway, thank God we've got rid of Ching! Quick! Hop
it!!"

Mrs. Neville was in the downstairs flat, sitting with two
women in shawls. A bottle of Martell's brandy stood on a small
round table between them, beside a solitary candle.

"O-oh, what a night, Phillip! My word, Gene, Desmond will have something to tell us tomorrow! Did you hear that bomb? They say it fell in the Strand, just outside a theatre. Another ten yards, and it would have caught the lot inside. The beasts! Do you know what they dropped over Highgate the other night? A hambone, with a label tied on it, saying, 'For Starving England'. Thank God someone can laugh!" she suddenly shrieked. Then in her creamy voice, "I am forgetting my manners, blame it on the Kaiser. This is Mrs. Tinkey, and this is her daughter, Miss Tinkey."

Phillip tried not to giggle; it sounded like Stinkey. To cover his laughter, he pretended to cough, thumping his chest, saying, "It's the gas, I got a whiff on the twenty-fifth." Then trying to be gallant, like Dr. Dashwood, he said to the elder woman, "I thought you were two sisters," whereupon the older woman said, "There now!" in a pleased tone of voice, while the younger said, "Go on, I don't believe you!"

"Now you've spoiled a pretty compliment!" cried Mrs. Neville.

"Well——" he said. "By candlelight, you know——" He stared at the bottle.

"It's no good looking at that bottle, Phillip," laughed Mrs. Neville. "That bottle is to be opened only in an emergency!"

She smiled coyly at Phillip, before turning to the older woman and saying, "That's our little safeguard, isn't it, dear? Oh yes, Phillip, that bottle is quite an old friend now. It's been three times on this table, beside that candle, during the past six weeks, hasn't it, dear?" with a wink at Phillip.

Footsteps sounded on the tessellated area in front of the flats. Phillip blew out the candle. "Hush. It's Ching! Don't move!" They heard the bell in the next flat ringing. At last footfalls went away, and after an interval, Phillip said he must go. He was going on the Hill, half way across, with Eugene, who lodged in Foxfield Road, he told Mrs. Neville. Saying goodbye, they left the three women sitting round the bottle on the table. What a night!

Distant guns broke out as they walked up Hillside Road. "I bet the bottle will be opened now, Gene!" as a broad lilac beam leapt above the roof of the Modern School before them. "I'll just call in to see if Mother's all right, I won't be a sec."

He ran up to the porch, key in hand, quietly opened the door in darkness, to hear from above, down the long passage to the end bedroom, Mavis's terrified voice calling, "Mother! Mother! I can hear one coming! Quick! Quick!" then Mother's voice saying, as she hurried down from the front bedroom, "It's all right, dear, Mother's coming!"

Phillip heard a faint high throb passing away in the sky. "Don't get the wind up!" he called up the stairs. "The chance of anything falling here is a million to one! I'm just going on the Hill, Mum, I won't be long. Cheer-ho!" and he was about to leave before she could say anything to stop him, when Polly came down the stairs in white bodice and bloomers. She carried her skirt and shoes in one hand, and coming to him beside the newel post, said with a little laugh, "Hullo. May I come with you?"

"You're not dressed."

"Yes, I am," as she got into the skirt. "I can put on my overcoat, see?"

"You'll catch cold," he said, feeling her knee, while her nearness drew the wire in him.

"That I won't!" She tossed her curls, and called out, "Aunt Hetty, I'm just going on the Hill for a minute with Phillip, to see the sights. It's all right, I'm already dressed."

"Polly, I don't think you ought to, dear. It is so very very late!"

"Only for five minutes, Aunt. I've got on my thick overcoat. Come on," to Phillip. She took his arm while he closed the door quietly by turning the Yale key. "Uncle won't be home until midnight," she whispered.

Arm in arm, exhilarated in comradeship, Phillip and Polly and Gene walked up the gulley. Phillip was glad that Polly was with him. She could walk fast, like a man. She was a bit of a sport. He sighed, thinking of Helena.

London lay around the Hill, dark with the smallest lights. Northward a tongue of flame arose, casting a pink haze in the darkness. Gunfire started again. They saw little red flashes high in the night over Woolwich; then searchlights were weaving, clustering, breaking apart, wildly searching. The beams went out, one after another, quickly, leaving the stars winking coldly in the wind, and bright points of light burning below.

"Thermite candles," said Phillip. They waited for flames;

when none appeared, they walked arm-in-arm towards the elms, where Phillip stopped.

"Father once saw a Camberwell Beauty on his strips pinned to this tree, with his dark lantern," he said, suddenly. "Before I was born. He used to collect butterflies." Loneliness overcame him for a moment, giving way to a desire for Polly. Yet he did not want to say goodbye to Eugene.

"We'll meet again, Phil?"

"Of course, rather! Well, goodbye for now, old man."

They shook hands. Holding on to Polly's hand, Eugene said, "Are you ever in Town?"

"Sometimes," said Polly, tossing her curls. "Why, may I ask?"

"I'd like to take you out to dinner one night."

"Perhaps," said Polly, taking back her hand.

"Well, so long!" said Eugene, fixing the monocle and raising his hat. "Till we meet again!"

They waited while his footfalls lessened in the darkness.

"It seems awfully sad, somehow, to have to say goodbye," said Phillip. "But life is like that, you know."

They walked back unspeaking until Polly said, "I am sorry about Bertie. Aunt Hetty asked us not to talk to you about it, but I want to say I'm sorry, Phil." She took his arm again.

"Oh, Mother doesn't understand, really. She always tries to hush things up. Was Aunt Dorrie very upset?"

"She didn't cry, Aunt said, but was very quiet. Gran'pa wants to take them both to Brighton, but there's Uncle Dick, with his special constable's work, to be considered."

"Yes, he's out until midnight, three nights a week. Poor old Father. What's the time now?"

The hands of his Ordnance wristlet watch, glowing phosphorescent, showed twenty past eleven. The wire between life and death drew him. He did not speak while they crossed the crest of the Hill; but at the top of the gulley he stopped, holding the sleeve of her coat. "Polly, shall we——?"

"If you like."

They went along the hurdles opposite the sheep-fold and sat down on the grass.

"You're shivering," said Polly. "Here, come inside my coat."

She held him. After a while she unbuttoned the top of her bodice. "Lay your head here." He fondled her warm softness, while all feeling for her stayed away with his thoughts. He clung to his thoughts, yet knowing them to be hopeless. It was ended; all he had ever hoped for was dead. He might as well have Polly. He put his lips to her breast, feeling roughness rising in him.

"Polly, has anyone else ever——"

"Wouldn't you like to know!"

"Not particularly. Come on."

"All right," said Polly.

The October night was quiet. From the Hill the distant shunting of ammunition trucks in Woolwich could be heard. It was half past eleven. Richard Maddison had another thirty minutes to go before he reported to the Randiswell Police Station. Each night he visited the dozen special constables on their beats, always at the same times and places, so that they could rely on him appearing regularly. He was tired, quite fagged-out, he told himself as he walked down a street, dutifully looking for cracks of light in doors and windows, and scanning roof-tops for sign of signalling by flash-lamp. He was cold, he had had but a scanty supper, he had arrived home from the office only ten minutes before being called out for duty. He had never been late yet. In the dreary course of his patrol he thought of his dark lantern, and wished that he had not given it to Phillip years before—the boy would have taken it anyway—for then it could have warmed his hands during the coming winter nights.

February 1954—May 1955
Devon.